HAZZARD: THE COMPLETE SERIES

Fred Davis

BOOKS BY FREDERICK C. DAVIS:

Hazzard: The Complete Series

Kirk: The Complete Series

Ravenwood: The Complete Series

HAZZARD:
THE COMPLETE SERIES

FREDERICK
C. DAVIS

BOSTON

ALTUS PRESS

2016

EDITED AND DESIGNED BY
Matthew Moring

ASSOCIATE EDITOR
Ray Riethmeier

PUBLISHING HISTORY
"Coffins for Two" originally appeared in the August 1935 issue of *Secret Agent X* magazine. Copyright © 1935 by Ace Publications, Inc.

"Juggernaut Justice" originally appeared in the September 1935 issue of *Secret Agent X* magazine. Copyright © 1935 by Ace Publications, Inc.

"Corpses' Court" originally appeared in the October 1935 issue of *Secret Agent X* magazine. Copyright © 1935 by Ace Publications, Inc.

"The Murder Crypt" originally appeared in the November 1935 issue of *Secret Agent X* magazine. Copyright © 1935 by Ace Publications, Inc.

"Terror Tribunal" originally appeared in the December 1935 issue of *Secret Agent X* magazine. Copyright © 1935 by Ace Publications, Inc.

"The Death-Chair Challenge" originally appeared in the January 1936 issue of *Secret Agent X* magazine. Copyright © 1936 by Ace Publications, Inc.

"About the Author" originally appeared in the July 22, 1933 issue of *Flynn's Detective Fiction Weekly* magazine (Vol. 77, No. 6). Copyright © 1933 by The Frank A. Munsey Company. Copyright renewed © 1960 and assigned to Steeger Properties, LLC. All rights reserved.

THANKS TO
Bill Thom

Visit *altuspress.com* for more books like this.
Printed in the United States of America.

TABLE OF

CONTENTS

Coffins For Two

By Frederick C. Davis

CHAPTER I

DEATH OF THE BENCH

MARK HAZZARD, District Attorney, with sickening heart, watched twelve men file in from the jury room to their place in the judgment box, anxiously studied the inscrutable faces of the twelve as the foreman faced the bench. A strange expression on Judge Goldman his face when he heard Judge Crombie gravely ask, "Gentlemen of the jury, have you reached a verdict?" The expression of the jurist's face became even more perturbed, the foreman answered "Yes."

The twelve had decided between Hazzard and the indictment of the accused defendant Sid Kelso. Hazzard's brief for grand larceny had followed three convictions on minor charges. If the foreman of the jury had pronounced one word, and not the to convict Kelso of a fourth offense in fact, under the drastic statute a thousand threats of imprisonment.

"What is your verdict, gentlemen of this jury?"

All eyes had preyed on the city. Kelso, backed by the crooked politicians he had bribed, had defied the justice of the courts and abroad. Crooked graft, with crooked lords... The good skill of a powerful legal lawyer. Crooked Sid had found one loophole after another in the law through which he had wriggled to immunity. John Mark Hazzard had declared his determination to get Kelso.

One by one Hazzard had stript predatory lieutenants. Step by he had fought toward the structure of the Kelso mob, the tombstone scene. The moment of loss or defeat had come. A strenuous "rock-long trial" of floor led the stricken hours of exhausted jury. The frenzied buttonized exhortation of bench law to bear and the distinguished judge, dressed the fateful question to the jury.

Dread filled Hazzard the Kelso might slide the law-hanged, handcuffed... drawn an expert to phone. In Kelso's neighborhood, massive blood money. His countenance was the...

BOOK I

COFFINS FOR TWO

Mark Hazzard, red-headed, fiery-tempered
district attorney, had the state's case sewed
up in a bag. The defendant was guilty,
and the jury found him guilty. But a wily
criminal lawyer twisted that verdict, and
let the guilty man walk from the courtroom.
That guilty man was now prey for Mark
Hazzard's own personal code of justice.
For the Juggernaut of Justice had his own
iron rules, and bucked the police and the
underworld—while keeping a secret that
would send him to burn in the electric chair.

DEATH ON
THE BENCH

MARK HAZZARD, District Attorney, with quickening heart, watched twelve men file solemnly from the jury room to their places in the judgment box.

He anxiously studied the inscrutable faces of the twelve as the foreman faced the bench. A strange premonition of danger tightened his nerves when he heard Judge Crosdale gravely ask: "Gentlemen of the jury, have you reached a verdict?" The drawn grayness of the jurist's firm face became even more pronounced, Hazzard noted with growing concern, as the foreman answered: "We have."

The twelve had decided between freedom and life imprisonment for the rat-eyed defendant, Sid Kelso. His indictment for grand larceny had followed three convictions on minor charges. If the foreman of the jury now pronounced one word, and not two, to convict Kelso of a fourth offense, he faced, under the drastic Kernan law, a mandatory sentence of life imprisonment.

"What is your verdict, gentlemen of the jury?"

The moment speeded Hazzard's pulse because it was the crisis of his long months of grim endeavor to stamp out the scourge of as evil a ring of extortionists and racketeers as ever had preyed on the city. Kelso, backed by the crooked connivance of politicians he had bribed, had defied the justice of the courts with shrewdly planted graft, with crooked bondsmen. The shady skill of a powerful trial lawyer, Hubbard Todd, had opened one loophole after another in the law through which he had wriggled to immunity—until Mark Hazzard had declared his determination to get Kelso.

One by one Hazzard had indicted, tried and convicted four of Kelso's predatory lieutenants. Step by step he had fought toward the supreme test of forcing justice upon the contemptuous Kelso. The moment of victory or defeat had come, after a strenuous week-long trial, with the door locked for eighteen hours on the exhausted jury. The greasy-faced, button-eyed extortionist faced the bench now, as pale and haggard as the distinguished judge who addressed the fateful question to the jury.

Dread filled Hazzard that again Kelso might elude the law. He had presented documentary evidence, proved by expert graphologists to be in Kelso's handwriting, letters demanding blood money. The defense's countermove was the testimony of witness after witness that Kelso was elsewhere on the night he had actually met Howard Brandon, broker, in a public park with a demand for one hundred thousand dollars. Eye-witnesses! The word brought sharper bitterness to the heart of Mark Hazzard than any other in the lexicon of the law.

Gravely Judge Crosdale had charged the jury: "Gentlemen, you have heard six witnesses state that they saw the defendant elsewhere on the night he is alleged to have extorted money from Howard Brandon. You have heard Brandon testify that the defendant is the man who demanded extortion money of him. You must carefully weigh this conflicting testimony and decide whether it condemns the defendant or clears him. You are to judge the credibility of these eye-witnesses."

Eye-witnesses! The words burned the mind of Mark Hazzard, echoed in his memory, as he watched the worn face of the foreman of the jury. Firm-eyed, clean-cut, with a temper as fiery as his brilliant red hair, Hazzard—the youngest man ever to achieve the important office of prosecutor of the district of King's County—heard the jury grant him a grim reward:

"Guilty."

Judge David Crosdale peered at the stunned Kelso and leaned forward painfully. Hazzard had seen the ashiness of the jurist's face become more pronounced during the progress of the trial. He was sure that the man on the bench was ill and suffering. He listened anxiously as the jurist mumbled:

"This court pronounces upon the defendant the mandatory sentence of—"

Abruptly a breathy, agonized gasp broke from Judge Crosdale's lips. His head dropped to the bench and lolled; his arms swung limp as he sagged. A soft, crunching sound passed through the hush of the court as the jurist sprawled to the floor. One moment of stunned

astonishment held reporters, counsel and spectators motionless while they stared at an empty chair.

Hazzard, the first to move, strode dismayed toward the bench. The bailiff sped with him; the stenographer sprang up; the courtroom broke into a dismayed babble. Hazzard bent anxiously over the limp jurist on the floor; he peered appalled into a face that was ghastly passive. He straightened, gazed at the startled men who had followed and said quietly:

"Judge Crosdale is dead."

THE COURTROOM became a bedlam as Hazzard thrust clear of the court attendants. His quick thrust opened the jurist's chambers behind the court. He snapped into the telephone, into the ear of the courthouse switchboard operator: "Hazzard speaking. Give me my office!" He waited with mind in turmoil for the voice of his secretary to answer.

He knew that Ann Nash should be at her desk. She was on duty every moment Hazzard was at work, night and day. Quickly efficient, with a mind tuned to match Hazzard's fast decisions, she should be answering this call without a moment's delay. But she was not. The distant bell purred repeatedly, but the line remained dead.

Hazzard spun from the telephone. "Call Crosdale's home and his doctor!" With the snapped orders, he pushed through the swinging doors of the courtroom and took the stairs four at a time. His hand gripped the knob of his office entrance hard and he opened the way to a sight that chilled his blood.

A ruddy-faced deputy sheriff, detailed to the guarding of state's evidence kept in Hazzard's office, lay with bleeding head under a broken-legged chair that had crushed him down. Scattered papers on the floor led Hazzard on a swift trail through a door with shattered pane. He glimpsed trim pumps and sleek silk past the corner of Ann Nash's desk and seized the girl's arm as she strove weakly to rise.

She clung to him dizzily, her clear blue eyes dimmed, her usually firm lips trembling, as Hazzard's gaze shot to the huge safe set into the wall of his inner office. In it he had stored the extortionist letters written by Kelso immediately after the jury had retired. Now the compartment in which he had placed them was empty. A wave of angry heat surged through him as he gripped Ann Nash's arms.

"Talk!"

"He—he came at me before I knew what was happening!" the girl blurted. "I heard the crash out there, and saw Hunter going down—then he hit me. A masked man—handkerchief across his face—a man in a top-coat. I tried to stop him, but—"

"Ann! Who was he? You saw him. You'd know him if—"

"It happened so fast!" the girl said rushingly. "I didn't see him clearly. I tried to pull him back—heard something rip, but—I'm sorry, Mark!"

"The rat who did this." Mark Hazzard declared grimly, "is going to be much sorrier!"

Quick steps in the outer office brought Hazzard's assistant, Frank Mayton, toward him. Mayton stared around, appalled, then blurted to Hazzard:

"Judge Cheever's taking the bench to pronounce sentence on Kelso. There's hell popping down there—"

"And here!" Hazzard snapped. "Beat it downstairs, Frank—out this building. Try to find a man in a torn top-coat. He's got the evidence against Kelso. Get after him!"

The amazed Mayton rushed from the office. Ann Nash was at the telephone now, asking for Inspector Trencher. Hazzard, in the outer office, pulled the broken chair away from Hunter as the deputy struggled up. He examined the ugly welt on Hunter's head and sent him staggering out for first aid. Hazzard's face was a furious red, his temper was flaming, when he strode back to the safe.

"Inspector Trencher," Ann Nash told him, lowering the phone, "is coming over."

"That's the way to handle this!" Hazzard said with bitter irony. "Just stand by until Trencher saunters into it!"

A quick examination of the safe verified his fears. Four extortionist letters, identified as Kelso's handwriting, were not in the compartment, nor among the papers scattered over the floor. Another drawer was open but empty; it had contained statements with which Hazzard hoped soon to convict one Nat Brock on the same charge that had brought a verdict of guilty against Kelso. Suspicion kindled in Hazzard's turbulent mind as he rapidly scanned the papers he picked up.

A spot of white on the rug drew his hand. He lifted a tiny white sphere that flaked when his fingernail dug at it, bringing a pungent odor to his nostrils.

"You tore the masked man's coat," he thought aloud to the breathless Ann Nash. "Ripped his pocket probably, and this fell out of it."

The thermometer bracketed outside Hazzard's window was registering the first sharp drop of temperature of the fall. It had brought many top-coats out of cedar chests and storage closets. Hazzard's own, for the first time this season, hung on the rack behind his desk. Hazzard peered at that little white sphere with disgust.

"Evidence," he declared. "And worthless!"

Ann Nash asked: "Why?"

"It means our masked man got his coat out of storage in such a hurry tonight he didn't have time to take the mothballs out of it, that's all. Did you smell anything like this when he hit you?"

"Yes." Ann Nash said it with certainty. Now she was her usual poised, capable self. "I did."

"Whoever was here won't keep that coat with him now. He'll get rid of it because of the torn pocket. That's no good. There might be an odor of naphthalene on him—but where will it be months from now, assuming I manage to find him, arrest him, indict him and bring him to trial? You can't preserve an odor that long— and it wouldn't be conclusive evidence if you could. It's no good!"

The girl said: "I tried to pull his mask down, but that was when he hit me."

Hazzard smiled tightly. "Thanks for trying. You're aces." He was rewarded with a quick smile, and it had the effect of cooling his temper. "Aces," he declared again with the utmost assurance. "As a secretary and as yourself."

Ann Nash said very quietly: "Thanks, boss."

There was a quick step in the outer office, and again it was Mayton. Hazzard's assistant was breathless and bewildered.

"He must have gotten away clean. Nobody noticed him. He took the evidence on Kelso? Good Lord! Well, we're not going to need it. Judge Cheever's going to pronounce sentence on Kelso right now."

"There's a damn' good reason," Hazzard asserted as he strode to the door, "why that evidence was taken—in spite of the verdict."

"Funny the way Judge Crosdale dropped, wasn't it?" Mayton asked as he followed. "Of course he's had Angina for years, but it's damned strange that—"

"Too strange!" Hazzard paused, looking back at Ann Nash. "Ann, I want you to go to Judge Crosdale's home in a hurry. You may have a tough time getting in because they'll be upset, but I want information. Crosdale was at home while the jury was out. I want to know what he did—everything about his heart ailment. I'll be along."

Mayton exclaimed: "Good Lord, do you think that girl's a machine that never eats or sleeps? She was here all last night and all today, living on sandwiches and coffee. I'll go to Crosdale's place instead and—"

"I like Ann's methods." Hazzard smiled through the door. "Do you mind, Ann? Can you make it?"

"Certainly I can make it," the girl answered. "Do you think I'm a sissy?"

SHE WAS slipping into a woolly coat, pulling a pert felt hat on her head, even as she spoke. Hazzard's eyes reflected the admiration and esteem he felt for her as he hurried from the door. He pushed into the courtroom to find it still buzzing, the attendants and counsel still stunned by the shock of Judge Crosdale's death. A gavel in the lean hand of Judge Joseph Cheever was rapping on the desk.

Into the hush that followed, the sharp-eyed juryman declared: "The jury has returned a verdict of guilty against the accused. The unfortunate death of Judge Crosdale turns upon me the duty of sentencing the defendant. Under the laws of this state it is mandatory that—"

"Your honor." Hubbard Todd, towering tall, with eyes that surveyed the world from the eminence of his height with the cold sharpness of an eagle's, stepped to the bench briskly. "I move for a mistrial."

Judge Cheever's gesture was sharp, impatient. "To attempt to take advantage of the catastrophe of Judge Crosdale's death, Mr. Todd, is, in my opinion—"

"I move for a mistrial, your honor," Todd persisted in his strident voice, "on the grounds that the present court has no jurisdiction to pronounce sentence upon the defendant. The trial is incomplete. Only the judge who presided thus far has the right to impose sentence. Under the laws of this state, a new trial must be granted."

Mark Hazzard studied the puzzled face of the jurist on the bench. Again his easily stirred temper sent surges of heat through his veins. His hand closed hot and hard, as he waited for the court to deliberate—hot and hard on a ball of naphthalene.

"Counsel for the defense and the Attorney for the State," Judge Cheever pronounced firmly, "will submit briefs on the motion for a mistrial. The hearing is set for December 8th. Court is adjourned."

Hazzard's eyes blazed at the offensive face of Sid Kelso—at Kelso, grinning malevolently. His fists clenched harder, his temper spurted his heart with rage as he faced Hubbard Todd. The towering, lean attorney smiled with studied contempt.

"Eye-witnesses," he declared, "can give powerful direct evidence, Hazzard. Perhaps you'll learn just how powerful, at the new trial. My client will be absolutely cleared, I promise you."

Hazzard asked with bitter, double meaning: "Honestly?"

He struggled to control his temper while the contemptuous Todd and the grinning Kelso strode from the courtroom. He went up the stairs, into the office, and his knuckles rapped hard on his desk.

Mayton, eyeing him, remarked dryly: "Some day, when you get as mad as that, you're going to explode."

"Damned good reason!"—the words were an explosion. "Frank, I'm facing defeat in my most vital case. Because evidence has been stolen. Because a judge dropped dead on the bench. Because of a ruthless lawyer taking advantage of a legal situation not provided for in the statutes. What chance have we got against that crooked machine—legally?"

Mayton admitted despondently: "Not much!"

"Kelso will win the new trial with his bribed eye-witnesses!"

The word stung Hazzard's lips as he spoke it. He peered at the scattered papers, grim determination strengthening in him minute by minute. He gazed at the little white ball of naphthalene on his hot palm—evidence valueless in the courts, but a thing that could become a pointer of doom outside them. He closed his hand tightly upon it, glared at Mayton and said:

"If the law can't get those crooks, I can. I will! If a defective law—"

Death whispered an interruption.

A flat, cracking sound echoed in the office as a white-rimmed hole appeared in the window-pane at Hazzard's back. A bullet went past his head with a breathy whine. A thump jarred the door frame. A swift succession of ominous sounds—and Mark Hazzard stood chilled by the wind of a killer's bullet.

CHAPTER II

STAIN OF MURDER

HAZZARD WHIRLED from the desk; even as he moved, a second splintering concussion marked the appearance of another white-bordered hole in the pane. He snapped, "Get out of here!" to Mayton and whirled through the connecting door. Quick strides carried him to the window of the adjoining dark room. He peered into the bleak street that separated the courthouse from police headquarters, alert for furtive movement, for the glint of a gun in the light. But he saw only darkness—the black of night from which a murderer's slug had sped.

Turning back to the staring Mayton, he said with ironic casualness: "Better go home and get some sleep, Frank. And have a talk with Cheever first thing in the morning."

Mayton blurted: "God, I saw that red hair of yours riffle as the bullet went past you!"—and he stared after Hazzard, speeding in hot anger down the stairs.

Hazzard's hand stole under his coat, to the 9mm Webley he always carried, as he pressed out the entrance and slowly went down the broad stone steps. Along the gloomy street he saw no one but a thick-shouldered, lean-hipped man coming out of the door of police headquarters. Hazzard waited grimly until this familiar, slow-moving figure became Inspector Trencher, stocky legs straddled, facing him. Trencher's eyes were blacker than the night, ominously deeper.

He said wryly: "No use getting excited, Hazzard. We'll find the man who robbed your safe. It's only a matter of time. Leave it to me."

"I'm probably too easily aroused, inspector," Hazzard answered tartly. "I'm pretty jumpy when I get worked up over a little thing like a killer shooting at me with a silenced gun!"

Trencher looked mildly surprised as Hazzard went up the steps at his side. "That so? Somebody did that? All right, I'll look into it. He's beat it by now, of course? Well, I'll hunt him up."

"Thanks, inspector, very much," Hazzard retorted. "But don't let it upset you. There's all the time in the world, you know. What's the use of trying to grab him now when he wouldn't be brought to trial for months?"

Trencher observed as he plodded up the steps: "When you've been going after crooks as long as I have, Hazzard, you'll know there's no good of going off half-cocked. I've been in this game too long to get excited about anything any more. Let justice take its course. The mills of the gods grind slowly, but they grind exceeding fine. Take it easy, Hazzard."

"The mills of the gods grinding slowly," Hazzard observed, "is one reason why crooks have time to scramble out of the works before they get pinched."

Trencher chuckled dryly as Hazzard led him into the office and indicated the documents strewn on the floor. "You're an interesting hot-head," he observed, moving about. "Maybe it's the heat in you that accounts for your traveling so far so fast. Why, a few years ago, nobody ever heard of Mark Hazzard, and now you're D.A."

Hazzard sensed the penetrating undertone of Trencher's statement. He knew this slow-moving plodder possessed a wit that was a dangerously keen weapon against any man he suspected. His mind was a rapier that thrust while his words drawled and he slouched. It was reaching now for a tender spot in Mark Hazzard, and they both knew it.

"If that's a compliment, Trencher," Hazzard smiled, "thanks!"

"Not at all, not at all, young fellow." The very simulation of affection in the words was a menace that Hazzard sensed. "You see, the department's got to take it slow and careful. We can't arrest a man without a warrant, and we can't issue a warrant without damn' good evidence. You—you go off like a firecracker, and if the force doesn't work fast enough to suit you, you take on the job yourself. I never could understand how a man like you could pop up so suddenly out of nowhere. You've certainly left your mark behind you all your life."

"I wouldn't be surprised, inspector," Hazzard parried. "I'm flattered by your interest in me personally."

"Naturally, I'm interested," Trencher went on as he looked at the scattered papers. "A fighting D.A., with two fists and fast legs and a terror to any crook he starts after—why, sure! Where's your home town, Hazzard? Where'd you go to law school? What did you do before you came here?"

Hazzard's smile tightened. "We're forgetting something, aren't we, inspector? State's evidence has been stolen from the district attorney's safe. A murderer took two shots at me with a silenced twenty-two. That's the business of the moment, isn't it?"

"That's right," Trencher drawled. "I've often noticed you don't want to talk much about yourself. You're too modest, Hazzard—too modest."

"Let it go at that," Hazzard suggested grimly.

Trencher leaned on the desk. "I'll head back to the office and see what I can do about this. There's one thing I've been meaning to mention to you, Hazzard. Just in a friendly way, you know. No hard feeling, of course. But the way you disregard the formalities and regulations and go out after crooks yourself—that's dangerous. You might get into trouble. Ever thought of that?"

"You mean," Hazzard asked, "that I might break the law myself, going after crooks as I do, and then you'd have the job of giving me the works—which you wouldn't like—is that the idea?"

Trencher's lips pursed. "Yes," he admitted. "That's it. Ever thought of that, Hazzard?"

Hazzard said levelly: "I'll take my chances. The law is imperfect, Trencher—we both know that. It's full of holes and flaws and sense-less procedures that help crooks defeat justice. Crooks use the law as a cover, and guilty men are acquitted, innocent men condemned. We're both in it. We know that 'law' doesn't mean 'justice' as it should."

"Well, we make mistakes," Trencher drawled. "But we do pretty well in the long run." He sauntered to the door, and turned his omi-nously black eyes back at Hazzard. "You might make a mistake, too, you know—and that'd be pretty bad."

MARK HAZZARD'S sharp eyes probed into the blackness of Tren-cher's, striving to read the inspector's inscrutable mind, chilled by a sense of danger. He kept staring at the door after Trencher left. He saw one pocket of Trencher's coat sagging strangely; and he lowered himself into his chair slowly, filled with a foreboding of disaster. His hand moved automatically toward a corner of his blotter where a glass paper-weight always rested, a thing he was in the habit of toy-ing with when lost in thought.

He stared, chilled anew—for the paper-weight was gone. Gone—
and Trencher had left the office with one pocket sagging heavily.

Hazzard spun his chair and turned alert eyes out the window. He
saw Trencher appear on the courthouse steps and amble slowly across
the street. After the inspector pushed in through the headquarters
entrance, Hazzard's eyes rose to the window of a corner office opposite. That was Trencher's. Across the chasm of the street they could
see each other's desks—the inspector with the ominous black eyes
and the district attorney who had been warned against a "mistake."

Hazzard's hand snapped out the light when he saw Trencher stride
into the office in the headquarters building. He could see only part
of the inspector, but he was aware that another man had entered the
room, that Trencher's arm was extending toward him. Hazzard's mind
ached to hear the words that were being spoken in that office as he
watched.

They were:

"Take this paper-weight and see what fingerprints you can find
on it. Give me good, clear photographs. Never mind whose it is. Do
the best job you know how, and let me have it quick."

He turned to the typewriter sitting on a leaf of his desk, fed in a
headquarters letterhead, and his face grew grim as he hit the keys.
Hazzard, peering across the street from the dark window, could not
see the words on the paper:

DIRECTOR, DEPARTMENT OF JUSTICE, WASHINGTON, D.C.

Sir:

I am enclosing photographs of a set of fingerprints of a man
I suspect of connection with some crime about ten years ago.
He claims to come from Pennsylvania. Please check your files
exhaustively and inform me of your findings at your earliest con-
venience.

I am, sir, yours respectfully.

Trencher put the letter before him and took up a pen. He gazed
out the window, at the dark office of the district attorney—but he
could not see Hazzard watching him in the blackness. Absorbed, he
tugged at his memory, tried to remember back through the years, to
connect Hazzard's face with another person, another name.

Strive as he might, Trencher could not find that elusive fragment of recollection. Had it been the line-up—a parade of the accused, in which a man with Hazzard's face had appeared? Had it been in connection with a crime in some other city—a photograph in the newspapers, perhaps? Trencher had searched the newspaper files in vain. He had relentlessly hunted through the police records, but each lead had become obscured in the darkness of the past. It haunted him—that indefinable memory—as he gazed at the dark window beyond where Hazzard stood unseen, watching.

He said aloud "This'll do it!" and signed his name to the letter.

HAZZARD FELT an uncanny apprehension as he drove rapidly toward the home of Judge Crosdale on the outskirts of the city—a persistent hunch that he was being followed. A coldness like the breath of the bullet, which had lightninged past his head in his office, played over his scalp. He searched the shadows as he turned his car into the broad driveway; but the blackness of the night was an enigma.

The maid who admitted him to the stricken home led him into the library where Ann Nash was waiting. She was at his side at once, giving him a neat array of notes already prepared. Her eyes were weary but alert; and Hazzard's hand lingered on her cool fingers as he scanned the neatly written lines.

"Mrs. Crosdale," the girl explained, "says that this wasn't entirely unexpected—the judge had been suffering from Angina. I tried to get more information. This note about the Scotch ale—"

Hazzard was rapidly reading it: "There was a personality sketch about the judge in the *Bulletin* recently. Home life of the great—that sort of thing. In it there's a line about the judge's always taking a glass of ale with his dinner. A case of an imported Scotch brand was delivered here soon afterward—compliments of the distributor."

Hazzard shifted to another note.

"The judge liked it, and ordered more. Tonight, while the jury was out, he came home for dinner and had the first bottle out of the new case. There's more in the refrigerator. Mrs. Crosdale didn't know what I was getting at—I'm not sure of it myself."

"But," Hazzard remarked dryly, "you're very close to being a mind reader, Ann. How did you—?"

"Perhaps it was an accident that the judge's collapse came at such a lucky time for Kelso," the girl answered crisply. "You suspect he was murdered. It would have to be poison. A mistrial, evidence stolen—and Kelso goes free—but Mark Hazzard's on the job."

"Ann." Hazzard asked it softly. "Do you like it—working night and day, missing meals, going without sleep, running the chance of some crazy crook getting you because you're with me in this thing?"

"I thrive on it," she answered.

His hand closed on hers. "You're the only one who knows what I'm driving at—who doesn't try to cure me of my obsession to make the law the instrument of justice it should be. It's in me, so deep-rooted that it can never be eradicated. Nobody understands that but you."

She began: "I lo—" and broke off, as the red of her cheeks deepened, with "—admire you for it."

"I need that."

"Mark." Ann Nash smiled. "I've a question to ask you—in eighteen minutes. Not until then. You can refuse, of course, but—please don't."

"Ask it now."

She shook her head firmly. "Eighteen minutes—can't until then."

"Then, in the meantime," he asked, answering her smile, "where's the kitchen?"

"This way," Ann Nash said, and led him toward it.

It was a fresh white room, with a huge electric refrigerator standing between two windows. Hazzard opened the door and cold air cascaded around his ankles. "More here?" he asked. "Where, Ann?"

The girl, stooped beside him, exclaimed: "There was—a few minutes ago! I saw it. Eleven bottles—half a case less the one the judge had for dinner—in the bottom."

"This time," Hazzard said grimly, rising, "the evidence is stolen before it gets into the hands of the state. It can't be far and—"

He broke off, listening. With a quick turn to the kitchen door, he opened a view upon spreading grounds, noting that the entrance would yield from the outside. A night wind, rustling through elms on the grounds, carried a crackling sound, softened by the distance. It was the noise of splintering glass.

Hazzard hurried; Ann Nash kept at his side. The estate of the late jurist reached over a wooded knoll. In the gloom a brook trickled musically. Hazzard gestured a warning to the girl, crouched when he reached the crest, peered at a winding line of water twinkling faintly in the starlight. His heart quickened as he gazed intently at a shadowy figure bending over the rippling bank. And again, more sharply, came the crash of shattering glass.

Hazzard bounded over. A bush rustled in the darkness. His hand slipped toward his Webley when the sound brought a gasp from the crouching figure. Gun-metal twinkled in the light as Hazzard broke into a run. A dart of flame flashed; a bullet whipped over Hazzard's shoulder; his Webley echoed.

The slugs crossed in the gloom, and the black figure leaped the brook. Hazzard's bound carried him across it. Hot wind fanned his cheek as another bullet whistled. As he followed the darting figure, bushes tripped him. He sprang up, muttering maledictions, hearing the snarl of a motor. When he reached the mesh fence, a car was speeding in the street without lights.

Hazzard aimed swiftly, fired twice; but the thick blackness obscured his target. The car roared around a bend in the drive as he sped back. Ann Nash's anxious call brought his breathless: "Okay! Call Trencher—the prowl cars!" He heard the girl running through the grass as he paused at the edge of the brook.

He tore off a paper match, hearing excited voices in the house. Studying the ground in the flickering light, he saw broken glass glittering among the rocks of the brook bed. Other fragments twinkled on an area of wet earth. Hazzard slipped the jagged neck of a bottle into his pocket, noting the plain cap. He scooped up moist dirt, found a used envelope in his pocket, packed it full.

Ann Nash hurried back, paused, anxiously watched his eyes glitter in the fading light of a second match. "Was it my imagination," he asked, "or did I smell naphthalene in the kitchen?"

"I thought I did!"

He declared tightly: "We've got to have something better than that. Take this envelope, Ann. Find Dr. Norton, wherever he is, and get him into his lab no matter what he's doing." Dr. Timothy Norton was the city toxicologist. "After that," he added, "you might use some sleep."

"You're not hurt?" the girl asked anxiously. "Mark—are you?"

"Missed me," he answered laconically. "I suppose Trencher's sending a man out—there being no hurry. Slip back to the car, Ann. I'll be right with you."

HE WENT into the house as the girl hurried off, and strove to reassure the distracted Mrs. Crosdale that there was no cause for alarm.

He looked again in the kitchen, for a possible clue to the prowler, but could find nothing. He returned thoughtfully to the car, slipped behind the wheel, and started off. Ann Nash looked at him, and said nothing while he drove.

"I'm going to drop off at home," he said at last. "Use this car to get to Dr. Norton's."

"Eighteen minutes are up," the girl said softly, looking at her watch, as Hazzard drew the car to the curb in front of the small house in which he lived. "That makes it one minute past midnight."

"Yes?" curiously.

"It's my birthday. I can do anything I want to now, can't I? I'm going to ask you a question."

"Is it important?"

"The most—the most important thing in the world to me, Mark!" She said it in a whispering rush. "I've got to ask you because you've never asked me."

"What is it, Ann?"

"Will you marry me?"

Mark Hazzard gazed at the girl's red cheeks, at her redder lips, at the shining light of her eyes—and agony pinched his heart. He sat silent, stunned by the answer he knew he was forced to make. He started to speak and could not. A rush of warmth from his heart coursed to the hand closed tightly on the girl's trembling fingers; and he sat wordless until Ann Nash asked:

"Don't you love me, Mark?"

"Ann! Ann, darling, listen. Love you? With all my heart. God, Ann, it's been burning in me for months—ever since I came to know you—that question. The question you've asked me—that I've wanted to ask you—and couldn't."

"Why couldn't you ask me?"

"Ann, there's no one else—you must believe that." His hand crushed hers and he gazed deep into her lucid eyes. "There's no one but you. There never will be, I swear it. God, there's nothing I want more—nothing!"

"Why can't we—"

"Marriage is impossible for me, Ann—impossible!"

"Why, Mark?" softly. "Why?"

Mark Hazzard's tortured mind flashed back through the years—it brought him a picture of a night bitterly cold, of a bleak railroad yard, of the end of an exhausting journey for a man more than ten years younger than Mark Hazzard was now—a journey on the rods of a freight car. The Christmas holidays had urged him to return to his home near Philadelphia by the only means available to him—the stolen ride of a tramp. Mark Hazzard saw himself in that painful flash of memory—penniless, shivering, aching for food—a being who had since ceased to exist, whose name was Dennis Grant.

He heard it again as he sat with fingers clinging yearningly to the hand of Ann Nash—the crack of a shot that had burned the brand of murder upon him.

The gun's report, carrying softly over the sooty snow of the railroad terminal, had sounded the death of a railroad detective. Flashing torches had swung damning beams upon the man who was then Dennis Grant—stabbed him as he strove desperately to elude the searching crew who came swarming through the yards. Hard hands had trapped him. Days of agony had followed. He had heard tragedy speak twice within an hour: the verdict of a jury pronouncing him guilty of murder in the second degree; and the news that the shock of his disgrace had ended his mother's life.

Mark Hazzard vividly remembered the words of the judge instructing the jury upon whose decision his entire life had depended:

"You have heard three witnesses declare that the defendant fired the fatal shot. They have each stated that they saw the defendant commit the crime of murder. Opposed to this, you must weigh the evidence that the revolver found in the snow did not bear the defendant's fingerprints, and his unsupported statement that he did not fire the shot. You must decide whether or not these three eye-witnesses to the tragedy are credible."

Eye-witnesses! The word brought bitterness to the heart of the man who had become Mark Hazzard. Eye-witnesses had seen him commit a crime he had not committed. Eye-witnesses had damned him with a sentence of life imprisonment—mistakenly. Yet no eye had been keen enough to balk the desperate attempt which had turned him into a hunted fugitive.

A swiftly swung chair, the crash of a splintering window blending with the barking of police guns, had sounded the overture to months of hungry hiding and furtive moves. While headlines declared GRANT ESCAPES COURTROOM WHEN SENTENCED, the man who now was Mark Hazzard had huddled in bleak holes, shuddering with the biting cold and the agony of starvation. The memory was delirium in the mind of the District Attorney of King's County.

Once safe beyond the boundaries of the state, once the furor had passed and a changed name had enabled Mark Hazzard to find a job, he had determined to make himself expert in the vagaries of the law which had condemned him while innocent. He had followed an unconquerable determination to make the word "law" mean "justice."

Not the slightest clue had ever come to light to point to the identity of the man who had actually fired the shot that had brought conviction for murder upon Dennis Grant. There was no hope that the truth would ever be learned. The years had formed a baffling maze that could not be penetrated to the real killer. Perhaps by now death had sealed the lips of the guilty man against confession. It was a scar of which Mark Hazzard could never rid himself.

Yet the years had not removed the danger that Mark Hazzard's real identity might become known. The charge of murder still held against Dennis Grant and time could never outlaw it. A life sentence still awaited him; and if the truth were learned, Mark Hazzard must serve it. If the secret of the District Attorney of King's County were ever revealed, Mark Hazzard would become Dennis Grant, convicted murderer.

He had exerted all the keenness of his mind upon the bonds that connected him with that dread past; he had severed them one by one; but the possibility that one might remain haunted him. In some way he could not dream now, the past might rise at any moment to damn him. He could never escape the danger that constantly hunted him; he could ask no one to share it with him—least of all the girl he loved.

And Ann Nash had asked: "Why can't you marry me, Mark?"

"God, Ann!" he blurted. "In all the world there's nothing I want more—but I can't! I can't!"

He shouldered from the car, blinded with anguish, and strode stiffly to the front of his dark house. He fumbled with the key, stepped into deeper gloom, and stood shocked with despair, heart pounding. He did not move until he heard the car move away; until the girl he loved had gone. Suddenly a wild impulse seized him, to rush after her, to tell her, to dare to ask her to share the danger with him. His hand gripped the knob hotly; but suddenly it went cold.

He remembered—saw as clearly as though they were staring at him now—the black, ominous eyes of Inspector Trencher.

CHAPTER III

SECRET CAPTIVE

MARK HAZZARD snapped lights, strode to the rear of the little house that was his home. He lived here alone, with a motherly old housekeeper to tidy the rooms with Hazzard's never catching a glimpse of her. He stepped into a closet in the hallway, and lifted the receiver of a little independent telephone, and touched a red button.

This line was less than a hundred feet long; it trailed into a room located above the garage at the rear of the grounds. There, Hazzard knew, Dan Carey was hidden. Carey was a hard-muscled, ruddy-faced young man who had become Hazzard's assistant in matters of extralegal justice. The room above the garage was a haven in which he lived in secret, always ready to obey Hazzard's slightest command with dogged, loyal zeal. His voice answered on the line:

"Okay, skipper."

Hazzard said quietly: "Danny, I want Nat Brock watched."

"Brock!" the hushed voice answered. "There ain't any guy I'd rather spot—you know that, skipper. What do you want him for?"

"No legal charge can cover the case at this point, Danny," Hazzard explained. "Perhaps I can find proof enough to charge him with murder—but I doubt it. Legally or not, we've got to get him somehow. Your job's to keep an eye on him. When you spot him, call me, either here or at the office."

"Right, skipper!"

Hazzard stepped from the closet and went into the living-room, to the telephone connected with the city system. He waited, listening to the hum of a motor from the garage. He heard Dan Carey drive away along the alley flanking the rear of the house, and smiled with cold satisfaction, knowing that Carey would stick to the trail with dogged persistence. As the sound of the car vanished, Hazzard dialed the number of police headquarters and asked for Inspector Trencher.

"Would I be rushing things," he asked wryly, "if I asked whether you've got any lead on the man who's trailing me around with a silenced gun, inspector?"

Trencher drawled over the line: "Take your time, Hazzard. We'll get him. Just leave it to me. What makes you think he's still trying to get you?"

"A feeling," Hazzard answered, "that I'm being watched. There's no legal proof, of course, inspector, but that would-be killer is a rod man for Kelso. Kelso is taking desperate measures to beat a life rap. Being shot at, inspector, is something that makes me mad."

"Sure, sure," Trencher drawled. "I'll take care of this. You're a better state's attorney alive than dead. I told you that before you ever started out to get Kelso. Have you got any evidence that one of his mob shot at you—evidence enough so's I can swear out a warrant to arrest him?"

Hazzard answered: "No evidence, inspector—except common sense, which is not admissible in a court of law. There are not," he added wryly, "any eye-witnesses."

Trencher drawled: "Well, I'll assign a man to guard you."

"No, thanks, inspector," Hazzard answered with a tight smile. "He'd only cramp my style."

"Hmpff!" Trencher said. "If one of Kelso's rod men puts a bullet into you, there probably won't be evidence enough to arrest him. How easily will you rest in your grave knowing that? Don't be a damned fool!"

"Being a damned fool," Hazzard observed, "is evidently my greatest talent."

He left the telephone and paced the room anxiously. Kelso's ruthlessness carried a bitter undercurrent through his flow of thoughts as he moved back and forth, baffled by the prospect of constructing a legally presentable case against that predatory crook. His anger stirred; a rankling torment filled him when, after an interval, the telephone rang.

His quiet "Yes?" brought an answer in the voice of Ann Nash.

"I'm calling from Dr. Norton's lab, Mark," the tireless secretary said breathlessly. "I got him out of bed and made him come here—and it was worth it. You're right—Judge Crosdale was poisoned!"

Hazzard heard the heavy voice of the toxicologist rumble over the wire. "Please understand that my findings are no proof that any murder has been committed. I have simply applied Reinsch's test to the wet earth you submitted, and I find traces of arsenic."

Hazzard asked swiftly: "Arsenic administered over a period of time will result in death through collapse, won't it, Dr. Norton?"

"In certain cases. But please remember I found the arsenic in the dirt. Probably the ale which Miss Nash mentioned, spilled there, accounts for it—arsenic is soluble in beer—but there's no proof of it. You have very slight evidence to justify an autopsy on Judge Crosdale."

The voice of Ann Nash returned. "Your mind reader is still on the job. The Scotch ale is imported by Hiker and Company in this city—a small concern. A man named Max Connor is sales manager. He's on his way to your office now."

"And you," Hazzard told the girl, "are on your way to bed. Aren't you?"

Softly came: "Good-night, darling."

HAZZARD LEFT the house hurriedly. His wary glance up and down the street found empty shadows. There was no suggestion of a lurking killer in the darkness; yet, while Hazzard sought a taxi, he felt that uncanny, cold prickling of his scalp which warned him that unseen eyes were watching him. It persisted even after a cab picked him up and carried him toward the formidable, white stone courthouse.

Entering his office, he glanced across the street to see the slow-moving but indefatigable Trencher still at his desk. He heard footfalls on the stairway and took up the telephone as it rang. The voice on the line was Dan Carey's.

"On the job, skipper."

"Good, Danny!"

"Nat Brock's at the Sunrise Bar, one of his hangouts. I can't get near him—he'd recognize me—but I've got him spotted. Do I keep him in sight?"

"You forget about sleeping and eating, Danny. Shadow him wherever he goes. I'm looking for a sniper who's trailing me around with a silenced gun, waiting for a chance to drop me, but Brock's probably not the man. Keep him in sight and—"

"Slick Perles is with Brock, skipper—another of Kelso's sneaky sidekicks."

Hazzard observed grimly: "I'll take care of that angle. Brock's your man, Danny—and phone if the trail gets hot."

"With a chance of getting that crook, I'll never let him slip me!" Carey promised grimly.

Knuckles were rapping the door when Hazzard lowered the phone. He opened the way and peered at the thin-faced, shifty-eyed caller. There was an edge of insolence in the squeaky voice which said:

"I'm Max Connor. What the hell d' you wanna see me about?"

Hazzard gestured Connor to a chair, dug into his top-coat pocket, and held the broken neck of a bottle toward his caller. He pointed to the plain cap which was still in place and asked crisply:

"Can you identify that?"

"No."

"You have the agency for Highland Ale in this city. This is a part of a Highland Ale bottle, isn't it? The name's stamped in the glass."

"I guess it is."

"Is that a Highland Ale cap, that plain one? That's a matter you'll have to tell the truth about, Connor, because I can check it a thousand ways."

Connor mumbled: "Highland Ale has caps with a picture of a girl in kilts on 'em."

"Which means this bottle of ale was opened, then recapped—is that it?"

"I don't know nothin' about it."

Hazzard straightened. "Make yourself comfortable, Mr. Connor. You have nothing to be uneasy about—only the charge of being an accessory before the fact of first degree murder."

Connor widened his shifty eyes and blurted: "What the hell're you talkin' about?"

Hazzard pressed his questions. "Did you send a complimentary case of Highland Ale to Judge Crosdale? Did you know the caps had been removed, poison dropped in, and new caps put on? What about the second case Judge Crosdale ordered—all bottles with this plain cap instead of the originals? Who made the switch? Tell the truth!"

Connor mumbled: "I'd have to look at the records, I don't know nothin' about it. I don't know nothin'—nothin'."

Hazzard leaned forward intently. "Have you ever been in the death house, Connor? Have you ever seen a man fry? Do you know how it's done? They shave the back of your head so you get the jolt in the brain. They strap you around the legs and put a mask on your face. It's cold in there—until they throw the switch. You feel it hit you, feel your flesh burn—smell it burning—while you sit there frying....Have you ever thought of that, Connor?"

Connor jerked up, staring, and Hazzard followed with gleaming eyes.

"What're you talkin' about!"

"I'm talking about what's going to happen to you for being an accessory to a murder. You know who put arsenic in the ale that was sent to Judge Crosdale. You're as guilty as the man who put it in. That's the law, Connor—and I'm the man who's going to send you to the chair if you don't talk!"

Connor blurted: "I ain't under arrest! You can't make me talk! I got a right to have a lawyer!"

Hazzard's open palm slapped Connor's face. Connor recoiled, whimpering, then made a crazy try to strike back. Hazzard's tempered muscles broke the attempt. His hand clamped hard on Connor's throat. Again his palm slapped blindingly across Connor's face.

"You're innocent, are you? You're fighting back like an innocent man. You're facing me without being afraid—like an innocent man. The law's on your side at this moment, Connor—why don't you make the most of it? Or would you rather talk and beat the rap? Talk—instead of frying in the hot chair and feeling your flesh burn?"

"God—God, don't!" Connor quailed against the wall. "I don't know nothin' about it. Brock took a case of ale, that's all, then had our truck pick it up and take it to Crosdale's. He had the second case ready the same way. I don't know nothin' else about it!"

Hazzard snapped: "You're coming with me!"

HIS THRUST sent Connor reeling into the outer office. His eyes blazed with contempt, his face flamed with the heat of his volcanic temper as he went down the steps after Connor. He forced Connor across the street, into the massive structure that housed police headquarters. He shoved Connor into an office and came grimly to a stop, facing the ominous black eyes of Inspector Trencher.

Trencher drawled: "Hello, Hazzard. What's coming off here? Is this man under arrest? Have you got a warrant for him? What's the charge?"

"A warrant," Hazzard answered quickly, "is exactly what I'm here for." He spoke rapidly, word crowding word, while Connor shifted in frantic uneasiness from foot to foot, Trencher's black eyes studying him shrewdly. "I want a warrant for Nat Brock's arrest, on first degree murder."

Trencher's head wagged. "From the looks of this bird you've brought in," he said, "he could have you up for assault and battery and get away with it."

Hazzard asked grimly: "Do I get that warrant, inspector?"

Trencher frowned. "Hazzard, you know the law—except when that hot head of yours takes fire, and then you're apt to forget it. If Crosdale was murdered, I want to get the killer as badly as you do—worse, because Crosdale was one of my dearest friends. I'll do it, too—in time. But you haven't got a case now, Hazzard. I can't give you a warrant."

"I'm certain that Judge Crosdale was poisoned by arsenic dissolved in the ale Nat Brock doctored—that Crosdale's death is saving Sid Kelso from life imprisonment."

"Listen, Hazzard." Trencher wagged a weary gesture. "Have you any evidence of arsenic in Judge Crosdale's body? No, you haven't. What're you going to do—order an autopsy? You've the power to demand it, Hazzard—but you won't do it if I can stop you. And I'm going to stop you—until you've a damned sight more proof than you've got now."

Hazzard exclaimed: "What?"

"Sure, you can demand it, Hazzard," Trencher drawled on, "but I don't think you'll get it done, as matters stand now. Crosdale and Dr. Autumn, the Medical Examiner, and me—we're the oldest men in the city government. We've seen so many district attorneys come and go, we can't remember the names of 'em all. Mark Hazzard started to set the world on fire about ten years ago, and the three of us—we've been close friends for three times that long. If I say to old Doc Autumn, 'I think Hazzard's going off half-cocked about this autopsy on the judge,' he'll agree with me, and find some way of getting around it."

"But—"

"Because he doesn't want the ghastly job of cutting into the brain and stomach of a man who was as close to him as a brother, and he won't allow any of his assistants to do it. I think that's how it stands, Hazzard. You'll have to have damn' powerful proof before you'll get an autopsy performed on Crosdale. It would be outrageous cruelty to Crosdale's family."

Hazzard declared tightly: "In spite of all that, I'm going to see Crosdale's murderer get what's coming to him—I'm going to prove he died of arsenic poisoning."

Trencher's eyes were searching. "Calm down, Hazzard. Doc Norton told me there's no conclusive proof arsenic was in the ale. If there was, you have no proof that Brock is the man who put it in. Even if he did, you can't prove that the ale he doctored is the ale the judge drank. That's pretty thin circumstantial evidence—and you have no eye-witnesses to any part of it, have you?"

Bitterly Hazzard echoed: "Eye-witnesses!"

"See how it stands, Hazzard? You can't connect Brock with this thing, and you're still farther from connecting Kelso with it. Better back down and leave this to me. You might have the strongest moral conviction in the world—but that's not legal evidence."

Hazzard agreed grimly: "That I know!"

Trencher turned to smile crookedly at the nervous Connor. "Well?" he drawled. "If you're going to charge Hazzard with felonious assault, this is the time to do it. If you're not—clear out!"

Connor's shifty eyes turned to Hazzard. The bruise across his jowl grew more vivid as his gaunt face paled. His swollen lips fumbled with words stopped by Hazzard's clear voice.

"Go ahead, Connor. Take advantage of your legal right. That'll bring the case to trial and get the facts about the doped ale into the court record. Why don't you speak up? Listen. If you're smart, you'll turn state's evidence. But if you try to skip, I'll follow you and drag you back no matter where you hole in. Felonious assault, Connor—how about it?"

Connor turned abruptly and snatched at the door knob. His quick steps sounded in the corridor as the door slammed. Hazzard smiled tightly into Trencher's smouldering eyes.

"My cards are on the table, inspector," the district attorney declared. "I'm out to get Brock and Kelso any way I can get them. You may get me in the process, but I'll get them first." He strode to the door, turned back grimly. "Some undertaker in town," he added coolly, "is going to get an order for coffins for two."

"It'd be too bad, Hazzard," Trencher drawled, "if you made a hot-headed mistake."

Hazzard's smile tightened. He went back to the desk, peering at a circle of glass that lay on Trencher's blotter. He asked ironically:

"Isn't that mine, Trencher—that paper-weight? I'm missing one exactly like it from my office."

Trencher's eyes glinted. "Yes, it's yours, Hazzard," he answered. "When I'm looking for evidence, I sometimes pick up things absent-mindedly. I carried this out of your office the other night. I thought maybe the robber's fingerprints might be on it."

"Were there," Hazzard asked tightly, "fingerprints?"

Trencher drawled: "I'm checking up on that now. I'll let you know."

Lips curved hard, Hazzard said bitterly, "Thanks!" He took the paper-weight from Trencher's steady hand. His fingers gripped it tightly as he strode from the office.

Trencher sat, smile fading, eyes brightening grimly. He touched a button on his desk and was still peering at the door through which Hazzard had gone when a blue-shirted man stepped into his office.

"I'm expecting a letter from the Department of Justice, Moore," he said in a low tone. "When it comes, see that I get it—no matter where I happen to be—the fastest way possible."

Then, slowly, shrewdly, he began to smile again.

HAZZARD STEPPED from a cab in front of his home—and again felt the prickling of indefinable dread which warned him someone was watching him—a killer lurking in the shadows. He pointed the key into the lock of the entrance; but to his surprise, the door swung open. He stepped in, startled, seeing a litter of papers on the floor of the room beyond. He moved toward his desk—and saw that it had been rifled.

Its drawers were out; papers were scattered. The desk clock had been knocked to the floor. Hazzard's glance, first at its face, then at his wristwatch, told him that the search had been made only a few minutes previous. He was striding out hastily, his temper flaming, when quick steps sounded on the rear porch and a husky voice called in: "Skipper!"

Hazzard hurried to the firm-bodied young man who sidled in. Dan Carey's eyes were wide with wonder. He paused to blurt:

"Brock broke in here, skipper—your own place! He sneaked in from the alley. I didn't know what to do—tried to call you—I was starting in after him when you showed up. For Lord's sake, skipper, what's Brock trying to pull off?"

"Trying to get something on me!" Hazzard answered angrily. "Where is he now, Danny!"

"He beat it out when your taxi stopped. I saw him going up the stairs to my place over the garage. He must be there now, skipper!"

Hazzard turned startled as a bell rang. On the pane of the entrance he saw a man's shadow, arm raised to the call button. He started toward it and ordered crisply:

"Slip out and watch your door, Danny. If Brock starts out again, nail him. Careful!"

"I'll get that guy!" Carey promised it grimly as he slipped out the back entrance.

Mark Hazzard quickly closed the door of his study as he looked again at the shadow on the entrance pane. "Careful!" he had warned Dan Carey, and now his head spun with dread. The need for caution bore upon them both, for Dan Carey was a fugitive from the law, an escaped convict charged with murder. Mark Hazzard alone held the secret of Carey's presence in the city. He was the district attorney who had sent Carey up the river—but the secret was one which would never pass his lips. He was thinking anxiously of the loyal Carey as he looked at the shadow on the door and took slow steps.

The bond that held Hazzard and Carey strongly together was the mutual danger of discovery—the constant, hovering threat of the chair for Carey and life imprisonment for Hazzard.

Once Dan Carey had been a cop under the orders of Inspector Trencher. He had built up an enviable record, then had resigned to accept an offer as detective with a private investigating agency. Working on a case of daring extortion, a dangerous trail had led him to Brock and Kelso. Carey's career had ended abruptly when the grim Inspector Trencher found his fingerprints on the police positive that lay beneath the body of a man shot through the heart.

Carey had desperately fought the charge of murder. District Attorney Mark Hazzard, handling his first homicide case, had listened to Carey's lawyer argue that Carey's gun had been stolen to use as a plant, that the victim, one "Ice" Cling, though a henchman of Kelso's, was also an underworld foe of Nat Brock. But the attempt to turn suspicion on Brock had ended in failure.

Hazzard's duty had obliged him to present the fingerprints on the gun as damning evidence, against Carey, though in his heart he had felt a moral certainty that the ex-cop was guiltless. The jury had brought Hazzard unwanted victory with a verdict of "Guilty"—a word condemning Carey to the chair.

Hazzard remembered, as he approached the door, reading with unconcealed satisfaction the startling newspaper headlines announcing the escape of Dan Carey while on his way to the state prison. He recalled the night when, on one of his investigating prowls among the dives of the city, he had found a bewhiskered vagabond quaking with cold, sickened with hunger, huddling behind garbage cans in an alley.

Mark Hazzard had looked at Dan Carey that wretched night, and had seen Dennis Grant, a hunger-tortured fugitive from so-called justice.

He had not revealed his discovery to Inspector Trencher because he was convinced of the innocence of the man he had convicted. Secretly he had brought Carey to his home. He had furnished the room above the garage as a haven for the man whom the law was hunting. District Attorney Hazzard had assumed the risk of harboring a fugitive from justice.

The pathetically grateful Carey had become Hazzard's undercover partner even while the law hunted him. In secret comradeship with the district attorney who had sent him up the river, Carey was crouched now somewhere in the blackness behind the house—hiding from the danger of discovery while at the same time watching a criminal enemy of Hazzard's.

HAZZARD PULLED the door open, smiled grimly at the fattish face high-lighted against the gloom of the street, and said: "Good evening, Flarigan."

Big Tom Flarigan rumbled: "I want to talk with you, Hazzard, about something important."

Hazzard's anxious mind was on Brock; his temper was still hot. Impatiently he began: "Suppose I see you at your office first thing in the morning, Flarigan, and—"

"This," the huge man interrupted heavily, "is too important to wait."

With sharp concern; Hazzard followed the big man into the living-room. He had known this man from the start of his career—Big Tom Flarigan, the political driver of the controlling machine. Flarigan's organization dominated the city. To oppose him meant political suicide—an axiom proven repeatedly at the polls. Hazzard, looking into Flarigan's dark blue eyes, saw condemnation now.

"Hazzard, I made you—you're not forgetting that, are you?"

"You put me in office, Flarigan—that's true."

"Sure." There was an ominous undertone of warning in the big man's fatherly manner. "The D.A. we had then was raising a bad smell. You were just the kind of a man we needed. We worked together pretty well then, didn't we, Hazzard? I got you elected."

"You made me," Hazzard said with eyes gleaming, "and you can break me—that's the point, isn't it, Flarigan?"

Hazzard's directness brought a conciliating gesture from the big man. "No need to put it that way, but it's true. You're a good man, Hazzard, but a little—impulsive. Sometimes you don't stop to think. You're going like all hell fire into something now that ought to be handled careful."

"Kelso?" Hazzard asked tightly.

Now Flarigan's fatherly manner vanished. "Be wise, Hazzard. Be smart. Why, if you play along with me, you can have anything you want. The voters like you. Anything you want—mayor, senator, maybe even governor in time—anything. If you play along with me, Hazzard— and be wise."

"That kind of wisdom, Flarigan," Hazzard answered, "doesn't seem to be a characteristic inherited with my red hair."

Flarigan came heavily to his feet. "Better think it over, Hazzard. Think it over. You said it—I made you and I can break you. Remember that."

Hazzard said tightly: "Listen. I won't be bribed with money and I won't be bribed with threats. Becoming mayor or senator or even governor doesn't mean a damn' thing to me. I'm where I want to be—District Attorney—with a chance to make the law mean what it should. If you're determined to break me, Flarigan, you can start now."

Flarigan warned again: "Be wise."

"I'm going after Kelso and Brock until I get them. That's a promise, Flarigan. Good-night!"

FLARIGAN STRODE out. Hazzard's flaming temper brought wrathful red to his face as he closed the entrance with a click. He turned swiftly, sped to the rear door, sidled into the gloom. The political boss' threats passed from his mind in his concern for Carey, in the danger of Brock's presence in his house. He drifted silently across the grass until a whisper stopped him:

"Skipper!" Carey came quickly to Hazzard's side. "He's still in there, skipper—my place!"

Hazzard said tightly: "We'll pay him a call."

They moved toward the door in the wall of the garage which opened onto stairs that could be raised and lowered from the ceiling. Through it Carey had seen Nat Brock slip. Now, as they neared it, they heard the soft rasp of a turning knob, and saw a dark figure silhouetted against the white wall.

"Get him!" Hazzard snapped.

The command sent Carey diving toward the door, and Brock bounding toward the alley. Hazzard heard the cracking of knuckles against flesh as he leaped to block Brock's path. He saw Carey staggering against the wall, Brock again leaping off. Hazzard bounded, Webley in hand, straight at Brock. A driving fist smashed along Hazzard's chin as he straight-armed with his left.

The skin of his knuckles split on the point of Brock's jaw. Brock sprawled back, arms flinging wildly, and crunched on the gravel walk. Carey, scrambling, plunged on him. Hazzard straddled, automatic leveled, his temper a raging heat. Carey dragged the struggling man up and Hazzard's voice crackled.

"Stop that!" Brock peered, and the glint of the Webley forced him to subside. His breath beat fast as he peered into Carey's face, then into Hazzard's.

Hazzard commanded evenly: "Go back up, Brock. You're just the man I want to see. If I'm not mistaken, there's an odor of naphthalene about you."

Brock gasped: "I know him! He's Carey! Carey!"

Carey's big hands grabbed at Brock's shoulders and he shook him viciously. "Shut up!" he ordered. "You heard that. Go back up!"

Hazzard's heart speeded as Carey hurled Brock against the garage wall. The glimmer of the Webley forced Brock through the door, back up the stairs. Carey kept close behind him; Hazzard stepped last into the little room under the roof. Brock whirled to face them, his ratty eyes flashing with fear and triumph.

"Turning Carey in, Hazzard?" he asked in a snarl. "Tellin' the cops there's an escaped convict here?"

Carey snapped: "Shut up, rat!"

Brock blurted: "He's been livin' here—I've found that out! Livin' here on the D.A.'s place! That's goin' to be good! The D.A. harborin' a fugitive!"

Carey snapped again, savagely: "Shut up!"

"I'll spread it! The D.A. with a convict in his place! How'll you like that, Hazzard? How'll you like goin' up the river for it? You're goin' to get the works for it—the—"

Dan Carey's hand slapped resoundingly across Brock's evil mouth. Brock staggered, dazed, terror shining in his eyes. Carey took dogged steps after him, fists clenched.

"You framed me, Brock—that's the reason I'm a convict. You drilled Cling and fixed it on me! I've been waiting for a chance to get my hands on you! Brock, you dirty—!"

Carey's fingers closed on Brock's throat. Brock's face flashed white as he clawed at the ex-cop's tendoned wrists. Cold fury tightened Carey's muscles as Hazzard seized his arm.

"Easy, Danny!"

Carey looked up, lips drawn, thumbs crushing upon Brock's windpipe.

"If you kill him, Danny," Hazzard said slowly, "you'll never have a chance to clear yourself of the charge of murder."

Carey's hands loosened. He stepped back and left Brock cringing against the wall. He began: "Him finding out about you and me, skipper—" and Brock cut in vehemently: "You'll have to kill me to keep it quiet! Murder me! That's the only way you can keep me from tellin' the whole—"

Again Carey's hard hand slapped stinging pain across Brock's mouth. Brock sagged, lips bleeding. Hazzard, looking into Carey's anxious eyes, said quietly:

"Tie him up, Danny. Make a good job of it."

Brock pushed for the wall, began a mad scramble toward the door. Hazzard sprang after him desperately; his arm hooked under Brock's chin and Brock squirmed helplessly. Carey, jerking a sheet from the bed, began tearing it into strips. Hazzard grimly held his man captive until Carey gasped, "Okay, skipper!" Then Hazzard twisted Brock's arms, forced him down, held him still while Carey wrapped white bands tightly around Brock's ankles and wrists.

Carey thrust a section of the sheet into Brock's mouth and bound it down with another strip. When he rose, Brock lay helpless on the floor, terrified eyes staring.

Hazzard's hands went into his pocket. He said, "This belongs to you, I think, Brock." A tiny sphere of white, clicking and rolling on the floor, brought wilder terror to Brock's eyes. Hazzard stood straight, gun returned to his holster, speaking tartly.

"You're going to have a chance to make up your mind, Brock—to tell the truth. Carey's going to stay right here, and wait for you to talk. The whole story, Brock—how you poisoned Judge Crosdale, how you robbed my office, how Kelso's put a killer on my trail. How you framed Carey for murder—all of it. A statement, signed and witnessed, that will stand as evidence in court. When you're ready, Brock, just let Carey know."

Hazzard strode stiffly down the stairs. Carey followed him, and in the darkness beside the garage they paused, peering at each other haggardly.

"God, skipper, I'll kill that rat before I'll let him get you into trouble—about me!"

"If you do that, Danny," Hazzard answered levelly, "there'll never be an hour when the law won't be hunting for you as a convicted murderer."

"I'll go to the chair before I'll see you take a rap on my account!"

Hazzard's tight lips clipped his words. "You can't do that, Danny—you can't! This is my job—my job, do you understand that? Even if it breaks me, I'm going to get Kelso and Brock. That's a promise, Danny—a promise I'm going to keep!"

CHAPTER IV

DEAD MAN'S HAIR

LIGHTS WERE burning in Hazzard's office next evening when he strode in quietly. Ann Nash, alert and bright-eyed as though she had not lost a moment's sleep, followed him to his desk. There was anxiety in her eyes, a sadness in her smile that pinched Hazzard's heart. She asked quietly:

"Now—can you tell me why?"

"Ann, it's something I can never tell you."

Her chin lifted. "Some day I'm going to find out, Mark, and make you see it doesn't matter—that nothing can matter that much."

"I hope you never find out."

"I'm going to try." She forced another smile. "In the meantime, then, between the district attorney and his secretary, strictly business. I've just tried again, on the telephone, to get Trencher to let down about the autopsy, but he won't. He's blocked every move."

Hazzard's knuckles rapped the desk angrily. He reached for the telephone, spun off the number of the telephone in Carey's hidden room. "Hat and coat, Ann," he said quietly. "I'm going to need you." He heard the receiver lift, but no salutation answered.

"District Attorney Hazzard speaking. Anything doing on the case you're handling?"

Carey's answer rang with anger. "Brock's holding out, skipper. He ain't made a move to talk yet. God, it's hard to keep my hands off that rat's dirty throat!"

Hazzard answered: "I'll handle that. Coming right away."

He left his desk with determined steps, and Ann Nash, in trim coat and pert hat, followed him down the stairway. As he went with her to his car, he felt again the prickling warning that he was being watched. To Hazzard it meant that a hired killer was still trailing him, that the moment was coming when a well-aimed bullet would hit him. He glanced around alertly as he took the wheel and started away.

The girl beside him said nothing as he took the shortest route toward the home of Judge Crosdale. He drew to the curb, noting that a patrolman was stationed on the porch. "Trencher," he observed wryly, "expects me to do something hot-headed!"

Ann's eyes followed him anxiously.

"Wait," he said. He went quietly across the sidewalk, alertly watching the patrolman, and eased through the gate. Still feeling that eerie warning of hidden eyes watching him, he kept to the shadows and walked across the grass. Circling silently to the side of the house, he peered through a curtained window and saw a familiar face—a man talking with Mrs. Crosdale. Trencher.

Cold purpose narrowing his eyes, Hazzard shifted to the side porch, to the French windows of the adjoining room. He peered in through drawn drapes, and saw, in the amber light, a casket.

Hazzard pried at the windows, drew one open silently. He stepped quietly into the room where the dead jurist lay; he went to the casket and peered down at the wax-like features of Judge Crosdale. His lips pressed as he brought a small pair of scissors from his pocket. He bent intently, and the blades snipped off a lock of the dead man's hair.

He slipped it into an envelope, which he pocketed—turned—and stopped short, staring. He had not heard the connecting door open. He had heard no step in the room. But now he was looking into the ominous eyes of Inspector Trencher—black condemnation.

Trencher drawled bitterly: "That's going too far, Hazzard."

Hazzard's answer snapped. "You forced it on me, by refusing—"

"I warned you about making a mistake. Mutilating a dead body is a serious crime. Where do you think it's going to get you?"

Grimly Hazzard countered with: "What are you going to do about it, Trencher?"

"We'll ask the commissioner," Trencher said heavily. "We'll ask him what we're going to do about it. Give me that, Hazzard." The inspector's hand extended for the envelope.

Hazzard straightened. "I'm keeping it, Trencher—and I'll answer to any charge for taking it. There's one procedure you forget, isn't there? You'll have to have a warrant before you can arrest me." He started angrily toward the open door.

"I think I'll have it, Hazzard."

Hazzard stepped out into the darkness—and into the menace of a killer's gun.

The whizz of the bullet past Hazzard's head was followed quickly by the muffled report that burst from the shadows of the lawn. Glass cracked behind Hazzard's head as he leaped aside, hand sliding toward his Webley.

Trencher blurted in consternation and charged into the open.

Hazzard, backing against the wall, warned swiftly: "Out of the light, inspector!"

Trencher bawled: "Adams!" and the patrolman came running from the front porch.

A rustle of leaves on the far side of the lawn told Hazzard that the sniper was rushing for cover. Grimly, deciding to leave the chase to Trencher, he started across the lawn toward the gate. Adams was running with bared gun. Trencher plodded wheezing and grim after Adams as Hazzard hurried to his car.

He remarked wryly as he slipped behind the wheel, Ann Nash's widened eyes upon him: "Kelso's rod man is a rotten shot!"

The girl's hand went to his hotly as he sent the car swinging around the bend in the drive. He headed into the business district, swung to a stop in front of a telegraph office. He wrote on a blank quickly:

> Dr. Norton:
>
> Please analyze this sample of hair for traces of arsenic and give your report to Inspector Trencher as soon as possible.
>
> HAZZARD.

The note was sealed in the envelope with the white lock when Hazzard pressed it with a bill in the hand of a messenger boy. "Hang onto that," he ordered, "and break all records getting there!" His face was set, his eyes shining with purpose, when he returned to the wheel and sent the car whizzing again.

ANN NASH'S eyes, reflected bewilderment when he swung into the alleyway behind his home. She followed him as he opened the garage door. He lowered the steps, went up and into the lighted room, followed by the girl who paused in consternation, peering at Brock, bound on the floor, and at the ruddy face of Dan Carey.

"You've seen Danny before, Ann," Hazzard said with quiet grimness. "You know now that the district attorney is guilty of harboring a fugitive."

The girl asked breathlessly, "Is that—is that the reason why you can't—"

"No," Hazzard said softly. "No, Ann. It's—something else." He turned to the bound Brock while the girl watched anxiously. His lips tightened when Carey blurted: "He's kept tight as a clam, skipper!" His hands fastened on Brock's arms as he said:

"You might get me for this, Brock—but that's not going to stop my getting you. Understand that? Listen. Carey's going with me. My secretary is staying here with you, ready to take any statement you want to make. This is your last chance tonight—understand?"

Brock glared. Hazzard straightened to say: "Get into that old uniform of yours, Danny. Ann, I'm forced to mix you up in this. Tonight's got to decide Kelso's case—there's no other way. If Brock wants to make a statement, take his gag off—don't loosen his hands or feet—and make him sign your notes. Will you do it, Ann?"

Ann Nash answered firmly: "I'll do anything you ask of me, Mark."

Dan Carey was quickly pulling into the blue uniform of a patrolman. Hazzard's mind flashed details of a plan while he waited. Before going to his office, he had been watching the building in which Sid Kelso lived. He had seen Kelso leave, and had followed to another building. There, Hazzard knew, lived one Helen Norcross, a blonde dancer at the Paradise Cabaret, upon whom Kelso lavished furs and diamonds. He gambled that Kelso was still there, and took up the telephone to dial the number of the Norcross apartment.

The woman's voice that answered was falsely cultured.

Hazzard, speaking in a whisper, asked: "Sid there?"

"Yes."

"Tell him he's wanted at home."

Brock stared at Hazzard with terror, Ann Nash with growing anxiety, as Hazzard spun the dial again. This time he ticked off the number of the apartment building in which Sid Kelso lived. In a voice cleverly disguised, Hazzard asked for Kelso.

"What?" came over the line. "You're kidding me, aren't you? I know your voice—you're Mr. Kelso yourself."

Hazzard said: "No, no. You're mistaken."

The doubtful answer was: "You sound just like Mr. Kelso. Either way, he isn't in."

"Take a message," Hazzard directed in the counterfeit of the extortionist's voice. " 'Come to 1010 Wharton Street. One of the boys is in trouble.' That's all. Thanks."

"You sure this isn't a joke, you're not Mr. Kelso?"

Hazzard cut the connection, smiling tightly. Carey was buttoning the tunic of his uniform. The girl took the gun which Hazzard pressed into her hand and smiled when he said: "Chin up!" His fingers lingered on hers as Carey ran down the steps; and when he turned to follow, his denied yearning for this girl was an agony.

Carey sat tensely beside Hazzard as he sped the car toward the business section of the city.

"Skipper, I can't figure this!" he blurted.

Hazzard smiled tightly, and turned the car into a street colored with the neon glare of cheap restaurants and shady hotels. "I'm playing a gamble to force the truth out of Kelso's hired men, Danny," he said quickly. "And if that gamble loses, there'll be no more of either of us."

"Skipper, I can take it," Carey answered earnestly. "But I'm not going to see you get it on my account!"

Hazzard's car stopped near the corner of Wharton Street. He walked with Carey quickly to the door of 1010. It was an empty store, its panes grimy. Hazzard's skeleton keys drew the bolt of the old lock. He eased in; Carey stood at his side in the darkness. Quietly he said:

"We'll see if Kelso takes the bait. Watch for him through the window, Danny—in that checkered coat and flashy green hat of his. Remember above everything else—we can't let Kelso catch even a glimpse of us. If he does, the whole plan's wrecked."

"He won't be able to see much through our knuckles, skipper!"

THEY WAITED while minutes ticked by with agonizing slowness. Each time a shadow passed the grimy windows, they tightened. Each time a step sounded on the pavement their breath quickened. Dread that the wary Kelso would not come made their hearts beat heavily while minute followed minute interminably. Hazzard's bitter despair ended abruptly with Carey's sharp whisper:

"Back, skipper!"

They huddled against the side wall, peering at the shadow which now lay motionless on the greasy panes. Shoes gritted down the cement stairs. Hazzard poised, seeing the evil face of Sid Kelso in the faint neon glow. He saw Kelso make a gesture that might be a signal to someone else in the street. The knob grated and turned; and Kelso took slow steps inward.

Hazzard leaped. His shoulder jarred the heavy-muscled man against the opposite wall. Kelso whirled with a stifled bellow and struck once, wildly. Hazzard's fists flashed with trained precision, three times, driving past Kelso's clumsy defense. The paunchy man went down with a wheeze, crunched to the floor, lay still.

"He didn't spot us, skipper! All clear!"

"Watch the door, Danny!"

Carey stood alert, hand ready on the butt of his gun, while Hazzard bent breathlessly over Kelso. He found Kelso's keys; he emptied every pocket. He pulled off Kelso's top-coat and hat, then took a roll of adhesive tape from his pocket. He plastered Kelso's mouth, bound Kelso's wrists and ankles with the sticky straps. He straightened at Carey's side, peered into the pink-green glare of the street and said tightly:

"You're coming with me, Danny."

Hazzard eased the door open. He took Kelso's coat and hat, went up the steps, glanced back and forth, started away. Shock stopped him—an explosion of cold sensations. It struck his senses like a sudden storm—the pinch of torn flesh, the hollow pop of a silenced report, the snarl of clashing gears. Stunned, Hazzard spilled down, feeling warm blood trickle, as a lightless car flashed past.

"Skipper!"

Carey's hands fastened hard, dragged Hazzard back into the room and jerked him half upright. Breath beating, Hazzard stooped, torn muscles refusing to allow him to stand. Hot blood was coursing down his side, and the sting of sharp pain was beginning to pulse through his body. He braced himself, and blurted:

"Kelso's rod man—is getting better with that gun, Danny!"

Carey was crouching at the door, police positive gripped, staring out. The rushing car had whirled around the corner and out of sight. He turned back in an agony of anxiety as Hazzard forced himself to stand erect. Hazzard's hand, pressed hard to his side, was streaked with red.

"God, skipper, he got you! We can't go through with it!"

Hazzard took a deep, cold breath. "Go through with it? Nothing's stopping me tonight, Danny."

Hazzard painfully bundled Kelso's top-coat and hat; he went up the steps with Carey anxiously following. His body throbbed with growing pain as he slipped into his car. Carey watched him in consternation as he pressed the motor hard.

Hazzard brought the car to a stop in the alley behind the apartment building in which Kelso lived. He stepped out, unrolling the coat, shaping the hat. As Carey watched, he assumed the appearance of Sid Kelso in the dim light from the windows. He took a folded newspaper from the car and directed Carey tightly:

"Come up a few seconds after me, Danny."

"Sure, skipper!"

As he approached the entrance of the apartment house, he lowered his head, pretended to read the newspaper, imitated Kelso's slouching walk. As he passed, the door man said: "Good evening, Mr. Kelso." In the elevator, the attendant remarked: "Nice evening, Mr. Kelso." Hazzard kept his face turned away, answered: "Fine evening" in Kelso's voice, and stepped to the door of Kelso's apartment.

Kelso's keys admitted him. He walked slowly through silent rooms into that which Kelso used as an office. He turned back as a rattle sounded; Dan Carey came in quietly. Hazzard shook off the coat and hat; he opened a drawer of the desk, though he scarcely hoped to find incriminating evidence in it; and his examination was stopped by the ring of the telephone.

Hazzard lifted the instrument.

The voice that came over the line was breathy, hushed. "Perles calling, Sid."

"Well?" Hazzard asked, in Kelso's voice.

"I got the D.A.! I trailed him into a store on Wharton Street and put a bullet in him when he was coming out."

Grimly Hazzard answered: "Good work, Slick."

"I'm getting rid of the rod, then I'm clearing out of town. But first I need some coin, Sid. How about sending me over a roll? I'm at the Sunrise."

Wryly Hazzard answered, again in Kelso's voice: "Stay there, Slick. I'm sending something over."

"Thanks, Sid! The D.A.'s not pinning anything on us or anybody else now!"

HAZZARD LOWERED the instrument with a tight smile. Swift decision again moved his hand toward it at once. Just as his fingertips touched, the bell shrilled with the signal of another incoming call. Hazzard tensed, and lifted the receiver. Immediately, before he could speak, a husky voice blurted:

"Brock talkin'—Brock!"

Brock! Hazzard had left him bound, in Carey's secret room with Ann Nash. He had been hoping until this instant that fear would force Brock to talk. A bewilderment of consternation struck him and pain stabbed in his wound as he gripped the telephone. His mind sped to meet the surprise. Simulating Kelso's voice, he asked: "Where you been, Nat?"

"No time to tell you now, Sid! We've got the D.A.—that's what I'm callin' to say! Got him cold! I'm comin' straight over, but I got to tell you now—Trencher's on his way to your place—Trencher!"

With difficulty, in his cold dismay, Hazzard maintained the disguise of his voice. "What's Trencher coming here for?"

"I'm tellin' you we've got the D.A. Carey—wanted for murder—the D.A.'s been hidin' him! Carey's been hidin' on Hazzard's place. That's why Trencher's comin' to your place, Sid—to hear what I've got to tell him about Hazzard!"

All the lingering fear of years of a lived lie stung Hazzard's heart at that moment. He felt the despair of the damned as he gripped the instrument and sat in silent torture. He managed to mutter into the transmitter:

"How much did you tell Trencher, Nat?"

"I didn't tell him anything—except that I've somethin' on the D.A. Just enough to get him hot-footin' it over to your place. When I get through talkin' with Trencher, Hazzard'll be startin' up the river! I'm comin' now!"

Hazzard sat chilled as the connection broke. Instantly he rattled the hook, demanded the number of the telephone in Carey's hidden haven. He waited an agonized minute until an answer came in Ann Nash's breathless voice.

"Ann! What happened?"

"Mark! He managed to get his hands loose, and I didn't know it. He knocked me down, and got out of here. I—I didn't know what to do, Mark. I followed him, saw him go into a store and a telephone booth. I managed to get into the next one and I heard him callin' Trencher—"

"Did he tell Trencher about Danny?"

"No—nothing definite. Oh, Mark, darling—"

"Ann! Are you hurt?"

"I'm all right," the girl answered with a sob. "Mark, what can you do—now?"

"Listen!" he urged sibilantly. "Call headquarters as soon as I hang up. You've been tipped off by someone who called my office—you know Slick Perles is at the Sunrise bar now, with the gun he's been sniping at me with. Perles is waiting there. Got that?"

"Yes, Mark!"

"Good girl!" He broke the connection. Then immediately, using the voice of Kelso, he asked for the number of police headquarters. His voice was his own when he asked for the office of Inspector Trencher. The answer sent a new chill through him:

"Inspector Trencher has just left the building."

It meant: "Trencher is on his way now to Kelso's apartment."

Hazzard pushed away the instrument which had sounded a pronouncement of doom on him.

CHAPTER V

HAZZARD'S WAY

HAZZARD ROSE alertly, his mind in turmoil. His nerves tightened as he heard an elevator panel click, and steps come toward the door. His signal sent Carey back through a connecting door. He waited, hand on knob, until a rap sounded. He asked again, in disguised tones, "Who is it?" and heard:

"Brock."

Hazzard pulled the door open. Brock started in and stopped. The click of the closing door turned him. He stared at Hazzard, and at the door in which Dan Carey appeared. He took retreating steps, his face ashy with dismay; and then his thin lips began to curl in triumph.

"Trencher's coming," he said. "That's your finish, Hazzard."

Hazzard answered, eyes levelled: "I think you're right, Brock. My finish and yours. Kelso's opened up. He's told his story. All of it—the whole rotten mess—it's all in the record, signed and witnessed. He's going down to headquarters now."

Brock rasped: "That's a lie."

"Have it your way," Hazzard answered easily. "But when Trencher leaves here, he'll be taking you along with me. You'll be starting on the last mile, Brock. They're polishing up the chair for you now."

Brock snarled again: "That's a lie."

"Trencher's coming," Hazzard reminded him. "You're staying until Trencher comes, and then you'll know it's the truth. There's only one way to escape the chair, Brock. You can save yourself by telling the whole truth about all of Kelso's deals. How about it, Brock?"

Brock's answer was a darting snatch at his arm-pit holstered gun. It flashed in the light as Hazzard's hand swung toward his Webley. The pain of his wound had stiffened Hazzard's muscles. His gun was still inside his coat when Brock's glinted level. He leaped to avoid the blast even as the report thundered.

Brock whirled away, firing again—and Hazzard felt the sting of it gashing his shoulder as he fell aside. At the same instant another gun roared in the room—the police positive in the hand of Dan Carey. A gun exactly like it, his fingerprints marking it, had condemned Dan Carey for murder. Now it dealt leaden vengeance on Brock—a withering fusillade of bullets crashed Brock lifeless to the floor.

"Danny!"

Mark Hazzard, crouched with pain, stared aghast at the limp figure on the carpet, at the trickling red on Brock's clothes. Dan Carey was standing with smoking gun in hand—and smiling. Hazzard's face was white with dismay—and Carey was smiling.

"That's a promise kept," the ex-cop said.

"God, Danny—you can never clear yourself now!"

"What I'm thinking of, skipper, is that Brock won't do any talking now—about you hiding me."

Hazzard listened in tortured anxiety. The explosions in the room had aroused an alarm across the hall. There were startled voices in the adjoining suite. Hazzard jerked open the entrance, and peered out—but the corridor was empty. He snapped over his shoulder.

"Get out of here, Danny! Down the fire-stairs—fast!"

"Not without you, skipper!"

"Get down!"

Hazzard's tone was an imperative command. He thrust Carey out the door. He stood, muscles tight, heart hammering, as the ex-cop sped around the bend, to the entrance of the fire-stairs. He held back, a thought blazing in his mind. Instantly it became a desperate plan of action.

"Eye-witnesses!"

Hazzard sprang across the room to the chair on which he had placed Kelso's checkered coat and green hat. He tugged into them quickly. He strode to the door, listened. Now the voices were subsiding; the alarm was passing. Deliberately Mark Hazzard raised his Webley. He opened the door, so that the reports might ring more loudly in the corridor, and, four times, swiftly, pulled the trigger.

The blasting concussions stirred a new response. A woman screamed; a man called out. A knob rattled, and a door opened. Shielding his face with low-pulled hat and hunched shoulders, Hazzard began a quick, breathless run along the corridor. He heard the clack of an elevator grille, glanced back swiftly, and saw, stepping out of an elevator cab—Inspector Trencher.

Hazzard fired back as he fled past the L of the hall. His slug whined off the tile as Trencher dragged at a hip-holstered service gat. Hazzard whirled into the fire-stairs, bounded down them. The baffling echoes of his own footfalls in the well made it impossible for him to determine if Trencher was following. He sprang from platform to platform; darting across a cellar room, he sped through a door held wide by Carey. Together they ran toward the waiting car.

HAZZARD SENT it flying. He swung it into the street, turned four times in a bewildering succession. While Carey steadied the wheel, he wriggled out of the checkered top-coat, snatched off the hat. He touched the switch of the radio and kept the car rolling rapidly while Carey sat breathlessly.

"Calling all cars!" The radio twanged. "Calling all cars. Pick up Sid Kelso. Use caution; he may resist. Calling all cars to pick up Sid Kelso, last seen escaping his apartment on Plaza Street and Fifth. Code thirteen. Code thirteen."

Code thirteen, in the lexicon of the police radio system, meant, "wanted for murder."

Hazzard swung the car sharply to the curb a block from the store at 1010 Wharton Street. Carey hurried with him along the dark alley while he grimaced with pain, carrying Kelso's coat and hat bundled against his throbbing side. They darted to the entrance of the empty store and shouldered in. Together they bent over Kelso.

Kelso was squirming in the dark, squealing behind his gag of adhesive tape. Hazzard ripped it off, pinioned him, stripped the bands from his ankles and wrists. As Kelso struck out, Hazzard's fist drove him flat against the wall. Carey whirled with Hazzard toward the rear of the store. Behind them Kelso's coat and hat lay on the littered floor.

They groped through black rooms to a back entrance. They darted across a bleak yard, swung over a board fence. Once in the car, Hazzard drove with a slowness that was torture in his anxiety. He kept listening to repeated radio alarms for Sid Kelso. When he turned into his garage, he saw a shadow moving in the light on the stairs, and rushed up.

Ann Nash went into his arms and sobbed. In dismay the girl examined Hazzard's wounds; she forced him to submit while she dressed them. It was not until they were cleaned and bound that the dance music on the radio ceased playing and an announcer's voice followed the clang of a bell.

"A special news dispatch, ladies and gentlemen. Sid Kelso has just been picked up by the police. He was found by squad car men and is now being taken to headquarters for questioning by Inspector Trencher, who saw him escaping the scene of a murder.

"A second flash, ladies and gentlemen. 'Slick' Perles, underworld henchman of Kelso, is dead as the result of a gun-fight with police who closed in on him at the Sunrise Bar a few moments ago. A charge of attempted murder of Mark Hazzard, District Attorney, was about to be lodged against him. Perles' attempt to escape cost him his life. A silenced gun was found on him which police expect to prove is the weapon he used in his attempts to murder Hazzard. A bullet embedded in the door of the office of the district attorney will establish—"

"Mark!" Ann Nash exclaimed as Carey snapped the radio off and grinned in cold satisfaction. "What have you done?"

Mark Hazzard answered: "Cracked a case!" He peered at Carey as he spun the dial of the telephone. "I've overlooked something in the rush, Danny. Thanks for my life. But—you'll never be able to get clear now."

"That's okay with me, skipper," Carey said, still grinning. "Okay, because you're clear!"

Hazzard's request brought the voice of Inspector Trencher on the wire.

"Hazzard! You listen! I've got Kelso here on a warrant for murder. Dr. Norton just phoned to say his analysis shows arsenic present in the judge's hair. How the devil do you know things like that—that arsenic can be detected in the hair? You've had it from the start—Nat Brock poisoned that old man. Considering that, Hazzard, forget what I said at Crosdale's house, will you?"

"Gladly," Hazzard quietly answered. "As for Brock, he'll never squeal on Kelso now. That's probably the reason Kelso got him, wasn't it, inspector? And the reason Brock is now roasting in hell—probably wishing for a cold glass of ale!"

MARK HAZZARD moved agitatedly back and forth across his office. The atmosphere of the courthouse was bustling, tense, expectant. Downstairs, a jury was deliberating behind a locked door on the most vital case Mark Hazzard had ever handled. He paused at his desk to gaze again at the headlines of the special editions which had roared off the presses since the jury had retired.

"KELSO VERDICT EXPECTED TONIGHT!" the black banner read.

Hazzard's eyes skipped to paragraphs which gave him cold satisfaction.

In his charge to the jury, Judge Joseph Cheever said:

> "The counsel for the defense has advanced the alibi that at the time of the murder of Nathan Brock, the defendant Sydney Kelso, was being held by kidnapers. You are to examine the statements of the telephone operator at the defendant's home that it was the defendant's voice which telephoned that night, asking for himself—which, according to the state, was an attempt to establish an alibi for premeditated homicide.
>
> "Defendant's statements concerning this alleged kidnaping are unsupported. No one saw the act committed as he states. He cannot name or identify the kidnapers. These statements you must consider against the testimony of six persons who said they saw Kelso flee his apartment at the time of the murder, a smoking gun in his hand. One of these witnesses was Inspector Trencher.
>
> "You must decide, gentlemen of the jury, whether defendant's alibi can stand against the testimony of these eye-witnesses."

Hazzard looked up to see Ann Nash quickly entering, her color high, her eyes shining.

"The jury's reporting!" she exclaimed. "And you have a caller—Mr. Flarigan."

Hazzard's eyes lingered on her face as he stepped out to confront Flarigan.

Flarigan was blinking, looking solemn. He said slowly: "Hazzard, you went ahead in spite of my—suggestion. It happens that you're coming through okay but—that's dangerous. Be wise. Get the idea? Be wise and be mayor or governor if you choose. Get the idea?"

"You made me, Flarigan," Hazzard answered with a wry smile, "and you can break me. I won't be surprised if you find occasion again to remind me of that!"

He felt Flarigan glowering after him threateningly as he ran down the stairs. He entered a courtroom hushed and tense. He saw the jury already in the box, the dignified Judge Cheever eyeing the foreman. The court's question came:

"Gentlemen of the jury, have you reached a verdict?"

"We have."

"What is your verdict?"

"Guilty."

The hush deepened; Judge Cheever's rumble was the voice of doom:

"This court pronounces upon the defendant, Sidney Kelso, the sentence of electrocution to be executed upon him, during the week of October 12th. Court is adjourned."

Bedlam! Reporters sped from the doors. Spectators sprang from their seats, chattering, crowding. Within the rail the District Attorney of King's County triumphantly faced the towering, scowling Hubbard Todd. He said with quiet firmness:

"You'll appeal, of course, but you can't win. Eye-witnesses, Todd. They're powerful, you know—especially when one of them is a man like Trencher. Powerful enough to make it a certainty that Kelso's going to the chair."

Todd's vulture eyes gleamed defiance. Kelso was sagging at the defense counsel table, mumbling bewildered protests. Flarigan was near, peering at Hazzard, wagging his head forbiddingly. At the rail Ann Nash was standing, her ripe lips curved proudly, her shining gaze on Hazzard. And at the gate, Inspector Trencher had paused.

A plainclothes man had come hurrying into the courtroom. He proffered an envelope to Trencher. Trencher glimpsed its return address—*Department of Justice, Washington, D.C.*—as he snatched it and ripped it open. He peered intently at neat, terse lines:

> The fingerprints submitted by you do not match any in our files. Pennsylvania, which you mention as the suspect's home, was slow to coöperate with this department in submitting fingerprints. Philadelphia did not begin sending them, for instance, until 1929.

Defeat sagged Trencher's shoulders. He glanced at the district attorney with a faint smile that said: "There are other ways—other ways."

Dennis Grant, convicted murderer, alias Mark Hazzard, District Attorney, looked into the ominous blackness of Trencher's eyes—and smiled.

BOOK II

JUGGERNAUT JUSTICE

*Mark Hazzard, fighting D.A., knew he'd sent
an innocent man to the death house. And now
to save that man from the last mile, he was
ready to become the corpus delicti that would
point death's finger at the real murderer.*

CHAPTER I

COURT OF DOOM

DISTRICT ATTORNEY Mark Hazzard climbed the black fire-stairs with the firm intention of breaking the law.

He paused on the platform at the twelfth floor and levered a sharp tool into the crack of the one-way door. He was the youngest prosecutor ever to battle the state's cases in King's County. His red hair was a warning of a hot temper that made fearful defendants squirm while he fought for legal justice in the court room. He was a two-fisted terror to those who faced him from the witness stand with guilt in their hearts. Yet tonight Hazzard was making himself as liable under the criminal code as they, by forcing his way through this sealed door.

He strode along the silent corridor to an entrance lettered *Lockridge, Culver and Hinton, Attorneys,* and slipped a skeleton key into the lock. That painted line might have read *Lockridge, Culver and Hazzard,* if the hot-headed young lawyer who was once slated for a junior partnership had not chosen to fight at the polls for the office of prosecuting attorney—and won.

When Mark Hazzard alertly entered the black law office, he stood in the rooms where his career as a lone wolf of justice had begun. The silent office recalled vividly the bitter mischance that first led him to study law.

He snapped a switch, swung a chair under a light fixture, and climbed up. He quickly unfastened the milk-glass bowl and unscrewed the bulb. The globe which he removed from his pocket and twisted into the socket looked quite ordinary; but it was not. Once it was gleaming, Hazzard spoke to it in a whisper:

"Are you there, Ann? Can you hear me? Keep listening."

Hazzard replaced the reflector bowl, slid the chair back and stepped

quickly to the wall switch. He unfastened the plate with a screw driver and hooked the leads of a small condenser across the terminals. Sure of the connection, he replaced the plate, and hurried into one of the partitioned offices. Again he spoke into empty air:

"Can you hear me now, Ann? I'm standing near Culver's desk. Adjust the knob so you can hear me plainly. I'm coming down to check and—somebody's coming!"

He had heard brisk footfalls in the corridor. He sped to the switch and clicked darkness into the office; he looked around swiftly for a place to hide. Shadows were moving on the pebbled pane of the entrance when he hurried to a door in the side wall. A key was turning in the lock when he closed himself in thick darkness. He stood in the supply closet, heart speeding, listening, while the entrance opened and two men strode in.

"There's nobody here," one of them exclaimed.

"That's strange. I'm sure I saw a light," the other insisted.

"Better look around, Larry," the first suggested warily. "There's been a petty thief working in the building."

Hazzard recognized the voices as those of Vinton Culver and Lawrence Hinton, partners in the law firm. Standing anxiously at the door, he heard the footfalls move into the adjoining offices. When both men were beyond other doors, he inched the closet open and tensed to speed across to the entrance and out. Instantly he drew back, dismayed and breathless. One of the men was returning.

"I don't like this, Larry," Culver said. "You saw a light. There's somebody in here."

"Hiding," Hinton's voice answered. "How about the supply closet? Watch it while I—"

Hazzard's tight lips suppressed a moan. He heard two quick steps and the sliding noise of a desk drawer. Knowing that discovery was a certainty, he twisted the inner knob. When he stepped out into bright light, Vinton Culver gasped and Lawrence Hinton whirled from a desk. Culver blurted "Hazzard!" as Hinton lifted the automatic he had taken from the drawer. It glinted dangerously at Hazzard as he smiled and said:

"Good evening, gentlemen. Weren't you expecting me?"

Culver snapped: "I expect any sort of trickery from you. Hazzard. What the devil are you doing here? What do you mean by sneaking into this office in the middle of the night?"

"I'll keep my purpose to myself, if you don't mind," Hazzard answered wryly. "I assure you it's quite unnecessary to point that gun at me."

Hinton's lips curled. "You deserve to be treated like a common burglar, Hazzard. That's what you've made of yourself by sneaking in here."

Culver added bitingly: "Exactly, Hazzard! The estimable district attorney is guilty of the crime of breaking and entering. Keep him covered, Larry—and call the police."

"ONE MOMENT, Hinton." Mark Hazzard stepped forward tensely, studying Culver's cold eyes, Hinton's scornful smile. "You are quite right. I have no search warrant. I am guilty of burglary. You have only to call the police, and I'll be forced out of office and made to face the charge in court. Before you do that—"

"You deserve that!" Culver straightened stiffly. "Duncan Lockridge took you into this office when you were down and out. He trained you as a trial lawyer because he had faith in you. He backed you at the polls, helped more than any other man living to elect you to office. You've repaid his generosity and trust by bringing him to trial and convicting him of murder!"

"True," Hazzard admitted, "but—"

Lawrence Hinton spoke through curling lips. He was the young attorney who had succeeded to the junior partnership which Mark Hazzard might have had. Hazzard's withdrawal had raised him to that position prematurely. Yet now his eyes were a denunciation and his words a lash:

"You know damned well his appeal will be denied, Hazzard. You tried to break Duncan Lockridge on the witness stand. You pounded at him with every piece of evidence you could find. That man was your friend—he made you—but all you thought of was making yourself a glorious hero in the eyes of the public. Lockridge is the squarest man who ever lived, but he's going to the electric chair—and you've sent him there!"

"Gentlemen," Mark Hazzard's face pictured keen pain. "I did convict Duncan Lockridge for murder in the first degree. If he goes to the chair, it will be because of the case I built up against him. It was my duty to do that. I was forced to present those facts to the jury. You may believe Lockridge is innocent of murder—but you're not half as convinced of it as I am."

"What!" Culver snapped in a rage. "How can you have the effrontery to say that after you, and you alone, sent him to the death house?"

Hazzard's eyes blazed. "Would Lockridge have come off better at the trial if I'd turned the case over to one of my over-ambitious assistants? Certainly not! He couldn't escape the facts the police built up against him. I wasn't trying to break him on the stand. No! I was doing my best to get at some clue, some little contradiction of circumstances that would bring the whole case crashing down. Whether you believe it or not, I'm still doing my damnedest to clear Lockridge."

Hazzard's knuckles clicked to the desk. "You don't need to remind me that he's my friend. I haven't forgotten that he gave me my chance. I know I have to thank him more than any other man, for being state's attorney. God, I'm not persecuting him! I'm trying to use the power he gave me to save him. In spite of all the evidence, in spite of the jury's verdict, I *know* that Duncan Lockridge didn't kill Walter Platt."

"Very pretty, Hazzard," Hinton sneered. "Very noble. But the fact remains you convicted him."

Hazzard moaned in despair. "A dozen times during the trial I moved that the charge be dismissed for lack of evidence, but each time the court overruled me. Twice since the conviction, I've gone to the governor and pled that the verdict be set aside, and he's refused. You've overlooked that, haven't you? I'm still trying. I'm going to stop at nothing until I've found evidence to clear Lockridge—and even your bringing me up for burglary, gentlemen, won't keep me from it!"

"Do you expect to find your evidence here?" Culver demanded coldly. "Do you think that Hinton or I are guilty? Do you dare hint that either of us would allow Lockridge to take the blame for something we did—the man who's closer to us than anyone else in the world? By God, Hazzard—!"

"I don't know who's guilty," Hazzard broke in, "but I know Lockridge isn't. I'd keep on trying to prove it if I suspected my own brother. Listen to me, both of you. What if Lockridge's appeal is denied tonight? What if Governor Bryant repeats his refusal to intervene? What chance will Lockridge have of escaping the chair then? One and only one—a district attorney who's doing his damnedest to serve justice above the written law."

Hazzard strode to the desk where Hinton stood, his temper raging hot.

"If you choose to charge me with breaking and entering, gentlemen, you have your case. You can force me out of office, and by doing so you'll destroy the last chance of proving Duncan Lockridge's innocence. If you two men—'closer to him than anyone else in the world'—are willing to shoulder the blame for his death, here's the telephone."

He lifted the instrument from the desk and held it toward Vinton Culver. Culver's eyes were still blazing with contempt, but a flicker of uncertainty had crept into them. Hinton's gun wavered. Hazzard's firm lips curved coolly as he replaced the telephone and strode briskly to the entrance.

"In that case, gentlemen, I trust you wish me the best of luck. Good-night!"

HAZZARD'S JAW muscles were lumped with anger, his pulse was still hammering, when the elevator cab dropped him from the twelfth floor of the Lambert Building to the eleventh. He heeded no skeleton key to open the office directly below the suite of Lockridge, Culver and Hinton. Through dim light, he strode toward the girl who was sitting with phones pressed to her ears at a recording microphone.

She searched Hazzard's eyes anxiously, and kept listening, while he listened through a second hand-set. The bulb he had screwed into the light fixture on the floor above was one which concealed a sensitive pick-up. The condenser he had mounted in the switch box was a device which passed the sound impulses even though the lights were off. Hazzard listened to voices traveling over the wires of the light circuit while his secretary watched a diamond stylus recording the words on a composition disc.

Culver's voice came: "I don't trust Hazzard. He's not trying to clear Lockridge. He came here hunting for evidence, all right, but not for Duncan's sake. I think he suspects us of jury tampering—he's trying to disbar us both and make himself Public Hero Number One."

Hinton's reply came through: "Certainly! If he makes the slightest move in that direction, I'll prefer charges against him for burglary. I'll break him out of office. God, it's awful—waiting to hear from the Court of Appeals!"

Culver spoke: "The decision is due sometime tonight. It will mean the chair for Duncan if they deny the appeal—in spite of what Hazzard says about trying to save him. I don't trust him!"

Hinton's voice lowered. "Listen, I think I know why Hazzard came here. He couldn't hope to find any documentary evidence. He's planted a microphone somewhere. He's got someone listening in on everything said here. Look around! We've got to find it!"

Hazzard tensed with alarm while he heard the sounds of movements in the office above, brought to his ears by the sensitive device. He lowered the phones while Ann Nash looked up with hurt eyes.

"They don't understand, Mark!" she exclaimed anxiously. "You told them the truth—I heard every word—and you *are* trying your best to save Lockridge. Will—will they find the microphone?"

"It'll take a good job of hunting." Hazzard's eyes narrowed. "I'm convinced either Culver or Hinton is guilty of that murder. The facts show it—there's no other answer. But finding proof—" His voice faded hopelessly. "Stick at that machine, Ann. I want a record of every word spoken in that room."

Ann Nash answered alertly: "On the job, Mark."

The silence in the phones meant that now both men were searching for the hidden microphone. Hazzard lifted the telephone, spun the number of his office. Frank Mayton, his assistant, answered.

"Any message, Frank?" Hazzard asked anxiously.

"Yes, from Inspector Trencher. He wants you over in his office as quick as you can make it."

"Trencher?" A chill tingled along Hazzard's nerves. "Ring him that I'll be right over."

His fingers warmly pressed Ann Nash's arm; he left the office with quick strides.

"Duncan Lockridge is innocent—innocent—innocent," had drummed through Mark Hazzard's mind since the moment of Lockridge's sensational arrest. "Innocent—innocent" all the while he had presented damning evidence against Lockridge in court because his duty demanded it. It had become an obsession that drove him day and night. "You've got to prove Duncan Lockridge did not commit murder. You and you alone must prove it—"

When Hazzard swung his car from the curb, newsboys on the corner were howling headlines that mocked him:

"Appeal Decision Due Tonight on Lockridge Murder!"

"Court Deliberating Lockridge's Case!"

"Noted Lawyer Awaiting Final Verdict!"

"Death or New Trial for Lockridge—Decision Tonight!"

In a squalid upstate town, Duncan Lockridge was caged in the grim death house. The bleak corridor which passed his cell ended at the door of the chamber where prisoners met their doom in the electric chair. There Lockridge was waiting for word of the decision to penetrate the gray stone walls of the prison while, in a stately building in this city, the Court of Appeals was sitting in extraordinary session. Tonight their judgment would be announced. Tonight the zero hour in a condemned man's life must come.

Mark Hazzard gripped the wheel hard and sent his car speeding across the city with grim, unconquerable purpose.

CHAPTER II

THE VOICE
IN THE DARK

RECOLLECTIONS OF that trying case—the most grueling he had ever handled—kaleidoscoped through Hazzard's mind with the speed of the spinning car wheels.

"The murdered man, Walter Platt, was last seen alive entering the Lambert Building." Hazzard's own words, uttered during his summation to the jury, came back to mock him. "He asked directions to the office of Lockridge, Culver and Hinton. The elevator operator noticed the man seemed very shaken. He entered those offices—and vanished from the world of living men. Those, gentlemen of the jury, are incontestable facts.

"When Walter Platt entered those offices, the junior partner of the firm, Lawrence Hinton, was there. You heard corroborative testimony that Hinton immediately left the office when Duncan Lockridge came in a moment later. Hinton testified that when he left, Platt was still there. Though Lockridge denies it, the testimony shows that he and Platt were left alone in that office. And when Platt was next seen, he was a water-sodden corpse which had been dragged from the river."

Each remembered word stung Mark Hazzard as he kept his car speeding across the metropolis.

"Dr. Autumn, the Medical Examiner, has testified his expert opinion that Platt was dead of suffocation before he was thrown into the river. Proof of this fact is that no water was found in Platt's stomach or lungs. Lockridge has denied killing Platt in the office, denied carrying him unseen from the building, denied throwing the dead man into the river. But, gentlemen of the jury, there is damning mute testimony to prove he did exactly that."

Inspector Charles Trencher, the deliberately methodical sleuth whose power extended all through the police department, had placed that evidence in Hazzard's hands. Three distinctive parallel, curving scratches had been found in the enamel of Lockridge's costly car, near the rear door. Three nails in the heel of Platt's right shoe matched those scratches exactly. Hazzard had been forced to build his most damaging argument in the case on those three etched lines.

"Platt's heel made those scratches on Lockridge's car, gentlemen of the jury—that is an established fact. They were made when Platt, already dead, was tumbled into the rear seat of Lockridge's car—that is a certainty. That the car was driven from the alley behind the Lambert Building, to the bank of the river, carrying Platt's dead body cannot be doubted. The man who drove the car then threw Platt into the river in an attempt to conceal the murder—no one can question that conclusion. That Platt had reason to fear going in that office was indicated by his manner on the elevator.

"Duncan Lockridge denies he is the man who killed Platt. You must decide which you believe, gentlemen of the jury—the silent testimony of those three scratches on Lockridge's car, or Lockridge's statement."

Hazzard remembered his earnest effort to present the case with scrupulous fairness. He recalled how he had avoided every accusing statement which the evidence did not inexorably force him to make. He had ended his summation with a plea that the evidence be weighed with the utmost care, had even called the attention of the jury to the law that Lockridge must be acquitted if there remained a "reasonable doubt" of his guilt. Now, as he drove, Hazzard again heard the verdict that meant he had won a sensational case, but condemned a friend to the electric chair:

"We, the jury, find the defendant, Duncan Lockridge, guilty of murder in the first degree."

Hazzard had clicked on the radio, and it had been playing softly while intersections flashed past. He listened alertly as a gong sounded and the music yielded to a news announcement:

"The latest word from the courthouse, ladies and gentlemen, informs us that the decision of the Court of Appeals will be announced within an hour. The judges are about to complete their study of the record, and their verdict in this startling case is being awaited anxiously. Governor Bryant has issued a statement that he will take no action in the case if the appeal is denied, and therefore the decision of the court may be considered as final, since Lockridge's counsel has declared that they will not carry the case to the Supreme Court of the United States. As soon as the decision is announced, it will be broadcast."

Hazzard swung into the street which separated the massive courthouse from police headquarters. He looked up at lighted windows. In the room behind them, the august tribunal of last resort was deliberating the fate of a man while the entire city awaited their word. His nerves burning with impatience, Mark Hazzard climbed to the office of Inspector Charles Trencher.

He stopped short just beyond the sill. The full-waisted, heavy-jowled man who rose from the inspector's desk was not Trencher. His eyes glimmered a threat while Hazzard stood stock still; his lips pursed into a mocking smile. He said in a heavy, throaty tone:

"How are you—Dennis Grant?"

THAT FULL-CHEEKED face, and the sound of that name, brought bitter memories flooding into the mind of the man who had been Dennis Grant.

A bitter cold night. A bleak railroad yard with sooty snow packed between gleaming rails. A man more than ten years younger than Mark Hazzard, crawling in agony from the rods beneath a freight car. It was the end of an exhausting journey for one then known as Dennis Grant—the stolen ride of a tramp, undertaken so that he might join his mother at Christmas. In that painful flash of memory, Mark Hazzard recalled that the freezing trip had not carried him to his home, but to the prisoner's dock.

He heard it again as he stared at the square, brutal face of the man standing at Trencher's desk—the crack of the shot. He saw again the gun thrown at his feet, the gun he had picked up before he knew what he was doing. He remembered blinding lights turned into his eyes and hard hands gripping him as a grimy yard crew trapped him. It was like a nightmare suddenly come to life again—the courtroom, the accusing finger of the prosecuting attorney damning him for the murder of a man he had never seen, with a gun a murderer had planted on him—and that word of doom uttered by the foreman of the jury:

"Guilty."

During the trial, a huge man, handcuffed to Dennis Grant, had led him back and forth between cell and dock. That same massive sheriff who had moved to Dennis Grant's side, and clamped a horny hand on his arm, while the judge had pronounced the sentence of life imprisonment upon him, was the man now facing Mark Hazzard.

Panic struck through Mark Hazzard's mind. He had made a desperate and successful attempt to escape from the courtroom in Philadelphia—from the clutch of the man now facing him. He had lived for months in terror of capture. At last, finding a job, he had studied endless nights so that he might understand the law that had condemned him for a crime he had not committed.

He had fought hard to place himself in a position to administer a justice that stood higher than the statutes. He had created a new identity for himself as Mark Hazzard, District Attorney. His whole world was now shaken by the quiet words spoken by the man at Trencher's desk:

"How are you, Dennis Grant?"

They meant: "Mark Hazzard, you're wanted for murder. There's a sentence of life imprisonment waiting for you."

He forced a smile. Moving quietly toward the man at the desk, he said, "I don't understand you. My name's Mark Hazzard. I'm the district attorney."

"I know you're the district attorney," the big man said. "But your name is Dennis Grant, isn't it?"

"I said my name is Hazzard."

He turned as a connecting door opened. Inspector Trencher came in slowly, a twisted smile on his lips. His black eyes showed an ominous smoulder that sent a piercing chill to Hazzard's heart. The huge man at the desk extended his heavy hand to Hazzard and said drawlingly:

"It's been a long time since I've seen you, Grant."

Hazzard's surging temper brought scarlet to his face as Trencher settled into the swivel chair behind the desk. His voice was a crackle:

"Who is this man, Trencher? Why does he insist on calling me by a name that's not mine? Is this your idea of a practical joke?"

"Not at all, Hazzard, not at all." Trencher seemed to gloat. "Shake hands with Horace Halsey, an old friend of mine. He used to be sheriff of Delphia County, Pennsylvania, about ten years ago. You know, Hazzard, I've always been interested in you, but I never could get you to talk much about yourself. So when Halsey showed up, I pointed out your picture in the papers, and asked him if he knew you. Do you remember him, Halsey?"

"Sure," the ex-sheriff rumbled. "I'd know him anywhere. But his name wasn't Hazzard then. It was Grant—Dennis Grant."

Trencher frowned. "Sure of that?"

"Sure?" Halsey showed a toothy, confident grin. "I couldn't forget that. I took him into the criminal court in Philadelphia, and back to his cell again, twenty times. I watched him all during the trial—that was my job. I was right at his side when the judge sentenced him. I tried to stop him when he threw a chair through the window and got away. Forget *him*—when I turned hell upside down for months, trying to find him? Not much!

"He's Dennis Grant—wanted for murder, with a life sentence waiting to be served."

MARK HAZZARD turned squarely to Trencher. The blaze in his eyes was so fierce that the inspector's smile faded. His voice was edged with cold fury.

"All right, Trencher. We understand each other. You're out to get me. You don't like the way I administer the law. You stick by the statutes in your routine way no matter if innocent men are jailed and guilty men go free. You're content, for instance, to let the Court of Appeals be the final judge of Duncan Lockridge while they think only of legal errors without considering the merits of the case. I'm not a slave to established procedure and I never will be. You don't like the way I work—so you're out for my skin. That's the truth, isn't it, Trencher?"

Trencher wagged a hand. "Take it easy, Hazzard. Sure, our methods differ. You stick your neck out and run your chances, and I hold to the regulations—but it's your neck. You set yourself up as a special police department and a special supreme court both in one—but if you overstep yourself, nobody's going to suffer but you. That's beside the point, isn't it? There's no use exploding if Halsey's mistaken. The thing is—*are* you Dennis Grant?"

Hazzard spoke through a dry throat. "You're clever, Trencher. Last month you checked up on my fingerprints, hoping to get something on me, and this time you're making a direct accusation through Halsey. You pretend to be as slow-witted and plodding as a pack mule while you're sly as a fox. As for your question—suppose you answer it!"

Again Trencher's hand wagged disarmingly. "Take it easy, take it easy, Hazzard. Don't go off like a firecracker. When you're in this game as long as I've been, you learn it doesn't pay to get excited. Halsey may be absolutely mistaken, sure. There's no use arguing about it, is there? We can check up on it in a few minutes, and then there won't be any question."

"I'm not making any mistake," Halsey asserted.

"Is that all right with you, Hazzard, if I check up?" Trencher asked.

"Go as far as you like, Trencher," Hazzard flared.

"Thanks," the inspector answered dryly. He reached for the telephone and lifted it slowly. He spoke into the transmitter casually. "Get me Brennan at Philadelphia police headquarters."

He broke the connection and his twisted smile came again. "Halsey wouldn't want me to take his unsupported word for it—not in a thing like this. Not the district attorney's being a murderer and a fugitive from the law. Would you, Halsey?"

"The records will show I'm stating facts," the ex-sheriff rumbled.

"It'll be tough, won't it, Hazzard, if it's true?" Trencher queried.

Hazzard smiled bitterly. The sensational disclosure would strip him of his honor and integrity. It would transform him from a respected public official into a convict. It would change the plaudits of the newspapers into scathing denunciations. It would bring tragedy to Ann Nash, the girl he loved, and utterly destroy his world. But he answered Trencher grimly:

"I don't happen to be afraid of anything you might find out about me, inspector. I'm still Mark Hazzard, the district attorney. As long as that's my job, I'm going at it with all I've got. I'm going to prove that Duncan Lockridge is not a murderer."

Trencher repeated quietly: "It's your neck."

"Do you mind, inspector," Hazzard asked huskily, "if I use your phone?"

"Go as far as you like."

Hazzard's eyes narrowed at Halsey as he spoke into the transmitter. "Connect me with the district attorney's office." He saw suspicion untinged by doubt in the ex-sheriff's stare when Frank Mayton answered. "Any call for me yet, Frank?"

"Another, just now, Mark," his assistant answered. "Damned if I know who left it or what it means. It's just 'he's come in.'"

"I've been waiting for that—thanks!"

Hazzard lowered the phone with a thump. His tight lips curved with a smile of defiance. "Trencher, I have no intention of waiting here, while you try to prove I'm a murderer. Let me remind you that you can't arrest me without a warrant, and you can't issue a warrant for me without a specific charge. From now on, if you want me, you'll have to find me. Good-night, inspector!"

Hazzard strode straight to the door. Trencher leaped up, snapped, "Come back here!" but Hazzard did not stop. The door slapped shut; the heels of the district attorney tapped down the corridor. Trencher's fist crashed angrily to the desk; his black eyes gleamed with triumph.

"I've got him!"

He grabbed at the telephone the instant it rang. "Philadelphia headquarters?" he rasped. "Brennan! That you Brennan?" Then, peering at the door through which Mark Hazzard had gone, he said levelly:

"Brennan, look up the records of Dennis Grant, convicted of murder about ten years ago. Read me his fingerprint classifications. I'll hold the line."

INSPECTOR TRENCHER sat tensely, his stubby fingers drumming. He opened a drawer of his desk, took up an envelope, and slid photographs from it. They were reproductions of Mark Hazzard's fingerprints. A month ago Trencher had taken them off a paperweight which Hazzard habitually fingered, and he had been rewarded by finding distinct impressions. He eyed them grimly, and the cryptic classification noted above them, while he waited for Brennan to report.

When the answer came, Trencher's hand crushed the phone: "Good Lord, inspector! We've got Grant's rogue gallery pictures, but his fingerprint record is missing!"

"What!"

"Missing! It should be in the file, but it isn't. Damned if I know what happened to it. It's gone—that's all."

"Gone!" Trencher echoed the word while Halsey stared with widening eyes. The inspector's mind sped while he answered: "Listen, Brennan. I want those pictures. Send a man up here with 'em as fast as he can make connections. And Brennan. Send along a blank fingerprint card. Got that? A blank."

"They'll be on their way at once, inspector."

Halsey blurted as Trencher broke the connection: "His prints are missing? I know the reason for that. He stole 'em out of the files."

Trencher straightened tensely. "What the devil makes you say that?"

"Listen. I remember, about a year ago, Mark Hazzard came to Philadelphia headquarters. He said he was making a personal visit to check up on some crook's record. Naturally, because he was D.A. here, they gave him a free hand. I didn't hear about it until afterward—I didn't see him at the time—but they told me they'd had the famous Hazzard in there. That's when he stole the fingerprint record out of the files!"

Trencher's eyes were black flame. "That won't stop me from getting him. I'll get proof he's Grant—legal proof. Nothing's going to stop me now."

He touched buttons on his desk as he spoke. Halsey blinked in bewilderment while the connecting door opened and a blue-shirted man appeared. Tensely Trencher handed him the photographs of Mark Hazzard's fingerprints.

"Get this straight," he commanded. "Arrange these prints in exactly the same positions as those on a record card. Have a photolithographic plate made of them and hold it. I want to have them reproduced on a special card in a hurry, soon as I say the word. And keep strictly quiet about it—it's important."

"Yes, sir."

When the connecting door closed Halsey blurted: "That's proof, isn't it? Hazzard's being there in Philadelphia headquarters—the card disappearing?"

"No. Not legal proof," Trencher drawled. "It's no good. We're getting Grant's pictures—but I'm going to do better than that. I'm going to break Hazzard. I'm going to force him to admit he's Dennis Grant—murderer!"

"How?" Halsey asked huskily.

"Philadelphia's sending a blank fingerprint record card. I've got Hazzard's prints. I'm going to transfer those prints to the card. When I show that to Hazzard—with the name of Dennis Grant on it, the right dates, everything—he's going to think it came out of the Philadelphia files and he'll know his game's up. He's going to break!"

Halsey declared: "That's it! He won't know the difference! He'll break!"

"His confession will be legal proof, Halsey," Trencher ground on. "I can't offer that fingerprint card as evidence, because it'll be a fake. The rogue's gallery prints might not be much good, because a man changes in ten years. But a confession will prove it!" Trencher's eyes smouldered as he said again: "The D.A.'s little game is up."

MARK HAZZARD swung his car to the curb in a neighborhood of old-fashioned rooming houses. His heart was hammering with dread, his mind still picturing the ominous black eyes of Inspector Trencher, when he stepped into a dark doorway. The man who moved quietly at his side was wearing the uniform of a patrolman.

"He's in there now, skipper."

"I got your report, Danny."

The blue uniform was a disguise which shielded Dan Carey, ex-cop and fugitive from the law, from the scrutiny of men who had once been his comrades on the force. As district attorney, Mark Hazzard had sent him up the river for murder. Carey's desperate attempt to escape had succeeded. Hazzard had found him starving in a dark alleyway while the law hunted him.

Because he was convinced of Carey's innocence in spite of the evidence—exactly as he was convinced of the innocence of Duncan Lockridge—Hazzard had sheltered him from the inexorable manhunt. Dan Carey had become Hazzard's under-cover assistant in the face of a danger that threatened disaster every hour of the day and night, not only for himself but for Hazzard as well. If it ever became known that the District Attorney of King's County was harboring a fugitive, Mark Hazzard's career would be brought to a swift and tragic end.

"Keep your eye on that door, Danny. I'm going in," Hazzard said quietly.

He crossed the street quickly, pushed through a paint-blistered door, climbed two worn flights. He turned to the door at the rear and listened to the sound of a newspaper crackling above soft radio music. He knocked, twisted the knob, and stepped in briskly as a thin-faced man sprang from a chair with startled eyes.

Hazzard spoke crisply. "Your name's Thomas Mackler. You're a cabinet maker. You served on the jury of the Leeds versus Carren case, with the man who was later killed, supposedly, by Duncan Lockridge. That's true, isn't it, Mackler? You and Walter Platt were two of the twelve who decided that case."

Mackler blurted: "Well? What if I did?"

"At the first vote, the jury stood two to ten in favor of the defendant Carren—that's true, isn't it? You and Platt argued for Leeds. The two of you kept that jury locked up until you argued them into a verdict in favor of the plaintiff, Leeds. Counsel for Leeds was the firm of Lockridge, Culver and Hinton."

Defiantly Mackler answered: "What if we did?"

"Did you force the jury to render that verdict because you were convinced of the merits of Leeds' case—or because somebody handed you a certain sum of money?"

"What's that?" Mackler gasped. "You accusin' me of takin' a bribe?"

Hot temper edged Hazzard's voice as he continued. "Listen. You attended every session of the Lockridge murder case. You know that I wasn't able to bring out any motive for the killing. The papers printed rumors of the reason Lockridge murdered Platt. Lockridge had bribed certain jurors on the Leeds versus Carren case. One of the jurors—Platt—was attempting blackmail on Lockridge, knowing that if the truth came out, Lockridge would be disbarred. In order to save himself and to keep the truth hidden, Lockridge killed Platt. That's the story. What do you think of it, Mackler?"

"I don't know nothin' about what Platt did, but I never took any money for—"

"Listen! I've been having you watched. You don't make much money in your shop, but you've been spending plenty. You buy whole cases of liquor. You get yourself a lot of new clothes. That radio there, Mackler, cost you three hundred and fifty dollars. How did you happen to have so much ready cash, all of a sudden—right after the close of the Leeds case?"

"That's none of your business!" Mackler blurted.

"Jury bribing is the state's business, Mackler. I've got enough evidence on you to charge you with it. I can indict you tomorrow morning if I choose, and send you up the river for the rest of your life." Hazzard's eyes were blazing, his words driving like steam under pressure. "You've got just one chance of beating that rap. Do you want to know what it is?"

Mackler stared in terror.

"You'll tell me, here and now, how much bribe money you accepted, and who paid it!"

Mackler swallowed hard, blinked dismayed eyes, tongued his dry lips. Hazzard stood tense while the radio played softly into the quiet. He watched Mackler's fear becoming a consuming corrosive burning away all reason. The thin wood-worker said in a sudden cackle:

"If I tell you, you won't have me arrested?"

"I promise you you won't have to answer for it—if you tell me the truth!"

Mackler's breath whizzed. "I—I'll tell you the truth, I took the money—so did Platt. We got it from—"

"Lockridge?" Hazzard urged desperately.

"No. No, from—"

Two quick shots barked from outside.

The reports drove splinters from the rear window. The bullets slapped past Hazzard, past Mackler, into the wall. Hazzard whirled, his hand darted to his arm-pit holster, while Mackler staggered back in terror. The cabinet maker's outflung arm struck the table lamp. It crashed to the floor and its bulb exploded. Hazzard backed with his 9mm Webley leveled, while the darkness fluttered with swift movement.

A shadow vanished from the fire-escape platform outside the window. The hallway door flashed open and shut as the terrorized Mackler fled. Hazzard took swift steps toward the window, but paused. The radio had ceased playing; and out of the silence an announcer's voice rushed:

"The Court of Appeals has handed down its decision in the Lockridge murder case, ladies and gentlemen! The appeal has been denied. The verdict of guilty must stand. Since the case will not be carried to the United States Supreme Court, and since Governor Bryant has declared he will not intervene, Duncan Lockridge must die in the electric chair!"

CHAPTER III

THE VANISHED
JUROR

HOT WRATH drove Mark Hazzard to the window where two white-rimmed holes shone in the pane. He thrust the sash up and crawled out. His Webley peered down the rusty flights as he alertly descended. Eyes flashing, he searched the black court, wary for any rustler that might betray the flight of the would-be murderer.

He dropped from the lowest platform and stood in black silence. Quiet steps took him past the rear door of a building fronting on the next street. Standing ajar, it hinted that the prowler had escaped to the street. Hazzard shouldered through it, ran along a hall, out a front door. He heard the hum of a car beyond the corner and knew that his man was fleeing.

Fury beat at his temples as he sped back. He slipped into the building where Mackler lived and bounded up the steps. Mackler's room was black and empty; the radio was playing dance music. The line of fire across the room strengthened Hazzard's conviction that the man at the window had intended to kill the cabinet maker. He sped down the stairs and out the entrance; crossed through quiet gloom to the doorway where Dan Carey was waiting.

"Did you see him come out, Danny?"

"Nobody's used that door except you, skipper. God, what's happened? I heard shots."

"There *were* shots," Hazzard answered wryly. "They've proved to me that Lockridge is innocent, but they can't make a case in court. Keep watching, Danny. If you see Mackler come out, shadow him. Phone any message to Ann."

"Right, skipper! Listen—I don't get it. You've been playing this jury bribing angle from the start. Couldn't you've used it to save Lockridge at the trial?"

Hazzard watched the door of the rooming house while he answered. "It would have made Lockridge's conviction all the more certain because it would have supplied the missing motive. Somebody bribed Platt and Mackler when they were jurors on the Leeds case. Platt turned it into a means of blackmail. The murderer was desperate to escape paying blood money—especially because it would mean disbarment if either Platt or Mackler talked. Got it, Danny?"

"Sure, skipper. But—"

"Platt was killed because he threatened to spill the works. The man who did it was watching Mackler tonight, and tried to kill him to keep him from telling the truth. It wasn't Lockridge, because Lockridge is in the death house. I'm morally convinced it's either Culver or Hinton—but a moral certainty isn't admissible in court as evidence. I've got to find proof, Danny—proof, before they strap Lockridge in the chair and throw the switch."

"How're you going to do it, skipper?"

"That's what I'm after, Danny. How."

Hazzard hurried to his car while Carey stayed to watch the rooming house door. He circled the block, though he realized that there was now no hope of spotting the man who had attempted to silence Mackler. He turned toward the Lambert Building. Again and again, while he drove, he was chilled by a haunting recollection of Inspector Trencher's accusing eyes.

The elevator carried him to the eleventh floor. He quietly entered the office he had rented, to find Ann Nash sitting alertly at the recording machine. Searching his face anxiously, she rose and seized his hand.

"Mark, what's the matter? You're worried. I can see it in your eyes."

"Nothing, darling." He kissed her lingeringly and the word echoed mockingly in his mind. "Nothing" he had said, when the ghosts of the past were rising to rob him of all his world and the girl he loved.

"There *is* something, Mark," Ann Nash said quietly. "I've seen it in your eyes again and again. Don't you know you can tell me anything, Mark, and I'll understand. Whatever is preying on your mind is keeping us apart—making us both unhappy. You've refused to marry me because of it. Won't you tell me what it is, darling?"

Grimly Mark Hazzard told her again: "It's nothing, Ann—nothing."

A CLICK came from the automatic trip of the recording device. The black record began to revolve under the diamond stylus, registering words spoken in the offices above. The girl turned at once, eyes and ears alert. Hazzard was reaching for the second pair of phones when the telephone purred. He heard the breathy voice of Dan Carey over the wire.

"Skipper, Mackler came out right after you left. He must've been hiding somewhere in the place. I followed him to your building, skipper—the Lambert. He's in there now."

"Good work, Danny. Keep on the job. When he comes out, follow him again. We're on a hot trail, old timer—we've got to play it for all it's worth."

The instant he lowered the instrument, Ann Nash whispered: "Mark! Listen!"

He adjusted the phones swiftly. A voice was carrying clearly over the circuit. Mackler was saying huskily:

"He's on to it. I tell you—but that ain't what's worryin' me. That's your funeral if it gets found out. Somebody shot at me in my place and I ain't goin' to—"

The answer was a whisper. "You fool, don't you know Hazzard's tried to scare you into talking? You have nothing to be afraid of."

Mackler: "Those bullets missed me by less than an inch! I'm not takin' any more chances. Platt got killed because of what he knew. How'll you like it if I go to the cops with the whole story? I know who it was that called Platt to this office. If you want me to shut up, you've got to pay me plenty!"

The whisper: "Keep quiet now! There's a microphone hidden somewhere in this place. Somebody might be listening in. Listen to me, Mackler. You're not going to talk, and you're not going to get any money. Clear out!"

"I guess you've got plenty in the safe. I'll take a good big wad of it right now if you don't want me to go straight to headquarters and spill—"

The words ceased with a sharp, cracking sound. Hazzard half rose, clamping the ear-phones tight, scarcely breathing. He heard a dull thud, then a gasp. The only sound during a long, quiet period, was a vague, scraping noise. Hazzard slipped the phones off and Ann Nash's eyes followed him anxiously as he strode to the door.

"I'm going up. Mackler's on the point of coming clean. Be sure you get it on the record, Ann—every word!"

"Mark—be careful!"

He smiled a wry answer. He hammered the elevator button while his temper flared. When the cab left him at the twelfth floor, he strode straight to the door of the firm of Lockridge, Culver and Hinton. He found the door bolted, and knocked. Impatience burned through him while slow steps answered. Lawrence Hinton looked out.

"What the devil do you want, Hazzard?"

"A statement from Mackler."

Hazzard thrust in. Hinton stood back, lips curling, while the alert eyes of the district attorney scanned the room. Hazzard stepped back to the gleaming front of the inset safe; he looked into each of the partitioned sections; he opened the supply closet. He was certain that Mackler had entered this office, certain that the cab could not have carried him down. Now he found not the slightest inkling of Mackler's presence.

"Looking for someone, Hazzard?"

"Mackler was here!"

"Here?" Hinton smiled thinly. "Besides burglarizing the place, are you spying on us? Very commendable, Hazzard—very. It happens you're wrong. No one by the name of Mackler has been here."

Hazzard asked quietly: "Quite sure?"

"No one named Mackler, or anyone else." Hinton stated flatly. "I've been here absolutely alone since Culver left, an hour ago. Just what makes you think, Hazzard, that someone was here?"

Hazzard did not answer. Instead, he asked again: "So you're quite sure?"

Hinton scowled. "Hazzard, I don't like your actions. I still think you're a lying, contemptible sneak—railroading Lockridge to the electric chair. You've no damned business here. Get out!"

Red filmed before Hazzard's eyes; his fists went hard; but he did not strike. He controlled his flaming temper with a desperate effort. He forced the tension from his muscles, the rasp from his voice, as he answered:

"Not yet, Hinton. Not quite yet. Before I go I want to ask you some questions about the very strange way in which Walter Platt met his death."

HAZZARD WALKED slowly into the partitioned section which he knew to be Hinton's office. He saw no indication that Mackler had been here. Hinton followed him, frowning. Hazzard confronted him, eyes narrowed, and asked:

"You told all you knew about it at the trial, didn't you, Hinton?"

"I knew nothing about it, and said so!"

"Shall we say only the murderer could know that secret?"

"What the devil are you driving at, Hazzard! Say what you have to say, and get out!"

The very softness of Hazzard's voice was ominous. "Walter Platt died of suffocation. His body showed all symptoms of it when he was dragged from the river. His whole face blue, his blood dark and fluid—but the only mark of violence was a bruise on his jaw, which certainly was not fatal. That's puzzling, isn't it, Hinton?"

"Stop, Hazzard!" Hinton snapped. "I heard you ask it over and over again at Lockridge's trial—'What did you use to smother Platt? What did you use to smother Platt?' Railroading him, every word! Showing the worshipping people that you're a man of justice to whom friendship can make no difference! Now you've got the contemptible effrontery to ask me—"

Hazzard interrupted gently. "What do *you* think Lockridge used to smother Platt?"

Hinton stared in mute indignation.

Hazzard smiled coldly, bent forward, and spoke rushingly:

"That was a puzzle all through the trial, wasn't it, Hinton? A strong man smothered to death, without a mark of violence to show how it was done. That murder occurred here, in this office—but how? What is here, in these rooms, that might have been used to suffocate a man without leaving a single mark? Do you know the answer to that?"

"I'll stand for no more of this, Hazzard! I'm not on trial. You can't force me to answer your damned insinuations. If you don't get out of here, I'll throw you out!"

"You'll find that," Hazzard answered, while his temper flared, "a fatal experiment." He leaned forward tensely, eyes blazing. "I know why Platt was killed. I don't know how, but I'm going to find out. I'm certain Lockridge is not guilty. You've heard my promise to clear him, Hinton—and I'm going to make my word good. Clearing Lockridge means getting the man who actually committed the killing. Does that interest you?"

"Listen—Hazzard—!"

"Just to make sure you know absolutely nothing about it, Hinton," Hazzard said tightly, "suppose you—"

A knock sounded. A black shadow was blotted over the pebbled pane of the entrance. The knob twisted as Hazzard straightened. Inspector Charles Trencher took slow, heavy steps toward the partition.

"Hello, Hazzard!" Trencher said.

Hazzard's mercurial temper raged. "Surprised to find me here, aren't you, Trencher? Quite surprised."

"No," Trencher drawled. "One of the boys happened to mention he saw you coming in here a minute ago."

"Happened to mention it," Hazzard asked acidly, "because you ordered him to watch me?"

Trencher smiled crookedly. "Well, the fact is, Hazzard, the commissioner wants to see you. Seems pretty anxious—guess it must be something important. Suppose we go over to his office together right now."

Hazzard answered stiffly. "Listen, Trencher. I'm here for a damned good reason. I want to see Hinton alone. Go back to the commissioner's office and wait for me there, will you?"

"We'd better go along together, Hazzard," Trencher answered ominously. "Right now."

Fury crashed Hazzard's fist to the desk. He strode out the entrance with face crimsoned and jaw clenched. Trencher followed him into the waiting elevator cab, smiling crookedly. At the lobby level, Hazzard shouldered out first. He walked swiftly to the sidewalk and glimpsed Dan Carey in the shadow.

"Out of sight!" his gesture warned. "Keep an eye on Hinton."

Trencher was stooping into the car when Hazzard's hand clamped on his arm. The inspector straightened warily. The tight lips of the district attorney clipped his words:

"The commissioner will have to wait."

Trencher warned: "Take it easy, Hazzard. You and I are going down there now and—"

"Not—quite—yet!"

Hazzard's thrust sent Trencher backward. The inspector lurched, grabbing for Hazzard's arm. Hazzard tensed on toe-tips and his knuckles hissed. His blow clicked to the point of Trencher's chin. The inspector dove to the pavement with a grunt. Hazzard spun, slipped behind the wheel, and kicked at the starter.

When Trencher pulled up, black eyes smouldering, hand groping automatically for his gun, the tail-light of Hazzard's car streaked red past the corner.

PONDEROUS IRON gates swung open before Hazzard's car and shut behind him. Guards escorted him to the office of the veteran warden of the State Prison. He strode to the desk of the man who had headed the institution for thirty years.

"Wharton, I want to see Lockridge."

The warden's milky eyes blinked. "Sure, you can see him if you want to—but you're wasting your time."

They walked silently along bleak cement corridors, up cold steps. Wharton led the way and his voice rumbled.

"Wasting your time. Innocent men don't get executed. You can search all the court records for three hundred years back, and you won't find a single authentic case of an innocent man's paying his life for a crime he didn't commit. When Lockridge gets the jolt, it'll be a guilty man frying."

Hazzard said wryly: "I'm doing my best to see that the precedent holds this time, warden."

The hall in the remote wing where the chair room was located rang rhythmically with their footfalls. Men condemned to die occupied these heavily fortified cells. Gaunt, haggard faces looked out at Hazzard as he passed—some of them the faces of men whom Hazzard had convicted with a grim certainty of their guilt. But when he paused, he gazed at the pallid features of a man he believed with all his heart to be innocent.

"Hello, old man," he said. To Wharton he added: "Put through a call to Governor Bryant for me, will you, warden? Thanks!"

Duncan Lockridge smiled wanly as Wharton tramped away, and extended a thin hand through the bars. Hazzard gripped it hotly. The man who had been one of the most highly esteemed attorneys in the city, who now was awaiting the opening of the green door of death, said quietly:

"I'm glad you've come, Mark. I want to tell you that I don't hold it against you. You were fair at the trial—fair to your job and to me, too. You're not to blame because I'm here."

"Duncan—" Hazzard's earnestness tightened his voice. "You've told me your story twenty times, but I want to hear it again. There might be something—some little thing we've overlooked—that can help clear you."

Lockridge smiled. "Certainly, Mark." He told it again, automatically, while Hazzard listened intently, how he had gone into his office just as Lawrence Hinton was leaving; how he had worked most of the night on an important case; how he had simply left, stopped in a nearby bar for a glass of beer and then driven home. He had seen nothing of Platt, had known nothing of Platt's murder, until the body was found in the river.

Testimony corroborating Lockridge's story had been disastrously weak. The elevator operator in the Lambert Building had not remembered the time of Lockridge's departure. The bartender who had served him the beer had not recalled him at all. This, and the fact that he had been alone in the office all the night, had provided him with only a feeble alibi.

Hazzard asked tensed questions: "Did you see any indication that someone else had used your car during the night? Did you notice the scratches on the side? Isn't there any way you can prove you were in that office all night without having once gone out? Can't you think of something I can work on, Duncan?"

To every query, Lockridge answered: "No."

"And you didn't see Platt at all that night—not at any time?"

"No."

Hazzard smiled. "Chin up, Duncan. I'm not giving up. I'm going to get you out of here, old man. That's a promise."

Again he gripped Lockridge's thin hand. Filled with a torturing bafflement, he walked slowly back along the cold corridor. When he entered the warden's office, Wharton, holding the telephone, grumbled:

"Governor Bryant's on the wire. I got him out of bed. You're wasting your time and everybody else's."

Hazzard gripped the instrument hard. "Governor Bryant? Hazzard speaking. I'm getting new evidence in the Lockridge case. I'm absolutely convinced Lockridge is innocent. Governor, in the name of justice, will you grant him a reprieve so that I can have more time to build up a case and—"

Bryant's angry voice interrupted: "What kind of evidence? Is it admissible in court? Is it strong enough for a new trial?"

Hazzard admitted grimly: "No. But if you'll give me a chance—"

"See here, Hazzard! You've badgered me on this case for weeks. I'll have no more of it! You've got to have damned strong evidence before I'll lift a finger to save Lockridge from the chair. That's final, Hazzard! Good-night!"

Hazzard lowered the phone slowly. His pulse pounded hotly as he left the warden's office. He peered back, in the direction of the death house, and pictured Lockridge in his bleak cell—Lockridge, waiting within sight of the green door, which was destined to open soon and beckon him to his doom.

HUSHED DARKNESS lay over the city when Hazzard stopped his car at the side of the Lambert Building. Eleven floors above the street, he knew, the tireless Ann Nash was still posted at the recording machine. Somewhere Dan Carey was keeping an eye on Hinton. He felt that the relentless Trencher had men looking for him, with orders to bring him to headquarters when seen—a prisoner. He was warily moving toward the entrance when furtive footfalls sounded behind him and a tense whisper came: "Skipper!"

Hazzard spun to Carey. The ex-cop's eyes shone startled as he peered back toward the alley entrance and said rushingly:

"I've been following Hinton. He left the office right after you did, and went home. A little while ago he came back. His car's around in the alley. Just now I spotted somebody sneaking out the back way. It's too dark to tell if it's Hinton, but he's carrying something heavy and—"

The sound of a starting motor whirred out of the alley blackness. Hazzard strode swiftly. Peering cautiously past the corner, he saw a car without lights spurting toward the far street. It swung out of sight as Carey blurted:

"That's it, skipper! It might be Hinton! He put something in the car—brought it down the fire-stairs and—"

"Come on, Danny!"

Hazzard whirled back. Carey clambered into his machine while he kicked it into action and they turned to speed after the car that scurried from the alley. He glimpsed it on the next street when he was three intersections beyond the Lambert Building, and twisted to follow. The zig-zagging chase led him out of the business district, through a section of warehouses, into river dampness. The bewildering turns of the mysterious car took it from sight until Hazzard chanced a swift run onto the ramp of the bridge.

Then he glimpsed it—a black, motionless shadow at the apex of the span. A dark figure with hunched shoulders was moving beside it. Hazzard pressed at the accelerator when he saw the man furtively lift something heavy and cumbersome to the rail of the bridge. It spilled over and dropped from sight. The black figure spun about as Hazzard's headlights flickered on him; and a gun glittered in his lifted hand.

"Look out, skipper!" Carey gasped as the gun spat fire.

The cracked windshield blinded Hazzard when the bullet struck. His one hand twined hard on the wheel and his other swung to his Webley. He swerved to run alongside the other car while the black figure sprang into it. Three swift flashes sent slugs clanging against Hazzard's machine. The lightless car spurted away, swung swiftly. A howl of alarm broke from Carey's lips when it came driving straight toward Hazzard's machine.

Hazzard twisted wildly to avoid the imminent head-on collision. Tires whined past him. He spilled down, with his car still rushing, at the warning glint of a gun. Twice more bullets ripped the night air. The slugs whizzed past Hazzard and Carey while they huddled. The other car was roaring away when they straightened to glimpse an iron girder directly ahead.

Hazzard flung his car aside, but the girder tore into his right fender. They spilled forward with the violence of the stop. Hazzard ducked out, Webley leveled; but the other car was speeding off the ramp, lights still out. Carey gripped the rail and peered over, at a foamy white spot on the black surface of the river.

"Skipper! It looked like a man's body he threw over! Did you see it, skipper?"

Hazzard snapped: "I saw it, Danny! Listen. The shots might bring a prowl car at any second. If they spot you, you're done for. Get off this bridge, Danny—make it fast! I'm going after that car!"

His ringing tone urged Carey into a run down the slope of the span as he backed and twisted to follow the lightless car. Wind whipped past him as he went down the ramp—and his temper flared with the conviction that he stood small chance of spotting the other car again. He swung past corners, searching vainly, lips pressed together and face hotly flushed, as he hopelessly searched.

SITTING AT his desk in police headquarters, Inspector Trencher ceased rubbing his jaw to listen. He recognized the quick footfalls sounding in the corridor. His lips twisted with a grim smile as he rose. He said to ex-Sheriff Halsey, who was slouched in a chair, and to Commissioner Brook, who was moving angrily back and forth:

"That's Hazzard coming."

Hazzard paused on the sill, eyes glinting from Trencher's crooked smile, to Brook's accusing glare, to Halsey's stubborn defiance. He came quickly to the desk, took up Trencher's pencil, scribbled on a pad. He said imperatively:

"Here's an automobile license number. I want to know who owns that car—and I want a warrant for his arrest."

Trencher drawled "Sure," and touched a button. "Warrant? What's the charge?" He handed the slip to a blue-shirted man who came in and immediately withdrew. "Why don't I make it two while I'm at it? Another for Mark Hazzard, charging assault and battery on an officer of the law."

"If you like, inspector," Hazzard said bitterly. "I want a warrant charging Lawrence Hinton with first degree murder."

"Hinton?" Trencher sat up. "Who's he killed?"

"Thomas Mackler."

"Where's the body?"

"You'll have to drag the river for it."

Trencher swiveled back. "Tell me, Hazzard, how can I charge Hinton with murder when we haven't got the *corpus delicti?*"

Hazzard snapped: "I saw Hinton sneaking out of the Lambert Building with a man's body. I saw him throw it off the bridge. My testimony will establish the *corpus delicti.* I want that warrant!"

Trencher countered: "Are you absolutely sure it was Hinton? Are you positive it was Mackler's body? If you're not, you don't get the warrant. A mistake would get the whole department into hot water. Eye-witnesses are sometimes wrong, you know."

"Stick to the procedure, be absolutely certain before you make a move, Trencher," Hazzard challenged, "—and give Hinton a chance to slip out of the state!"

"There's plenty of time, Hazzard," Trencher drawled. "If we find Mackler's body in the river, that'll be plenty of time. How'd Hinton kill him? Got any idea? If you didn't actually see the murder committed, if your proof isn't conclusive—why, I can't do anything, Hazzard, until we've got the body."

The door opened again, while Hazzard strove to control his raging fury, and a blue-shirted man brought a slip to Trencher's desk. The inspector said "Humph!" and handed it to Hazzard. He peered at a scrawled address, and a name: Vinton Culver. Speechless, he watched Trencher lift the telephone and ask: "Get me Vinton Culver's home right away.

"Better cool off, Hazzard," he suggested. "Culver's car, but you're accusing his partner, Hinton. You can't have any warrant."

"It means only that Hinton used Culver's car tonight—just as he used Lockridge's to dispose of Platt's body."

Trencher said "Humph!" again and "Where's your proof of that?" He asked into the transmitter: "Mr. Culver? Inspector Trencher talking. Have you been using your car tonight? Has anyone else been using it? Just take a look at it, will you, to make sure?" To Hazzard he explained: "He's going out to the garage now. We'll know in a minute."

Commissioner Brook was facing Hazzard grimly. "Look here," he said. "Are you trying to pull the wool over our eyes by pretending to be on fire about the Lockridge case? You'd better let that go, Hazzard. You're through being the D.A. Explain this, will you?"

He handed Hazzard two photographs. Hazzard started. They depicted the drawn face of a young man ten years younger than Hazzard. A number identified the prisoner of the law known then as Dennis Grant. Hazzard remembered, with a pang of pain, that photograph being taken. It brought the agony of the past into the present as he gazed defiantly into Commissioner Brook's eyes and asked:

"Who is this?"

"Don't you recognize yourself, Hazzard?" Brook asked. "Can't you see it's Dennis Grant?"

"A resemblance, yes," Hazzard countered. "It's why Halsey made his mistake. Since the law demands positive evidence, you've got to admit that picture is not conclusive."

Trencher, smiling crookedly, put down the telephone and remarked: "Culver says his car is in the garage. You're having another of your brainstorms, Hazzard."

"If it's there, it's just been put back!" Hazzard retorted. His knuckles pressed the desk. "You're taking Halsey's word that I'm the man in that picture—taking it after a lapse of ten years. You said a moment ago, Trencher, 'eye-witnesses can be wrong, you know.' Halsey's statement is worth nothing."

Halsey grumbled: "I know you're Dennis Grant—don't try to bluff out of it."

Hazzard whirled on him. "Have you studied the science of criminology, Halsey? Are you familiar with the experiments of Munsterberg, Dauber, Gross, Dupre, Heindl, Hellweg—all proving how unreliable eye-witnesses are? Do you know it's been proved that witnesses on the average make an error of about five inches in the height of a person, and mistake the age by eight years?

"Do you know it's an established fact that eye-witnesses are wrong about the color of the hair in exactly eighty-three per cent of careful tests? Those errors were made in only a matter of minutes, and you claim to identify me positively as Dennis Grant after more than ten years!"

Halsey reiterated stubbornly: "You're Grant."

Hazzard faced Trencher. "You'll have to have better proof than that, inspector. Until you get it, I'm still the D.A. Gentlemen, goodnight!"

Trencher leaped up and snarled: "Come back here, Hazzard!" as the district attorney snapped through the door. He sprang after Hazzard and followed swift footfalls down the stairs. When he reached the street, Hazzard's car was speeding away. Trencher tramped back grimly. Once in his office, he punched push-buttons as he snarled commands.

His orders brought eight hard-faced plainclothes men to his desk. His voice droned at them ominously:

"Keep this strictly under your hat. Any man who lets it leak out will get broken. I want Mark Hazzard. Find him. Watch his office, and grab him. Bring him back here. Start looking for him right now!"

Eight grim detectives went out the door while Trencher peered at the rogue's gallery photographs of Dennis Grant, convicted murderer, and smiled twistedly.

CHAPTER IV

STILL MAN-HUNT

ANN NASH looked through the window of the district attorney's office, across the sunlighted street at a window in police headquarters, and saw Inspector Trencher at his desk. She knew that the plainclothes man posted in the corridor was there at Trencher's orders. Dread certainty that Hazzard was in grave trouble filled her, but she could not guess the reason. Since Dan Carey had relieved her at the recorder in the Lambert Building, she had neither seen nor heard from Hazzard.

Each empty hour was agony to the girl. The day was an eternity of consternation and anxiety. She remained at her desk with torture showing in her eyes—until, long past sunset and after a period of trying silence, the telephone rang.

"This is Vinton Culver speaking," a voice said. "Will you come to my home right away? It's very important."

Ann Nash caught a faint hint of Mark Hazzard's inflection through the disguised tone. She went from the office breathlessly, pulling on her coat while she ran down the stairs, tugging an impertinent hat on her head while she slipped into her car. She sensed that she was being watched by Trencher's men as she turned in the direction of the attorney's home.

She crisscrossed the city until she was sure she had shaken off anyone who might be trailing her car. She followed the bends of a boulevard and braked in tree-shadows near Culver's residence. As she hurried to the entrance, a shadow stepped from the hedge and said:

"Good girl, Ann. I'm going to need you."

"Mark!" She whirled to him breathlessly. "Where have you been, Mark? What's happened?"

"No time to explain now, Ann." His hand closed on hers snugly while they went to the door. "I'm in a spot, that's all. Don't worry about me—it's Lockridge I'm thinking of. I've got to get the evidence to clear him tonight, no matter what it means, or he'll go to the chair. If Culver—"

He broke off as the entrance opened. A maid escorted them into a library, and they waited tensely. The girl saw that Hazzard was carrying a small suitcase which was very heavy, that he had something bulky in his pockets. He grimly resisted the mute question of her anxious eyes until Vinton Culver strode toward them stiffly.

Hazzard said quickly: "Mr. Culver, I'm pressed for time. Please trust me as much as you can. I'm more convinced than ever that Lockridge is innocent. You want to help me clear him, don't you? You want to see the man who is actually guilty get the chair instead?"

"Certainly," Culver answered coldly. "Certainly. But how—"

"When Trencher called last night, about your car, you didn't feel the radiator to see if it was hot? You merely made sure it was in the garage and—"

"Naturally. Trencher merely asked—"

"Have you seen any indications that your car was used late last night, without your knowledge—taken out of your garage, and then put back?"

"No."

"Mr. Culver, I want the combination of your office safe."

"What? Why? What the devil, Hazzard, are you—"

"Give me the combination of that safe! It's vital. Then call Lawrence Hinton and ask him to meet you at your office in half an hour. You're not going there to see him, but I am. Anyway, give him that message."

Culver hesitated; but the sting of Hazzard's words and the blaze of Hazzard's eyes decided him. He wrote cryptic symbols on an envelope and handed it over. He spun the dial of the telephone. Hazzard, taking up the heavy suitcase, heard him say:

"Larry? I'd like you to meet me at the office in half an hour. Yes, it's important." Culver's eyes widened. "You are? You think it best? I'll talk it over with you. Half an hour, yes." The lawyer rose and explained: "Hinton insists on preferring charges against you, Hazzard—for burglary."

"That," Hazzard declared as he strode to the door, "is literally the least of my worries. Good-night, Mr. Culver."

Ann's hand kept warmly on his arm as they hurried to her car. He put the heavy suitcase in the rumble compartment and clicked on the radio while he turned toward the center of the city. The girl asked anxiously:

"Won't you tell me, Mark? You know I'll understand—anything."

Hazzard smiled. "I know, Ann—but I can't. Listen. I want you to relieve Danny at the recorder. Whatever comes over the wire tonight is going to be of the utmost importance. I'm positive Hinton is guilty of the Platt killing, but there's only one way of pinning it on him."

Hazzard listened intently to the voice of a news commentator issuing from the radio:

"Thomas Mackler, who was a juror in the Leeds case, is still missing from the rooming house where he lives. Police have been unable to locate him. Though no information is forthcoming, it is believed that the men now dragging the river are searching for Mackler's body. Whatever they are searching for, they have not found it so far. The swift current of the river, and its unusual depth has in many cases made the task of dragging it unsuccessful."

Hazzard said wryly: "I can't count on that." He turned to the girl: "Ann, Hinton killed Platt in an unusual way. I think I know how, but there's no evidence to back me up. The only way of getting that evidence is to allow Hinton to try to kill me in the same strange way."

"Mark!"

"A chance," Hazzard answered. "It may not work. But if it does, it's going to nail Hinton—even if I become the *corpus delicti* that proves him guilty."

The girl studied his face in wide-eyed alarm as he swung into the alley behind the Lambert Building. He sent her ahead and searched the sidewalks before he followed her. Certain he was not seen, he lugged the heavy suitcase into the elevator cab. Ann Nash was tensely silent while they rode up and opened the office where Dan Carey was attending the recording machine.

"Nothing worth a damn came through today, skipper," Carey announced as he rose. "The office is empty now."

"Okay, copper," Hazzard said with a tight smile. "Ann's on the job. Get some sleep, then come back and relieve her at five in the morning. Watch yourself. Trencher's got men watching for me all over town, and one of them may spot you."

"Why, Mark?" Ann Nash insisted. "What has Trencher got on you?"

"Please, Ann—let it go. I've kept clear of him so far, haven't I? I've been busy all day, ducking his dicks and getting certain important jobs done. Now, stick at that machine and catch every word. On your way. Danny—and if you know any prayers, say 'em for me."

The girl's gaze followed him anxiously as he left the office. When the elevator cab left him at the twelfth floor, he carried his heavy case to the door of Lockridge, Culver and Hinton. His skeleton key admitted him. He clicked on the lights and stood alertly listening. The rooms were empty. The way was clear.

HAZZARD CAREFULLY turned the combination dial of the inset vault, following the cryptic notations made by Vinton Culver. He tugged the heavy slab of a door open and stepped into the musty air within the steel walls, carrying the heavy case. He sought a place to hide it, and slipped it behind thick ledgers in a low compartment.

He reached to the single electric bulb in the vault and unscrewed it. The globe he twisted into the socket was a duplicate of that he had placed in the light fixture in the outer office—a sensitive microphone. He looked at it as he said quietly:

"Hear me, Ann? Are you getting it? Stay at the machine—I'll call you in a minute."

He stepped out and thrust the heavy door into its frame. He spun the dial to scatter the combination, and brought a bottle from his coat pocket. With a brush he dusted its powdery content over the dial and the handle; it left an almost invisible film of white. He pocketed both bottle and brush, stepped to the office switchboard and dialed the number of the phone in the room below. "Did you get it, Ann?"

"Yes, clearly."

"Good! Listen. Hinton's almost due. Get every word that's said up here—it's absolutely vital. The whole case may depend on those records. There isn't time to explain now—you'll get it later, over the wire. On the job!"

She echoed: "On the job," and her voice was strained with anxiety.

Hazzard shrugged off his coat, tossed his hat aside. His watch told him that almost half an hour had passed since Culver had telephoned Hinton. He walked back and forth tensely while the minutes crawled. He turned abruptly, facing the door, when the elevator grille clacked open in the corridor. Steps sounded; a shadow blurred over the pebbled pane of the entrance.

Lawrence Hinton paused, eyes narrowed at Hazzard. He came in slowly, without speaking, his lips tightening maliciously. Hazzard saw desperation in the deeply graven lines of Hinton's face. He said quietly:

"I've got a theory I want to talk to you about, Hinton."

Hinton retorted: "You've gone too far with your highhanded methods. You're going to face a charge of breaking and entering. I'm calling the police right now."

Hazzard smiled: "Go ahead." Hinton strode quickly to the switchboard. "Culver and I will both testify that you're guilty of committing a burglary."

The dial spun under his flicking finger. "You're through as the district attorney."

Hazzard suggested: "Ask for Inspector Trencher. He'll be quite interested."

The receiver clicked. "Headquarters?" Hinton asked with a rasp. "Give me Inspector Trencher." He glared defiance at Hazzard. "Trencher? Lawrence Hinton calling. I want to prefer a criminal charge against Mark Hazzard. He's here, in my office now. Good!" He jerked the plug from its socket and rose. "Trencher's coming right over."

Hazzard said: "While we're waiting for him. I'll tell you why I came. I've got a theory—I mentioned that. I think I know how Platt was killed. It's the answer to the whole nasty business, Hinton."

Hinton's eyes narrowed.

"Platt came to this office. The bruise on his jaw, found in the necropsy, showed he'd been hit hard—knocked unconscious. The man he was trying to blackmail did that—the man who bribed him as a juror on the Leeds case. You did it, didn't you, Hinton?"

Hinton challenged: "Can you prove it, Hazzard?"

Hazzard admitted: "No. Platt's dead—and so is Mackler, in the same way. You were in this office with Platt. You knocked him down. You thought you'd killed him on the spot, didn't you, Hinton—that wizened little man with heart trouble. You were terrified, and you tried to think how you could cover yourself. You were here, with Platt on the floor, supposedly dead, when you heard the elevator stop— Lockridge coming up."

Hinton's eyes were glaring. "Go on, Hazzard," he bade huskily.

"Your only thought, when you heard Lockridge coming, was to hide him. The safe was standing open. You dragged Platt into it and locked him in. You pretended to Lockridge that nothing had happened, and went out. That's what killed Platt, Hinton—all the post-mortem symptoms show it—suffocation while he was locked in that safe."

Hinton snarled: "You're talking damned nonsense!"

"Am I? You had to wait until Lockridge left the office before you could get Platt out of the safe. You used Lockridge's car that night—and Culver's to get rid of Mackler. You've sneered at me for convicting Lockridge, but you're letting him go to the chair for a murder you—"

Hinton struck with savage desperation. Hazzard had seen that fist grow hard. He had seen it begin driving toward his jaw. He was a trained boxer who could have parried that crushing blow with ease but he deliberately let Hinton's hard knuckles jolt him to his heels. He collapsed like a dropped length of chain.

Hinton stood stiff, knuckles bleeding. He bent over Hazzard; he made sure that Hazzard was unconscious. With feverish haste he strode to the safe and turned the combination dial. He tugged the heavy door open. He dragged Hazzard into it. His moves became frantically swift as he shoved the slab into its frame and scattered the combination—for footfalls were sounding in the hall.

CHAPTER V

FINGERPRINT TRAP

THE SAFE locked. Hazzard was imprisoned in it. Hinton made sure of that while he steadied himself and answered the rap of knuckles on the entrance. He stepped back as Inspector Trencher came in with eyes blackly ominous.

Hinton blurted: "Hazzard knocked me down when I was turning from the telephone, inspector. He ran out—maybe he used the fire-stairs. I'll charge him with burglary when you find him."

Trencher drawled: "Beat it, did he? Don't worry, Hinton. I'll grab that hot-head."

Hinton followed Trencher into the corridor. He stood rigid, watching the inspector charge down the fire-stairs. When the footfalls were no longer audible, he peered into the office, eyes narrowed in wonder. The microphone haunted his mind. It must be hidden somewhere. He touched the elevator button, tensing with a growing determination, his eyes gleaming with the same savage light that had filled them when he had trapped Hazzard in the vault.

He stepped tensely through the opened grille and asked of the night elevator operator: "Did he come from the street, that man you brought up first? Do you remember where he came from?"

"No, he came from the eleventh floor," the operator answered. "He's got an office there. Eleven-twenty."

"Take me down."

Hinton's slitted eyes turned to 1120 when he left the cab. He took slow steps toward it and silently twisted the knob. It held. He listened through, to a faint rustle of movement. His face became a mask of murderous intent—and he knocked.

Ann Nash heard the sharp rap through a voice that was speaking over the wire. She had clearly heard Mark Hazzard's accusation of

Hinton. She had caught the thud of the driving blow and the thump of Hazzard's falling body. Trencher's voice, and Hinton's again, had followed a strained interval. Again there had been a period of baffling silence, but now a voice was speaking in the phones; and it was the voice of Mark Hazzard.

"Can you hear me, Ann? It's all right. Hinton knocked me cold for a few minutes. Did you get it all, Ann?"

Again the imperative knock sounded. The girl turned anxiously, slipping off the phones. She rushed to the door, drew the bolt, whispered, "Come in, Danny," and hurried back. The voice was sounding again when she replaced the phones. She heard quiet steps behind her while it said:

"I'm inside the vault, Ann. Hinton has locked me in. He plans to leave me here until I've died of suffocation. It won't be long before—"

An unseen hand snatched the phones from Ann Nash's head. Another clamped across her eyes as she turned frantically. She tried to spring up as an arm crushed her and dragged her back. The shattering crash she heard was the fall of the desk lamp. Blackness filled the office and blinded the girl while the pressing hand lifted from her eyes to her mouth. She strove to escape the mad strength of the man who held her—until a paralyzing blow struck the side of her head.

The girl became a limp burden in Lawrence Hinton's arms. He lowered her, and sent the recording machine crashing to the floor with a savage kick. Its turn-table jammed to a stop. He clawed at the girl's dress, ripped it open, tore off the sleeves. He used one to bind Ann Nash's slender ankles, the other to pinion her wrists. He stuffed a silken gag into her mouth and tied it tight; and he left her unconscious while he turned to the automatic recorder.

It was broken. He took the composition disc from the turn-table and broke it in his hands. In a compartment in the lid he found other records; and he cracked each one apart. He made certain that he had destroyed every one before he stole for the door. He carried the fragments out with him. Ann Nash, peering through the haze of returning consciousness, vaguely saw him go, though she couldn't distinguish who it was.

A dim voice echoed in her mind—Mark Hazzard's. "I'm in the vault. Hinton has locked me in. He plans to leave me here until I've died of suffocation."

The girl strove desperately to break from the silken bonds. She tried to cry out, but her muffled voice was inarticulate. With all the strength she could summon, she tried to tug her wrists free, to kick her ankles loose—but the knots were hard, the bands painfully tight.

"I'm in the vault…. Hinton locked me in… to die of suffocation."

The corridor beyond the door was silent. When the elevator hummed, the cage passed the level of the eleventh floor without stopping. The nearest offices were empty; and beyond the window was heavy darkness. Ann Nash could not know how many endless minutes passed while she tugged at her bonds. She could think only of the voice of Mark Hazzard as it had come over the wire:

"Locked in the vault… die of suffocation."

Tears streamed from Ann Nash's eyes while she lay exhausted. The faint shine from the street vanished on the pane, and told her that dawn was near, that hours had passed. Again and again she renewed her attempts to break free, but each sapped her strength. She lay faint, heart pounding, aware of nothing but that voice, conscious of no feeling save the dread of the death it had promised Mark Hazzard.

"Locked in the vault… to die… die…."

ANN NASH scarcely heard the sound that came at last to disturb the crushing silence. Her eyes turned dimly toward the shadow that appeared on the pane. She heard a key click, saw the blur of a square face, heard a blurted expletive.

It was Dan Carey. She summoned her strength as she felt the knife in his hand sawing at the silk. She ignored his questions as she struggled to her feet. She tottered to the door and gasped:

"Danny—call Culver—Culver. He's got to open the safe—Mark's in it. Get Trencher. They've got to—open the—safe."

An amazed elevator operator carried the exhausted girl in her torn dress up one floor. She tugged at the knob of the entrance of the suite of law offices and implored the attendant to open it. She waited in agony until the pass key drew the bolt; and she stumbled to a stop, gazing in terror at the shining door of the vault.

"Mark—Mark!"

She was trying with unreasoning hopelessness to find the combination on the dial when Dan Carey shouldered in. Carey exclaimed: "I got 'em both—Culver and Trencher. I told 'em to come fast as they can make it." He shuddered. "Is he in there, Ann—the skipper?"

"He's been there for hours—hours," she wailed. "He may be dead,

Danny—it's been so long." A noise in the corridor brought alarm to her eyes. "You've got to keep away from Trencher, Danny. Please go. There's nothing we can do—but wait."

Dan Carey grimly remained until the hum of the elevator warned him. He sped to the fire-stairs door and peered back through a crack to see Trencher and Culver hurrying into the office. He heard Ann's desperate: "Open it—open it!" and grimly crept down.

In the office, Culver raised his hand to the dial and hesitated. "Hazzard's in there?"

Trencher gripped the girl's arms and demanded: "How the devil did he get in there? What's happened? Speak up!"

She tried to turn from him and implored again: "Please open it—please! It's been so long—"

Culver tensely began turning the disc.

"Hinton put him in there!" the girl exclaimed wildly. "Hinton hit him, and dragged him in, and left him there to die. If—if Mark's dead—if it's cost him his life—he's proved Lockridge is innocent just the same."

Culver exclaimed: "That's right." Ann peered as the lawyer thrust at the huge steel handle. A moan of despair broke from her trembling lips when she saw that it would not turn. Trencher blurted blasphemy—for Culver, in his nervous anxiety, had missed one of the points of the combination by a hair.

THE INSPECTOR snapped: "Try it again—quick! No—wait!"

He listened alertly. A faint hum was issuing from the elevator shaft. A cab was coming up. Trencher pushed Culver away from the vault. He seized the girl's arm firmly. With a sharp gesture toward one of the partitioned offices he snapped:

"Get out of sight! That might be Hinton coming. If he's guilty—if it's cost Hazzard's life to prove it—I'm going to get him cold! *Get in there!*"

He thrust Culver into the office. He forced the girl with him, and quickly closed the door. Ann Nash scarcely breathed when the click of the opening lock sounded. Trencher brought his service gat into his crusty hand while slow footfalls moved across the office. Silently he opened the door a crack; and his black eyes narrowed on Lawrence Hinton.

Hinton's eyes shifted warily right and left as he stood at the vault, listening. His lips curved with malevolent triumph as he reached to the dial. He paused to glance at his wristwatch; and he mumbled: "Seven hours—seven hours." There was no sound in the office while Trencher watched Hinton through the crack as the man selected the combination of the vault on the dial.

The last number stopped under the mark. Hinton seized the handle, thrust it down. He tugged the great door slowly open, retreating with if. Light gleamed on the floor in a spreading fan, and Hinton stepped into it. He expected to see Mark Hazzard lying twisted on the floor, face swollen, eyes protruding, dead of suffocation. He did not expect the sight he beheld—Hazzard standing erect, smiling calmly, Webley firmly leveled.

"Raise your hands, Hinton," Hazzard said. "I think this case is closed."

Hinton stood stock still, shocked icy cold, staring at the apparition who came at him out of the vault. He scarcely heard the swift movement behind him. He retreated slowly, almost unaware that Trencher's hard hand was closed on his arm. He heard a girl's: "Mark—Mark!" and saw the frantic girl fling her arms around the ghost who continued to level an automatic at him.

"Hold him, Trencher!" Hazzard's arm tightened snugly around Ann. "It's all right, darling. Didn't you get it on the wire? I told you I'd brought in two small oxygen tanks in the suitcase—didn't you get it? I've been waiting for Hinton to come back. Ann, it's all right!"

"He broke the machine!" the girl sobbed. "I didn't know, Mark—I didn't know!"

Trencher growled while Hinton still stared: "You'll testify that Hinton locked you in there, will you, Hazzard? Was that the way he finished Platt—and Mackler?"

"Exactly," Hazzard said. "I'll testify to it, and so will the stuff on his hands. I powdered the dial and the handle with naphthionate of sodium when I first came in here. It's still on his skin even if he's washed his hands in the meantime. It'll shine under ultra-violet light. You're familiar with that thief-trap, aren't you, Trencher?"

Trencher snarled: "If that's so, Hinton, you're nailed beyond all doubt!"

Suddenly Hinton wrenched away. He spun to drive a wild blow into Trencher's face. He tore his arm loose and whirled to the door as Hazzard went from Ann Nash's arms with automatic twinkling.

He bounded after Hinton into the corridor. He stopped short, straddled, when Hinton crouched at the entrance of the fire-stairs with a revolver glinting up from his pocket. Hazzard leaped aside at the first thunderous report.

Screaming lead caromed off the corridor walls. Gunsmoke gusted in the dim light. Stinging flecks hit Mark Hazzard's face while his automatic crashed. He took slow steps forward, peering narrowly at Hinton, sprawled on the floor, whimpering with the pain of a broken arm. When Hazzard paused it was because Trencher's big hand closed on his arm.

"There's your man, inspector," Hazzard said. "Pick him up."

Trencher answered: "All right, Hazzard. From now on this case is entirely mine. I'm taking Hinton to headquarters, and I think you'd better come along. How about it, Hazzard—considering this?"

"This" was a card Trencher had slipped from his pocket. Hazzard saw fingerprint smudges on it. He saw blank spaces filled in with haunting dates, under a black line indicating the card belonged to the records of the Philadelphia Police Department. A sigh of utter despair drained his lungs as he gazed haggardly at the lettered name: *Dennis Grant;* and, following *Convicted of,* that dread word: *Murder.*

The card went back into Trencher's pocket.

BLUISH LIGHT filled the room in police headquarters where Hinton's tired voice droned. Ultra-violet light, shafting from a reflector, bathed Hinton's hands while officers held them during the confessional. The brilliant phosphorescence on the fingers was a shine that proved a killer's guilt.

"Lockridge gave me the Leeds case to organize. If we lost it, it would be my fault. That's why I bribed Platt and Mackler. Lockridge and Culver didn't know anything about it," Hinton recited as the police stenographer's pencil sped. "I couldn't pay blood money to Platt. If he talked, it would mean the end of me as a lawyer—maybe send me to jail. I didn't mean to kill Platt. But Mackler—"

Mark Hazzard turned at a touch on his shoulder. "Governor Bryant on the wire," a whisper said. He went quietly out the door, into the office where Trencher, Commissioner Brook and ex-Sheriff Halsey were waiting. He smiled tightly and took up the phone.

"Hazzard, you were right from the beginning," Governor Bryant said. "I'm issuing a pardon to Duncan Lockridge at once. Thank God you found out the truth before it was too late."

Hazzard said "Thank you, governor," and turned to face Trencher. The inspector's ominous black eyes were upon him; that crooked smile meant victory. Trencher slowly handed the fingerprint card to Hazzard and asked: "What have you got to say to that—Dennis Grant?"

Hazzard's eyes went over that card like a microscope. His smile had grown when he tossed it to the desk. "That's not worthy of you, Trencher," he said "not a palpable fake like that."

"Fake?" Trencher snapped. "What do you mean—fake? Those are your prints, aren't they?"

"My prints," Hazzard admitted. "The date of arrest on that card is December 4, 1924. Down here in the corner is a little code imprint made by the printer. See it?"

He pointed to the tiny type: 45-100M-3-4-35.

"It means that this fingerprint record card is Form 45 in that shop. The order called for a hundred thousand of them. They were run through the press on March 4, this year. That card didn't come into existence until eleven years later than the date of arrest written on it. You overlooked that, didn't you, Trencher?"

Trencher jerked to his feet. "All right—but you can't get away from these photographs! That's you—Dennis Grant, murderer! Can you deny that, Hazzard?"

Hazzard leaned forward tensely. "That fingerprint card is a fake. These photographs are questionable. You've heard of the case of Will West and William West, both convicts at Leavenworth Penitentiary in 1903, both Negroes, one a murderer and one guilty of manslaughter—two men absolutely identical in appearance, impossible to tell apart, though they were absolutely no relation to each other. Amazing, Trencher—but such similarities happen. Realizing that, can you pin this thing on me?"

Trencher retorted: "There's a man who identifies you absolutely as Dennis Grant," and he gestured to ex-Sheriff Halsey.

Hazzard gazed at Halsey levelly. He said quietly: "Listen. The charge you've made is enough to wreck my whole life. It's come down to this—your word against mine. All right, Halsey. Are you willing to answer a few questions?"

Halsey challenged: "Ask me anything you please. I know you're Grant."

"You were sheriff in Delphia County when Grant was convicted of murder in Philadelphia, more than ten years ago, weren't you?"

"I was."

"How long were you sheriff there?"

"Four terms."

"You remember me—remember me distinctly as Dennis Grant—among all the men who become your prisoners during that time?"

"I do. You're Grant."

"Then you'd remember all the others as well, wouldn't you, Halsey?"

"I'd know 'em anywhere. I never forget a face. I haven't forgotten yours."

Hazzard smiled as he removed a photograph from his pocket. He offered it to Halsey and asked: "Then you remember this man?"

Halsey peered at the photograph and answered gruffly: "No, I don't remember him."

"What!" Hazzard's voice rang with surprise. "You never forget a face, yet you don't remember the man in that picture?"

The ex-sheriff shifted uneasily in his chair. "Wait a minute now. I'm gettin' it."

"What's the matter with your perfect memory, Halsey?" Hazzard demanded. "Don't you remember his name—the crime he committed—anything about him? Do you confess your recollection is faulty—that it can't be relied on?"

"No, I don't!" Halsey snapped. "It's comin' back to me. His name—"

Hazzard asked swiftly: "Was it Frank Harker or Ernest Berger or Henry Flint—which of the three was it, Halsey?"

"Flint!" Halsey exclaimed. "That's his name, Henry Flint!"

"Flint," Hazzard echoed. "What was his crime? Murder, burglary, kidnaping, or—"

"Murder! That's him. He killed an old guy named Moses Abrams. He was sentenced to the chair. You can't fool me, Hazzard! I remember him, just as sure as I remember you!"

Hazzard straightened, smiling. "Henry Flint, once a prisoner of yours, sentenced to electrocution for murdering one Moses Abrams. You remember him—just as sure—as you remember me." And Hazzard laughed.

Trencher snapped: "Cut that out, Hazzard! You can't get away from it! You're Grant—"

"One moment, inspector!" Now Hazzard was not laughing. His eyes were blazing, his face reddening as his temper dared. He took the photograph from Halsey's fingers and turned to the desk. "You heard Halsey identify this picture definitely. It's his word, and his word alone, you're trying to use to ruin me. Look at this picture, Inspector Trencher. Study it well.

"I spent hours this morning finding it. I spent more hours waiting while a photographer copied it to make it look like a rogue's gallery picture. Perhaps you'll recognize it more easily than Halsey did!"

He turned on Halsey and his words rang sharply. "That photograph was made ten years ago—of the very man you're looking at now. Henry Flint, murderer? That's not his picture. You—the man whose word might send me to prison for life—you identified that man as a killer— and it's an old picture of Inspector Charles Trencher!"

Trencher sat stunned. Commissioner Brook stared in baffled amazement. Halsey shrank sheepishly, the mumble on his lips an inaudible protest. Mark Hazzard, his eyes shining sharply, turned to the door and opened it.

"Good-night, Inspector Trencher," he said. "Or, shall I say, 'good-night, Henry Flint?'"

When he closed the door, he saw Ann Nash hurrying up the stairs. She came to him anxiously. In his arms she asked quickly: "What is it, Mark? Please—what's the matter?"

Hazzard was listening through the door. He heard Commissioner Brook growl: "You damned fool, Halsey!" And Trencher's voice was a roar. "Get out of here, you halfwit! Get out of this office before I break your neck!"

Hazzard stepped aside as Halsey charged out and went stumbling down the steps. His quiet laughter came from his heart; but the girl asked worriedly again:

"What is it, Mark?"

"Nothing, Ann—nothing!"

This time the word meant—*nothing*. The spectre of Dennis Grant, convicted murderer, had fled into the darkness of the past.

By Frederick C. Davis

Corpses' Court

BOOK III

CORPSES' COURT

*Mark Hazzard, double-fisted, fighting
D.A. of King's County wax out to nail
a racketeering rat. Three times he had
the evidence that would send this man to
the chair. But he did not use it. Instead
he jeopardized his entire career to give
this man an alibi—to escape the law!*

CHAPTER I

SNATCH TRAP

MARK HAZZARD, red-headed District Attorney of King's County, rolled his car into the garage that sat at the rear of his modest home. He slipped from the wheel, moved through thick darkness, rapped three times on the wall. He expected a responding knock from the room hidden overhead, but only silence answered him. He signaled again, listened while his nerves grew taut with a foreboding of danger, and called softly:

"Danny! Are you up there, Danny?"

Ominous quiet strengthened Hazzard's anxiety as he lifted a counterweight. A hinged flight of steps swung down from the ceiling. Dim light spilled over him while he climbed. When he poised, head and shoulders in the glow, peering around the secret room, his hand moved with angry quickness to his arm-pitted Webley automatic.

A desperate struggle had left the hideaway in chaotic disorder. Fragments of a chair lay beside a cot that was ripped apart. A broken lamp leaned drunkenly across an overturned table, its light shafting into the empty bathroom. Scuffling feet had kicked the carpet into a heap. A red spatter glistened on the floor near the head of the stairs—blood.

"Danny!"

Hazzard's heart trip-hammered as he sprang up. He jerked open the door of a closet and saw the blue tunic of a patrolman's uniform hanging in its place. A gun harness lay on the dresser, a police positive still clipped in its holster. It told Hazzard at once that the occupant of this secret room had been overwhelmed by the surprise of a savage attack. A red trail led down the stairs—and Dan Carey was gone.

Mark Hazzard's anger flamed as he took up the telephone and spun off the number of his office. His mercurial temper made him a terror to the witnesses he faced in the courtroom. He was a two-fisted fighter whose relentless questions made the guilty squirm in the box. Crooks feared him more than the police because again and again he had defied the musty procedure of the courts and taken a lone wolf's trail into the underworld after criminals he had marked for his own brand of legal justice. Wrath now sent his blood pounding through his temples because his truest friend had been snatched.

"Ann!" he exclaimed when his efficient secretary answered. "Listen, darling. Danny's in trouble. There's been a fight in his room, and he's missing. If Trencher's behind it, he's probably there in the office now, waiting for me with a warrant."

Dan Carey, comrade of the District Attorney of King's County, was a fugitive from the law. Hazzard had himself tried Carey on a charge of first degree murder. His duty had forced him to present damning evidence against the ex-cop while in his heart he had believed Carey innocent. The jury's verdict of guilty had brought the district attorney an unwanted triumph. The news of Carey's escape, while being taken up the river to the death house, had gladdened Hazzard's heart.

Hazzard had found the hunger-sickened convict hiding miserably from the manhunters directed by the relentless Inspector Trencher. He had not turned Carey over to the police. Instead, he had given the fugitive the security of this hidden room. Carey had become his under-cover assistant in the administration of justice outside the law.

Inspector Trencher's search for the escaped convict had not been abandoned. Months had passed since Carey's sensational getaway, but the inspector's standing orders were keeping every man on the force constantly on the lookout for him. Circumstances had made it impossible to prove Carey's innocence. His capture must mean death in the electric chair. The violent disruption of this secret room filled Hazzard with dread that Trencher's men had found the hideaway and made Carey a prisoner.

Found it—on the property of the district attorney? If it was the police who had seized Carey, Mark Hazzard must face a charge of harboring a fugitive. It would mean the end of him as state's prosecutor. It would mean dishonor. It would bring tragedy to the girl he loved, and destroy Mark Hazzard's whole world. Yet it was not concern for himself, but a consuming anxiety for Dan Carey, that prompted his call from this private phone.

Ann Nash answered with a restrained exclamation of dismay.

Hazzard knocked the revolver from Norvell's fingers as it blasted.

"Trencher isn't here, Mark," she said quietly. "He's in headquarters. I can see him through the window, at his desk. He keeps looking across, as he always does. Darling, you know you've got to be careful! Trencher's out to get you."

"Then it wasn't the police." Hazzard thought swiftly, eyes narrowed. "You're right—Trencher wants my scalp—but I can't let that keep me from seeing this through. We've got to play it as though nothing's happened. Better run along home, Ann. I'll handle this alone. Goodnight."

"But Mark—"

Hazzard broke the connection. The angry color persisted in his clean-cut face as he made a swift inspection of the room. He found not the slightest clue to point to the identity of the man who had fought Carey. He was doggedly following the trail of red spots on the steps, in the hope of finding telltale tracks outside, when the purr of the telephone startled him. He sprang to it with caught breath.

"Danny?"

The instrument was connected to a private line. Its number was known only to Hazzard, Ann Nash and Carey. Hazzard's heart sped with the thought that it was the ex-cop calling, but he heard only a humming quiet on the wire.

"Ann?"

The voice that answered was neither Carey's nor Ann Nash's. It was a man's whisper: "Hello. Is that you, Dennis Grant?"

SOUND OF the name chilled Hazzard's blood. He was shocked into silence during a moment of bewildered turmoil. He straightened tensely and answered in a disguised tone: "Wrong number. Nobody here by that name."

The voice asked ominously: "Sure *your* name isn't Grant?"

Hazzard gripped the instrument in corded hands and broke the connection. He stood dazed, a long, agonized breath draining his aching lungs. *Dennis Grant*—the name rang mockingly in his brain. It was a threat rising out of the darkness of the past. It menaced Mark Hazzard with disaster even worse than a charge of harboring a fugitive. It brought a haunting dread to the district attorney's heart—but he forced it from his mind and thought again of Dan Carey.

The red stains led him grimly down the stairs. In the garage he found a metal spool on which adhesive tape had been wound. He followed the gleam of his pocket torch along the gravel path and into the alley. Eyes glittering, he studied faint tire impressions in the black grit. The patterned lines curved into the street. Hazzard's sharp gaze followed them over pavement glistening with a light sprinkle of rain. They marked the way Dan Carey had been taken away—a captive.

Hazzard hurried to his car and backed out the drive. He swung past the corner and began to trace the wet tracks. At the corner they blended into a baffling confusion left by many cars that had passed. He leaned out, driving slowly, striving to find the trail again. Moments later he straightened in despair, coldly convinced the attempt was futile.

He was being watched. A strange prickling of his scalp warned him that hidden eyes were following his movements. His quick glance around disclosed no figure lurking in the shadows, no other car on the street, yet when he drove on, slowly, the sensation persisted.

Trencher's men? The unknown who had dragged Carey from the hideaway? The man of the ominous voice who had spoken the name of Dennis Grant over the secret wire? Hazzard could not know. But

the certainty that he was being tailed stirred his temper and strengthened his haunting dread of disaster.

Suddenly he thrust at the accelerator. He zig-zagged across the
city in an attempt to escape the spying eyes. He slowed as he passed
the courthouse entrance, and swung around the corner. He left his
car and walked back through the gloom, glancing up at the lighted
window of Inspector Trencher's office, in the big headquarters building across the street. He waited on the courthouse steps for the
trailing car to appear—in vain.

Baffled, troubled, he climbed the steps to his office. He found it
dark. Ann Nash had gone. A yellow slip on the sill told Hazzard a
telegram had been brought since her departure and taken back un-
delivered. He tossed it aside, sat at his desk and stared out the window
with fingers drumming. Across the street, in the lighted office in
headquarters, he saw Trencher at work. After a moment the inspector
looked across and made an ironically cordial gesture of greeting.

"Never impatient," Hazzard murmured bitterly to himself. "Always
slow and methodical while you're thinking like a fox. Waiting for a
chance to hang the district attorney's scalp to your belt. That's the
program, isn't it, inspector?"

A knock spun Hazzard in his chair. He opened the entrance quickly
and drew back, intently studying the sly face of the man who slowly
came in. Diamonds glittered on the caller's hand as he opened a
jeweled cigarette case. He did not offer it to Hazzard. He clicked a
gold lighter and inhaled deeply, his gaze coolly insolent.

"Have you come here, Norvell," the district attorney asked heatedly, "so I might have the pleasure of throwing you out?"

Arnold Norvell smirked. "Better hold your temper, Hazzard. I want
to know why I'm being shadowed."

"That's curious. I want to know the same thing—about myself.
Perhaps you can explain who's been tailing me tonight."

"What makes you think so? And if I could, what would you do
about it?"

The contemptuous words clouded smoke into Hazzard's face. His
fists crushed white with anger. His muscles ached to drive a blow at
Norvell's leering mouth, but he forced himself to control the impulse.
Gesturing toward the desk, he managed a tight smile.

"Sit down, Norvell. I'll tell you why you're being shadowed. I'll explain how I'm going to send you and Machen up the river for twenty years—gladly."

Norvell's sneering eyes glinted threateningly as he followed Hazzard into the inner office. He slouched in a chair as Hazzard slapped a folded, engraved document to the blotter. The edged voice of the district attorney did not disturb his elaborate air of casualness.

"A month ago," Hazzard snapped, "you and Cliff Machen began to operate the so-called Universal Life Guaranty Association. It offers low cost insurance to its members. You send high-pressure salesmen after people of limited income who can't afford as much insurance as they'd like in the big established companies. You're collecting thousands of dollars every day in payment for fake protection. It's nothing but dirty robbery."

Norvell said insinuatingly: "Is it, Hazzard? But it's not murder."

"Meaning what?" Hazzard's eyes sharpened when Norvell answered with only an evasive gesture. "Here's one of your policies. It's so full of holes, deliberately put there, that you can evade paying the face value in a dozen different ways. You talk to your clients about saving the expense of a medical examination, but lack of an examination is exactly the way you trap them."

"Unlike a certain public official," Norvell retorted slyly, "we're not hiding anything. It's all down there in black and white. Anybody can see it."

SHARP APPREHENSION stung Hazzard's heart. He unfolded the policy while he defiantly met Norvell's insolent gaze.

"This provision, for instance?" he asked bitterly. " 'It is distinctly understood that the person to whom this certificate is issued is in good health at the time of issuance; otherwise the Association is under no obligation whatever.' That clause forces the beneficiary to assume the responsibility of proving the dead person was in perfect health the day he bought this policy, perhaps years previous. You know it can't be done. You'll refuse to pay, and keep the thousands the policy cost."

Norvell shrugged. "I wouldn't advise you to make any trouble about it, Hazzard. You might be making trouble for yourself at the same time."

Hazzard rounded the desk with clenched fists. "Your innuendoes and threats won't stop me, Norvell! I'm getting the facts. I'm going to wreck your racket and send you and Cliff Machen up the river. You wanted to know why you're being shadowed. That's the reason. Now clear out!"

Norvell sneered. "Nor just yet, Hazzard. Let's talk this over, and leave the poor widows and orphans out of it—shall we?" His words drawled shrewdly. "I think we can reach an understanding, you and I."

Again Hazzard fought a tempestuous impulse to drive his fist into Norvell's insolent face. The purr of the telephone turned him away. His face was flushed when he raised the receiver, but the voice that whispered over the wire turned it deathly white.

"Skipper! Skipper, it's Danny."

Hazzard's blood pounded while he looked warily at Norvell and answered: "Go ahead. I've been upstairs—understand? I want to know—"

"Listen, skipper!" Carey's words rushed. "It's a house on Planter Street—got it? The name on the mailbox is Adams—I saw that much when I was dragged in. There's nobody here now but me, but I'm tied up so I can't—"

Hazzard said swiftly: "I'm on my way!" He lowered the telephone, still gazing defiance at Norvell. "Just what are you driving at—an understanding? The only understanding I ever have with a dirty crook like you, Norvell, is that I'm going to get you. Is that enough?"

Norvell answered calmly: "We'll settle all that in a few minutes, Hazzard. If you're in a hurry, don't let me detain you. I'll be waiting here when you come back—if you don't mind."

The glitter in Norvell's sly eyes chilled Hazzard. He stifled a hot retort and strode past. Anxiety for Dan Carey urged him into a run down the stairs. Norvell's insinuating tone rang mockingly in his ears as he hurried to his car. Starting away, he was tormented by a recollection of the strange tone on the wire asking for Dennis Grant.

"Sure *you're* not Grant?"

Someone knew. Someone had come out of the past with the secret that the man known as Mark Hazzard was wanted for murder.

CHAPTER II

BLOOD TRAIL

H**AZZARD BRAKED** cautiously near a small house on Planter Street. His hand shifted from the wheel to his Webley as he slipped out. He paused at the gate, where the mailbox bore the name *H.C. Adams,* and searched the gloom. He went past dark windows, to the rear entrance, and listened.

There was no sound beyond the door. Hazzard brought out a pack of skeleton keys and tried one after another in the lock. The bolt drew back and he opened a crack. His Webley peered into thick darkness. He shouldered through, breathing deep of musty air. He was going quietly along a bleak hallway when a whisper came out of the blackness:

"Skipper!"

Hazzard spun to the door at his side and thrust in. He whispered: "Okay, copper," and groped to a switch. The snap of the switch revealed Dan Carey lying hunched in the corner beside a telephone he had dragged from a stand. Adhesive tape was strapped around Carey's wrists and ankles. More of it had been bound across his mouth, but now it was dangling. Hazzard strode to him swiftly.

"Anybody else here, copper?"

"Nobody else!"

Hazzard began peeling the sticky bands. "Go ahead, Danny. Tell me what happened."

Carey grinned ruefully. "I'm not sure yet. He hit me from behind before I even knew he was there. All I want's a chance to get at that guy."

"Who, Danny?"

"Norvell."

"Norvell!"

"Sure. He didn't try to hide his face, either. There's something funny about that. He had that car of his, big as a locomotive. I didn't begin coming around until he carried me into this place. I got rid of the tape on my mouth by running my face against the floor. Look at the splinters, skipper! God, I'm glad I found you at the office!"

"Norvell." Hazzard's eyes gleamed as he rose. "Did he use that telephone after he brought you in, Danny?" he asked as Carey scrambled up. "Can you remember?"

"He used it, but he whispered—I couldn't make it out."

"I think I heard what he said, Danny," Hazzard mused grimly, "—on the other end of the line. Was Machen with him, or did he pull this trick alone?"

"I'm ashamed to say he managed it alone, but the next time I get near that mug he's going to need help! Listen, skipper." Carey squinted anxiously. "What's behind it? How did he find out about me? I'll kill him if he uses it to get you into a jam!"

"He's playing a crafty game, Danny. We've got to watch our step. Slip out to the car now, and keep out of sight. You're going back."

A sharp sound brought Carey to a stop on the sill. It made a statue of Mark Hazzard. They waited during a tense moment and it came again—the shrill ring of the telephone. Hazzard reached for the instrument slowly while Carey watched breathless. Hazzard brought the receiver to his ear and said nothing, but a voice came over the line.

"Good work, Dennis Grant."

A click broke the connection. Hazzard's eyes glittered as he lowered the dead receiver. A jerk of his head sent Carey to the front entrance as wrath colored his face. Following Carey, he glanced through open doors into unfurnished rooms. He was convinced when he reached the car at the curb that Arnold Norvell had provided the house for the express purpose of keeping Danny Carey prisoner. And he was certain now it was Norvell's voice that had spoken over the wire.

Carey crouched out of sight while Hazzard turned the car toward his home. His eyes questioned Hazzard, but he did not speak until the car swung to a stop near the garage from which Carey had been carried unconscious.

"Skipper, it's too much of a chance—my staying here now," the ex-patrolman protested as he climbed out. "What if Norvell tips off headquarters, and Trencher finds me here? I'm not worrying about myself, but—it would play plenty of hell with you, skipper!"

"It's too much of a chance for you to hide out anywhere else, Danny," Hazzard answered firmly. "If Norvell doesn't talk, you're safest here—and he may keep quiet. He had this trick all planned. He had to shake his shadow in order to pull it. He's playing a slick game of waiting—but I'm going to force his hand."

"If he spills it, skipper, all I want, before the cops grab me, is a chance to give the rat what he deserves!"

Hazzard smiled wryly. "You may get it, Danny. Upstairs now, and keep out of sight. Camp by that telephone—because I think I'm going to need you."

HE BACKED the car. Carey vanished inside the garage before he swung into the street. He speeded along the drive, eyes thoughtfully narrowed. When he parked in front of the courthouse, he saw that Trencher's window, in headquarters, was still alight. He climbed quickly to his office and thrust in.

Arnold Norvell was slouched in the chair beside the desk. He crushed his cigarette into an overflowing tray and rose, smiling thinly, as Hazzard strode toward him. Hazzard's temper flared again at the studied insolence of Norvell's manner. He was about to speak when a knock sounded at his door.

A telegram messenger wagged a salute when Hazzard looked out. Hazzard took the yellow envelope, scrawled on the receipt blank, and turned back. Heavy footfalls hurrying on the stairs made him pause again. He saw the heavy-shouldered, grim-faced Inspector Charles Trencher. Trencher ignored Hazzard as he strode into the district attorney's office. Black eyes glittering dangerously, he tramped to a stop facing Arnold Norvell.

"All right," he said in his chesty, threatening tone. "You're the man I'm looking for."

"I?" Norvell asked with mild surprise. "What for, inspector, if I may ask?"

"Yes, you may ask," Trencher drawled. "I'll gladly tell you. I want you on suspicion of murder."

Hazzard, ripping the edge off the yellow envelope, jerked to a stop. The torn strip fluttered from his numb fingers. He knew this elaborately casual manner of Trencher's—knew it masked a dogged determination. His foreboding sense of disaster grew stronger as he watched Norvell smile crookedly and ask:

"That's interesting, inspector. Who am I supposed to have murdered?"

"A man whose death means plenty of cash for you, Norvell," Trencher answered easily. "Your partner in the Universal Life Guaranty Association. Cliff Machen."

Norvell's sly smile tightened. "Is that so? When did I do it?"

Trencher glowered. "Don't try to bluff out of it. I've been having you watched day and night. You've managed to slip my shadow several times, but I've got a pretty good record of what you've been doing. For one thing, you've opened new joint bank accounts with Machen and put plenty on deposit. The money's payable to you or Machen— or survivor. That's interesting too, isn't it, Norvell? Or survivor."

Norvell asked again, shrewdly: "When am I supposed to have killed Machen, inspector?"

"Twenty minutes ago." Trencher's glare turned on Mark Hazzard. "This is a good one. I get word that Machen's been shot to death, and I send out an alarm to pick him up, and then where do I find him? I look across the street and see him in this office. Do you usually do that, Norvell? Pay a call on the district attorney right after you've killed a man?"

A new chill passed through Hazzard's heart as Norvell's calculating eyes turned on him. He slipped the telegram from its envelope while he moved to his desk. He was unfolding it when Norvell observed easily:

"Twenty minutes ago, inspector? I think that lets me out. I've been here in this office, with Hazzard, for at least an hour."

Trencher snapped: "What? That's your alibi, is it? Is that true, Hazzard?"

Again Hazzard felt the cold threat in Arnold Norvell's gaze. He saw Norvell's eyes flicker suggestively to the telegram, and he looked down at it. One cryptic line held him spellbound with dismay and silent. While he automatically dropped the yellow envelope into the waste-basket, he ignored Trencher and peered at those few startling words:

'TWAS THE NIGHT BEFORE CHRISTMAS

A.N.

The night before Christmas—more than ten years ago. A recollection of it flashed with painful clarity into Mark Hazzard's mind. He felt again the sting of the winter wind howling around him as he rode the rods of a freight car into the gloomy railroad yards of Philadelphia. Penniless, hungry, he had stolen the ride so that he might join his mother at Christmas. During those wretched hours on the rods, one then known as Dennis Grant had dreamt of the cheery warmth of home. He had never reached it. His destination had become, instead, the chill cell of a prisoner of the law.

He recalled the crack of the shot in the railroad yards. In blind fear he had desperately attempted to escape the men who had swarmed upon him. A man whom Dennis Grant had never seen had died before a gun he had never touched, but he found himself branded with the crime of murder. He had protested hopelessly that he knew nothing of what had happened, that some other tramp had killed the yard detective in order to escape an arrest for vagrancy, but no one had believed him. Twelve good men and true had returned a verdict of guilty.

"This court sentences the defendant, Dennis Grant, to imprisonment for life in the state penitentiary."

The words of the sentence mocked Mark Hazzard after more than ten years. He felt again the surge of frantic revolt that had gripped him. He had snatched up a chair, flung it through the courtroom window, scrambled past the jagged glass while guns blasted at him. He had escaped through a bleak and hostile night while bloodhounds bayed on his trail.

When, at last, he had found safety in a distant city, a driving determination had filled him to make the law an instrument of true justice. He had studied countless weary nights after working each day at backbreaking labor for starvation pay. He had created a new identity for himself. Mark Hazzard, alias Dennis Grant, escaped convict, had become the youngest prosecutor in the history of King's County—a man of integrity and honor.

NOW THE new world he had built was threatened by a crook who had somehow learned his secret. He stared numbly at the warning ironically concealed in the child's jingle of the telegram while Inspector Charles Trencher demanded again:

"Is that true, Hazzard?"

Norvell said coolly as Hazzard raised haggard eyes: "Of course it's true. I came in here an hour ago. I've been with Hazzard every minute of the time. I couldn't possibly have killed Cliff Machen—could I, Hazzard?"

Trencher growled. "Better be sure of it, Mr. District Attorney. Be absolutely sure you were not out of this office even for five minutes. If you did leave, I intend to blow Norvell's alibi to pieces by checking every move you made."

Hazzard clearly read the threat in the glint of Arnold Norvell's narrowed eyes. It said: "Did you hear that, Hazzard? If you say you went out, Trencher's going to check your movements. He's going to ask you, first, where you went. What will you answer? Will you say you were helping a friend of yours—a man wanted by the law? Will you admit you're harboring a fugitive? If you do, it's the end of Mark Hazzard—you realize that full well."

As plainly as though Norvell were speaking the words, Hazzard caught the meaning of the silent warning. "If you admit you left the office, you'll have to lie to Trencher about what you did while you were gone. He'll pick that falsehood to pieces. He'll learn the truth. He'll find out the district attorney has been hiding a man wanted for murder—if you say you left the office."

But Mark Hazzard was not thinking of himself. Concern for Dan Carey filled his tortured mind. Carey had been sentenced to the electric chair. If ever he were captured, he must traverse the last dread mile to the death house. It was impossible now to prove the ex-cop was innocent. Once the dogged Trencher made him prisoner, Carey would inevitably face the horror of the copper straps and the black hood of doom.

Trencher was glowing. "Well, Hazzard? Why don't you answer? Was Norvell here in the office with you every minute of the last hour, or wasn't he?"

"He was here."

Huskily Hazzard spoke the words. Norvell's thin lips twisted evilly in triumph. Trencher planted himself firmly, his black eyes smouldering at Hazzard.

"Sure of that?"

Hazzard forced himself on. "Positive, Trencher. There's no question of it. At the time Cliff Machen was murdered, Norvell was right here with me."

Coolly Norvell remarked: "Thanks, Hazzard. I think that lets me out. You'll have to look elsewhere for your murderer, Trencher. Good-night."

The diamonds on his hand glittered again as he opened his jeweled cigarette case. Smoke streamed from his thin lips as he strode easily to the door. He turned a sharp, contemptuous glance back at Hazzard, then went out. Trencher faced the district attorney grimly during a moment of tense silence.

"We'd better look into Machen's killing right away, inspector—hadn't we?" Hazzard asked in a strained tone.

He went past Trencher, and out the door. Trencher hesitated, eyes narrowed shrewdly. He searched the top of the desk for the telegram Hazzard had received, but it was gone. His hand dipped swiftly into the waste-basket and he brought up the yellow envelope. His heavy eyebrows arched when he glanced at it. He thrust it into his pocket. The blackness of his eyes grew dangerously deeper as he tramped after Hazzard down the stairs.

"And I thought I had a case cracked," he drawled. "Norvell's killing Machen looked like a natural. Nobody else in the world has a better motive. Why, it seemed open and shut. Now I haven't any case against Norvell at all. The district attorney, of all people, has given him an alibi."

The telegram was crushed in Hazzard's fist.

"Of course, you're right about it, Hazzard," Trencher went on with a casualness that disguised a strengthening suspicion. "If it was anybody else, now—why, giving a man an alibi, knowing he's guilty, makes one an accessory after the fact. If the alibi broke down, it would be damn' tough on the man who gave it. It might mean the chair for him. If it was anybody else, understand. Of course, the district attorney wouldn't fake an alibi for a killer."

Hot fury beat through Hazzard's veins. He did not miss the veiled threat in Inspector Trencher's words. He realized it as clearly as though Trencher had said:

"The district attorney has faked an alibi for a killer—and I'm going to prove it!"

CHAPTER III

THE CHECKERED CLUE

T **RENCHER AND** Hazzard walked side by side, without speaking, to the spot where murder had been done. Cliff Machen's apartment was located not three blocks from the district attorney's office. As the elevator carried them to the third floor, Hazzard realized grimly that during his absence Norvell had had ample opportunity to hurry to this building, commit murder, and return. His dread that Trencher would penetrate the falseness of the alibi became a gnawing torture as he entered the room where Machen had died.

The murdered man lay crumpled beside a chair, red blotting the front of his shirt. His garb was as flashy as Norvell's. The malevolence of his fattish face persisted even in death. Behind the chair, the wafting curtains of an open window disclosed the platform of the fire-escape. While the official photographer focused his camera, and members of the homicide wandered about, one of them reported to Trencher:

"Plenty of cash still in his wallet. It wasn't any sneak thief who did this. His killer got away through the window and out the court. There's blood on the platform—evidently he was hurt somehow."

Hazzard asked quickly: "You're sure of that? The murderer was wounded?"

"Must have been—and badly."

To Trencher Hazzard remarked: "That bears out Norvell's alibi, doesn't it? He wasn't bleeding when you saw him. How about that, inspector?"

Trencher growled: "There's an answer to everything," and tramped into the adjoining room. Hazzard found two detectives facing a woman who was slumped in a chair, the mascara of her beaded lashes streaking her face with her tears. She was wearing a light coat. A suitcase sat near the door. The plainclothes man who was taking notes said to her gently:

"Now, just tell Inspector Trencher what happened, Mrs. Machen."

Hazzard listened intently to the woman's hesitant story. "I—I was coming back from a visit with my mother in Toledo. I took a taxi—from the station. I was in the hall, unlocking the door, when I heard the shots."

Her eyes widened with terror. "I was so frightened I didn't know what to think—but I rushed in. I saw Cliff lying on the floor, with red all over him. I was so horrified I stood there staring for a minute. Then I rushed to Cliff, and saw he was dead. I looked out, and saw the man again, in the light of one of the lower windows. Then he got out of sight—and I telephoned for the police."

Trencher asked carefully: "Did you get a good look at him? What did he look like?"

"I didn't see his face, but he was wearing a brown checkered suit."

The inspector snapped: "Don't make any mistake about that!"

"I'm not mistaken," the woman answered in a whisper. "I'll never forget. He was wearing a brown suit with big checks. I'd know it anywhere—if I saw it again."

Hazzard smiled tightly. "Norvell's wearing a plain blue worsted tonight, inspector. You couldn't confuse that with a loud brown check. It's another thing that lets him out."

Mrs. Machen looked startled. "Arnold Norvell? You can't believe he did this! Why, he was Cliff's best friend. Arnold is the last man in the world who'd do it. You're mistaken—I know you are!"

Trencher growled: "Don't worry now, Mrs. Machen." Hazzard followed him from the room. A gleam burned in the depths of his black eyes as he studied the district attorney's face. "It apparently lets Norvell out, but appearances are sometimes deceiving. I'd still think it was Norvell—if it wasn't for your alibi, Hazzard. Being in this game as long as I have, you get so you don't trust anything."

Hazzard tightened. "Including an alibi given by the district attorney?" he asked.

"Let's suppose, for a minute, Norvell hasn't any alibi," Trencher suggested ominously. "The blood on the fire-escape doesn't necessarily mean the killer was wounded. It might've been somebody else. For instance, that sneaky little stool Jake Keats—because I had Keats shadowing Norvell tonight. Suppose Norvell came in here and killed

Machen. He had to beat it out the window because Mrs. Machen was coming in. Suppose Keats was on the platform, watching Norvell. Then the blood would mean that Norvell hit him with a bullet on his way out. Get it, Hazzard?"

Hazzard smiled wryly. "I get it. But where's Keats? And you're overlooking the matter of the loud checked suit."

"I haven't forgotten that," Trencher droned. "Maybe Norvell's got a room close to this place. He could have gone to it, put on that checked suit, come here, killed Machen, then changed back. All to confuse any possible eye-witnesses. You see, Hazzard, neither the blood nor the checked suit really proves Norvell didn't do it. Only one thing actually clears him—the district attorney's alibi."

Hazzard's lips curved bitterly. "And being so long on the force, Trencher, you don't trust anything—including that."

Trencher pretended surprise. "Did I say that? Not at all. Why, I wouldn't want to believe Mark Hazzard was faking an alibi for a killer. If you were, and the truth came out, it would send you up the river. You wouldn't do that—even if Norvell had something on you—would you?"

Hazzard's eyes snapped. "Trencher, I'm calling your bluff. You think the alibi is false. You believe Norvell forced me to protect him. You're going to do your damnedest to prove it. You're out to break me. That's the fact, isn't it, inspector?"

Trencher gestured disarmingly. "Take it easy, Hazzard. I don't approve of your methods, because I'm an old plodder who sticks to the routine. You're a hot-head who likes to make himself judge, jury and executioner all in one. We don't get along very well together, but we understand each other—don't we?"

Hazzard forced himself to control his flaming temper. "I understand perfectly," he retorted, "that you're never going to stop trying until you've got me where you want me—in prison. This killing has given you a new chance, and you're going to play it to the limit. Our cards are on the table, Trencher. It's a fight to the finish between us."

HAZZARD TURNED away abruptly, while the inspector's black eyes blazed. A girl entered the room at that moment. Sight of Hazzard's drawn face brought her to a dismayed stop. She went to him with anxious quickness and asked in a whisper that no one else could hear:

"Mark, darling—what's the matter?"

Hazzard forced a smile. "Our esteemed friend, the inspector, is determined to prove the district attorney is an accessory to this murder, Ann, that's all. Don't let it frighten you. I'm glad you've come. Listen—"

Ann Nash's clear eyes widened with alarm. "But Mark! What possible reason has he for thinking—"

"An excellent one, I'm afraid." Hazzard alertly drew her aside. "I can't explain here, but Trencher's going to do his utmost to prove Arnold Norvell killed Cliff Machen. If he does, I'm finished. I need your help, Ann."

The girl said promptly, studying Hazzard's lined face: "I'm on the job."

"Good. Go to Norvell's place right away. Call from the lobby, to find out whether he's there, then wait. I'll be right along."

Ann Nash's lips pressed anxiously as she hurried out. Hazzard saw that Trencher was again questioning Mrs. Machen. He went past the dead man, to the window, and crawled out. The light of his pocket torch played over the bars of the fire-escape platform. He studied the sticky glisten of fresh blood.

The gleaming spots led him down the ladder, to the lowest platform. The bottom section was swung down to the pavement of the court. Hazzard's light played upon another stain on the cement, then flashed over the rear walls of the surrounding buildings. Piled ash cans made black shadows as he strode to a door. He walked quickly through the lobby of the apartment house, and slipped behind the wheel of his car.

The drawling tones of Inspector Trencher haunted his mind as he swung around the corner. "Suppose Norvell hasn't any alibi? Suppose he went to a room near here, and changed into the checkered suit, then killed Machen?" Hazzard's nerves burned with anxiety because he was convinced that Trencher's theory was the truth.

He braked near the entrance of the apartment building in which Arnold Norvell lived. When he entered the lobby, Ann Nash slipped out of a telephone closet. He stepped inside as she reported quietly: "Norvell is out."

"Good." Hazzard slotted a coin. "Keep your eye on the elevators. I want to take a look at his wardrobe before he gets back." He was dialing the secret number of the phone in Dan Carey's hideaway.

A whisper came over the wire. "All safe, copper?" Hazzard asked. "Listen. I want Arnold Norvell spotted. No matter where he goes from now on, Danny, tail him. It's a risk, but there's no one else I can count on for the job."

"Never mind that, skipper," Carey answered. "I'll watch that mug."

"Good! Start now, at his apartment on Audubon. Keep your head down, Danny!" He broke the connection, and dialed another number. The phone sergeant at headquarters answered. "Give me Mulligan, Hopper." When Trencher's assistant answered, Hazzard asked: "Has there been any report from Jake Keats since Machen was bumped off?"

"No word from him. He was watching Norvell tonight, and probably he's still on the job."

Hazzard said: "Thanks!" and stood a moment in thought. He slipped out, took Ann Nash's arm. They strode to the elevators. Hazzard's eyes were narrowed shrewdly when the cab started up. He waited until they left it at the seventh floor to say:

"A nice building, Ann. How'd you like to live here?"

"Mark, what are you thinking of?"

"A long shot." He paused at the door of Norvell's apartment and opened his pack of skeleton keys. "First thing in the morning, you're going to rent an apartment here. The one you want is directly above or below Norvell's or right next it." He straightened alertly as the bolt drew back. "Soon as you have it, you're going to buy the most sensitive radio in town, and move it in."

"But why, Mark?"

"Norvell's collecting thousands every day from the poor—premiums on his bootleg insurance policies. He's probably rented half a dozen places around town for use in emergencies. He snatched Danny and took him to one of them tonight. I want to find out about the others."

HE STEPPED quietly into the apartment. He signaled Ann Nash to remain at the door while he went through a modernistic library, into a bedroom. He immediately opened a closet and quickly examined each of Norvell's suits. He turned to another where he found more. When he closed the doors, his lips were drawn doggedly tight. In neither had he found a suit answering Mrs. Machen's description of that worn by the murderer.

"Too far from Machen's anyway," he murmured to Ann as he glanced around. "Norvell's got at least one other place. It's going to be your job to find it."

"Mark!" The girl retreated from the door in alarm. "Someone's coming!"

Hazzard urged: "This way!"

The girl hurried past him as a key clicked into the lock of the entrance. Hazzard swung to the door in the bedroom which gave into the corridor, and drew the bolt. Ann Nash slipped out as steps sounded in the library. Hazzard signaled her to call the elevator, and closed the door silently. When the cab opened, she entered it alone. It was carrying her downward when Hazzard went quietly to Norvell's entrance. He knocked.

Norvell opened the way and stood back, eyes narrowed. Hazzard sauntered in, glancing around. Norvell followed him, opening the jeweled case, lighting a cigarette. Hazzard studied his sinister face through clouding smoke.

"Rather clever, Norvell," he said quietly. "Your finding out about Dan Carey."

Norvell said nothing.

"You were going to keep him hidden and hold him over me as a threat, weren't you? If I didn't stop the investigation of your bootleg insurance racket, you'd tip off the police and they'd find him. They'd match his fingers with prints found in the room above my garage, and that would nail me for harboring a fugitive. You came to my office tonight to tell me that."

Norvell said insolently: "I think we understand each other, Hazzard."

"But Danny was able to reach a telephone, and it spoiled your set-up. You couldn't go through with it after Danny phoned me. You think pretty quickly, Norvell—and act just as fast. You changed your plan completely in a few seconds. You had another one all ready, and you pulled it off while I was out of the office. My going after Danny gave you the chance you wanted to kill Machen."

Norvell's thin lips streamed smoke. "Nice of you to alibi me, Hazzard," he said levelly. Suddenly he leaned forward, eyes glinting. "You're going to keep on backing up my alibi. You're going to see to it that Trencher never touches me. If you don't, it's going to be just too bad for the honorable and respected district attorney. We understand each other, Hazzard."

Hazzard's hands became fists. He strove to keep himself from smashing his knuckles into Norvell's contemptuous eyes. The heat of his temper brought flaming color to his face as Norvell uttered a scathing laugh. He forced himself to reason clearly, to allow Norvell to think he was completely subjugated by fear of the truth leaking out. Suddenly he strode past Norvell and slammed through the door.

When he left the lobby, and joined Ann Nash in his car, he saw a man in blue uniform sauntering through the shadows with nightstick twirling. He smiled grimly. Dan Carey was on the job.

CHAPTER IV

SATAN'S CEREMONY

DISTRICT ATTORNEY Mark Hazzard paced anxiously back and forth across the office. Each time he turned at the window, he could see the grim-faced Trencher across the street, seated at his desk in police headquarters. Hazzard kept moving, burning with impatience, waiting for the telephone to ring.

Four empty days had passed since the murder of Cliff Machen. Detectives working under the direction of the dogged Trencher had found no clue to the identity of the man in the checkered brown suit. No new evidence had come to light. The newspapers were sarcastically promising that the case would be another to go into the unsolved file. Why, the editorials demanded—since the police were getting nowhere—wasn't the two-fisted district attorney hot on the trail of the killer this time?

"That's right, Hazzard," Inspector Trencher had drawled, calling his attention to the mocking black type. "They expect it of you, you know. They want spectacular action because it makes big headlines. I'm no good to 'em because I'm just a plodder. You're not losing your grip, are you? Say, who do you think really killed Machen—since your alibi clears Norvell?"

Hazzard thought of the accusing light in Trencher's smouldering black eyes as he snatched up the telephone. The number he called was that of headquarters. He asked for the inspector. Gazing through the window, he could see Trencher answering the call. They studied each other across the dark chasm of the street while they talked.

"Trencher, I want information," Hazzard snapped. "How the devil can I make any progress on this case if you hold out on me? What about Jake Keats? He's still missing, isn't he?"

"You want to know about Keats, Hazzard?" Trencher's voice droned over the line. "Why, sure, I'll tell you. One of the best stoolies we've ever had, but he didn't make his report on Norvell the night of Machen's murder, and we haven't had a word from him since."

"You've been trying to find him. Haven't you any idea where he is?"

"Stoolies are shifty birds, Hazzard. They scare easily. Maybe Keats saw the murder and skipped because he'd have to testify, and that would mean getting a bullet in the back, some dark night, with the compliments of any number of crooks he's spied on."

"Do you really believe that, Trencher?" Hazzard snapped.

"Well, now," the inspector drawled, "when you've been in this game as long as I have, Hazzard, you'll realize it's wiser to keep your theories to yourself until the right time."

Hazzard angrily replaced the phone. He paced back and forth again, nerves throbbing. A jangle of the bell jerked his hands to the instrument. He asked, tensely, "Yes?" and heard the cautious tones of Dan Carey.

"I've got it, skipper! I've spotted Norvell going to a new place. It's a room on Division Street—Number 30, first floor back—in the same block with Machen's place! He just went in, and came right out again."

"Good work, Danny! Keep watching him."

"Trust me, skipper. I'm sticking to that mug's tail, all right. Listen. He's been seeing a lot of Mrs. Machen. Being the so-called best friend of her deceased husband, I guess he thinks it's up to him to console her. God, what a rat! This is the first place he's been, on his regular rounds—and right next door to hers."

"Go after him, Danny! When he stops again, phone Ann."

Grim hope tightened Hazzard's mouth as he hurried from the office. Quick steps took him down the stairs, out the entrance, to his car. He rounded corners and braked to a stop near the apartment of the late Cliff Machen. Division Street cut across that on which the building stood. Hazzard went straight to the door of Number 30 and thrust in.

He paused alertly at the door of the rear apartment on the ground floor. An exit nearby opened into the court. Looking out, Hazzard saw the fire-escape which led past the Machen apartment in the other building. He brought his skeleton keys into play, and stepped into the darkness of the rear room.

The air was oppressively close and acrid. Hazzard snapped a switch.

The apartment was bare. A soft hissing sound drew him toward the door of a bath. When he opened the door, suffocating fumes clouded into his face. Again he snapped a switch, holding his breath. He peered at a steaming, brownish liquid which half filled the tub.

A large brown bottle, empty and corkless, lay on the tile floor. Hazzard read its label: *Sodium Hydroxide, Commercial.* He grimaced as he drew back his right sleeve. He reached into the odorous fluid in the tub. It felt slimy, and brought a sting to his skin. His fingers closed on soft fabric. He dragged it up, dripping—a brown coat of checkered pattern.

Hazzard's eyes gleamed. He dropped the coat into the soapy solution. He knew the chemical would soon dissolve the wool fabric and leave only meaningless remnants—pockets and buttons. Coupled with Dan Carey's word, it was damning evidence—but evidence that Mark Hazzard, District Attorney, could never use. The ex-cop, wanted for murder, could never offer his testimony from the witness chair. If Hazzard dared legally to establish Norvell's connection with the checkered suit in some other way—

"We understand each other, Hazzard," the murderer had warned.

HAZZARD THOUGHT rapidly as he washed his stinging arm at the bowl. He left the incriminating garment in the caustic solution when he closed the door behind him. He shouldered into a telephone booth and dialed the number of a phone which had just been installed. Ann Nash's voice answered.

"Is there a report from Danny?" Hazzard asked.

"Yes, just now," she answered wearily. "Norvell and Mrs. Machen are in a house at Five-Ten Nassau Street—Danny doesn't know whose. He's watching it now. Mark, you've got to be careful, darling. One of Trencher's men is watching Norvell, too!"

"Naturally, Ann," Hazzard observed bitterly. "The inspector's trying to get Norvell because it's one way of nailing me."

"Danny saw him make a call from a signal box. He was probably reporting to Trencher at headquarters. It means trouble, Mark—I'm sure of it!"

Hazzard was peering through the glass of the booth. The click of a latch had surprised him. The entrance of the building was opening. Two men came in cautiously, their eyes shining alertly in the light. Suddenly, without answering the girl, Hazzard pronged the receiver and crouched down.

The two men who walked past the booth were plainclothes men working under Inspector Trencher's orders. They paused at the door of the rear apartment and one said quietly: "This is the place." A turmoil of uncertainty filled Hazzard's mind while he heard them working at the lock. After an eternity of torment, he heard the door swing open, then shut. He raised to see that the two detectives had gone inside. They were certain to find the suit worn by a killer.

Norvell's warning haunted Hazzard as he hurried out. "You're going to see to it that Trencher never touches me. If you don't, it's going to be just too bad for the honorable and respected district attorney. We understand each other, Hazzard." The threat brought fury storming to Hazzard's heart as he sent his car speeding away.

He swung into Nassau Street and braked in front of the modest home numbered 510. Norvell's massive limousine was sitting at the curb. Somewhere in the shadows, Hazzard knew, a headquarters man was watching. Dan Carey, he felt certain, was still on the job of tailing Norvell and keeping out of sight. Hazzard strode to the door and knocked. Though there were lights inside, and the sound of a voice, no answer came.

Hazzard went in quietly. Words being spoken in a sing-song tone drew him toward an open door. He paused in amazement, peering into a room hung with Biblical pictures. Arnold Norvell was standing at the side of Grace Machen, and both were facing a man whose hand was upraised. A gray-haired woman and a sallow-faced young man were standing at one side, smiling beneficently. Eyes closed, the minister of the gospel solemnly proclaimed:

"I pronounce you man and wife."

An expectant flutter filled the room while Mark Hazzard drew back. He went out the entrance quietly. He was about to leave the porch when a car swung swiftly to a stop in front of Norvell's. Hazzard recognized it as a police machine. He stepped aside, into a patch of deep shadow, as Inspector Trencher ducked out. The door of the house was opening when Trencher came to a stop on the porch.

Arnold Norvell smiled slowly at the inspector as the woman paused, startled. His insolent confidence remained unshaken when Trencher growled:

"Come along to headquarters, Norvell, I've got a lot of questions to ask you, about some places you've rented under assumed names."

Norvell asked levelly: "You're still after me, aren't you, Trencher?

In spite of the alibi the district attorney gave me, which clears me completely, you persist in—"

"That's right, Norvell," Trencher droned. "I persist. That's me all over. I sent my men to one of the places you rented. It's right around the corner from Machen's apartment. They've just reported. They found a brown checked suit there—in the process of being destroyed."

"That so?" Norvell asked slyly. "What good does it do you? That's not evidence against me."

"Mrs. Machen saw the murderer wearing a suit like it," Trencher pointed out grimly, "and we found it in a place you rented under a false name. That's enough evidence—"

"It's a frame-up," Norvell countered casually, "and even so, you can't use it. Let's talk this over with the district attorney, Trencher. He'll explain the law on that point."

Trencher had angrily begun: "I don't need Hazzard to explain—" when Hazzard stepped from the shadows. Trencher turned in surprise. Arnold Norvell's startled look faded into contemptuous confidence. Hazzard's face was drawn, his eyes glittering, when he paused with defiant gaze on Trencher's flushed face.

"WHAT THE devil are you doing here, Hazzard?" the inspector demanded. "When Norvell needs help, you're right on hand, aren't you?"

"Perhaps you do need me to explain a point of law, inspector," Hazzard answered tightly. "No one saw the murderer of Cliff Machen except Mrs. Machen. She alone informed you of the checked brown suit. Her statement is not an affidavit. Nobody who heard her give the description can testify about it in court because that would be hearsay—inadmissible evidence. In short, the suit is absolutely worthless unless this woman testifies concerning it on the stand. She can't do that now."

Trencher snapped: "Why not?"

"The significant point of law, Trencher, is that a wife cannot testify against her husband."

The inspector growled: "What the devil has that got to do with—"

Norvell interrupted with a gesture of introduction. "Allow me, Inspector Trencher. Mrs. Arnold Norvell. We were married not five minutes ago."

Trencher stared. The woman who had become Norvell's wife looked confused, fearful. Mark Hazzard's lips crushed together as Norvell's sneering smile grew.

"Do you wish to see the marriage license, inspector?"

Trencher's only answer was an inarticulate growl. Norvell took the woman's arm. They went past the inspector, toward the heavy sedan. Hazzard uttered a bitter laugh as the car drew away, and Trencher swung on him. The inspector's black eyes glowered a threat.

"You're behind this, Hazzard! You're covering Norvell at every turn. First an alibi, now a legal trick to make my evidence inadmissible. That's pretty clever, Hazzard—but an old dog of the law like me can't be stopped by a thing like that."

Hazzard answered grimly: "This marriage was Norvell's own idea, inspector. He probably induced the woman to do it by saying it was the only way he could keep you from using her against him—her husband's best friend."

Trencher's lowered lids veiled his ominous eyes. "Well, maybe the suit wouldn't have been much good in court anyway. Maybe there are other ways of nailing Norvell. If I can prove his alibi is no good, for instance, I've got him cold. Somehow, I might find evidence to show he was out of your office, Hazzard—and you, too—at the time of the murder. That would go hard on you, because you swore he was there all the time."

Hazzard challenged: "How can you do that, inspector?"

Trencher drew a yellow envelope from his pocket and fingered its ripped edge. "Suppose a telegram was brought to your office when nobody was there. The boy would make a note about the attempted delivery and try again later. The envelope with the time written on it would be evidence the office was empty then. The messenger might come back three or four times. Suppose he was there, knocking on your door, without getting an answer, at the very moment Norvell was killed. His testimony and record would prove Norvell's alibi is a fake, wouldn't it, Hazzard? You're the district attorney. You should know."

Cold dread struck at Hazzard's heart. "You can scarcely expect me to help you show my own word can't be relied on, Trencher," he answered bitterly. "That's your job, you're the brains of the plainclothes division. You should be equal to handling it."

Trencher's smouldering eyes followed him as he strode past.

His hands gripped the wheel furiously while he sent his car spurting away. He knew Dan Carey had followed Norvell from the minister's home. Gambling that Norvell had returned to his apartment, Hazzard angled toward it. When he left the car near the entrance of the building, he saw Dan Carey strolling on the opposite side of the street and knew his deduction was correct.

The heat of his anger persisted while the elevator carried Hazzard to the level of Norvell's rooms. The new Mrs. Norvell answered his knock. Hazzard strode past her, into the library. Arnold Norvell faced him scornfully as the woman came to his side.

"I—I haven't done anything wrong, have I?" she asked anxiously. "I'm only trying to help Arnold. He was Cliff's best friend—the police have no right to accuse him. You can't possibly think he killed—"

Hazzard broke in ringingly: "I want to see your husband alone."

Norvell's curling lips taunted Hazzard while the woman left the room. When the door closed, Hazzard spoke with quiet tenseness.

"Listen to me, Norvell. Get every word. So far I've let you think I'm afraid of you. You think I defended you before Trencher because of your threats. You're dead wrong. I did it because it's a point of law that can't be escaped. Trencher's not trying half as hard to nail you for murder as I am."

Norvell answered easily. "You haven't any doubt of it, have you, Hazzard? You know I killed Machen."

"I know you killed him and I'm going to—"

"You're going to keep your mouth shut!" Norvell took a threatening step. "You don't remember me, do you—but I recall you distinctly. Eleven years ago I was slaving at a typewriter in the office of the Prosecuting Attorney of Delphia County, Pennsylvania. I handled all the papers in the case of Dennis Grant, convicted of murder. I can tell Inspector Trencher exactly how he can prove you're Grant—and I will if you don't keep me covered."

Hazzard's fists clenched hard.

"If I'm brought to trial for murdering Machen, you won't handle the state's case, Hazzard. I'll spill all I know about you the instant I'm arrested. When I'm brought into court, you'll be back in Pennsylvania, serving the life sentence that's waiting for you. Mark Hazzard won't exist!"

Hazzard exerted a straining effort to keep his fists out of Norvell's leering face. "That can't stop me, Norvell. I expect you make your threats good. You won't hesitate an instant to destroy me the moment

Trencher grabs you. Until that happens, you can be absolutely sure of one thing. I'm fighting you under cover and going the limit. I'll get you before Trencher gets me. I think we understand each other now!"

He spun to the door and slammed out. The fury that beat through his heart was driven away by a chilling dread. He felt a dank coldness in his lungs like the air of a prison. He remembered with a shudder the ominous eyes of Inspector Trencher, black as the doom he faced.

CHAPTER V

MURDER BRAND

HAZZARD QUICKLY climbed two short flights to the next floor of the building. He knocked at the door of the apartment directly above Norvell's. He stepped in quickly when Ann Nash opened the way. Her eyes shone wearily as she followed him into the room furnished only with a chair, a cot and an elaborate console radio.

"Nothing, Mark," she said in a tired tone. "I've checked every call, and there isn't a single lead."

She had kept a nerve-straining vigil in this room for four interminable days and nights. The radio had played softly every moment of the time. Even when no programs were being broadcast, she had kept it on, listening to every clicking noise that issued from the speaker. It sent the rhythm of a dance band into the room as Hazzard moved nervously back and forth.

"Trencher's found a list of places Norvell rented under assumed names," he told the girl. "He'll be going through every one of them, trying to find evidence—evidence that will break me as well as convict Norvell. Danny found one, but Trencher won't let me know where the others are—depend on that. Ann, we've got to—"

"Listen, Mark!"

A swift series of clicks was sounding in the radio. The girl whirled, picked up a pencil, tapped it swiftly on a pad each time. A shorter series followed the first, then a longer. They meant that someone was spinning the dial of a telephone in one of the nearby apartments. Each group of clicks indicated an integer of the number being called. When the girl's pencil poised, she studied the dots she had made and exclaimed:

"He hasn't called this one before, Mark. It's Central 7834." She took up the telephone as she spoke. "I'll check it through and—"

"It might be one of Norvell's secret places, Ann!" Hazzard said quickly. "If it is, we've got to get to it before Trencher does. It's a race between him and me for evidence against Norvell, and if he gets there first—"

The girl interrupted, speaking quickly into the transmitter. She demanded immediate connection with the chief operator. The name of the district attorney elicited information not available to the public. Ann Nash replaced the instrument and said breathlessly:

"It's a house on Grosvenor Street—number Six-Forty. Shall I phone and try to find out—"

"No! We're going there now."

Hazzard slipped out while the girl hurried after him, tugging a perky hat on her head. They waited impatiently while an elevator cab hummed up. Stepping in, Hazzard saw the number of the next lower floor glowing on the annunciator. It warned him that Norvell was also coming down. He gripped the cab control and snapped at the startled attendant:

"You're going down without a stop!"

As quick steps took him out the foyer with Ann, the cab began to ascend in response to Norvell's ring. Hazzard hurried to his car, helped Ann in, glanced around alertly. He stepped into the shadow of a building as Dan Carey, in patrolman's uniform, came to his side.

"Norvell's coming down. This time don't follow him. Come after Ann and me in the car, and keep an eye out for the police. We're heading for a place on Grosvenor Street. If you spot Trencher near it, warn us somehow that he's coming."

"Trust me, skipper!"

Hazzard peered into the lobby of the apartment building as he slipped behind the wheel. Norvell was striding out when he spurted from the curb. He turned at the corner and pressed the accelerator down hard. Blocks farther on, he looked back at the headlamps of a trailing car. He realized with a shock it was not Carey's light roadster, but Norvell's heavy sedan.

Hazzard sped. A series of swift turns took him into a street paralleling Grosvenor. Hard-pressed brakes stopped his car a block from 640. Ann Nash hurried with him along a driveway, through a hedge, across the un-trimmed lawn of the house Norvell had phoned. It was dark and silent. A sign on a porch post read *For Rent*. Hazzard was moving quietly toward the entrance when a twist of the knob, by a hand inside, startled him.

He swung off the porch and flattened against the side wall. Ann Nash huddled breathless at his side as the entrance closed and foot-falls crossed the porch. A lean man hurried out the gate and into the shadows. Hazzard let him go. He peered up and down the street as he glided to the entrance. Norvell's car was not in sight, but another turned at the corner as Hazzard tried his skeleton keys in the lock.

When the car slowed, lights out, Hazzard knew it was Dan Carey's. He drew the bolt. His hand swung to his Webley automatic as he cautiously opened the way. Ann Nash went in slowly after him. They stood in the dim light reflecting from an open door, and listened. Not the slightest rustle of movement came out of the silence.

"Norvell phoned to warn his man off because Trencher's looking into these places," Hazzard said quietly. "I've an idea that man was a jailer."

HE WENT alertly along the hallway. He repressed an exclamation of dismay when he stepped into the shaft of light. A man was lying on a cot in the room. Straps of adhesive tape bound his ankles and wrists, and sealed his lips. His shirt was crusted with dried blood. He moaned in agony and looked up as Hazzard strode in.

"Jake Keats," he murmured.

He bent over the exhausted man. Bullets had torn an ugly gash in the stool pigeon's side. It was untreated and unbound, an infected horror. Grimly Hazzard tugged at the strips of adhesive. He had freed Keats' wrists, and was peeling the bands from Keats' ankles, when quick steps sounded on the porch.

Hazzard whirled as Ann Nash exclaimed: "Norvell!" She retreated into the room while Keats struggled up, groaning. Hazzard was facing the door, tight-lipped, when Norvell appeared in the light. Norvell came in slowly, eyes narrowed. He reached to his arm-pit holster and brought a blue revolver into his hand as Hazzard spoke.

"Trencher *was* right. It was Jake Keats' blood on the fire-escape of Machen's place. He's an eye-witness to the crime of murder."

"That's right, Hazzard." Norvell brought the revolver level. "He saw me do it. I forced him down the fire-escape and into the room where Trencher found the checkered suit. I kept him there until the next night, then brought him here. I don't mind telling you what happened, you see, because you're not going to talk about it."

Keats staggered up and stood swaying.

"*He* can talk," Hazzard said grimly. "And Trencher knows about this place. What're you going to do about that, Norvell."

"I came here to do something about it," Norvell answered gratingly. "This!"

Hazzard struck out as Norvell's finger tightened on the trigger. He knocked the revolver down as it blasted. Norvell lurched against him, snarling with fury. Hazzard's head struck the sharp edge of the door jamb. He tottered, dazed. The thunder of Norvell's gun was a shock that cleared his mind. He tensed to spring again at Norvell, but his muscles froze. He stared paralyzed with dismay at Jake Keats.

Keats was sagging against the wall, jaw gaping, eyes following. New red gushed from the hole made by Norvell's bullet just above his heart. He drew a single, choking breath, then dropped to the cot. As he rolled to the floor, dead eyes staring, a stifled cry of horror broke from the lips of Ann Nash.

Norvell said tersely: "He won't talk now!"

Hazzard straightened tightly. He thought he heard quick footfalls on the sidewalk, but the furious pounding in his ears made him uncertain. A crazy rage possessed him as he grasped the blue revolver and tore it from Norvell's hand.

"Better wipe my fingerprints off it, Hazzard," Norvell suggested in a threatening tone. "You wouldn't want Trencher to connect me with this."

Hazzard blazed: "Cold-blooded murder!"

"That's right. What does it matter? You didn't want Keats to talk, did you? You and your girl aren't going to do any talking either—are you?"

Ann Nash's terrorized eyes pled with Hazzard's. Fury boiled through his veins as he jerked out his handkerchief and polished the weapon of murder. Again he heard quiet steps outside the house. Nerves burning tight, he listened while he handed the revolver to Norvell.

"Getting rid of it will be your job, not mine!"

Norvell sneered: "Why bother? It's not registered in my name. Anyway, I needn't worry—with the honorable district attorney looking out for me."

Anger filmed Hazzard's eyes with red as he faced Norvell. A sudden knock, shocking through the silence of the house, sent a chill to his heart. He spun from the room and saw a shadow blotting over the glass of the entrance. The knock sounded again and Dan Carey's hushed voice called through:

"Skipper! Trencher's coming!"

The shadow vanished from the pane. A fast rustle in the grass told Hazzard that Carey was running to the rear of the house for his car. He gripped Ann Nash's arm and forced her toward the back entrance. Again there were steps on the sidewalk—ominously slow—as he opened the way. He hurried out with the terrified girl. Norvell strode swiftly after them to the hedge. They slipped through as another knock sounded—Trencher's knuckles rapping at the entrance of 640.

Ann Nash kept breathlessly at Hazzard's side as they sped through the shadows. Glancing back, he saw Norvell vanishing in the gloom near the farther corner. When he slipped behind the wheel of his car, a muffled grinding told him that Norvell was starting away. Dan Carey would follow him. Hazzard swung his car from the curb as he heard startled voices inside the house where murder had been done. He knew then that Inspector Trencher had found Jake Keats' dead body.

Hazzard's heart pounded heavily with dread as he sped.

ANN NASH'S hand was closed pleadingly on Hazzard's arm when he braked at the curb near the entrance of the apartment building in which Norvell lived. The massive car at the curb told them Norvell had already returned. As Hazzard began to duck out, the girl said wretchedly:

"Mark, I don't understand. What hold has Norvell on you? It must be something stronger than his knowing about Danny. Won't you tell me, so I can help you, somehow? No matter what it is—I've got to know."

Tell her? Hazzard's eyes pinched with agony. Tell her that he was a convicted murderer? Tell her that a few words spoken to Inspector Trencher would destroy him as Mark Hazzard, District Attorney, and transform him into Dennis Grant, fugitive from the law? Turmoil beat through his mind as the girl's hand clung pleadingly to his.

"I can't tell you that!" he answered huskily. "You've got to trust me, darling. I'm not thinking of Danny now, nor of myself—but you. No matter what else happens, you've got to be kept out of this. Leave my car here and wait at the office until you hear from me."

He turned from her in agony, and hurried into the lobby. When the elevator cab left him at the seventh floor, he found Mrs. Grace Norvell waiting for it in the corridor. He strode past her without speaking and touched Norvell's button. The car was carrying the woman down when Norvell, smiling with cool contempt, ushered him in.

"Not worried, are you, Hazzard?" he asked slyly.

Hazzard's jaw-muscles lumped. "Listen, Norvell. This is strictly between you and me. You can break me if you wish. You can force me to cover your dirty tracks and laugh at me behind my back. But you've got to keep Ann Nash out of it!"

Norvell's lips curled. "Why should I? She was a witness to the murder, wasn't she? She hasn't reported it to the police, has she? Under the law that may be construed as sheltering a criminal. It makes her an accessory after the fact. You don't want her to go to the chair, do you, Hazzard?"

Hazzard's fingers itched to crush around Norvell's thin neck. Norvell uttered a mocking laugh that blinded him with fury. He fought his flaring temper as a heavy knock sounded on the door and Norvell turned. Suddenly urged by a chill alertness, he backed toward a connecting door. He closed it to a crack as he heard the gruff voice of Inspector Trencher at the entrance.

Covered with darkness, Hazzard watched in agony as Trencher came to the center of the room. The inspector thrust his big hands into his coat pockets and turned his back to the connecting door. Norvell was again smiling with contemptuous confidence. He drew a cigarette from the jeweled case and struck the flame of the gold lighter as Trencher asked:

"Been out, haven't you? Just got back? Or has Hazzard got another alibi for you?"

"Why ask?" Norvell countered. "You've got a man watching him."

"You beat it out of here so fast a little while ago he couldn't follow you," Trencher drawled. "Where'd you go, Norvell? To the house on Grosvenor Street?"

"What house, inspector?"

"The place where we just found Jake Keats dead. He was killed with a revolver, because I didn't find any automatically ejected shells in the room. Do you own a revolver, Norvell?"

"I don't know what you're talking about."

Trencher peered shrewdly through the smoke curling from Norvell's thin lips. "Well, maybe I've got you all wrong—you and the D.A. Maybe I'm wasting my time. It'll only take a minute to prove you didn't have anything to do with killing Keats—if you're willing to submit to a test."

"Anything you say, inspector."

"All right, Norvell." Trencher drew a small, wide-necked bottle from his pocket. He reached for Norvell's right hand. "We use this occasionally at headquarters. Got any objections to trying it now?"

"Not at all, inspector," Norvell answered quietly. His gaze turned to the door behind which Hazzard was standing frozen. "Maybe the D.A. won't think so much of it as evidence."

"Maybe not." Trencher opened the bottle. A limpid drop fell from the brush attached to the cork as he lifted it. "Nothing mysterious about this, you know. It's a solution of wax, sulphuric acid and diphenylamine crystals. It's called the nitrate test."

Hazzard watched the brush touch the forefinger of Norvell's right hand. Growing consternation stopped his breath as he began to reach through the crack of the door. He had seen this test used on criminals at headquarters. He knew the reaction that Trencher was expecting. Grimly he reached toward the light switch near the door.

"You see, Norvell," Trencher drawled, "when a man fires a revolver, most of the burning powder flies out through the barrel, but some of it spits out through the socket of the trigger. A bit of burned nitrate gets on the skin of the trigger finger. See that, Norvell? Look at the bright blue ring around your finger. Interesting, isn't it?"

Norvell stood tense, eyes slitted. Mark Hazzard reached farther toward the light switch. Trencher stepped back, corking the bottle, slipping it into his pocket, his black gaze smouldering.

"The blue ring proves you fired a revolver a short time ago, Norvell! It goes a long way toward pinning Keats' murder on you. This test is going to send you to the chair."

Hazzard snapped the switch. He flashed the door open and leaped into thick darkness. Trencher whirled at the sound of his swift movements.

Hazzard glimpsed the glitter of the inspector's gun and snatched at it wildly. Clenching it, he smashed his fist to Trencher's blunt chin. Trencher lurched against him, driving out heavy blows. Hazzard danced on toe-tips, striking with trained precision. His terrific straight-arm clout exploded full in Trencher's face. Trencher went down.

Hazzard stood breathing fast. His right hand slipped to his Webley as he reached again for the switch. Norvell's cigarette was a red spark that vanished in a flood of light. Hazzard straddled beside the unconscious Trencher and brought his automatic level at Norvell.

"Trencher's got you cold!"

"He's got you too, Hazzard," Norvell answered with a rasp, "unless you get me out of it."

"I can't get you out of it now! You're facing a conviction for murder. Listen, Norvell! I told you when I came in here that you're to keep Ann Nash out of it—even if I have to put a bullet through you. Understand that? I'll let Trencher nail me for a brand new murder before I'll let you drag that girl into court."

Hazzard's whipping words turned Norvell's face white with fear. He slipped the Webley into his pocket with his finger still on the trigger. Keeping its muzzle pointed at Norvell through the fabric, he rushed on. "You're going out that door with me. You're going to do exactly as I say. If you don't, Norvell, I'll kill you and gladly take the consequences. Now move!"

CHAPTER VI

BULLET VENGEANCE

TRENCHER SQUIRMED on the floor, the light of return-ing consciousness flickering in his brain. Hazzard's Webley forced Norvell to the entrance. Trencher was moaning, striving to rise, when Hazzard closed the door.

Going down the elevator, the Webley pressed threateningly to Norvell's side. Hazzard's eyes were a blazing danger that kept Norvell fearfully silent. Outside, he prodded Norvell toward the car and glanced around for Dan Carey. His signal brought Carey hurrying from the gloom as Norvell ducked in. He passed the Webley.

"Keep him covered, Danny," he cautioned grimly. "If he makes a move, pull that trigger."

Slipping to the wheel, Hazzard brought the blue metal revolver from his pocket. He had carried it with him during the swift escape from the house on Grosvenor Street—a weapon that had blasted the life out of a helpless man.

While Hazzard turned corners and sent the car angling into a bleak section of the city, Dan Carey kept the Webley pressed to Norvell's side. Norvell's thin smile of triumph was gone now. Growing fear glittered in his eyes as Hazzard swung the car to a stop beside a black, massive building. Hazzard slipped from the wheel, the blue revolver leveled, while Carey prodded Norvell out.

Norvell demanded with a rasp: "What are you trying to do, Hazzard?"

"I'm trying to keep from killing you on the spot. Take him in, Danny."

The inky water of the river rippled beyond the end of the blind street. Broken windows in the gaunt structure stared into the gloom like blind eyes. A dark ramp led down the side of the building that had been abandoned as a brewery during prohibition and never re-conditioned. The Webley in Carey's hand forced Norvell to a door that hung on broken hinges. Hazzard's blue revolver glittered in the shafting moonlight as they walked across a cavernous room in which old vats stood like fat, gigantic ghosts.

The spectral silence was broken only by the gritting of their heels as they passed through an inner door. Norvell turned, his face pasty in the dim glow. Hazzard straddled, backing him against a moldy brick wall, the blue gun leveled.

Again Norvell demanded raspingly: "What are you trying to get away with, Hazzard?"

"Murder, perhaps," Hazzard answered tightly. "This is an excellent spot for a killing, Norvell. Your body could be thrown through a window, into the river, and it would never be seen again. You're forcing me to it."

Carey said grimly: "Don't take the risk, skipper. Let me have the pleasure of putting a bullet in this mug's heart. I owe him something."

Hazzard smiled bitterly. "Not you, Danny. You're going to skip. If Trencher gets me now, I want you out of his reach. Don't waste any time about it. Change your clothes and get across the state line tonight. First, phone Ann at the office, will you, Danny?"

The blue weapon in Hazzard's hand covered the white-faced Norvell while Carey stared a frantic protest.

"Warn her to say absolutely nothing about what happened tonight. She wasn't in the house on Grosvenor Street tonight. She knows nothing whatever about it. Even if the district attorney is charged with being an accessory to murder, she's got to keep quiet to save herself. Tell her that, Danny."

"Okay, skipper—but I'm not clearing out. I'm coming back to handle this mug."

Carey broke into a run that took him toward the ramp. He glanced back once, to see Hazzard keeping Norvell backed to the mossy wall, to hear Hazzard caution grimly: "Steady, Norvell!" He loped crazily along the street to a lunch wagon that sat near the corner. A storm of consternation was raging in his mind when he shouldered into the telephone booth and spun the number of Hazzard's office.

The purr of the bell jerked a quick response from the girl sitting tensely at the district attorney's desk. She heard Dan Carey's strained voice rush over the wire. The color drained from her cheeks and her fingers whitened on the instrument as she heard:

"The skipper's in a spot! He's trying to get me to clear out because it's all up with him. He wants you to keep quiet about the killing tonight. He says you've got to or Trencher will nail you for—"

"Where is he, Danny?" the girl interrupted anxiously. "Where is Mark?"

"He's got Norvell in the old Pioneer Brewery at the end of Whaling Street. He's snatched Norvell to keep him out of Trencher's hands. God knows what the skipper's going to do. Norvell's forced him to it—and it might be murder!"

"Danny!" Ann Nash frantically rattled the contact as the connection broke. "Danny!" She dropped the dead phone and sprang up, her eyes flashing with alarm. Suddenly she snatched up her purse and opened it. The little pearl-handled automatic nestled inside it was a weapon she always carried. She gripped the bag firmly as she hurried from the office.

ONCE IN her car, she pressed the accelerator hard. At each intersection she hammered the horn button and flashed past. She slipped swiftly from the wheel at the entrance of an apartment building. Ignoring the elevator, she ran up the stairs. She heard a radio playing softly in the Norvell apartment as she rapped.

She thrust in the instant the latch clicked. The woman who had been Mrs. Machen, who was now Mrs. Norvell, gazed in fright at her flashing, determined eyes. Ann Nash seized her arm and demanded breathlessly:

"I want to know what hold Norvell has on Mark Hazzard? Do you hear me? You've got to tell me that!"

The woman gasped: "I don't know!"

"Tell me!" The girl's fingers pressed desperately as the woman squirmed fruitlessly to escape her grip. "Norvell's forcing Mark Hazzard to cover him. He tricked you into marrying him so you can't testify against him, and now he's—"

"I did it to help Arnold," the woman protested fearfully. "The police are trying to frame him and I did it—"

Ann Nash laughed bitterly. "You're a blind fool. Norvell killed your husband, and yet you believe in him! He admitted it to Mark Hazzard, and he's forcing—"

"He didn't!"

"It's true! Arnold Norvell killed your husband. He talked you into marrying him, to save his skin, just as he's forcing Mark Hazzard to protect him. You're going to tell me how he's able to do that." Ann Nash pulled the little automatic from her bag and grimly leveled it.

The woman shrank away in horror. "I didn't know! I thought the police were framing Arnold. I couldn't believe—"

"You know it now!" Ann Nash reached for the knob. "You're coming with me. Do you hear? You're coming with me now—or I'll shoot you."

The woman stood trembling, staring, bewildered. An expression of cold fury came into her eyes as the import of Ann Nash's words gripped her. She straightened with fists clenched.

"I'll go with you. You don't need to force me with that gun. I'll go!"

Ann Nash jerked the door wide. She replaced the little automatic in her purse as she hurried along the corridor with the woman. They hastened down the stairs, to the girl's car. Grace Norvell sat tense, fingers entwined, eyes blazing with furious hatred, as Ann Nash sent the car speeding. Her destination was the abandoned building on Whaling Street.

FACING NORVELL with the blue revolver leveled, Mark Hazzard heard quick footfalls on the ramp. The stocky figure of Dan Carey hurried through the shafting moonlight toward him. Carey stopped breathless at his side as Norvell spoke a rasping challenge:

"You're not bluffing me, Hazzard. You're not going to kill me. Trencher will nail you for it if you do. He knows I've got something on you. You'll be the first he'll grab if I disappear. You're facing a murder rap, either way—if you don't alibi me out of both killings."

Hazzard's wrath sent hot blood pounding through his taut body. "Look around, Danny," he ordered huskily. "Find something to tie Norvell with." He straightened as Carey groped away through the darkness. "You know I can't keep you covered now, Norvell. Trencher's got you absolutely cold. Nothing I can do can clear you."

Norvell leered. "That's your hard luck, then, Hazzard," he drawled. "Your hard luck."

Hazzard stood with eyes glittering while sounds came out of the depths of the cavernous, black room—Carey searching for rope. Long minutes of straining tension passed. Carey was still groping through the gloom when footfalls sounded again on the ramp. The ex-cop swung toward the broken door, as two slight figures appeared silhouetted against the moonlight. He stopped short and blurted:

"Skipper! It's Ann, and—"

Hazzard moaned with despair. A swift glance across his shoulder showed him Ann Nash hurrying into the huge room, Grace Norvell following breathlessly. The girl stopped in dismay at Hazzard's side. Norvell scowled as the woman faced him. Hazzard kept the blue revolver steadied as she said with icy fury:

"You killed Cliff!"

Norvell sneered. "What are you going to do about it? You can't take the stand against me now. No matter what you say, it can't be used against your husband."

The words stung Grace Norvell to a mad fury. She stood trembling, her small fists clenched, her eyes filled with loathing. She said, very quietly: "You rat." Possessed with an insane hatred, she repeated: "You rat."

Her sudden turn surprised Hazzard. Sharp-nailed fingers were clawing at the blue gun before he was aware of her purpose. He drew back alertly, striving to keep the gun, but the woman's anger was a savage madness. As she tore at the weapon, Arnold Norvell flung himself from the wall. He was running desperately toward the door when the woman whirled with a revolver in her hand.

Three fast shots thundered through the shrouding darkness. The woman's face shone white and drawn in the flashes of flame. Hazzard leaped to her side and knocked the gun downward as she laughed. Arnold Norvell had stumbled to a stop in the doorway. He was clinging to the frame, moaning. The moonlight beaming through a broken window gleamed on the bright red gushing from his neck. He fell into the grit—and the woman laughed crazily again.

Startled voices echoed from the street:

"Those were shots!"

"Inside that building!"

"I'm going to call the police!"

Mark Hazzard twisted the blue gun from Grace Norvell's hand. Ann Nash was staring with one hand lifted in dismay to her parted red lips. Dan Carey had rushed to Norvell, now was straightening with a wag of his head that meant, "He's dead." Hazzard whipped out his pocket handkerchief and frantically polished the blue metal as his words rushed:

"Ann, take her out of here! Get some alcohol and ether and wash the nitrate stains off her finger. Go to my office and stay there. Be sure nobody sees you going in with her. You've been there together for the past hour—understand? She didn't kill Norvell—she doesn't know anything about it. Quick, Ann!"

The girl grasped Grace Norvell's arm and pulled her toward the door where the dead man lay. The woman shrank past, then broke into a run. Hazzard spun to Carey as quick footfalls sounded up the ramp.

"Get under cover, copper! Back to my place! Nobody else can help me now. This is strictly between me and Trencher. On your way, Danny! The police are coming!"

Hazzard's lashing tone forced Carey into a run. His quick steps followed Ann's and Mrs. Norvell's toward the street. Hazzard stood tense, pocketing his handkerchief, gazing at the motionless body of Norvell, as motors hummed outside the building. The sound moved away quickly. Then, almost at once, tires whined around the corner toward the ramp. Hazzard knew it was a prowl car.

When the two uniformed men ran into the musty rooms, their lights flashing, their service gats in their hands, Hazzard was standing near the dead man.

"Self defense," he said succinctly as they stared. "Let's go to my office and talk it over with the inspector."

INSPECTOR TRENCHER leaned tensely across the desk of the district attorney. The two radio patrolmen who had found Hazzard with Norvell were stationed at the outer door. Ann Nash was seated alertly at her typewriter. Grace Norvell stood white-faced near her, listening intently. Hazzard smiled tightly while Trencher's words growled.

"You're not bluffing me. I'm pretty old in this game, and I know my way around. First, Norvell killed Machen. Next Norvell killed Keats because Keats was a witness to the first murder. Then this woman found out the truth, that Norvell tricked her into marrying him after shooting her husband, and she got Norvell for it. That stacks up—and it puts the D.A. in a spot. Because, Hazzard, you gave Norvell a false alibi to cover his killing of Machen."

Hazzard answered quietly: "Wrong, inspector, all wrong. I didn't falsely alibi Norvell, because it was Keats who killed Machen. You'll have to find the motive, but a motive isn't a legal necessity if the circumstances prove the rest of the crime. You'll find Keats' fingerprints in the room where you found the checkered suit. Following Norvell around, he'd learned of it, of course, and he used it to cover himself after killing Machen. That clear?"

Trencher challenged: "Go ahead, Hazzard!"

"Gladly. Then, of course, it was Norvell who killed Keats. Again you'll have to find the motive. Perhaps it was because Machen was Norvell's best friend—revenge. Perhaps it was because Keats was getting evidence against Norvell in the bootleg insurance racket. Let that go. You know Norvell killed Keats and, since you're an old hand in the game, that ought to be enough. Do you follow me, Trencher?"

Again Trencher growled: "Go ahead!"

"I was watching Norvell tonight when you went into his apartment. Then I saw him beat it out. That meant you'd got him cold for the Keats killing, and he was making a getaway. I trailed him to the old brewery, where he was intending to hide until he could skip. I went in after him, and he turned his gun on me—the same gun he used to kill Keats. I tried to get it away from him, and in the fight it went off. That, Trencher, constitutes self defense."

Trencher was smiling ominously.

"We both know the law, Trencher," Hazzard went on levelly. "As an officer of justice, I can't be touched for Norvell's death. Furthermore, in a case of self defense, the burden of proof lies with the state, not the accused. Under the circumstances, I think we may consider the case closed. How about it, Trencher?"

The inspector's smouldering eyes narrowed. "I'm not so sure. Norvell had something on you. He was forcing you to cover him. This ought to tell what it was. This telegram. And this envelope I found in your waste-basket proves neither you nor Norvell was in this office at the time Machen was killed. Look it over, Hazzard."

Hazzard glanced at the notations on the yellow envelope. He saw a time jotted down coincident with the time Machen was killed—a note showing that an attempt to deliver the telegram then had failed. He brushed it aside with a smile.

"It doesn't prove Norvell and I weren't here, Trencher. It only shows we were talking so earnestly, about the bootleg insurance case, we didn't hear the messenger knock."

Trencher snarled. "You can't bluff your way out, Hazzard. This wire is a copy I got from the telegraph office. Just what does it mean? Explain it, if you can—and those initials."

Ann Nash came anxiously to Hazzard's desk as he gazed at the line that chilled his blood.

'TWAS THE NIGHT BEFORE CHRISTMAS

A.N.

It had warned Mark Hazzard that Norvell had known his secret. It had recalled that bitter night before Christmas when Dennis Grant had been seized for a murder he had not committed. Chill dread came again to Hazzard's heart as he read the words that threatened to annihilate the world he had created, to destroy his identity as a respected district attorney. His mind was groping for an answer when his secretary observed:

" 'Twas the night before Christmas, inspector, and all through the house not a creature was stirring, not even Ann Nash." She laughed softly. "It simply means that I chose that way of telling Mark I was lonesome and would be delighted to go somewhere to dance. The initials, you see, inspector, are mine."

"And Ann's manner of communicating with me," Hazzard added promptly, "is not police business, Trencher!"

Trencher snarled. He crumpled the copy of the telegram in one huge hand. His blunt finger leveled a threat at Hazzard's face, but he controlled his anger. He straightened, black eyes shining dangerously, and forced a smile.

"All right, Hazzard," he said quietly. "Good-night. I guess I've been mistaken all along."

He paused at the door to send one sharp, dark glance at the district attorney. It said: "I'm not through trying to get you, Hazzard. The time's coming when I'm going to nail you cold. This time you've won—but I'm not through trying to get you." And the glance left a chill in Hazzard's heart as Trencher tramped out.

He rose alertly. "Stiff upper lip," he cautioned Mrs. Norvell. "Say nothing—because it's all over." He led her to the door. She went out, confused, strangely happy. Hazzard smiled tightly as he returned to the desk. Ann Nash's hand went warmly to his as she searched his eyes.

"Thanks, Ann, for some very fast thinking."

"Mark—what is it?" she asked anxiously. "What does that telegram really mean? You know you can tell me anything—and I'll understand."

"I know, Ann. You wouldn't let it matter. You'd stick by me just as you always have. But it's a secret I can never tell you, darling." He took her snugly in his arms. "It's a secret I hope you'll never know."

He paused in the deep gloom that
blanketed the graves and anxiously
whispered: "Danny!"

The Saxon fraud trial was the culmination of months of arduous labor
on Hazzard's part. Until he had
brought the present indictment, the
cunning operators of the real estate
racket had defied all previous attempts
of the law to stamp it out. Hazzard
had challenged Saxon because Saxon's
slickest plan had mulcted scores of
home owners with the cooperation of
the civil courts.

Hazzard's investigations had revealed that Saxon's first step in the
predatory scheme was to profess to
have a handsome offer for a certain
parcel of property, and to present a
contract to the owner for signature.
The victim rarely read the document
carefully enough to discover that it
provided for the payment of a substantial sum to Saxon in case "unforeseen events" prevented the closing of
the sale.

In each instance, these "unforeseen
events" had occurred, and no sale was
made. If the property owner refused
to pay the staggering fee regardless,
Saxon invariably sued, and always
won the case. The racket had robbed
deserving men of their life savings,
had even cost them their homes, and
in several cases had led to suicide. It
was Saxon's use of the law to further
his fraud that had made Hazzard
swear to crush him. Razzed to rug-
wall at last, Hazzard believed, Saxon
had deliberately conspired to defeat

BOOK IV

THE MURDER CRYPT

*When Mark Hazzard, battling D.A., found
two corpses in a graveyard crypt, he set
out to catch a gold-greedy killer. For those
corpses were not yet cold, and with them
had died important testimony. But the only
clue he had to start on was a few grains
of dust, and the murderer had already
planned a grave for Mark Hazzard.*

CHAPTER I

DEATH AMONG
THE DEAD

HE CREPT through black shadows along the cemetery wall. Gun in hand, he peered warily through the brooding gloom that shrouded the headstones and monuments. Climbing over, he followed a path with soundless step, toward the only light gleaming in the graveyard. He paused furtively beside a shining window, listening, his eyes narrowed with desperate purpose.

He was not a ghoul, a thief, nor a fugitive from the law. He was the red-headed, two-fisted prosecuting attorney of King's County, Mark Hazzard.

Hazzard heard a voice speaking from a radio inside the caretaker's cottage.

"The jury in the sensational Saxon fraud case is still out. They have now been deliberating behind locked doors for more than five hours. Though the state's case was seriously weakened by the mysterious disappearance of several important witnesses, a verdict of guilty is momentarily expected. If Howell Saxon and his associates in the Saxon Realty Corporation are convicted, it will mean the break-up of a vicious racket and a new triumph for the fearless district attorney."

Hazzard turned from the window, smiling tightly. While he followed another path through the darkness he heard the announcer continue:

"Prosecutor Hazzard undertook the most difficult assignment of his career in demanding the indictment of Howell Saxon. His task has been to prove criminal intent behind contracts which are unquestionably legal. He was severely handicapped during the trial when the court ruled that several affidavits, made by alleged victims of the fraud, were defective and inadmissible as evidence. The vanishing of two of Hazzard's key witnesses against Saxon was another staggering

151

blow to the state's case. Though police have failed to find the missing men, the district attorney doggedly persisted, and tonight a verdict is expected for the People."

The police had failed to locate the vanished witnesses, but Mark Hazzard was still on the job. The same relentless determination that made him a terror to the guilty in court had sent him on a lone wolf's trail. He had marked Saxon for his own brand of legal justice, and no musty rules of procedure could keep him from forcing the case through to its deserved conclusion. He had persisted in the hunt after headquarters had abandoned it. Though a verdict of guilty was promised, his grim intent was to find the missing witnesses tonight.

He paused in the deep gloom that blanketed the graves and anxiously whispered: "Danny?"

The Saxon fraud trial was the culmination of months of arduous labor on Hazzard's part. Until he had brought the present indictment, the cunning operators of the real estate racket had defied all previous attempts of the law to stamp it out. Hazzard had challenged Saxon because Saxon's shrewd plan had mulcted scores of home owners with the coöperation of the civil courts.

Hazzard's investigations had revealed that Saxon's first step in the predatory scheme was to profess to have a handsome offer for a certain parcel of property, and to present a contract to the owner for signature. The victim rarely read the document carefully enough to discover that it provided for the payment of a substantial sum to Saxon in case "unforeseen events" prevented the closing of the sale.

In each instance, these "unforeseen events" had occurred, and no sale was made. If the property owner refused to pay the staggering fee regardless, Saxon invariably sued, and always won the case. The racket had robbed deserving men of their life savings, had even cost them their homes, and in several cases had led to suicide. It was Saxon's use of the law to further his fraud that had made Hazzard swear to crush Saxon. Backed to the wall at last, Hazzard believed, Saxon had deliberately conspired to defeat justice by abducting two of the state's key witnesses.

"Danny," he whispered into the darkness again.

A dark, soundless shape appeared behind one of the monuments. A man drifted to Hazzard's side. His powerful body was clothed in a policeman's uniform which he had no legal right to wear. Dan Carey, ex-cop, convicted murderer, fugitive from the law, was Mark Hazzard's assistant in the dangerous task of administering a justice higher than the written law.

When headquarters had abandoned the search for the missing witnesses, Hazzard's orders had put Dan Carey to watching Eric Miner, one of Saxon's crooked associates. Carey had kept on Miner's trail night and day. The hunt had produced no results until his telephone call to Hazzard's office tonight. His whispered information had brought the district attorney into the silent gloom of the cemetery.

"I followed Miner to his house more than an hour ago, skipper," Carey reported quietly. "A few minutes later somebody slipped out. I don't know whether it was Miner or somebody he met there. I trailed him here. He sneaked into the Wellington crypt."

"Good work, Danny," Hazzard answered grimly. "We know Miner's had some dealings with 'Fancy' Frank Phalon. Could it have been Phalon you saw?"

"Maybe, skipper. Whoever it is, he's in the crypt now."

Hazzard said wryly: "We're paying him a call."

HE WAS conscious of the Webley automatic, holstered under his left arm, as he followed Carey past headstones that stood like staring ghosts. The path led them deep into the cemetery. When they paused, with the wind sighing through the trees whose shadows sheltered them, the lights of the caretaker's cottage had vanished.

They faced a stone house of the dead which bore the carved name of Wellington. Its forbidding bronze door was shut. No glow shone from its colored glass windows. But, while Hazzard listened alertly, he heard furtive sounds that told him someone was moving about in the dark inside.

He drifted into the open, gesturing Carey to keep at his side. The prowling sounds came again when they entered the deeper gloom of the portico. Hazzard pressed the latch slowly, carefully, and found the way barred by a bolt. He stepped back and brought his Webley snugly into his hand. He sent its butt against the bronze panel—a sharp, quick rap.

A tense moment of silence followed. Silence—until, inside the crypt, two muffled shots blasted!

Hazzard stepped back swiftly, the automatic leveled. Carey flattened beside the door, police positive gleaming in the gloom. They stood motionless, breath caught, listening—but now there was no sound beyond the metal door.

Apprehension prickled across Hazzard's scalp as once more his hand slowly tried the latch. When he released it, and pressed the door, his pulse sped. The bolt was no longer barring the way. A hand in the dark had silently drawn it from its socket. The way into the crypt was open—into the blackness where an armed man lurked.

Hazzard quickly stepped through. A corroded hinge on the door rasped a warning of his move. Instantly a blinding beam of light sprang out of the gloom. It stabbed into Hazzard's eyes as he sprang back. His automatic was swinging toward the dazzling spot when the unseen gun thundered again.

The bullet crashed glass behind Hazzard's head at the instant the light vanished. Heels swiftly beat the marble floor. Hazzard gasped: "Stop him, Danny!" and leaped blindly toward the entrance. He collided with the heavy door as it clanked shut. Outside a gun rocked again. Hazzard groped to the handle and pulled as a moan sounded and rapid footfalls rustled the grass.

He slid to the wall outside the door, baffled by the blackness and the elusive rhythm of someone running. Another groan mumbled from a spot near him. He slipped his fountain-pen torch into his hand. Because he knew it would make him a target, he gave the contact only a brief touch, and leaped aside. The flash showed him Dan Carey, on hands and knees, face streaked with red.

"Get after him, skipper! I'm okay!"

Hazzard broke into a run. The shadows and the headstones were a bewildering maze. The fluttering of leaves overhead made the running footfalls an untraceable confusion. Hazzard sprinted along a black path toward the wall he had climbed. Certain the escaping man must have a car, he scrambled toward the roadster he had left on the road.

When he scaled the wall, he saw the roadster moving. One door, swinging open, told him his quarry had thrown off the hand brake and shifted it out of gear. Its wheels were turning with increasing speed down the steep slope. Hazzard's mercurial temper sent hot blood beating through his brain as he raced after it. Even while he flung himself along at top speed he knew that he could not reach the roadster. He glimpsed a dark movement, fluttering against the bank at a point beyond, and brought up short. His Webley spat twice. The bullets did not stop the ghost. Hazzard sprinted again, as his car careened crazily on the grade, while a starter snarled at the bend ahead.

Hazzard's roadster, lurching toward the ditch, cut off his line of fire. The hot motor of the other automobile instantly caught. A surge of power spun wheels in the grit. Flaring wrath drove Hazzard into an even faster run. He fired once more, at a movement which disappeared before his bullet could reach it. Then, as the other car sped, his roadster crashed.

It wrenched into the ditch, one running-board tearing against an outcropping rock. Its bumper drove against a stout tree. Metal cracked and the car rebounded violently. It reared like a fighting horse, then rolled on its side. Wood splintered and metal ripped again as it lurched down with wheels still spinning.

THE ANGRY beating of blood in Hazzard's ears almost covered the whine of the fleeing car. He whirled back grimly. When he climbed the bank and leaped the wall, lights were flashing near the Wellington crypt. A man in cover-alls—the caretaker, drawn by the shots—was standing at the bronze entrance, staring in wildly. Hazzard saw his face was deathly white as he thrust past.

He stopped short in dismay. Dan Carey, face still streaked with blood, was turning his torch upon two men who lay against the far wall. Their hands and ankles were bound with torn strips of stout cloth. Gags were stuffed in their mouths. The head of one was broken by a slug that had driven completely through. A round, black hole, a single red tangent flowing from it, marked the other's forehead.

Straightening, Carey blurted: "Murdered! We heard the shots, skipper!"

Hazzard, peering around, said grimly: "Crawford and Lewis—the missing witnesses."

The inside surfaces of the colored glass windows were thickly painted black. A score of empty milk bottles stood in one corner, and dried crusts of bread were scattered over the floor. A bag, placed near the dead men, contained an unopened quart of milk and several untouched sandwiches. Countless cigarette butts lay crushed on the marble.

"They've been held prisoners here since the trial began," Hazzard declared grimly. "They'll never testify against Saxon now. He's behind this—and he's going to get the chair for it!"

He grasped Carey's arm. The spot of his torch showed him an ugly cut on the ex-cop's forehead, caused by the vicious blow of a gun-butt. While the caretaker stared, they hurried along a dark path. Hazzard abruptly stopped, his temples pulsing with fury, his eyes anxiously on Carey.

"Danny, you've got to skip. If inspector Trencher asks questions about the cop who was here, I'll cover you. Get back to your car right away. Where'd you leave it?"

Carey gestured dizzily. "That side."

"Go back to Miner's house, Danny. If he's the man we want, he's had a head start, but keep your eye on his place. After an hour, phone my office until you get me. Okay, copper?"

Carey sighed: "Okay, skipper!" and stumbled away. Hazzard watched him totter out of sight in the shadows. At the entrance of the care-taker's cottage he waited until the sound of a motor came out of the gloom. It told him Carey was safely off, and a surge of relief pulsed through him.

Mark Hazzard had rushed Carey from the scene because recognition by the police would mean the electric chair for the ex-cop. Hazzard had himself convicted Carey on a charge of first degree murder. While in his heart he had believed Carey innocent, he had been forced as prosecutor to present damning evidence at the trial. The verdict of the jury had been a bitter triumph for Hazzard: "Guilty."

Dan Carey had been framed, and the only man who could prove it was dead. Carey had managed a desperate escape, while being taken up the river to the death house, and the news of it had gladdened Hazzard's heart. Still a fugitive, hunted by the relentless Inspector Trencher, Carey must, if he were captured, go to the chair for a crime of which he was innocent.

On one of his lone wolf prowls into the dives of the city, Hazzard had found the starving convict hiding miserably from Trencher's men. He had revolted at the thought of turning Carey over to the police. Instead, he had given the ex-cop the security of a room hidden above the garage of his home. Carey had served him loyally in the cause of true justice. Mark Hazzard stood ready to take any desperate extreme to protect the fugitive who had become his closest friend.

As the sound of Carey's car faded into the distance, Hazzard hurried into the caretaker's cottage. He spun the number of his office on the telephone dial. He was waiting impatiently for the connection to click through when the dance music of the radio ceased abruptly at the clang of a bell. Tensely Hazzard listened to a news announcement that struck a chill through his heart.

"A sensational development in the Saxon case, ladies and gentlemen! Judge Joseph Cheever has declared a mistrial. While the jury was still out, the defense attorneys seized upon a legal technicality to halt the case. They also entered a motion that the indictment be dismissed because of lack of sufficient evidence. If this motion is denied, the entire case must be tried again. If it is granted, Howell Saxon will go free and Prosecutor Mark Hazzard will stand defeated."

CHAPTER II

MURDER ACROSS
THE LINE

THE ZINGING bell in the district attorney's office brought
the hand of Ann Nash, his secretary, quickly to the telephone.
Alert, efficient, tireless, she had remained at her post in the criminal
court until Judge Cheever had dismissed the jury in the Saxon case.
She answered quickly as Hazzard asked: "Ann! What the devil happened?"

"Mark, darling, I'm terribly sorry. You couldn't have stopped it if
you'd been here. Saxon's lawyers pretended to discover, at the last
minute, that the jury was considering evidence which had been ruled
out by the court. They took the exhibits into the jury room with them,
of course, and among the papers was one of the affidavits which was
declared incompetent."

Hazzard snapped: "Who made the mistake of mixing them up?"

"It was a deliberate trick, I'm sure of it. Saxon's attorneys shuffled
the papers around and put the incompetent affidavit in with the
admitted exhibits. No one knew it, and no move was made until the
jury was about to report an agreement. I talked with the foreman as
he went out, and he said they had a verdict of guilty ready. You've got
to look out for Saxon, Mark! He's desperate enough to—"

"To kill—and has," Hazzard interrupted angrily. "Now I'm going
after him for murder! I've found my missing witnesses, both shot
dead. Tell Trencher he'll find the bodies in the Wellington crypt in
the Kindly Light Cemetery. Get John Price on the job, Ann. I want
him to turn that microscope of his on every bit of evidence. Ask him
to report to my office at the soonest possible minute."

"Mark, please be careful," Ann Nash urged anxiously. "You know
Trencher's after your scalp. What are you going to do?"

The crackling answer was: "Get Saxon!"

Dismay shone in the girl's eyes when the connection broke. Turning, she looked out the window, at the police headquarters building directly opposite. In one of the corner offices she could see Inspector Charles Trencher at his desk. The grim veteran of the force, whose power extended through every division of the police system, was Mark Hazzard's deadly enemy. She was lifting the telephone again, to report the murder of the two witnesses to Trencher, when steps sounded in the outer office.

She paused, opening the connecting door, an indignant flush coloring her cheeks. Three men had entered with swaggering insolence. One was Humphrey Todd, the diabolically clever trial attorney who had conducted the defense in the Saxon case. The second man was Todd's assistant. The third—portly, hard-faced, cruel-eyed, smiling now with leering contempt—was Howell Saxon.

Saxon demanded: "Where's Hazzard?"

Each word significantly clear, Ann Nash answered: "He is personally investigating the murder of his two most important witnesses in your case, Mr. Saxon."

Saxon stared defiantly. "I've got a message for Hazzard."

"I'll take it."

"It's this." Saxon's eyes narrowed insolently. "I'm going to prove Hazzard's used trumped-up evidence against me. I'll show he's faked affidavits and bribed witnesses. I'll prove *he's* responsible for the disappearance of Lewis and Crawford, because their testimony would have been in my favor. I'm going to break him for it. Tell him that!"

The girl answered levelly, coldly: "Every word you've said is a lie."

Saxon countered gratingly: "It's a promise."

He strode from the office with the other two men following. Ann Nash's eyes were widened with concern when she turned back to the desk. As she raised the telephone to report to Inspector Trencher, she shuddered at the memory of Saxon's evil leer and the threatening glitter in his eyes.

ELECTRIC TORCHES gleamed inside Wellington crypt. The dead men lay on the chill marble floor, side by side, with their bonds removed now. Uniformed men kept guard outside while Mark Hazzard stood in the door, grimly watching the start of the official investigation.

Ann Nash's call to Trencher had brought the homicide squad, the medical examiner, the official photographer and the criminologist,

John Price, to the cemetery. Flashing bulbs had recorded the scene on a series of films. The preliminary examination of Dr. Autumn was completed. With painstaking care, Price had supervised the wrapping of every milk bottle in newspaper, so that all latent fingerprints would be preserved. Every crust of bread had been collected. The scores of cigarette ends had been swept into a container. Price was examining the strips which had been used to bind the prisoners when Hazzard stepped alertly to his side.

"Can't hope for much," the criminologist said. "Whoever came here to feed these men was certainly masked, and he must have used gloves. The scraps of bread won't show anything, and the cigarettes are a brand that millions smoke. These pieces of cloth are the best bet. Something was ripped up to make them. It's very ordinary material, but—"

Hazzard urged: "Don't overlook the slightest possibility, Price."

Price murmured: "Dust. It's getting to be more and more valuable as evidence. You know the procedure, Hazzard? I'm going to put these pieces of cloth in a bag, and beat them with paddles. I'll do the same with the clothes those men are wearing. I'll take the dust that collects in the bags, and examine it under a microscope. It may tell a very interesting story."

He went on, absorbed, as Hazzard intently listened:

"There's dust on and in everything. The dust in these strips of cloth may tell where they came from. If I find tiny wood splinters, for instance, it may mean it came from a carpenter shop. Coal particles would mean something else. Various kinds of earth, mixed, might make a valuable clue. I'll get at this right away, Hazzard, and let you know what I find."

Hazzard insisted: "It's our best bet, Price—tiny bits of dust too small for the eye to see. Go after it for all it's worth!"

He strode grimly from the crypt, along the path to the gate. While waiting for the arrival of the police, he had telephoned for a wrecking crew and a taxi. His roadster was still out of commission, but the cab was waiting in the road. As he climbed in he snapped orders that sent it whirring toward the city.

Hazzard's temper, as fiery as his red hair, was a force he was obliged to fight in order to think clearly. The news of Saxon's crafty legal trick had set his blood to pounding hotly. He steadied himself, while the cab sped, with an unalterable determination to pin the guilt of a double murder on Saxon.

Hazzard faced baffling difficulties. It was certain Saxon himself had not fired the fatal shots. Neither Hazzard nor Carey had glimpsed the face of the guilty man. There was scant hope of finding substantial evidence to link Saxon with the crime. Yet Hazzard was sure the men had been kidnaped at Saxon's orders, that they had been killed at the moment of discovery in order to silence them. Hopelessness weighed upon Hazzard even while the strength of his dogged purpose grew.

His orders sent the taxi into a quiet side-street in a new and ostentatious residential district. Ordering the driver to wait at a corner, he walked quickly along the block in which the home of Eric Miner, Saxon's associate in the real estate racket, was located. As he went through the shadows, a uniformed figure appeared quietly and fell into step with Hazzard.

"No sign of Miner, skipper."

Hazzard paused, peering at the dark windows of Miner's house. "It was either Miner or Fancy Phalon at the cemetery, Danny," he said quietly. "My job's to prove one or the other is a murderer, with Saxon behind him."

Carey's head wagged. "Looks like a dead end, skipper. If it was Miner, he didn't come back here."

"Then we've got to try a new lead." Hazzard's fingers snapped impatiently. "Shift over to Saxon's place. Watch him, and keep in touch with my office. It's a million to one gamble, but we've got to play it."

"On the job, skipper."

HAZZARD TURNED back while Carey hurried to a light car standing at the curb. His orders sent the taxi weaving toward the courthouse. Glancing up, as he climbed the broad stone steps, he saw a light in the window of Inspector Trencher's office in the headquarters building across the street. He strode quickly to his office. When he opened the door an exclamation of astonishment stopped him.

Frank Mayton, chief assistant of the district attorney, rose from his desk in surprise. "How'd you get back so fast? Ann went out of here in a hurry, a few minutes ago, because you phoned her to meet you right away in St. George."

Hazzard felt a chill of apprehension. "I don't know anything about that. I didn't call her, Frank."

"That's strange," Mayton stared. "I was here when she answered the phone. She said you wanted her to take an important statement—new evidence in the Saxon case—and she left in a rush."

Hazzard's eyes sharpened. "It's a trick," he declared. "Fake call! Where'd she go?"

"She didn't tell me any address—just St. George. It was an hour after you phoned about the murders. She must be there now."

"Frank, listen!" Hazzard knuckled the desk as his temper flared. "Ann's in danger. Saxon's capable of anything. It's probably too late now, but get on the phone and try to trace that call. If that's no good, camp right here until we have some word from Ann. I'm seeing Trencher."

Mayton was spinning the dial of the telephone when Hazzard hurried out of the office. New anxiety stung his heart as he hastened down the stairs. Quick steps took him across the street, into headquarters, to the door of Trencher's office. He rapped, swung in, and strode directly to the inspector's desk. Trencher studied him with dark, ominous eyes as he snapped:

"I want Eric Miner and Frank Phalon picked up on suspicion of murder."

Trencher asked in a drawl: "Think they bumped off your two witnesses, Hazzard?"

"I'm positive one of them did. I want them brought in here and grilled. Force them to open up, Trencher! I'm not after Saxon for fraud any more. I'm going to send that crook to the chair."

Trencher asked shrewdly: "Got any evidence against 'em, Hazzard?"

"I'm counting on you to get a confession. If you don't, I'll beat it out of the guilty man myself!"

"Here, here." Trencher gestured disapproval. "There's no good in going off like a firecracker. Take it easy, Hazzard. We're on the job. If one of those men killed Lewis and Crawford, and if Saxon is implicated, we'll get 'em in good time. Your temper's going to get the best of you some day if you don't watch yourself."

Hazzard insisted hotly: "Pick those two men up and grill the truth out of them!"

"Why, we can't do that, Hazzard, and you know it. We can't treat 'em like crooks with records. Miner's supposed to be a respectable business man. Phalon was tried for forgery once, but he was acquitted. Their lawyers would be on the job in half a minute, and stop us cold. Your blood pressure's up so high you're not thinking straight."

Hazzard's fist smashed down. "Trencher, listen! We understand each other. You're satisfied to stick to the rules of the book and take your time. I'm not. Tonight I'm out to get a filthy crook in any way possible. If I make a slip, you'll have my scalp for it, but that's not stopping me. I'm going to get Saxon—do you understand that—in spite of you!"

Trencher's black eyes smoldered. "Take it easy, Hazzard," he warned again. "You've given yourself a dangerous job—being judge and jury and executioner all in one. These cases are matters of prescribed law, and we've got to stick to the procedure. I'm too old in this game to be reckless. If I had to collar you for running wild—for dealing out your own idea of justice regardless of the statutes—that would be too bad, Hazzard. Too bad."

Hazzard straightened. "Let's have the truth, Trencher," he retorted heatedly. "You're waiting for the chance to get me. You pretend to be a tired old plodder while you're actually quick and sharp as a fox—and absolutely relentless. You've promised yourself to break Mark Hazzard, and you're not going to stop until you do it. I'll take my chances on that. Right now I'm demanding you to pick up two men because it's certain one of them is a murderer."

Trencher gestured again. "All right, all right, Hazzard," he drawled. "I'll take care of that—in good time."

"We'd have a killer's confession tonight," Hazzard burst out, "if you were half as determined to get him as you are to get me!"

HIS STORMING temper had become a fury that utterly possessed him. He stood with fists clenched, blood pounding in his temples, while Trencher studied him. The moment of strained silence was broken by the jangle of the telephone bell. Trencher reached for the instrument casually as Hazzard wrathfully turned away. A startled exclamation from Trencher stopped him on the sill.

"Murder?"

The inspector's dark eyes lifted, hard light glinting in their depths. "Hold on a minute, Hazzard," he suggested throatily. "You'll be interested in this news." He listened over the line while Hazzard came back cold with a foreboding of disaster. His rushing breath caught when Trencher looked up to say quietly:

"Yes, you'll be interested, Hazzard. One of your suspects—Frank Phalon—is a dead man at this minute. That's not all. Your secretary, Ann Nash, is being held in St. George for murdering him."

Hazzard snapped: "What!"

"Ann Nash," Trencher repeated slowly, "is being held by District Attorney Shepard in St. George for having killed Frank Phalon."

A new surge of heat beat through Hazzard's brain as he snatched the telephone. He heard, in answer to his crackling demand for information, the peculiarly hollow voice of Amos Shepard, District Attorney of Essex County, in which the city of St. George was located. Hazzard's swift, angry questions were interrupted when Shepard cut in: "She's here now if you want to speak with her."

"Put her on the phone!" Hazzard stood rigid, stunned, until he heard the voice of the girl he loved. "Ann! What's happened, darling?"

Her answer was a plea. "They won't believe me, Mark. I went there because you phoned me to come—and they found me with him. He was dead, but—oh, I've told them the truth over and over, but they won't listen. What can I do, Mark? Won't you come and tell them—"

"Coming!" Hazzard answered ringingly. "Coming, Ann!"

While Trencher watched, a slow smile curving his lips, Hazzard crashed the telephone down and strode swiftly from the office.

CHAPTER III

EVIDENCE DESTROYED

A **TAXI SPED** Hazzard out of the city and across the invisible line that separated King's and Essex Counties. It whirled through the outskirts of St. George and bucked to a stop in front of the mouldering courthouse. Hazzard tossed a bill to the driver and hurried toward the door where two uniformed patrolmen were standing. The tempest of his temper was still raging when he thrust in.

Ann Nash hurried from a chair near the imposing desk in the corner. Her face was pale and her eyes frantic. Her lips trembled with anxiety as he took her hand snugly, and turned to the man behind the desk. Amos Shepard, who held the same position of authority in Essex County as Mark Hazzard in King's, rose to confront him.

"Before I hear a single detail of what's happened, Shepard," Hazzard snapped, "let me tell you that this girl was tricked into coming to St. George by a fake telephone call. There's absolutely no doubt she's been framed."

Shepard was coldly hostile. "To my mind, there's no doubt she's guilty of homicide. I'm going to press the case because the evidence warrants it." He gestured pompously. "Remember, Hazzard, you have no official status here. You're a private citizen in this county, a friend of Miss Nash, that's all. I'm under no obligation to explain this matter to you. I suggest you keep that in mind—and calm down."

Hazzard strove to control his anger. He knew Shepard as a politician of the old school, a cog in the party machine that controlled Essex County. His tactics, opposed in principle and substance to Hazzard's, were to endeavor to obtain as many convictions as possible regardless of the merits of the cases handled. He was known to be resentfully jealous of Hazzard's admirable record for fair play. His attitude now was an open challenge.

"Very well, Shepard," Hazzard answered tightly. "Exactly what is the evidence in this case?"

Shepard answered icily: "It's quite simple and conclusive. An hour ago a complaint was telephoned to police headquarters that there was a disturbance in Apartment 5D of the Rossmore Arms apartment house. The report said a violent quarrel was in progress. A radio car was instructed to investigate. The two patrolmen found a woman hurrying from the apartment just as they arrived. It was your friend, Miss Nash. She had a gun in her bag which had just been fired. Frank Phalon was lying in the room, shot dead."

Hazzard asked the girl tensely: "Were you in there, Ann? What actually happened?"

"I went there because it was the address I was given on the phone, when I thought it was you calling, Mark," she answered with weary despair. "I heard a shot after I knocked. I went in because I still thought you were there—you might be hurt. Frank Phalon was lying in the bedroom, and I caught a glimpse of a man climbing off the fire-escape platform."

"Did you see his face, Ann?" Hazzard asked alertly. "Did you recognize him?"

"I think it was Eric Miner."

"Miner!"

"I'm not sure, but whoever he was, he'd just killed Frank Phalon, using my—"

Shepard interrupted coldly, gesturing to a tiny automatic lying on the desk. "This is the weapon found in Miss Nash's purse. She admits it is her property. It is the same caliber as the gun used to kill Phalon. Our ballistics expert will prove the bullets in Phalon's body came out of it, you may be sure. Don't touch that, Hazzard!"

The sharp command stopped Hazzard's hand as he reached for the automatic. He stared at it in dismay. There was no possible doubt that it was Ann Nash's. Hazzard had given it to her a year ago, together with a permit for carrying it. His haggard eyes, meeting the girl's begged for an explanation.

"I don't know how it got there," she said faintly. "I haven't carried it for weeks. It must have been stolen from my apartment, because I found it on the floor, beside Frank Phalon. It's the only way I can account for it, Mark. Please believe me!"

"It's preposterous that anyone shouldn't believe you, Ann!" Hazzard snapped. "Is that all you're building your case on, Shepard—that gun? Ann didn't even know Frank Phalon. What possible motive could she have for—"

"We're led to believe," Shepard interrupted again, "she knew him intimately. Phalon's apartment has been thoroughly searched. In a drawer of his desk, we found these letters." He gestured toward a packet of them lying beside the automatic.

"All of them are signed with the name Ann. The handwriting agrees exactly with specimens she just wrote here in this office. They are indiscreet love letters, showing that this girl was carrying on a secret affair with Phalon months ago."

Hazzard exploded: "That's impossible!"

Ann Nash said in almost a whisper: "I didn't write them, Mark. You know I didn't."

Shepard continued pompously, while Hazzard's hands clenched: "What happened is perfectly clear. Miss Nash's clandestine affair with Phalon was over, and she was desperate to get back the letters she wrote him. She went to his apartment tonight to demand them. His refusal led to a violent quarrel. During it, she shot him. She was caught almost red-handed."

HAZZARD LEANED tensely across the desk. "Look at the facts, Shepard! If you investigate this thing fairly, you'll find that the report of the disturbance in Phalon's apartment was made before Ann Nash arrived there. She told you of seeing a man running off the fire-escape—probably Eric Miner—but you're ignoring that. You say she went to Phalon's apartment to get these letters, but you found them in the desk, not in her bag. If she'd committed murder to get them, she wouldn't have started away without them. If—"

"Having just killed a man," Shepard countered frigidly, "she was too terrified to look for the letters systematically. Her search was interrupted when she heard the squad car men coming to the apartment. You're wasting your time, Hazzard. This girl is going to face a charge of murder and nothing you can say will help her."

"Listen!" Hazzard's knuckles rapped. "You're overlooking one other vital fact. Ann Nash denies writing these letters—and Frank Phalon was once tried for forgery!"

"The authenticity of these letters, Hazzard, is a matter for expert graphologists to decide at the trial. A judge and jury will consider the weight of this evidence. I warn you that if you attempt to interfere—"

Blinding anger drove Hazzard's fist to the desk. "You can't bring this girl to trial for a crime she didn't commit! Not without evidence!"

"Don't touch it!"

Hazzard moved with desperate swiftness. Shepard's warning came as he snatched the letters and the gun from the desk. A wild, unreasoning fury possessed him as he backed away. Even as Shepard bounded toward him, he ripped the forged letters through. He struck out once, and his fist slammed hard between Shepard's eyes. Ann Nash stifled an alarmed cry when Shepard sprawled down. Hazzard whirled, thrusting the torn paper and the automatic into his pocket, and bounded to the door.

The two patrolmen at the door turned, startled, as he thrust out. He was sprinting toward the building entrance when Shepard staggered from the office. A bellow: "Arrest that man!" burst behind him while he bounded down the steps. He sped along the dark street knowing the patrolmen were rushing in pursuit.

Amos Shepard, turning angrily back, reached swiftly for Ann Nash's wrist. The anguished girl had started out. She recoiled from Shepard, twisting desperately to free herself as Shepard's hand closed on her arm. She thrust him back frantically, and felt his fingers slip loose. He lost balance when he struck a chair, and tottered down. When he straightened, and spun to the door, Ann Nash's footfalls in the hall were a quick, disappearing rhythm.

Shepard snarled with anger as he strode to his desk. He jerked up the telephone and snarled "Headquarters!" While his connection went through his narrowed eyes searched the floor and made sure no fragment of the incriminating letters had dropped from Hazzard's hands. His face was an ugly, fixed mask until a voice answered over the wire.

"Shepard calling—radio alarm!" he snapped. "Flash all cars! Ann Nash, secretary of District Attorney Mark Hazzard of King's County, is a fugitive. Brown hair, brown eyes, about five feet four, no hat or coat. Wanted for murder! To be brought to my office under arrest immediately she's taken!"

He was breaking the connection when heavy footfalls sounded near the door of his office. The breathless man who hurried in was one of the two officers who had rushed after Hazzard. He reported in a burst of breath:

"Looks like he's slipped us!"

Shepard's lips pressed to a hard, cruel line. He lifted the telephone again. He harshly demanded: "Connect me with Inspector Trencher!"

MARK HAZZARD peered warily through the rear window of the cab as it followed the dark by-street. He had escaped the vicinity of the Essex County courthouse through a series of unlighted alleys. He had slipped unseen into a taxi and, after circuiting St. George, had changed to another. Now past the dividing line, he was being carried rapidly to his office.

A quick word to the driver stopped the cab in the middle of a deserted block. He slipped out and walked back to the cover of a manhole. Slipping his fingers into the grips, he swung it away. He smiled grimly as he brought the torn letters from his pocket, ripped them again, and dropped the bits into the black hollow. Ann Nash's automatic splashed after them into the water of the sewer. Hazzard replaced the cover, hurried to the cab, and repeated: "King's County courthouse!" as he climbed in.

When the taxi stopped at the familiar broad steps, he glanced up to see Inspector Trencher's office in headquarters lighted. He hurried to his own. Frank Mayton rose from the desk as he entered.

"No luck on tracing the call, Mark," Hazzard's assistant reported. "Dial phones make it next to impossible. I've heard about Ann. It's a damned outrage, and you can count on me to the limit."

"Thanks, Frank." Hazzard took up the telephone as he answered. "I'm a hot-headed fool who's got himself into a devil of a mess." He spun off the number of headquarters. "No need of your getting involved, old man." Into the transmitter: "Give me the lab."

Mayton had gone when John Price's voice responded. The criminologist answered Hazzard's questions with: "We've got something important, Mark, but damned if I know what. The microscope shows one strange element in the dust I got out of the strips the two men were tied with. There is pollen from the common plants in the cemetery, but there's also a spore I can't identify. I've never come across it before. Some sort of fungus, perhaps, but—"

"If I can find where the spore came from," Hazzard broke in, "it will prove the cloths came from the same place, won't it?"

"Absolutely," Price assured him. "It points directly to the murderer or an accessory—but it's absolutely worthless unless you can find the source of the spore."

Hazzard promised grimly: "I'll find it! Hold that evidence!" He was replacing the telephone, eyes narrowed shrewdly, when the bell rang. He asked: "Hello?" and tightened apprehensively when the only answer was silence. "Hello!" he demanded again. His breath stopped when he heard a hushed question:

"Are you alone, Mark?"

"Ann!" Hazzard tightened. "Where are you?"

"I'm calling from a pay station in a rooming house in St. George. They're hunting for me, Mark. What can I do?"

Hazzard smiled wryly. "Good girl," he whispered. "Listen. Call a cab from the phone you're using now. Try to get to my place. You know the room above the garage where Danny stays. Keep out of sight there. Listen, darling. I'm going to get you out of this."

"There's no one else I can count on, Mark."

"Keep your chin up. Don't talk any longer. Some one's coming. I'll see you—"

Hazzard broke the connection as the entrance opened. Inspector Trencher sauntered toward him, black eyes smoldering. A queer smile played on Trencher's lips as Hazzard rose.

"I've orders to arrest you, Hazzard. Too bad, but Amos Shepard is doing it all according to the book. The charge is destroying and removing evidence, and being an accessory to the crime of murder."

Again Hazzard fought a surge of wrath. His lips quirked bitterly as he answered: "You're holding the trumps, inspector. You warned me my temper would get me into trouble, and now it has. Shepard is justified, except for one important detail. He has first to prove Ann Nash is guilty of murder."

Trencher retorted: "In the meantime, you'll be kept in a cell."

THE TELEPHONE jangled during a strained pause. A cautious voice asked: "Hazzard?" He waited with growing concern until it whispered on: "Don't try to trace this call. You'll find out who I am when the time comes. There's an eye-witness to Phalon's killing to prove the girl didn't do it. Got that much?"

Hazzard alertly turned the receiver away from his ear and gestured to Trencher to listen. "Go on!"

"You've got certain important evidence in the Saxon case. It's a small price to pay for getting hold of that eye-witness. I'll give you about an hour to think it over. When I call back, your answer's got to be final. Remember, you're deciding whether or not the girl goes to the chair."

The connection broke. Hazzard peered into Trencher's enigmatic eyes.

He rounded the desk with each word ringing:

"Unlike Shepard, you've got a brain that works, inspector. Listen to this. Eric Miner and Fancy Phalon helped Saxon kidnap my two key witnesses. Saxon's legal trick to end the trial was already planned. Framing Ann—including the letters Phalon forged—was all worked out, as a means of forcing me to abandon the case entirely. That's the strategy of a devilishly clever crook."

Trencher said: "You're guessing."

"Keep listening, Trencher. My finding Crawford and Lewis drove them to desperate measures. Miner killed the two men to silence them. Phalon didn't know his own death was part of the plan to frame Ann, but tonight he got it. Miner again—also to keep him quiet about the kidnapings. That must have been Miner on the phone a minute ago. The only way I can clear Ann is to pin the killings on Miner and Saxon."

"You haven't a particle of evidence, Hazzard."

"I want a chance to get the evidence! Shepard's only interest is in convicting Ann. The police department here is out of it because the murder was committed across the county line. I'm the only one she can count on for help. Trencher, if I don't find that evidence, if I'm kept from it by Shepard's throwing me into a cell, that girl will go to the chair—innocent!"

Trencher asked shrewdly: "Are you suggesting a bargain between us, Hazzard?"

"I am! I give you my word of honor I won't leave the state. I'll surrender to Shepard at the end of a reasonable period of truce." Hazzard's knuckles rapped imperatively. "Promise me a free hand, Trencher, and I'll agree to any stipulations you set upon me!"

The inspector's eyes craftily narrowed. He drawled, studying Hazzard's glinting eyes: "Maybe we can strike a bargain—but it'll be on my terms."

"State them!"

Trencher slowly smiled. "I've always wondered about your past,

Hazzard. I know your record for about ten years back, but no farther. I've always had the idea, somehow, you're hiding something. Maybe I'm wrong. If I am, meeting the terms of my bargain will be easy, Hazzard. Easy."

The face of the district attorney had gone white. He demanded huskily: "Well?"

"I'll give you twenty-four hours. If you've cleared Ann Nash at the end of that time, you'll be out of this mess yourself, and you'll have cracked a murder case. I'll be the first to congratulate you. But if you haven't—" Trencher's tone lowered ominously—"before I turn you over to Shepard, to answer his charges, you'll give me a complete, truthful history of yourself, up to the time when you first appeared in this city as Mark Hazzard."

Hazzard straightened. "You're still out to get me, aren't you, Trencher—and you think that'll do it!"

"Of course," Trencher went on, gesturing disarmingly, "there may be no reason at all why you should hesitate to tell me. But that's my bargain, Hazzard. You won't get your chance unless you agree to it. The deadline is midnight tomorrow!"

Hazzard smiled wryly. He extended his hand. As Trencher gripped it he said: "I agree. My word of honor." They searched each other's eyes, avowed foes, hands still clasped—and in Trencher's, Hazzard saw a gleam of grim triumph. He strode quickly from his office, his face lined with despair. The door slammed behind him.

CHAPTER IV

HOURS OF TRUCE

THE TAXI left Mark Hazzard in front of his modest home. As it ground away, he walked cautiously along the drive to the garage. Heart heavy with dread, he stepped past the second of his cars, a coupe, into the deep darkness of a corner. He raised a counterweight which lowered a hinged ladder from the ceiling. Looking up into the gloom he called softly:

"Ann?"

"Mark—"

The anguished whisper hurried him up. He pulled the flight back into place before he snapped a switch. Ann Nash, her face white, her lips trembling, came to him quickly. She flung her arms around him; she clung close and sobbed. He listened alertly, suspicious that the place was being watched, until she stepped back. She sank exhaustedly into a chair and asked imploringly:

"Is there any way out, Mark?"

"There is, and I've got to find it—within twenty-four hours." He bent over her intently. "Listen, Ann. Aren't you sure the man you saw on the fire-escape platform was Eric Miner? Isn't there something else you might tell me that will help clear you?"

She answered in a distressed whisper: "I'm not sure. There isn't anything else."

He straightened, his anxiety a gnawing pain. "Then it's strictly up to me. You've got to stay here, out of sight, until I find something." He repeated the word bitterly: "Something! Whatever it is, I've got to find it fast!"

The girl watched with wide-eyed concern as Hazzard stepped on the hinged flight and forced it down. He descended into darkness, and pulled the counterweight to close the opening in the ceiling. His heart pounded as he backed the coupe into the street. Glancing around sharply, to make sure he was not spotted, he sped.

He let the car roll along the curb, ignition off and lights out, when he neared the home of Eric Miner. Braking in deep shadow, he glanced at the glowing dial of his watch. The anonymous voice on his office phone, demanding the Saxon evidence, had warned: "I'll give you about an hour to think it over." The hour was almost up when Hazzard slipped from the car and drifted into the grounds of Miner's house.

He glided soundlessly to a lighted window. Gazing past drawn drapes, he saw the thin-faced Miner seated at a desk. Miner's fingers were drumming a nervous tempo. Hazzard watched tensely until, abruptly, Miner rose and strode from the room.

The click of the entrance latch sent Hazzard skirting into the shelter of a garden. He saw Miner cross the porch and stride through the gate. Hazzard rose as his man turned toward the lighted windows of a block of stores two streets away. He sped from the grounds, darted across the street, and went in Miner's direction, keeping in the deepest darkness. He was out of sight when Miner entered a pharmacy.

Through the window, Hazzard saw the suspect shoulder into a telephone booth. He hurried to the entrance, hat pulled low to shield his face. Sidling into the booth next Miner's, he heard the telephone dial clicking. Hazzard studied the dial in his own booth. Then the dial in the next booth whirred again. Alertly Hazzard counted the clicks.

Miner was calling the office of the District Attorney of King's County—and there was no answer.

Hazzard slipped out, hurried by a new, desperate hope. Miner was still in the booth when he left the store. He walked swiftly to the house. He opened the door, listened alertly, and concluded the house was unoccupied. He went to the desk Miner had left and began a grim wait.

A long minute passed. Hazzard had determined upon a gamble when steps sounded on the porch. The door opened and closed. A man's stride sounded in the hallway. Eric Miner paused just over the sill, his narrowed eyes startled, shocked motionless by sight of Hazzard.

"What the devil are you doing here?" he demanded.

Hazzard answered levelly: "Investigating three homicides. That means two alibis are necessary for you, Miner. If you haven't got them, you're going to headquarters and be booked on charges of first degree murder."

Miner snapped: "You can't bluff me!"

Hazzard smiled. "Where were you at the time Lewis and Crawford were killed tonight? Where were you when Phalon got it? Shall I tell you? First in the crypt at the cemetery, then—"

"You can't prove that!"

Hazzard parried: "Would I be taking you into custody, Miner, if I weren't absolutely sure of myself? Would I be risking a heavy damage suit for false arrest? I leave that to you to decide. The rest is up to the judge and jury. You're coming to headquarters with me now."

Miner stared appalled, speechless.

"You've got just one chance of saving your skin, Miner," Hazzard went on shrewdly. "You can turn state's evidence against the man who planned the kidnapings and the murders. That offer of clemency is withdrawn the moment you leave this house. Are you going to talk?"

Miner still stood mute with dismay.

Hazzard carried his strategy through. "All right, Miner. It's your one chance to escape the chair, but if you don't choose to take it—come with me."

He grasped Miner's arm. Miner followed him into the hall, staring, dazed. A mumbling sob broke from Miner's lips as Hazzard reached for the entrance knob. The door was opening when Miner suddenly tore away. He wrenched from Hazzard's grip, whirled, started back with a crazy lurch.

The library door slammed shut an instant before Hazzard reached the sill. He shouldered against the panels and felt the resistance of a bolt. He spun back and dashed into the adjoining living-room. He sped to the connecting door and gripped the knob. He was twisting it, tensing to thrust through, when the blast of a shot froze him.

A stifled moan came from the library. A sliding, thumping sound followed. Hazzard pushed in, breath caught, and stopped short again. A puff of smoke was floating near the desk lamp. A dark stain marred the blotter. Miner had rolled off the chair. The fuming revolver lay loosely in his hand. The bullet had cleaved the top of his skull.

Hazzard stood staring, dazed and heartsick. He was scarcely conscious of the quick, heavy tread on the porch, of the hammering at the entrance. Taking a bewildered step into the hall, he saw two startled patrolmen coming in. Their prowl car was panting at the curb, visible through the door. Seeing Hazzard, they paused. One of them blurted:

"We were passing the house and heard a shot."

Hazzard could not answer. He made a stunned gesture toward the library and moved past. The two squad car men stared as he went out of the door and walked blindly into the night.

ANN NASH'S eyes turned again, with dread fascination, toward the clock that indicated twenty minutes past eleven. Her red mouth was drawn with anxiety. Her eyes were dulled with exhaustion. Each endless minute of hiding, in this secret room above Mark Hazzard's garage, had been an ordeal. Since her frantic escape from the office of the District Attorney of Essex County, more than twenty-four hours had passed.

She rose, startled, as a metallic creak sounded. The hinged flight of stairs swung downward as she watched in alarm. A sigh of relief came from her tight throat as she heard Mark Hazzard's whisper of reassurance from the darkness below. His face shone dark-lined as he climbed up. She went into his arms and clung close.

"Chin up, Ann," he said softly. "There's still a chance."

The despair in his eyes brought her new pain. "I'm not thinking of myself, Mark. I'm so tired of hiding. I'd give myself up if it weren't for you. Darling—Trencher gave you until midnight tonight, and it's not long now."

"Forty minutes!" Hazzard said grimly. "Forty minutes left to crack a murder case, without a single bit of admissible evidence!"

The girl said softly: "He's been trying to get something on you for months. What is it, Mark? Won't you tell me? You know I'll understand."

"Not yet!" Hazzard said vehemently. "He hasn't got anything on me yet. Ann, I can't tell you what Trencher suspects, what he's trying to find out about me—that doesn't matter. I've done my damnedest to try to clear you, and I've gotten nowhere. Worse than that, I've destroyed your best chance to prove the frame-up."

"How, Mark?"

"Because I bluffed Miner, and the bluff worked too well. I was trying to get him to talk, and he killed himself—the one man who could tell the truth about Phalon's killing. He did it—I'm absolutely certain of that—but he'll never confess now. Oh, Ann, I'm sorry! There's only one hope now—only one."

Breathlessly: "Yes, Mark?"

"Proving somehow Saxon was behind it. Showing he was an accessory to the kidnapings and the murders. I'm sure of that, too, but it's not enough. I've got to have legal proof—evidence that a court can admit and a jury consider. There's nothing, Ann—nothing but some strange kind of spore, found in the dust taken from the clothes that bound Crawford and Lewis—little things too small for the eye to see, that we haven't been able to trace."

The girl said, her voice steady, her eyes clear: "I'm not afraid, Mark."

Hazzard smiled bitterly. "I gave Trencher my word of honor that if I hadn't cracked the case by midnight tonight—" His fists clenched as he repeated: "My word of honor!" Abruptly he turned, tearing his eyes from the girl's anguished face, and went down the stairs.

He strode into his house, sat at his desk, stared haggardly into space. The long day had mocked him with repeated defeats. All his logical reasoning, all his investigating, had come to a dead end. Dan Carey had telephoned hopeless reports. Hazzard was still haunted by the necessity of finding legal evidence—evidence admissible in court, strong enough to withstand the attacks of Saxon's shrewd defense attorneys. The hands of the clock on his desk were creeping inexorably to the hour of doom.

THE PURR of the telephone aroused Hazzard. Lifting the receiver, he heard Inspector Trencher's crafty drawl. Despair stung his heart as he listened to a damning pronouncement:

"It's eleven-thirty, Hazzard. You have exactly half an hour. If you haven't found evidence to clear Ann Nash by that time, I'm going to hold you strictly to your promise."

Hazzard snapped: "I intend to keep my word, Trencher."

"All right. I want that statement of your past at exactly midnight."

"You'll have it at exactly midnight," Hazzard retorted sharply, "if I've failed. But I still have thirty minutes, Trencher!"

Thirty minutes. The words rang ironically in his mind as he pushed the telephone away. He had labored fruitlessly on the case all day and all night. He had already spent forty-seven times thirty minutes in a desperate endeavor to clear Ann—in vain. His heart ached with hopelessness as he turned to the typewritten stand beside his desk. Thirty minutes—and the world of Mark Hazzard would collapse into chaos around him.

As he stared at the keys, he thought of Dan Carey. The disaster

Hazzard faced would engulf not only the ex-cop, but the girl he loved. Why hadn't Carey telephoned for more than an hour? Hazzard wondered while he fed a sheet of paper under the roller. He lifted leaden hands. Each click of the keys was a blow that rocked the foundations of his existence.

To Whom it May Concern:

This statement is a true record of the man known as Mark Hazzard, now District Attorney of King's County.

I was born Dennis Grant. My home as a boy was in Philadelphia, Pennsylvania. I left it at the age of fifteen with high hopes of somehow wresting a fortune from the world. My mother lived alone while I went from job to job, trying to get ahead. Perhaps it was my violent temper, my insistence upon just treatment in the face of a world of injustice, that kept me penniless. It was not long before Dennis Grant became little better than a hobo.

On the night of December 24, 1924, I rode the rods from New York City to Philadelphia. My purpose was to spend Christmas with my mother. The freight train reached the Philadelphia yards, and I was crawling off the car, when I heard a shot. I was seized by the yard crew and placed under arrest. The charge brought against me was second degree murder.

It does not matter now that I am entirely innocent of the murder. I never saw the man I was charged with killing. I never touched the revolver that killed him. He was a yard detective and I believe he was shot by another ride-bummer in a desperate attempt to escape arrest for vagrancy. There was and is no evidence to support this theory. There was absolutely no way at the trial, and none now, of proving I am innocent of the crime.

Mark Hazzard stared at the lines that damned him. His fingers tapped the keys again:

I was tried and convicted. The judge of the Criminal Court pronounced a sentence of life imprisonment upon me. I managed, by a desperate attempt, to escape from the courtroom by throwing a chair through a window and climbing out. For weeks I was hunted as a fugitive.

At last, when the search died down, I was able to find a job as checker on the loading dock of the packing plant in this city.

I spent my nights studying law. The injustice of my arrest, trial and conviction haunted me. I was driven by an unconquerable determination to make the law an instrument of true justice. I was finally admitted to the bar as Mark Hazzard.

My record as district attorney speaks for itself, but it is of no importance in light of the fact that I am a fugitive and a convicted murderer. The conviction stands. The sentence of life imprisonment still remains to be served. As Dennis Grant, I am surrendering myself tonight to Police Inspector Charles Trencher.

The lips of the District Attorney of King's County pressed grimly as he read the statement that condemned him for the rest of his days to prison. With cold hands he signed the name of Mark Hazzard to it, and below, that of Dennis Grant. He folded the sheet, slipped it into an envelope, and sealed the flap. Across the face of the envelope he scrawled the name of Inspector Trencher.

Precious minutes had ticked by. Mark Hazzard reached for the telephone. He dialed the number of police headquarters and asked in a hollow tone for Trencher's office. When he heard the inspector's drawl, he said levelly:

"My statement is prepared and signed, Trencher. I will put it into your hands, as promised, at precisely midnight, if by that time I have failed to find evidence to prove Ann Nash innocent of murder. I gave you my word of honor and I'm keeping it."

Trencher insisted quietly: "Midnight, Hazzard. Not a minute later."

Hazzard answered grimly: "It's here, Trencher, at my home. Will you come? I'll deliver it to you at twelve o'clock sharp—if I have failed."

Trencher promised: "I'll be there, Hazzard. I'll be there!"

The connection broke. Hazzard sat rigid, numb, staring at the inscribed envelope that contained his self-written warrant of doom.

CHAPTER V

INVISIBLE EVIDENCE

A QUICK STEP at the rear of the house startled Hazzard. He hurried from his desk. The trim figure of Ann Nash was silhouetted at the open entrance. She hurried toward him anxiously and spoke in a rush:

"Danny's on the phone, Mark. On the private line. He's got something important."

Hazzard half turned back, intent upon getting the statement from his desk, but a quick glance at his watch urged him into a quick run toward the garage. He dashed up the hinged flight, into the secret room. The girl's rapid footfalls followed as he snatched up the telephone.

"Danny!"

Carey's words sped over the line. "Skipper! I'm in Saxon's place. Inside his house—understand?"

"Go on, Danny!"

"I've hunted all over the grounds, trying my damnedest to find some unusual growth that might have given off the spore Price found, but it's no good, skipper. There are only ordinary plants and flowers in the gardens. They don't prove anything. Saxon went out a minute ago. The servants are away, so I slipped in on the chance—"

"Search that place, Danny!"

"Right, skipper. First thing, I'm going to hunt in the cellar. I've seen lights down there tonight, but when I looked in the window, Saxon wasn't in sight. There's something strange about it. Saxon might be coming back at any minute, but I'm not going to stop until I find—"

"The cellar!" Hazzard interrupted. "That's it! Price said the spore might be from some kind of fungus. Watch yourself, copper! You know if Saxon catches you in there, it will mean the chair!"

"I'll risk it!"

180

"Get to work, Danny! I'm coming over there now. Leave the rear door open so I can get in. Coming!"

Hazzard whirled from the phone. As he sped down the stairs he called to the alarmed girl: "Stay there, Ann!" With desperate urgency he climbed into the coupe. He backed quickly along the drive, spurted into the street, whirled past the first corner. He was pressing the accelerator to the floor boards when a sudden realization chilled him.

The statement! He had left it on his desk, marked with Trencher's name. The house was open. Trencher had promised triumphantly: "I'll be there—at midnight." Hazzard fought a wild impulse to turn back, but a glance at his watch tightened his anxiety. The zero hour was not long away. Each moment was precious. He kept the gas pedal pressed down.

Intersections flashed past. Hazzard's horn blared other cars aside as he sped in the direction of Howell Saxon's estate. Once he was near it, he drove more quietly. He swung to the curb near the drive and ducked out. His blood pounded in his ears as he skirted across a broad lawn to the rear of the immense house.

Saxon's place flaunted wealth. The money he had tricked from modest owners had enabled him to build this estate, far greater than any of his victims'. Spacious gardens framed the walks and fountains. The grounds were silent as Hazzard went cautiously past lighted windows. He paused at the rear door, nerves singing, and listened.

Gambling that Saxon had not returned, he entered quietly. Lights were burning in the luxurious rooms along the broad hallway. Hazzard did not disturb the silence of the house as he sought his way to the cellar entrance. A door beneath the winding stairs was standing open, a bright shaft fanning from it. Hazzard glided down and called anxiously:

"Danny!"

A whisper answered. A rasping sound, as of a rusty hinge, followed. Hazzard descended into a huge, cement-walled cellar, and saw Dan Carey hurrying from a far corner. Carey's face was white, his eyes gleaming. He gestured wildly as he blurted:

"Over there, skipper! Tunnel behind that door. Look at this!"

HE THRUST a cloth bag toward Hazzard. Hazzard peered at it intently one brief moment. The fabric of the bag was ordinary cotton. To the naked eye it revealed no possible connection with the strips which had been used to bind the kidnaped witnesses. But the dust in its threads? The inexorable pressure of time would not allow Hazzard even to complete the thought. He rolled the bag as he crossed toward the iron in the corner of the cellar.

"I got it out of there, skipper! The damnedest thing I've ever seen!" Carey blurted as he followed. "Maybe we can prove—"

Hazzard whirled, jaw clenched, eyes blazing. "Listen, Danny! I'll handle this alone. Go back to my place in a hurry. On the desk in my office you'll find a sealed envelope addressed to Trencher. Trencher's on his way to the house now for it. If I haven't got anything by midnight, he's entitled to have it—but not until then. If he gets hold of it, it's the end of me, Danny—understand that?"

Carey's stare widened. "I'm on my way, skipper!"

"If I don't get word to the house by midnight, I'm bound to let Trencher have it. If I've cracked this case in a few minutes, Danny— and if Trencher gets that envelope anyway—it's all over. Go ahead, copper!"

Carey started for the stairs. He stopped short on the bottom step. He looked back, face turning whiter, and whispered:

"Listen, skipper."

A sound came from above. It was a metallic rattle. A dull thump followed it. The rhythm of footfalls moving across the floor above Hazzard's head was a warning that stopped his breath.

Carey spoke under his breath: "Saxon's back!"

Hazzard urged: "Get out of here without his seeing you, Danny— if you can!"

He stood motionless, frozen with apprehension, as Carey crept up the basement flight. Saxon's footsteps were shifting into one of the rooms above. They paused, and a rattle of papers came through the open door as Carey neared it. Hazzard anxiously watched the ex-cop glide through, and into the hallway. He remained motionless until another slight sound came from the rear of the house—then the stealthy closing of a door.

Carey was out.

Hazzard took quiet steps toward the corner of the basement. An exultant hope filled him as he carefully gripped the rusty handle of the iron door. He drew the slab open with infinite care. Each rasp of the corroded hinges was sharp as a warning cry in his pounding ears. He listened to the movements of the man in the room above, while he opened the way inch by inch.

He drew his fountain-pen torch from his pocket as he slipped through. He glided into the air that was cool and heavy with moisture, carrying a peculiar rich odor. The beam of his light played along an earthen wall. He saw several other bags, like that rolled under his arm, before the spot turned upon an electric switch. He snapped it and stood tense in the glare, peering along a tunnel that led deep under the grounds.

Amazement filled him when he saw that the passage branched into others. Each was broad enough to pass an automobile, with footpaths leading between carefully tended beds of earth. Garden tools stood against the walls and, at intervals, mounds of fertilizer. Hazzard stared amazed at row after row of weird growths in the sectioned plots—mushrooms!

They grew in clusters of buff-white and orange, of various strange shapes, as far as Hazzard could see along the tunnel. He hurried ahead, and found that each branch was cultivated. Here, in the damp darkness, he knew, where the fungus growths flourished, Howell Saxon had practised an unusual hobby. And here, in the rich air, a strange spore must be floating, depositing a brown-black, invisible dust upon everything in the passages.

Hazzard turned back with heart pounding triumphantly. He was nearing the iron door when a gritting step—a heel grinding on cement—brought him to a startled stop. He straightened as an exclamation of astonishment sounded, and a shadow moved at the opening of the passage. Howell Saxon paused, peering in.

They stood motionless a moment, eyes narrowed, studying each other like wild animals about to leap. Saxon's cruel face hardened into a mask. Hazzard's eyes blazed victoriously during the moment of silence. He made no move—until Saxon's hand swung swiftly.

The stocky man sprang to the door, intent on slamming it shut, as he jerked a revolver level. Hazzard's hand closed on the cold butt of his Webley at the instant Saxon fired. Two blasting reports echoed along the tunnel. Two slugs slashed into the bare wall and sprayed earth. The revolver cracked again as Hazzard leaped.

Hazzard's Webley spat. The bullet spanged near the edge of the closing door. The black bore of Saxon's weapon was staring in at him. He was directly in the line of fire when he flung himself against the swinging slab. His Webley cracked again, beaded upon Saxon's upper arm. A gasp and a jerk told him his bullet had sped true.

Hazzard thrust out as Saxon whirled into a crazy run toward the stairs. A line of red spots marked the way Saxon went. He fumbled the revolver into his left hand and twisted back as Hazzard ran after him. The wild swiftness of the shot clashed with Hazzard's answering bullet. The district attorney staggered to a stop, blinded by the pain of torn flesh near his temple, red streaming down his face.

Hazzard flung himself savagely. Saxon's gun glittered up for another shot. Hazzard struck crazily at it as the explosion rocked through the rich air. Hurling himself against Saxon, grabbing at Saxon's wrist, he struggled while a crimson haze filled his eyes. He clamped his hand across the hammer of the revolver, wrenching back desperately. A gasp broke from Saxon's lips as the weapon twisted from his fingers.

Hazzard flung the gun aside. Quick, gritting footfalls were moving toward the stairs. He sprang forward again, groping. A blow caught him on the jaw an instant before his arms clasped around Saxon's body. He was dragged up two steps. Another backward lurch by Hazzard destroyed Saxon's balance. They spilled down and sprawled on the concrete floor.

DRAGGING UP, Hazzard holstered his automatic. Through the red blear he saw Saxon, eyes widened with terror, striving to rise. Hazzard let him draw up. Saxon began a savage blow as Hazzard drove his fist out. Hazzard's knuckles clicked squarely to the point of Saxon's chin. The stocky man moaned, dropped to his knees, melted down.

Hazzard gripped his shoulders and drove a command through closed teeth: "Talk!"

Saxon rolled and crawled. Again Hazzard straightened, and let him rise. He staggered up and backed to the cold wall as Hazzard advanced. The eyes of the district attorney gleamed with merciless determination. The whiteness of his clenched fists was marked by blood seeping from his torn knuckles. He commanded again: "Talk!"

Recoiling in terror, Saxon attempted another blow. Hazzard's straight-arm drive flattened him against the wall. His head sagged and his eyes rolled. He covered his head with his arms and moaned.

"Listen, Saxon! You helped Miner and Phalon kidnap my two witnesses. You're an accessory to the murders. I've got proof of it now! I'm going to nail you for that—and for planning Phalon's killing with Miner. I'm going to beat the truth out of you, Saxon!"

Saxon groaned: "Don't hit me!"

Hazzard pressed his head up. "That's the truth! You tore up a bag from your mushroom cellar to make strips to tie those men with. A microscope will prove that in court. Spore, Saxon—tiny mushroom spore in the fibers! Your clothes are covered with them now. Everything in the tunnels is full of them. You haven't got a chance of escaping the chair!"

Again Saxon pled: "Don't hit me."

"I'll beat the life out of you if you don't talk!"

Saxon attempted to twist away. Hazzard's clubbed fists drove him back. Three terrific blows sagged Saxon against the wall. He cried imploringly: "Yes! Yes! I admit it!"

"You'll make a written confession, Saxon!"

"Yes!"

"You'll admit you framed Ann Nash. You'll say Miner murdered Phalon! You'll swear to every detail of it, Saxon."

Saxon mumbled: "I'll do anything if you'll let me alone—let me alone!"

Hazzard gave him a push that spilled him to the floor. He caught Saxon's arms and dragged him to the iron door. Saxon squirmed on the floor while Hazzard jerked a cloth bag from its peg—a bag used for transporting picked mushrooms from the cellar—and ripped it to strips. He worked over Saxon swiftly, skillfully. When he straightened, Saxon was bound.

A glance at his watch filled Hazzard with a wild desperation. He sped from the tunnel, clanked the door shut, made sure the latch was firm. He bounded up the stairs, hurried into Saxon's library. He scarcely breathed as he lifted the telephone and spun a number.

It was that of the instrument in the room hidden above his garage. He waited in torture until the distant bell rang. In agony he stared at his watch—at the little black hands indicating one minute of twelve o'clock midnight.

THE PURR of the bell in the hidden room brought a quick response from Ann Nash. Even as she raised the receiver, she heard Mark Hazzard's voice rushing.

"Ann! Quick! Has Danny come?"

"No, Mark!"

"Is Trencher on the place?"

"Wait!"

Ann Nash listened intently. In the street she heard the purr of a motor. She turned quickly to the dormer window and jerked the curtain aside. She saw that a car had stopped near the driveway. Inspector Charles Trencher was alighting from it. He was striding toward the front entrance of the house when the breathless girl turned to the telephone.

"Trencher's here now!"

"Stop him, Ann! Don't let him in the house. Don't let him touch an envelope I left on my desk. If he does—" Hazzard's voice rasped off. "I'm on my way!"

The girl left the telephone and hurried down the hinged flight of stairs. As she ran from the garage, she heard Trencher knocking at the front door of Mark Hazzard's home. She scarcely heard another sound that came out of the darkness—the gritting of tires in the alley behind the garage. She hurried along the side of the house, to the porch.

Trencher was opening the door. The girl sprang up. She thrust him back, grasped the knob, then turned to confront the inspector defiantly. His ominous black eyes stared. His lips quirked wryly at the girl.

"Hello!" he drawled. "I think you know the police are looking for you. The charge is murder."

Ann Nash declared: "You're not going in!"

Trencher's dark eyes sharpened.

"No? That means there's something inside you don't want me to get my hands on. Perhaps you don't know about the little bargain between me and the district attorney. He promised me a statement at exactly midnight. It's midnight now."

The girl insisted frantically: "You're not going in!"

The inspector drawled: "Why not? I'm here at Hazzard's invitation. His agreement is backed by his word of honor. He can have only one basis for refusing to give me that statement now—cracking the murder case. Has he done that?"

Ann Nash blurted: "I don't know! But you're not going in. I won't let you in!"

"You can't keep me out now," Trencher drawled. His head lowered belligerently. "You're under arrest, young woman. Stand aside!"

The girl's tight hand on the knob was a challenge. Trencher seized her arm. She moaned a protest as he forced her fingers to loosen. She strove to keep her place, but Trencher's greater strength overwhelmed her. He backed her against the wall. Tears streamed from her eyes as he gripped the knob.

"I know that statement's in there," he said grimly. "I'm going to get it right now. I promise you it's the end of Mark Hazzard."

He stepped quickly into the vestibule. Ann Nash struggled to follow him, but he pushed the door shut against her, and clicked the bolt into its socket. Turning, black eyes smoldering, he stepped into the room which served as Mark Hazzard's office. The bright light of the desk lamp shone upon an envelope. From the doorway, Trencher could see his own name scrawled across its face.

He stepped toward it—and stopped short, startled. His eyes jerked up at a quick movement in the darkness beyond the open door of the next room. He glimpsed the glitter of a gun, the shine of widened eyes above a white mask. His hand swept toward his service gat.

Splashing flame tore the gloom in the next room. The bullet crashed into the desk lamp. Spattering fragments of glass flew about Trencher as he crouched down in sudden darkness. He fired once. The flame of his gun limned a man moving swiftly near the desk—a man whose face was covered with a tightly drawn handkerchief. The blinding glare of another shot sent Trencher stumbling into a corner while broken plaster dropped.

He sprang up, flinging himself toward the connecting door. Breath burst from his lungs in an expletive of rage as he collided with it. The masked man had shut it while spinning from the room. Trencher snapped it open, plunged through into darkness. He leaped toward the open rear entrance. As he bounded into the yard, the snarl of a motor came from the alleyway.

Trencher slashed his legs through the hedge. A swift black shadow was moving along the alley—a car traveling at increasing speed. Trencher aimed with deadly steadiness. His finger jerked off the trigger when a flash and a roar challenged him. The bullet gashed the air at his ear as he ducked. When he aimed to fire again, the car had whirled out of sight into the cross-street.

THE INSPECTOR loped back. He was nearing the rear entrance when a car shot into the driveway. The coupe bucked to a stop under slammed brakes. Trencher straightened grimly as Mark Hazzard ducked out. He lowered his smoking service gat when Ann Nash hurried to Hazzard's side. They went toward Trencher together.

"According to the terms of our bargain," the district attorney said tightly, "you are not entitled to any statement from me, Trencher."

The inspector's narrowed eyes shone like black diamonds. "You're not going back on your word, Hazzard. You haven't cracked your case, and your promise to explain yourself stands. I saw that statement on your desk, and I'm going to read it now!"

He thrust into the house. Hazzard followed him anxiously, at Ann's side, into the forward room. A match scratched, and Trencher held the flame high. He clicked a switch that brightened a globe on the ceiling. He turned to the desk, reaching—and paused, jaws clenched.

The inscribed envelope was not where he had seen it. He glanced at the floor, dragged chairs aside, and searched beneath the desk. When he rose his eyes were gleaming dangerously.

"You can't get away with a trick like that, Hazzard—having somebody steal the statement from under my nose! That's what your word of honor is worth, is it?"

Hazzard turned from the next room. He had snapped another switch and had looked around quickly. He smiled tightly as he answered:

"Evidently I've been visited by a burglar, inspector. The drawers where I keep my silver are empty. My wall-safe is opened and rifled— see for yourself. Probably the burglar took the envelope thinking it contained money. That's a matter for the police, isn't it?"

Trencher answered grimly: "Whether that statement was stolen by a burglar or not, I'm going to hold you to your word."

Hazzard's eyes glinted. "I'm keeping my word. I'm holding to my bargain. You're getting no statement from me, Trencher, because the Saxon case is cracked."

Trencher challenged: "That's another bluff!"

"That, also, you can judge for yourself," the district attorney retorted. "You'll find Howell Saxon bound, as my murdered witnesses were bound, in his mushroom cellar. John Price's microscopic examination will prove the strips used to blind Crawford and Lewis were once a bag used in Saxon's place. He's confessed to me that he planned to frame Ann, in order to get the evidence I have against him in the fraud case, and he'll put it in writing. You'd better take the case in hand without delay, Trencher."

Trencher glowered. Again Hazzard looked about the adjoining room. When his glance turned upon Ann Nash, he saw her red lips form a soundless name: "Danny!" He suppressed a smile. He knew that before long the stolen silver would be in the secret room above the garage. He knew Dan Carey would return the envelope to him unopened. Profound relief surged through him as he faced Trencher.

"It appears, inspector," he said quietly, "that Mark Hazzard, District Attorney, is going to send Howell Saxon to the chair."

HAZZARD STOOD at the desk of inspector Trencher in police headquarters. Ann Nash was at his side. They intently watched the bruised face of Howell Saxon while Saxon slumped in a chair beside Trencher's. The inspector's black eyes followed the lines of Saxon's confession. An all night grilling had elicited every detail of the crimes from their instigator.

Trencher slapped the pages in front of Saxon, proffered a pen and drawled: "Sign that."

There was no sound save the scratching of the pen while Howell Saxon's trembling hand scrawled his signature on each page of the confession. He dropped back when the task was completed. Two men in civilian clothes witnessed the document as Saxon despairingly covered his face with his hands.

Amos Shepard, prosecutor of Essex County, standing behind Trencher, made a gesture of dismissal. Blinking at Hazzard he said:

"All credit to you. You saved me from sending an innocent girl to the chair. Considering that, I—I'll overlook the matter of assault and battery. The evidence you made away with, of course, isn't necessary now. The confession is enough."

Hazzard bowed. "I hope we will be in accord on the next case, Shepard!"

Trencher, folding the confession, grimly rose. He saw Mark Hazzard smiling—but he did not smile.

"Mr. District Attorney," he said quietly, "Saxon's trial will be only a formality. You've made certain he'll be convicted. What's more, you've kept your bargain and your word. We're not exactly friends, you and I, but—I owe you my congratulations."

"After all, inspector," Hazzard chuckled, "though we serve the law with differing methods—we serve it together."

He clasped Trencher's extended hand. Ann Nash stood at his side, her hand warmly on his arm, as Hazzard's eyes studied the inspector's. The smoldering darkness he saw was a threat that must forever haunt him. But now—with Ann cleared, with Dan Carey safe in the secret room, Mark Hazzard smiled.

During the night the written statement that the district attorney was in reality Dennis Grant, convicted murderer, had become scattered ashes.

BOOK V

TERROR TRIBUNAL

*Labor racketeers crossed the trail of
District Attorney Mark Hazzard, fiery
petrol of justice. They killed a man but
left no corpse. And it was on this point of
law that Inspector Trencher red-taped the
hands of Mark Hazzard. When Hazzard's
manhunt led to a beautiful woman, he
could make no arrest. For that woman
was Inspector Trencher's own daughter.*

CHAPTER I

KILLERS FOR HIRE

THE SAVAGE voice of a stampeding mob roared around the Equity Cooperage Works. Torches flared in the evil faces of men who ran in packs, wielding clubs, hurling stones. Windows crashed while patrolmen, whistles shrilling, massed against the overwhelming attack. Rifles spat at the police squad and service revolvers cracked in answer. The howling onslaught struck the building like a sudden storm.

Shattered glass flew into the dark office two stories above the blood-spotted street. The burst wrung a stifled cry of alarm from a girl huddling against the far wall. An older woman, crouching behind a desk, moaned with anxiety. At the inner door three men stood, their eyes haggard in their bearded faces. For two days, while merciless "strikers" patrolled the streets, they had not dared go to their homes. Hungering, exhausted, they had been kept prisoners within the plant.

A sudden flare at the window startled them. A twirling torch, flung up from the street, spun inward through the broken window. Sparks burst from it as it struck the floor and rolled. Dripping oil spread flame in a pool as the women sprang away in terror. The eldest of the three men spun to a fire-extinguisher bracketed outside the door and hastily released a hissing stream. The glare etched deep lines in his face—until the torch lay sputtering and dead.

John Dillworth, owner of the coöperage works, grimly turned back to the hall into which the women had fled.

"You can't stay here any longer," he told them huskily. "It's too dangerous. My car is in the garage just around the corner. We'll try to make it before they get any worse. We might be able to slip out the side door without being seen."

Another sudden crackle of glass sounded. Sharp thuds told of

Roberta moved back from Leroy, saying: "I won't help you!"

bullets striking into the wall. The rioters in the street were firing in. The click of the bullets urged a desperate nod of assent from the two trapped women. Dillworth turned to direct the executive who had spent two anxious days in the plant:

"We'll have to move fast. I'll lead the way. Both of you follow Miss Moore and Miss Webster. Once we're out, we'll have to get them to the car no matter what happens to us."

They went quickly along a dark corridor and descended a flight of iron steps. From all points in the huge works the crashing of glass and the impact of hurled stones warned of the growing violence of the mob. They paused tensely at a narrow door. Dillworth, drawing the bolt, opened a crack to peer out. His breath caught while dark-visaged men ran past. When they were gone he urged:

"Now!"

He stepped out first, with the two women close behind him. The two fearful men followed quickly. As the door latch snapped into its socket, they started across the curb, refugees of terror. The sharp sound was a signal that brought rushing figures out of the darkness. Evil-faced men with clubs in their fists, guns brandishing, sped toward them at a shout:

"They're gettin' out! Show 'em we mean business!"

John Dillworth whirled. "Get them to the garage!" He choked it out as he flung himself at the attacking rioters. The other two men, gripping the arms of the women, sped past the curb while Dillworth parried the slashing clubs with upthrown arms. Again, as the savage blows forced him back, a snarling voice commanded:

"That's Dillworth—give it to him good!"

A merciless blow tottered Dillworth to his knees. A revolver butt was swinging toward his head when a hand struck it aside. He peered up to see a lithe, fast-moving man flinging himself into the fight. An automatic spat a warning and a clear voice snapped:

"Get back!"

DILLWORTH DREW up as the square-shouldered young man thrust the rioters back. He wheeled, dazed, as the same crackling tone commanded: "Try it—you can make it now!" Two more quick shots, flying skyward, scattered the grim-faced mobsters. When the young man with the automatic glanced back, the street was clear and Dillworth had vanished past the corner—safe.

Mark Hazzard, red-headed, two-fisted, the youngest district attorney in the history of King's County ever to battle the People's cases, smiled tightly.

Approaching the embattled plant, Hazzard had swung his car sharply to the curb to make way for prowl cars that came screaming. He had glimpsed the dark door opening cautiously, had realized that the prisoners in the plant were attempting an escape. Now, fury flashing in his eyes, his Webley leveled, he hurried past his car.

He caught sight of known faces among the leaders of the snarling crowd—floaters with criminal records, hireling thugs. This destructive violence was the culmination of weeks of strife engineered, Hazzard knew, not by the striking coöpers, but by paid terrorists. No recognized labor union had taken part. Mercenary agitators, fomenting the strike, had made workers jobless and then preyed on them. Professional strikebreakers, precipitating an industrial war, were thinking only of the thousands to be earned. Hazzard saw them earning their blood money tonight—betrayed workers sprawling with broken heads, falling with bullets in their bodies, paying their lives to traitorous ringleaders.

A riot call was rushing cordons of police reinforcements into a mounting battle.

Guns spat, whistles screamed, glass crashed, while Hazzard hurried into a drug-store a block away. The spinning dial of the pay telephone connected him with his office. "Ann!" he exclaimed when his efficient, tireless secretary answered: "Is there any report from Danny?"

"A minute ago, Mark," Ann Nash told him quickly. "He followed Hallan to a house at Sixty Edgecombe Street. He says Sorley's there, too. It's what you suspected, Mark—what you need to pin it on them—but please be careful! Those men are wholesale killers, and they'll stop at nothing to—"

"So far as getting those crooks goes," Hazzard said grimly, "stopping at nothing is exactly my own program. Thanks, Ann—and stay on the job."

Torch-carrying men were swarming upon the outnumbered police when Hazzard hurried back to his car. Missiles hurled from the fists of brutal-faced men at the parade of squad cars pouring toward the plant. Clubs slammed at Hazzard's car as he spun past the corner. The din echoed behind him while he sped. Possessed with a grim hope that he might find evidence to convict those responsible for the outbreak, he drove at top speed toward 60 Edgecombe Street.

A newsboy howled from the corner when a red light stopped Hazzard: "Eighty Wounded, Six Killed, Total in Strike Battles! Mayor Calls Militia! District Attorney Balked!"

THE DISTRICT ATTORNEY had been balked by hidebound legal procedure. At the beginning of the trouble, Mark Hazzard was convinced the devil's brew had been cooked by Miller Hallan, organizer of the strikebreakers, and Sam Sorley, captain of the revolting workers, in an under-cover cabal. Desperately trying to restore the impoverished workers to their jobs, Hazzard had gathered evidence to support his suspicions, and had presented it to the Grand Jury. Their decision of "no true bill" had stopped him short.

While the families of the ousted men hungered, while the plant remained paralyzed, Hazzard had sought further witnesses. He had petitioned the court to resubmit the case to the Grand Jury. Again he had been frustrated, by denial of his motion. "Insufficient evidence" were the words that mocked him. Hazzard had found himself left with no legal recourse. Now, determined anew to brand the conspiring crooks with their guilt, he was taking a lone wolf's trail of justice.

Hazzard eased to the curb in a gloomy, quiet neighborhood. The windows of the house at 60 Edgecombe Street were closely blinded. Hazzard scanned the house from the shadows, then glided onto the lawn. When he approached the garage, a stocky man moved soundlessly toward him. They stood silent, making sure they were not seen, until Hazzard asked:

"They're still in there, copper?"

Dan Carey, clad in a trim patrolman's uniform, nodded grimly. "Hallan and Sorley and two others—one of 'em a girl."

Hazzard asked in astonishment: "A girl, Danny? Who?"

"Didn't see her face. She went in with Jacques Leroy. Take it easy, skipper. Those rats will kill to keep themselves covered."

Hazzard whispered: "Keep watching, Danny. I'm going in."

Carey melted back into the shadows as Hazzard took soundless steps across the grass. At the rear entrance Hazzard paused, alertly listening. He found the door bolted. He turned to a cellar bulkhead next the porch. A padlock fastened it. Every nerve tense, he slipped the barrel of his Webley through the hasp. His muscles strained as the screws pulled from the wood. He raised a leaf, listened again, then went down.

Groping through blackness, he reached the basement stairs. With the utmost care he twisted the knob of the door at the head of the flight. Vague voices sounded as he opened a crack. They floated into the hall with a glow of light from another door directly ahead. Webley leveled, Hazzard crept toward it. Abruptly he stopped, nerves icy, staring at a girl standing in a corner of the room.

Dismay stunned him. Mark Hazzard knew all too well the unflagging relentlessness of the man whose power extended all through the police organization of the city—Inspector Charles Trencher. The crafty, unforgiving, merciless veteran of the law was Hazzard's vowed enemy. They had clashed again and again, foes by their very natures, and the battle of wits would never end until Trencher destroyed the district attorney. Hazzard peered appalled into the room where predatory crooks were meeting in secret conclave, because the girl he saw was the inspector's only daughter—Roberta Trencher!

CHAPTER II

TORTURE HEAT

IN HIS shocked astonishment, he was scarcely aware of the voice of Miller Hallan:

"Dillworth will cough up, don't worry. He can't depend on the police. It'll all be over by the time the militia get here, and he's got to depend on us. He's coming through with plenty."

The gruff tones of Sam Sorley answered: "It's time we're cleaning up and clearing out. The men want to go back to work, and we can't hold 'em out much longer. After tonight we've got to collect fast and—"

A loud knock silenced those in the room and spun Mark Hazzard. He jerked his eyes from the white-faced girl to see a shadow moving on the pane of the entrance. The tattoo again beat through the hush as Hazzard retreated. He shouldered into the darkness of the cellarway as Hallan growled: "See who that is, Jack." Closing the door to a crack, he watched Jacques Leroy stride along the hall, one hand gripping a pocketed automatic.

A bolt clicked back. Leroy jarred on his heels as the entrance thrust open. A man strode in, ignoring the jerk of Leroy's weapon. Face drawn, hands tightened into fists, he paused in the lighted doorway. The dangerous gleam of his eyes grew sharper. Tight silence held until Sam Sorley exclaimed huskily:

"Dillworth!"

Miller Hallan's ominous drawl invited: "Come right in, Dillworth. Come right in."

The owner of the Equity Cooperage Works stiffly crossed the sill. Jacques Leroy, following with eyelids drooped, kept his automatic leveled inside his pocket. When Leroy stepped in, Hazzard silently moved up. In cold amazement, during another moment of tense hush, he peered into the room. He saw Dillworth facing three men whose features had the mask-like hardness of killers.

Roberta Trencher had retreated in dismay to a connecting door. She opened it quickly, frantic to escape Dillworth's scrutiny, and vanished from sight. With cold deliberation, Dillworth removed a pair of rimless glasses from a case and pinched them on his nose, as though to study more intently the brutal men confronting him. He said frigidly:

"I have evidence enough to send you three to prison for a good many years, and I'm going to put it into the hands of the police tonight."

Concern for the girl turned Hazzard from the door. She had gone into a rear room. It was closed. Hazzard gripped the knob, turned it slowly.

He paused as Miller Hallan's threatening voice came along the hall:

"What're you talking about, Dillworth?"

Dillworth's voice rang with contempt: "My men were happy at their jobs until this strike began. I know now what brought it about. Your agitators forced it on them, Sorley—robbed them of work they wanted to keep. You, Hallan—I agreed to pay you fifty thousand dollars to break the strike you engineered through Sorley. You're vicious crooks who've preyed on my men and my business like jackals."

MARK HAZZARD eased through the door as Hallan taunted: "Go ahead, Dillworth—what's the rest?" Roberta Trencher spun to face Hazzard. Her anguished eyes widened in her pallid face. Utter despair held her speechless while the voices in the next room continued:

"I suspected it soon after I made the contract with you, Hallan. You put thugs and crooks into my men's places. They've done no work—they've only fought my men, to prolong the strike, so you can collect more thousands. It's meant death and injury and privation. I've had you watched. I've got strong, legal proof of what I say. Your being here together tonight is part of it. I'm going to make you pay for what you've done!"

Mark Hazzard listened as he went slowly to the frantic girl. He whispered: "Why are you here—with those men?" The girl's answer was a desperate shake of her head, entreating silence. He seized her hand, his eyes forcing the question. She recoiled in dismay, entreating silence—and Hazzard listened.

In the next room three leering-eyed men had drawn closer, with menacing deliberation, around John Dillworth. Hallan's lips curled coldly. Sorley's stained teeth were bared in a snaky smile. Leroy's slitted eyes were poisonous. Dillworth pinched his eye-glasses more firmly on his nose and grimly went on:

"I came here to demand that you call off the strike tonight—at once. After that, you're going to face criminal charges and—"

Hallan struck swiftly. His knuckles crashed to Dillworth's mouth. Dillworth staggered and collapsed into a chair. Instantly Hallan and Sorley gripped his shoulders, forcing him to remain seated. As Leroy's hand began to glide toward the table lamp, Hallan rasped:

"You're going to tell the D.A. things about us, are you, Dillworth? Maybe you'll change your mind. You'll find out talking hurts. The way we look at it, it'll hurt a lot."

Dillworth protested staunchly: "You can't intimidate me. I'll tell the full story—"

Again Hanan's knuckles drove. Dillworth straightened back with lips bleeding, fragments of his broken teeth glittering in the red. Quickly Jacques Leroy knocked the shade from the table lamp. The bared bulb glared blindingly as he brought it near Dillworth's face. Suddenly he thrust the sizzling hot globe under Dillworth's chin and pressed it hard.

Dillworth choked in agony. Fumes wisped across his contorted face as his skin scorched. Mercilessly Leroy pushed light against Dillworth's throat while Hallan and Sorley held the plant owner motionless. The tortured man's face went white as his scalding throat wrung out a strangled cry.

"How about it, Dillworth?" Hallan sneered, bending close. "Talking's going to hurt, ain't it? It's going to be lots easier to keep quiet. What do you think about that now?"

Dillworth gasped: "I'll tell it all!"

Suddenly Leroy dropped the light. His lean face twisted into a mask of fury as" he jerked his automatic out. Sorley and Hallan backed, baring their guns. Dillworth, rendered strengthless by the torment in his throat, remained slumped in the chair as they shouldered through the door. Their weapons raised to the tortured man's heart....

Mark Hazzard, in the next room, had heard Dillworth's choked moans of pain. Roberta Trencher shrank from him with a whimper as he took swift steps toward the hall, Webley glittering. Another groan sounded as Hazzard jerked the door open and whirled to the adjoining room. Through the doorway he saw Dillworth struggling up, eyes closed in agony. Then—shots!

Explosions blasted in the front room. Bullets screamed through the connecting door. Appalled, frozen, Hazzard saw Dillworth's face become a red horror. Glass splinters flew as the plant owner's eyeglasses split into fragments. One of his eyes became a sightless hole. Dillworth poised, masked in crimson, then spilled back. And in the next room fast footfalls sounded—killers fleeing.

HAZZARD BOUNDED to the door through which the bullets had streaked. In the glow from the street he glimpsed the lean face of Jacques Leroy. Leroy, his automatic wisping smoke, gasped the name of the district attorney. He sprang into the vestibule as his automatic flashed blinding flame into Hazzard's eyes.

The bullet slashed past Hazzard's head. He leaped aside. Black shadows blotted over the door. Hallan and Sorley crowded out, guns gleaming. A withering fusillade, crashing across the hall, forced Hazzard to retreat. He leaped to the rear room, firing as he moved, and slammed the door.

Heels hammered the hallway. Voices rasped. Hazzard, opening the door a crack, was driven back by a slug that sent splinters flying from the jamb. He glanced around to see Roberta Trencher gripping the table, staring wildly. From somewhere outside came a scream. It was repeated while Hazzard backed to the girl and gripped her arm.

"Neighbors have heard the shots. You've got to get out. Where's your car?"

The girl stared wordless. Hazzard's quick glance around told him the only exit was the door barred by the killers' guns. He snapped the light out, strode back to it. The girl moaned in the darkness as he eased it open. He leaped across the hall, glimpsing black movements at the entrance. It slammed shut as he started toward it.

Through the pane he saw a man ducking behind the wheel of a sedan sitting in the driveway. Two others were hurrying toward it, carrying a limp body between them. When Hazzard slipped out, a gun seared the darkness. The entrance pane shattered behind him. Two more savage shots forced him to leap back. He whirled into the gloom as a snarl sounded:

"Get that girl!"

FAST FOOTFALLS in the grass told him one of the men was running toward the rear of the house. Hazzard sped to the back door. Easing out, he snapped: "Danny! Stop him!" Near the garden a black figure moved through black shadows. Hazzard's gun cracked out a defiant bullet. Spitting flame answered. He stepped back again, grimly intent on guarding the girl, as a motor began to roar.

Hazzard ran along the hall. Reaching the front porch, he saw the sedan whirling into the street, one door gaping, a man pulling in. As it whined around the corner, headlights appeared in the opposite direction. The speed of the approaching glare warned Hazzard it was a prowl car. Concern for Roberta Trencher again took him quickly into the house. He saw her, still speechless with anxiety, venturing from the room.

"The back way!" he ordered. "You can't let yourself be found here. Get out before those men come in!"

One agonized moment she searched his eyes. Then she ran wildly, sobbing, to the rear door. She hurried out as the brakes of the prowl car squeaked at the curb. Hazzard followed her, looking back to see two uniformed men hurrying to the shattered entrance. She fled into the black alley behind the house. As her swift steps receded, Hazzard hurried toward the garage.

"Danny!"

Breathlessly out of the gloom: "Okay, skipper!"

"Did you get the number of that car?"

"Didn't get a chance, skipper!" Carey gasped. "Bullets started coming so fast—"

"Get out of sight!" Hazzard ordered tightly. "The cops are in the house now. Go back to your room and wait for a call!"

A cop warned away from the police! Dan Carey had no legal right to wear his trim patrolman's uniform. Once he had been one of dogged Inspector Trencher's most promising men, but a charge of murder had stripped him. District Attorney Mark Hazzard had convicted him of the crime, had sent Carey up the river with a sentence of death in the electric chair—but, instead, the ex-cop had become Hazzard's assistant in the task of meting out a justice higher than the law.

His duty as district attorney had forced Hazzard to present damning evidence against Carey at the trial while in his heart he believed Carey innocent. He had felt grim satisfaction at the news that, while being taken to the death house, Carey had made a desperate and successful break for freedom. The searching police, under Inspector Trencher's relentless orders, had failed to recapture him, but the sentence still hung over him—death in the chair if ever he were caught.

Carey had paid Hazzard complete loyalty since the night the district attorney had found him starving in an alley and befriended him. Certain Carey had been framed, knowing no legal proof of his innocence could ever be found, Hazzard had, instead of turning him over to the police, sheltered him from the manhunt. Carey's was a danger Hazzard now shared. The revelation of the secret that the District Attorney of King's County was harboring a fugitive would mean the end of Mark Hazzard.

Hazzard whispered: "Keep watching, Danny. I'm going in."

Carey sped into the shadows of the alley as Hazzard returned to the rear door. Two uniformed men were in the hall. They stared amazed at Hazzard as he hurried into the room where the girl had gone. He had seen a telephone there; now he snatched it up. His swift words flashed an alarm to police headquarters which in turn broadcast lightning orders to every prowl car in the city. His temper sped hot blood through his body as he strode into the forward room. He stood gazing at red spots on the rug, at a faint twinkle of broken glass, as his mind hummed:

"Roberta Trencher—here! Inspector Trencher's girl—mixed up with a gang of killers!"

CHAPTER III

KILLER'S
STALEMATE

MARK HAZZARD paused just inside the door of Inspector Trencher's office in police headquarters. The cold dismay lingering around his heart was strengthened by sight of a girl standing beside the inspector's desk. Roberta Trencher's eyes pled with Hazzard's during a tight moment—pled for silence. She waited in agony as Hazzard went in slowly.

He had expected to find her here. Coming to headquarters, following a quick and fruitless search for the killers' sedan, he had seen Roberta Trencher's roadster parked in front of the building. She studied him with desperately imploring eyes as she strove to control her agitation.

Inspector Trencher—a massive man, with eyes like black diamonds, whose lazy manner masked a brain that could think fast as lightning—smiled slowly and said: "Our hot-headed district attorney has something on his mind, Bobby. Better run on home. I'll be along later."

The girl went hesitantly to the door. A slight, frantic shake of her head as she went out beseeched Hazzard to be silent. He faced Trencher as the door closed, and saw the inspector still smiling quizzically.

"Mixed right into the middle of more trouble, aren't you, Hazzard?" Trencher drawled.

Hazzard answered grimly. "I was after evidence, and I found it. Hallan and Sorley together tonight—that proves criminal conspiracy. I all but saw murder committed in that house. I want a warrant, inspector, charging Jacques Leroy and Hallan and Sorley with first degree homicide—for killing John Dillworth."

Trencher sat up. "Dillworth? Where is he?"

"I saw Dillworth shot," Hazzard hurried on. "I saw Leroy with a smoking gun in his hand. Dillworth walked into that house, but he was carried out. They killed him because he'd found evidence enough to send them up the river. If they haven't disposed of the body by this time—"

Trencher interrupted with elaborate patience. "Hazzard, you're letting your impulsiveness run away with your better judgment. You know very well I can't issue a warrant for those men on the basis of what you've just said."

Hazzard's temper flared. "I tell you I saw—"

"You didn't see the actual shooting. You're not certain Dillworth is really dead. There can't be a murder charge without the *corpus delicti.* As for the rest, of course Hallan and Sorley and Leroy will flatly contradict you. Your word against theirs, that's all—and theirs backed up by the cleverest lawyers in town. As usual you're going off like a bunch of firecrackers.

"Calm down, Hazzard. If Dillworth's been murdered, I want to get the killers as badly as you do. That's my job. It's been my job for longer than Mark Hazzard has lived." A sly light came into his eyes. "I'll get 'em—in due time, and if your charges are substantiated. Until then, my hands are tied."

Hazzard straightened, striving to control his anger. "I promise you Dillworth is dead—because a crook like Leroy shoots to kill. It was cold, deliberate murder. Are you going to sit back and do nothing— give the crooks a chance to hide the body so we'll never find it? If you do, we'll never have a case. You've got to go after them—"

"Take it easy, Hazzard," Trencher drawled. "The prowl cars are on the job. If we find Dillworth's dead body, we'll take the usual steps in due time. I've got men at the house now, and maybe they'll find a clue that'll give us a case. Why, you haven't any corroborative witnesses, Hazzard. You can't even back up your statement that those men were at the house, can you?"

HAZZARD SMILED bitterly. He could back up his statement with two witnesses—but both forced silence upon him. Dan Carey, convicted murderer, fugitive from the law—his word could never be used. Roberta Trencher, the inspector's own daughter—Hazzard could not bring himself, at least until he learned the full circumstances, to involve Trencher's girl in a murder. His eyes flashed wryly as he answered:

"I have nothing to say to that—now."

Again Trencher gestured. "There you are. No good going off half-cocked in this game, Hazzard. I've been in it so long, I've learned to take it slow and sure." He smiled shrewdly. "My way isn't yours, Hazzard, but it works. I rather admire the way you go after crooks single-handed, regardless of the regulations—but it's dangerous."

Hazzard declared levelly: "I'm going after Leroy and Hallan and Sorley until I get them, inspector—in spite of the rules of the book."

"Sure," Trencher nodded. "Sure you will. You're very interesting, Hazzard—doubly so, because you're so reticent about your past. By the way, remember the chap who was here several months ago—the man who was sheriff of Delphia County, Pennsylvania, about ten years ago?"

Hazzard peered into the ominous blackness of Trencher's eyes and said: "I remember him very clearly, inspector."

Trencher went on slowly: "Have you ever heard of a Judge Middle-brook? Old timer, Hazzard. He sat on the bench of the Criminal Court in Philadelphia ten years ago when a murderer named Dennis Grant was convicted. He tried the case. He's the man who sentenced Grant to life imprisonment. He'll be in town soon."

Hazzard's heart went icy cold. "At your suggestion, inspector?" he asked grimly.

"Just a casual visit—he's an old friend of Judge Cheever. Thought you might like to meet him."

"I shall be delighted, inspector," Hazzard answered levelly. "But until then I expect to be very busy—cracking a murder case!"

TRENCHER'S OMINOUS eyes smouldered as Mark Hazzard strode from the office. The heart of the district attorney beat heavily with dread as he went down the stairs. He realized full well the masked hostility behind Trencher's slow smile. He knew the inspector was bringing Judge Middlebrook for the express purpose of identifying the district attorney as Dennis Grant. Cold anxiety filled Mark Hazzard because—it was the truth.

Ghosts of the past rose in Hazzard's aching mind to mock him. Almost eleven years ago—it was a haunting nightmare that Hazzard could never escape. A cold night, its bitter wind piercing the ragged clothing of one then known as Dennis Grant. Christmas eve, with the Philadelphia railroad terminal covered with sooty snow. He had bummed his way home on the rods, to spend the holiday with his mother—and instead he had been thrown into a clammy cell, charged with the crime of murder.

The shot had sounded in another part of the yards. Searching men, their flashlights stabbing into his eyes, had mobbed upon Dennis Grant. Another tramp had killed the yard detective in a crazy attempt to escape arrest for vagrancy. Dennis Grant had never seen the dead man, had never touched the revolver, but he had stood trial for the homicide. Over the span of years, he could hear the crisp verdict: "Guilty!" And a solemn voice sentencing him to imprisonment for life—the voice of Judge Middlebrook.

Kaleidoscoping memories in the tortured mind of the man who had been Dennis Grant—a chair flying from his hands—the crashing window—his leap into darkness—days and nights of agony while bloodhounds bayed on his trail. Finding a job at last so that he might keep from starving while studying law earnestly night after night— building up a new world and a new identity. Mark Hazzard, the evening he was elected District Attorney of King's County, had vowed to make his office an instrument of true justice.

Now the whole existence of Mark Hazzard—all he had achieved and all he held dear—was threatened with destruction by a name that tauntingly echoed out of the past—Judge Middlebrook.

A hand seized Hazzard's arm as he went down the steps of headquarters. His aching eyes turned into Roberta Trencher's. She glanced around furtively to make sure she would not be heard. She asked in a pleading whisper:

"Mark! You didn't tell him?"

Hazzard smiled bitterly. "No, Bobby. But you'd better tell me, hadn't you—why you were there? If it comes out—"

"Don't tell him, Mark—please! Never! Don't you realize, if dad ever learns about it—what it will do to him? If it got into the papers— Oh, Mark, it would ruin my whole life. I beg you not to tell dad—or anyone."

Hazzard answered levelly: "Your father's handling this murder case. So am I—in my own way. I'm out to get Hallan and Sorley and Leroy. I'll do everything I can to keep you out of it, but you've got to play square with me and tell me why—"

"I can't, Mark! I can't!"

Tears glimmered in the girl's eyes as she hurried blindly to her car. Hazzard hastened after her as the gears clashed, but she ignored his urgent call and spurted away. Deeply troubled, he watched her roadster swing out of sight. His clear eyes clouded, he crossed to the stone courthouse and climbed to his office. As he entered, the deep lines etched in his forehead brought a worried light into Ann Nash's eyes.

"What's the matter, Mark?" she asked anxiously, hurrying toward him. "Is it—Trencher?"

He warmly took her hand, forcing a smile. "Don't worry, darling. It's something I can't tell you. Please trust me."

"There's nothing you can't tell me, really, Mark. You know I'll understand. What is it Trencher's trying to do to you? What *can* he do?"

Looking into Ann Nash's eyes, Hazzard saw admiration and pride. But if he told her he was Dennis Grant, convicted murderer, what would he see in them then? He stifled the thought, his fingers tightening on hers, his lips curving grimly.

"I hope you never learn, dear, because—" Because he yearned to keep her, as whole-heartedly as he wished to safeguard his identity as Mark Hazzard, to preserve the new world he had labored ten grueling years to build. The girl he loved and the work he must do—they were Hazzard's whole existence. "No more questions," he whispered. "Get Danny on the wire will you?"

HE SAT at his desk, fingers drumming, while Ann called an unpublished number. When Dan Carey's voice came over the secret line he said crisply:

"New orders, copper. You're to watch Inspector Trencher's home. Keep your eye on his daughter. She's probably there now. If she goes out, follow her and report. If anything new comes up, let me know right away. It's important, Danny."

"Okay, skipper," Carey answered promptly. "That's rich! Me watching Trencher's place—for you!"

Hazzard's fingers tattooed again as Ann Nash studied his anxious eyes. "Strictly under the hat, Ann—Bobby Trencher's mixed up with Hallan and Sorley somehow. Mixed right into the middle of a murder! She's spoiled and willful, but she means the world to Trencher. It'll break his heart if he ever finds out. He's absolutely merciless at his job. He's promised himself my scalp and he'll stop at nothing to get it. But he's mad about that girl. Nothing else in the world could hurt him as much as finding out about her now. I can't tell him the truth—not that!"

Hazzard's knuckles clicked to the desk. "But her being mixed up in this case isn't going to stop me. I'll keep her out of it if I can, but I'm going after that crooked crowd just the same. Going after 'em in spite of Trencher. Look at him in his office over there! Sitting at his desk, reading reports, biding his time, while killers go free!"

Hazzard's temper stirred as he peered out the window, into the inspector's office across the street. "An embodiment of all the written rules and established regulations. A man who enforces the law strictly according to the book. A disciple of the axiom that lies at the very root of our Penal code—'Give the criminal every break!' One of our most prominent business men was murdered tonight by a pack of human wolves, and Trencher sits in his office!"

THE DISTRICT ATTORNEY paced his office while his secretary watched, her rich red lips queerly quirked. He was unaware of the passing of time, until the telephone jangled. Ann Nash said quietly: "It's Danny, Mark." He snatched up the instrument to hear:

"Skipper, I've been at Trencher's place a little while. The girl's there, and Leroy just went in. Think of it, skipper—that crook daring to go into the inspector's home! Shall I—"

"Stay there, Danny!" Hazzard snapped. "I'm leaving now."

He snatched up his hat and strode to the door, Ann Nash's eyes following. He paused, looking back, first at Trencher in the opposite window, then at the girl. He asked with a mirthless smile:

"Do a bit of checking up for me, will you, Ann—without the inspector's knowing it? Find out if Judge Middlebrook of Philadelphia is coming to this city, and when he is expected. That's all."

"Wait, Mark." Ann Nash's eyes shone with a strange, clear light as her hand on Hazzard's arm brought him to a stop. "There's something about Bobby Trencher you don't know. I've realized it all along—since you first met her—but you haven't dreamed it."

"What is it, Ann?"

"She's in love with you."

Hazzard started, then laughed. "Bobby Trencher—in love with me? Nonsense, Ann! Sheer nonsense!"

Quick strides took him down the steps and to his car. His blood pounded hotly as he drove across the city. He swung into an old-fashioned, conservative neighborhood and pulled to the curb directly in front of Inspector Trencher's home. When he slipped from the wheel, he noted a blue-uniformed man standing nearby twirling a nightstick.

Dan Carey's nod said: "Still there."

Grimly, Hazzard strode to the entrance. As he raised his fist to knock, the door opened.

A thin-faced, stoop-shouldered man jerked to a stop on the sill. Hazzard surveyed Jacques Leroy with open contempt, while Leroy's narrow-set eyes squinted with consternation. His temper flaring, Hazzard thrust him back. He gripped Leroy's arm, tugged him into the living-room, faced him squarely. He glanced around once, saw no sign of Roberta Trencher, and said gratingly:

"What are you doing here, Leroy?"

The sharp-faced man straightened defiantly. "Keep your hands off me, Hazzard. It's none of your business why—"

The little veins in Hazzard's temples had begun to pulse. "Pinning a murder charge on you is exactly my business! Listen, Leroy. I have no tangible proof that you killed John Dillworth tonight. His body hasn't been found. We haven't got the bullet that killed him. We haven't got the gun you used. I admit all that—but I know you killed Dillworth."

Leroy blurted: "Stay away from me, Hazzard. I'm warning you!"

Hazzard smiled tightly. "I haven't got a case—but I'm going to have one very soon. You're going to give me all the evidence I need. Start talking right now, Leroy—or I'll beat it out of you!"

Leroy challenged: "You're forgetting where you are, aren't you? You won't do a thing to me, Hazzard. You can't bluff—"

Leroy's teeth clicked on the word. Hazzard's swift jab snapped them together. Leroy recoiled, eyes flashing threats. He swung at Hazzard. Again the D.A.'s fist smashed out. The blow spun Leroy toward the door. He staggered up, peering into the vestibule. Hazzard, grimly following, brought up short.

Roberta Trencher, lips parted in dismay, was looking terrified at Hazzard. She came into the room slowly, while Leroy smiled thinly in triumph. As Hazzard made a gesture of apology, the disconcerted light at the girl's eyes gave way to cold reproof. She said tensely:

"You've gone too far, Mark. You can't do that here—not to Jack, You've got to let him alone."

Hazzard asked softly: "Why, Bobby?"

The girl's lips pressed against words she dreaded to utter. While she stood speechless, tears flickering in her eyes, Leroy straightened with a swagger. Hazzard ignored him while he rasped:

"Don't try that again, Hazzard! If you do, you might get it where it hurts. Understand? And if you get it that way, nobody's going to touch us for it. We don't happen to be afraid of you, Hazzard, or of the cops either. You're going to keep hands off."

Hazzard retorted: "I understand, Leroy. Now you listen. I'm not keeping hands off. I'm going to see you get the chair."

"Don't try it!"

LEROY'S EYES glittered ominously as he turned to the girl. His stare made her wince like the lash of a whip. Smiling with contempt, he strode from the room. The front entrance slammed as Hazzard stood gazing in consternation at the girl. She begged again, her voice almost breaking:

"You've got to let him alone! You've got to!"

Hazzard repeated gently: "Why, Bobby?"

"Because he—he's my husband."

Mark Hazzard stood stunned. Roberta Trencher seized his arms while tears welled in her eyes. There was desperation in her breathless plea as her words rushed on:

"Dad doesn't know! Nobody knows but you! Don't you realize how frightful it will be if it comes out? Inspector Trencher's daughter married to a crook—a murderer!"

Hazzard snapped: "You little fool! Why did you marry a man like that? Why didn't you think of this before—"

Roberta Trencher's chin lifted, the defiant gesture of a spoiled, rebellious child. "Because I liked Jack—because dad forbade me to see him any more. We were married secretly, in Chicago, weeks ago. What does it matter now—why I did it? He's my husband. You've got to let him alone!"

Hazzard raged: "He's a cold-blooded murderer! You went into it with your eyes open. I told you I'll try to keep you out of it, but you've got to take it if—"

"Mark, please—please don't! I was there tonight—when it happened. Jack admitted it to me—he did it. And I've got to keep quiet. If it comes out, Mark, I'll be an accessory. They—they can send me to the electric chair for it! You can't go ahead now—you can't!"

Roberta Trencher's voice had risen to a hysterical cry. She shook

Hazzard in wild protest as tears streamed down her cheeks. She sobbed uncontrollably, turned away. He stood appalled, dazed, as she ran up the stairs. Her sobbing became a far-away sound, behind a closed door. He was turning slowly toward the entrance when a grim thought struck him. He strode to the telephone in the living-room and dialed the number of his office. When Ann Nash's voice came over the line, he asked wryly:

"Have you the information I asked for, Ann?"

"Yes, Mark. Judge Middlebrook is coming to the city as a guest of Judge Cheever. He's expected day after tomorrow. He's to call at headquarters that evening to see Inspector Trencher.... What does it mean, darling?"

Hazzard broke the connection automatically, without answering Ann's anxious question. Pausing at the entrance, he gazed up the stairs, listening to Bobby Trencher's hysterical sobbing. His heart was weighted with lead as he walked bewildered into the night.

CHAPTER IV

DEATH RAID

FOUR MEN, early next evening, sat facing the desk of the District Attorney of King's County. Mark Hazzard's urgent summons by telephone had brought them. Their faces were grave with the importance of their mission. They waited anxiously while Hazzard's fingertips rippled on the desk. The sound stopped abruptly at the opening of the door. Mark Hazzard strode toward the dark-eyed Trencher.

"You know these men, inspector," he said crisply. "I asked you to come here to listen to what they have to say. It will be enough, I promise you, to merit drastic action against Hallan and Sorley, in strict accordance to the book."

Trencher drawled: "Glad to hear it, Hazzard."

"Glad," Hazzard said dryly, "because you've made no headway? You've satisfied yourself that John Dillworth is missing, but you haven't located his body. You have evidence indicating the murder, but you're checking it thoroughly before you make a move. So far, according to your respected code of procedure, you haven't dared touch Hallan and Sorley."

Trencher challenged: "Take it easy. It'll come in good time."

"Not fast enough to satisfy me, inspector," Hazzard smiled. "That's why I've asked these gentlemen to tell you what they know. They'll give you an opening to arrest Hallan and Sorley on a charge of criminal conspiracy to defraud. Once you grab them, you can sweat the truth about the murder from them. Is that, inspector, according to the regulations?"

Trencher growled: "Go ahead."

Edward Powers, an executive of the Better Business Bureau, leaned forward to say earnestly: "Hallan and Sorley work hand in glove, though they keep it covered, inspector. We've taken pains to find out the facts, and we've got them. Sorley dupes the laborers with high promises and arranges the strike. Hallan collects twenty-five or fifty thousand for having his hoodlums break it. It's a vicious racket that has cost scores of lives—that hinders our return to prosperity. And we have strong evidence now to back up what I say."

T.M. Nugent, operator of a huge plant manufacturing wire wheels, added grimly: "Sorley is the man who engineered the strike at my factory months ago. I hired Hallan, just as Dillworth did, because I was desperate. That pair are out and out crooks, and they cost me and my men a quarter of a million, not to mention the property damage and bloodshed."

William Graw, head of a national federation of labor organizations, rose with clenched fists. "Our purpose is to further the welfare of the working man. We know the conditions in the plants here. There was no just cause for any of these strikes. We urged our members to ignore Sorley's agitators, but it was no use. This thing will go on and on, costing hundreds of lives and millions of dollars, if we don't stamp it out now!"

The eyes of Vernon Ives, an executive of the Equity Cooperage Works, blazed with indignation. "Dillworth gave me the job of investigating Hallan and Sorley. I had to do it strictly under cover because of the danger. I gave Dillworth the facts when I became certain Hallan and Sorley were working together. Hallan's books and Sorley's records will prove it. I happen to know they're kept in the same safe, inspector."

Trencher's eyes had widened. He snapped: "What?"

MARK HAZZARD spoke swiftly. "Exactly. There's only one way to get those books and records—a raid. It will be conclusive evidence. You can listen to the full story of these gentlemen if you wish, Trencher, but there's no time to waste. Tonight is the time—"

"I've heard enough!" The inspector's jaw squared. "Gentlemen, I'm a literal-minded man. I make sure before I act. But once I'm sure, I don't waste time." He glowered at Hazzard. "I'll get that evidence. I'll arrange a raid right now. I give you a promise. Within an hour we'll have those records, or be in possession of Hallan's safe. Good-night!"

The telephone jingled as Trencher strode out. While Hazzard's eyes gleamed with satisfaction, Ann Nash looked in to say: "A Mr. Carey on the wire." Rapidly Hazzard shook hands with his callers as they expressed their heartfelt thanks. They were hurrying out when he lifted the receiver to hear:

"Listen, skipper. I've been on the job right along. Until a few minutes ago the girl was staying at home. She left to go to headquarters. She's there now, to see Trencher."

Hazzard looked through the window. In the inspector's office he could see Roberta Trencher, nervously moving about. He saw her turn anxiously as the door opened. Her father's imperative gesture cut short her approach. Trencher talked, busying himself at his desk, while the girl stared. Still watching, Hazzard spoke over the line:

"She's in hotter water than ever, Danny. Trencher's going to raid Hallan's office. He's arranging it now. If Leroy is picked up and talks—" The thought pinched Hazzard's lips. "Stay where you are. I'm coming down."

His jaw-muscles bunched angrily as he ran down the courthouse steps, searching the shadows for Carey. The grim manhunt had never relented but the fugitive, trim in his blue uniform, was standing in the gloom opposite headquarters. As Hazzard paused at his side, a girl appeared across the street. Roberta Trencher, her movements anxiously quick, hurried down to her waiting roadster.

Carey whispered: "I saw her get several telephone calls at home, skipper. She's almost crazy with worry. She must have come to headquarters for some special reason and—"

"We're going to find out what it is, copper," Hazzard answered levelly. "Stick with me."

THE GIRL'S car was starting from the curb when Hazzard and Carey hastened to the coupe near the courthouse steps. Once behind the wheel, Hazzard spurted it. He swung at the corner, eyes intent on the girl's roadster, careful that she would not see him. He hung back when red beacons stopped her progress. On the corners, newsboys were shouting headlines:

"Dillworth Still Missing!"

"Strike Violence Grows!"

"Four More Killed, Twenty Hurt!"

The girl's car led Hazzard into a secondary business section. She swung past the entrance of an office building, parked in the gloom at its side. When she hurried in, Hazzard and Carey were out of the coupe, watching from an opposite doorway. Roberta Trencher stepped into an elevator cab and vanished.

"She's going to Hallan's office!" Hazzard exclaimed. "Danny, keep an eye out for Trencher. The raid will break at any minute. If that girl is caught in there—"

He broke off grimly to rush across the street. The indicator of the elevator turned downward as he fingered the button. When the cab opened he snapped orders at the attendant which sent it upward again at once. He stepped out at the eighth floor, eyes narrowed at the only door through which light was shining. *Business Relief Service* its legend read. It was the headquarters of the professional strikebreakers—and Hazzard knew the girl had gone in.

Voices drew him to the door. Hand gliding unconsciously to his Webley, he listened. He heard a breathless whisper from the girl:

"Tonight—right away. There's no way to stop it!"

Hallan's rasp answered: "You'll stop it, all right. We've got to have time to move the books out of here. Get on that phone. Call your father at headquarters. Tell him—"

"Oh, no!" the girl protested. "What can I say to him? How can I ask him—"

"Use that phone!"

The brittle snap of Jacques Leroy's voice silenced the girl. Hazzard heard the telephone dial spinning. The girl whispered: "Inspector Trencher, please." Hazzard's mercurial temper flared as he heard her words rush:

"Dad—Bobby calling. You—you mustn't order the raid tonight. Please, dad—not yet.... Because I'm here—in Hallan's office. I can't leave. If your men pick me up in the raid, don't you see— I can't explain, but—please don't do it. Please!"

Hazzard straightened as the connection broke. The man in the office uttered guttural exclamations of satisfaction. He turned, hurried to the fire-stairs. He went down them rapidly, bounding from platform to platform. Crossing the foyer breathlessly, he shouldered into a telephone booth. His finger spun the dial to the number of police headquarters and he snapped, "Trencher—quick!

"Hazzard speaking, inspector. I've been watching Hallan's office. I heard the call you just got. Pay no attention to it. It's a trick. Bobby didn't make that call. It's some woman working with Leroy. She imitated Bobby's voice, that's all. Go ahead with the raid, inspector!"

TRENCHER'S VOICE boomed. "Glad you called, Hazzard! I was stopped cold. I didn't get it, but now I understand. I'm starting out right now. We'll bag those crooks!"

"Make it fast!" Hazzard urged.

His lips curved wryly as he stepped into the elevator cage. Again it whisked him to the level of the eighth floor. Pausing in the corridor, he heard voices still speaking inside Hallan's office. The distance from headquarters, he knew, was short. A few minutes would bring Trencher's men. Easing to the corridor window, Hazzard looked down into the street to see two prowl cars quietly rounding the corner—the advance guard, following radioed orders. Uniformed men were slipping from the machines, stationing themselves near the building entrance, when Hazzard turned back.

Hazzard passed the lighted door. The next—dark—he knew also opened into the suite. He brought out his pack of master keys and expertly tried one after another in the lock. The fourth opened the way. Hazzard stepped into a glow. Light was streaming through a connecting door. He glimpsed Roberta Trencher, her face white with terror, as Miller Hallan rasped:

"He'll hold off. We can get these books out of here in a few minutes and ditch them where they'll never be found. Get busy, Jack! Watch the street, Sorley." To the girl: "You're staying right with us, sister. If they try to grab us now, you're finished."

Hazzard shifted. He saw the evil-faced Sorley peering out the window. Jacques Leroy was carefully turning the dial of an inset safe. Hallan, fingering a gun, was glaring threateningly at the girl. Hazzard was moving toward the connecting door when Sorley whirled to blurt:

"The cops're down there! Four cars stopping in front of the building now! I saw Trencher getting out of one and the others—"

A savage snarl broke from Hallan's twisted lips. As Leroy whirled in dismay from the safe, Hallan's hand slapped across Roberta Trencher's pallid face. The blow made Hazzard's temper break like a storm. The girl was quailing back when he stepped grimly into the light. His Webley flashed out as he snapped:

"Don't do that again, Hallan!"

His left hand jolted to Hallan's jaw. Hallan swayed back, arms upthrown. Sorley, whipping around from the window with slitted eyes, grabbed toward his arm-pit holster. The glitter of Hazzard's Webley paralyzed him. Hazzard's hand flashed out to Jacques Leroy's right wrist and clamped. Hallan's eyes gleamed venomously as he drew up with red trickling across his cheek.

He snarled: "Get Hazzard!"

THE SHARP flutter of a police whistle pierced from the street at that instant; Sorley, hand still poised, gasped: "They're coming up!" Whirling, Leroy snapped the corridor door open. "They're using all the elevators!" Hazzard, lips tightened, kept his automatic leveled as Roberta Trencher came frantically to his side.

"Out," he directed her tightly. "Use the fire-stairs."

Sorley's swift draw stopped his words. His automatic spat flame. The bullet slapped past as Hazzard fired. The window behind Sorley spattered tinkling fragments into the street. The shot was a signal that bared Leroy's gun. Two slugs slashed at Hazzard. Hallan dropped behind a table. The D.A. desperately thrust the girl out of sight and leaped back from the blast of murderous gunfire.

He snapped the connecting door shut. Bullets splintered through it while he rushed the girl into the corridor. Lights were flashing above the elevator doors, signaling the ascent of the cars. At the fire-stairs, Hazzard swung the door wide. The frenzied girl paused at his side on the platform. Quick footfalls sounded below. Police were rushing up the well. Hazzard ordered:

"Up!"

The girl quickly ascended two short flights while Hazzard held the door open. Plainclothes men carrying fire-axes bounded up. Hazzard ordered: "They're in there—break in!" They shouldered past, jerking up their guns. An automatic spat from one of the office doors when the elevator grilles slid open. Hazzard glimpsed Trencher springing out.

Trencher bellowed: "Smash in!"

A shattering burst. The pane of the office door cleaved. Bullets slammed across the hall. Through the jagged fragments of glass, Trencher saw Hallan crouching with a machine-gun. Hailing bullets scattered the patrolmen. Trencher blasted his service gat into the office as other guns echoed his. The tile floor showed red.

Slugs raking across the open elevator cage spun the attendant back. In terror he slid the grille shut and sent the car plunging down. The corridor panel remained open, gaping into a deepening well. Blue-shirted men sped past, seeking cover. The tattooing machine-gun exploded at them. One jerked to a stop as the line of bullets crossed his neck. Toppling, head almost severed, he spilled into the open well.

"Look out for that gun! They're coming out!"

The deafening thunder of the gun beat in Mark Hazzard's ears. He whirled on the fire-stairs platform. His hand closed hotly on Roberta Trencher's arm. Uncontrollable sobs broke through her trembling lips as they rushed down. Hazzard hurried the girl into the basement. He pressed her against the wall, opened the side door wide to shield her and called to the two plainclothes men stationed outside:

"Go up!"

THE MEN bounded to the landing and out of sight. Hazzard hurried across the sidewalk, his arm about the girl. As he climbed into her car, he glanced past the corner at his own. Dan Carey was at the wheel, shadow-covered. Hazzard swung away, Carey followed. Guns were rocking high in the building and shattered glass was falling when Hazzard sped along the street.

The girl sat silent at his side, lips pressed in anguish, her one arm curled through his, while he drove rapidly to her home. When he swung into the drive, Carey skirted past and stopped in the shadows beyond. The terrified girl hurried ahead of Hazzard into the house.

She stood rigid in the living-room, white-faced, widened eyes searching his. Hazzard strode to the radio and clicked it on. Dance music tinkled softly when he turned back. He faced the girl with angry blood pounding. She winced from the fury in his eyes. He snapped:

"You didn't make that call—understand? It was some other woman imitating your voice. You don't know anything about it—you were here all the time. You've got to stick to that!"

"I understand."

"You were crazy to tip them off! What hold have they got on you? Why are you so insanely loyal to Leroy? You know he's a rat—a murderer—yet you—"

"I had to do it!" the girl blurted. "I didn't realize Jack was like that when I married him. He didn't get mixed up with Hallan until later. I know I don't love him—now."

Hazzard's voice crackled. "If they try to force you to protect them in any other way, you've got to refuse. For your own sake and Trencher's you've got to do it. They're finished. This raid is the end of them, but they may try—"

"It wouldn't have happened," the girl interrupted in a strained tone, "if you'd only realize that—that I love you."

Hazzard's fists curled. "Listen to me! They'll put pressure on you to get them clear. You've got to ignore them—defy them. It's your only way out now, if they bring your name into it. No matter what they try—"

The girl's words rushed: "You wouldn't even look at me. You didn't even know I existed. If you'd only realized it, I wouldn't have turned to—"

He seized her arms angrily. The fierce pressure of his hands made her wince. "I'm to blame for it all—is that what you're trying to say? Listen, Bobby! There's one girl for me—no other. It can never be any different. Stop your sobbing! I'm thinking only of getting you out of trouble—of keeping your father from finding out—"

Swiftly, the girl slapped her palm across Hazzard's face. His quick surge of temper tightened his fists; he stood rigid. Roberta Trencher backed from him, her eyes blazing, her lips tightened furiously.

"You can't throw her in my face—Ann Nash. I hate her! I hate you now. I'll hate you the rest of my life."

Grimly Hazzard answered: "You've got to leave that out of it. Do you want this thing to wreck your whole life—to break your father? You've got to do exactly what I tell you, or—"

He broke off, turning tensely toward the radio. The dance music had ceased at the clang of a bell. A breathless voice began a news announcement. Roberta Trencher stared at Hazzard unhearing, a consuming hostility flashing in her eyes:

"A special report, ladies and gentlemen. Police under the direction of Inspector Trencher are even now raiding the headquarters of Miller Hallan, professional strikebreaker. They are in possession of the offices following a gun battle. In the desperate fight, three men managed to blast their way out—Hallan, Sorley and Leroy. In their rush from the building they shot down two detectives and gravely wounded a patrolman. Leroy wounded Inspector Trencher. They are at large in the city at this moment. Orders have been flashed to all radio cars to search for them. This sensational raid—"

Roberta Trencher interrupted in a venomous whisper: "With all my heart I hate you, Mark Hazzard!"

Hazzard smiled grimly. "Did you hear that? Your father is

wounded—by the man you married. Nothing will stop Trencher now. He's going to find Leroy, and when he does—"

"I tried to get dad to let you alone, Mark," the girl interrupted bitterly again. "I wanted him to stop hounding you." She laughed tauntingly. "That's all over now. Now I'm going to help him. I'll show you how much I hate you!"

THEY STOOD with eyes clashing—and the telephone rang. It purred three times before the girl turned her contemptuous gaze from Hazzard. Chilled, he let her answer the call. Her hushed tone, her furtive glance at him, jerked his nerves tight. He stepped from the room, seeking an extension instrument. In the hallway he raised a receiver carefully and heard:

"Got that address? We're here now. We're going to stay under cover until the excitement dies down, then we're going to blow the town. You're in on that, baby. We need a car, see—need it bad."

Leroy's hushed voice.

"Get this straight. Tomorrow night, midnight. The address I just gave you. Be at the corner with the car. Nobody'll stop us if you're driving—Inspector Trencher's daughter. And if they try it, it's going to be just too bad. You and your old man will wish you never got into this case!"

The connection broke. Hazzard hurried back to find Roberta Trencher standing rigid at the other instrument, eyes widened with dismay. She stared up haggardly as he took her arm. Dogged determination rang in his voice as he said:

"You're not going to do that."

She whispered: "I've got to. I've got to do it."

"Leroy himself warned you!" Hazzard protested. "What if you're seen sneaking those crooks out of town? What will happen to you then? You know it'll make you even more of an accessory. You know your father lives by the rules of the book. You'll force him to press charges against his own daughter if you do that!"

Again, breathlessly: "I've got to do it. They've used me all along to shield themselves. They've held something over me from the very beginning, and I can't get away from it. They'll keep their promise if I don't obey them—and it will break dad."

Hazzard demanded: "How will it break him?"

"Jack gave me money after we were married," the girl said in a whisper. "That was all right, wasn't it—a man giving money to his wife? It was always by check—big amounts. They've had them back from the bank a long time. Don't you see the construction that will be put on it? Graft money, paid to Inspector Trencher, through his daughter."

Hazzard snapped: "You little fool!"

"Dad's job is his whole life, Mark. I know he seems tough and heartless to you, but if he's broken off the force it will kill him. That's why I've got to do what Jack says. I've got to get them safely out town—"

"You're not going to do that!" Hazzard exploded. "I can't let you. I'll do anything—"

The girl cut in defiantly, her eyes glittering with hostility: "How can *you* stop me?"

"You're not going to do it!"

"I *will* do it!"

Hazzard's jaw-muscles lumped. The raging of his temper filmed red before his eyes. He was scarcely aware of the flash of his knuckles to the girl's chin. He saw her stiffen back, then begin to crumple. He caught her. He raised her yielding body, looked at her white face, said softly though he knew she could not hear: "I'm sorry, Bobby—sorry!"

Grimly he carried her to the entrance and out. Making sure he was not seen, he strode to the waiting coupe. Dan Carey, hastening toward him, stared in amazement. Hazzard ducked in, holding the girl close, as Carey took the wheel. His crackling voice sent the car whizzing away. The line of her jaw showing crimson, Roberta Trencher lay softly against him.

HAZZARD'S DIRECTIONS turned the car into the drive of his home. Carey stopped it inside the garage. While Hazzard carried the girl, the ex-cop hurried to the rear entrance of the house. The girl trembled as consciousness returned to her while Hazzard carried her in. He took her into a bedroom, lowered her gently, and put on her forehead the cold cloths which Carey brought.

Her eyelids fluttered. The confusion of her gaze gave way to a stronger hatred as she gazed at Hazzard. Her head turned and, as she glimpsed Carey, her eyes widened. She drew herself up quickly, her red lips tightened with triumph, her whole bearing challenging Hazzard.

"I remember him! He's Dan Carey. You convicted him of murder—

he escaped. My father will be glad to learn that, Mark Hazzard. The district attorney harboring a fugitive!"

She laughed crazily, hysterically. Hazzard looked in dismay at Carey, and saw the despairing dullness of the ex-cop's eyes. He seized the girl's arms and shook her in an attempt to quiet her. She kept laughing defiantly, wildly, at Hazzard.

"Listen to me!" he snapped. "I'm doing this for your own good—for Trencher's. I'm going to keep you here so you can't help those killers get out of town. Danny's going to watch you. No matter what you might do afterward, you're not getting any deeper into trouble. Listen, Bobby!"

She would not listen. She was still laughing when Hazzard left the room. His gesture ordered Carey to guard the girl. The despondent sag of the ex-cop's shoulders sent a pang of grief through his heart. He said, quietly: "I'm sorry, copper."

Carey forced a smile. "That's okay."

Hazzard was thinking of the dread electric chair for Carey, of the destruction of the district attorney's whole world as he left the house— with Roberta Trencher's mocking laughter still ringing in his ears.

CHAPTER V

DRAGNET DOOM

BANNER HEADLINES blackened the front pages of the extra editions that flooded from the newspaper presses next day. A million radios echoed frequent flashes of the developments in the sensational Hallan-Sorley case. Nervous tension electrified the city while grim police kept up their relentless search for three hiding killers.

Crooks Still in Hiding!

"The raid last night, ladies and gentlemen of the radio audience, produced conclusive evidence that Hallan and Sorley have long been preying on workers and business alike. The Grand Jury, no longer skeptical, has just returned indictments against the two men and Jacques Leroy. They will stand trial on a staggering number of charges once they are captured."

Police Continue Crook Hunt!

"Through the Press Radio Bureau we are informed that every road, bridge, railway and bus terminal is under scrutiny. All automobiles leaving the city are being stopped. The search for Hallan, Sorley and Leroy is the most dogged in the history of the city. It can be only a question of a few hours before they are located. Police are ready to make swift and desperate efforts to seize them once they are spotted. Their attempt to escape, if made, is certain to be balked by the orders and strategy of the officer in charge of the manhunt, Inspector Trencher."

Dillworth's Body Dragged From River!

The startling news, flashed at once to the office of the district attorney, brought grim satisfaction to Mark Hazzard—and new dread. The strengthening of the state's case added to the threat of tragedy for Roberta Trencher, heartbreak for the inspector, the destruction of

Hazzard's whole world. When the information reached him, the district attorney peered through the window to see Trencher telephoning, grimly intent.

Ann Nash's eyes shone with anxiety as he urged, "Wait here," and hurried from the office. When he arrived at the inspector's desk, Trencher was just replacing the phone. The dark-eyed man gazed at Hazzard piercingly, his lips wryly quirked. He drawled:

"Dropping in to meet Judge Middlebrook, Hazzard? He'll be here soon."

A chill pang shot through Hazzard's heart. He fought down his consternation as he answered: "Are you satisfied now a murder's been committed? We might have had the killers forty-eight hours ago. Now they're under cover. What're you doing about it, Trencher?"

Trencher challenged: "The tried and true methods are producing results, Hazzard. I take it slow and sure, and now I've got a case. Dillworth was shot three times in the head. I've found proof that Hallan rented the house on Edgecombe Street through a fake name, and I can show Dillworth was killed there."

"Excellent results, Trencher," Hazzard retorted, "if a bit late!"

Trencher scowled. "A little splinter of glass was found in the room where Dillworth got it. Blood and a bit of brain matter on it. Chemical tests take time, you know, Hazzard—and following down leads. That bit of glass is part of a pair of eye-glasses ground to Dillworth's prescription. It's competent, conclusive evidence!"

"And where," Hazzard asked bitterly, "are your killers now, Trencher?"

The inspector rounded the desk, his black eyes smoldering. "Look here, Hazzard. You've been in the thick of this case from the very start. I think you know more about it than you pretend to. You're holding something back. Open up, Hazzard. What is it?"

Hazzard answered wryly: "Perhaps you're right, inspector."

TRENCHER'S EYES narrowed. "Bobby's missing. Did you know that? She wasn't home all night—she hasn't been all day. I haven't had a word from her. I've tried to find her, but I can't. I'm so worried about her I can hardly keep my mind on this case. Do you know anything about that, Hazzard?"

Hazzard countered: "What could I know about it, Trencher? No doubt she's perfectly safe."

"I hope so." Trencher's tone became ominous. "If anything has happened to her, I'll give the works to the man responsible for it. He'll wish he never—"

The inspector's voice drawled off as he scrutinized Hazzard's drawn face. He turned slowly to the ringing telephone. Thrusting the instrument toward Hazzard, he growled: "For you."

Ann Nash's anxious voice came over the wire. Looking across the street, he could see her at the phone in his office.

"Mark! A call just came from Danny. He said the girl's slipped away. She got past him somehow and was gone when—"

"Good Lord, Ann!" Hazzard blurted. He glanced warily into Trencher's questioning eyes. "Where is he now?"

"He's taken the roadster—trying to find her. You know what it will mean if she tells her father—about Danny. Has Trencher had any word?"

"No." Hazzard's mind raced. "If he has any further information— understand?—he'll call back. Stay there, Ann."

He gazed at the desk clock as he broke the connection. Eleven-forty. Last evening Jacques Leroy's threatening voice on the telephone had said: "We need a car—tomorrow night—midnight." The girl's protest echoed in Hazzard's mind: "I've got to do it!" He knew fear had driven Roberta Trencher to slip away from Carey in order to obey Leroy's command.

The entire city was ringed with alert police. Every road was being guarded, every car stopped. And Inspector Trencher's daughter was desperately intent on smuggling three killers across the sentry lines.

Hazzard was turning anxiously to the door when it flashed open. A plainclothes man, dogged chin outthrust, strode to the inspector's desk. Hazzard stopped short in the doorway, chilled with dismay, when he heard the grim announcement:

"We've spotted 'em, inspector! Hallan and Sorley and Leroy. They're hiding in an empty store across from the railroad yards. Eighty-six Terminal Street!"

Trencher snapped: "Who reported that?"

"Thayer just phoned it in. You can rely on any report he makes. He's holding off for your orders. They may be getting ready to skip. We can't waste time. If we ring the place and—"

Trencher's instructions clicked. "Order the special squad to stand by. I'll lead 'em myself. Load the cars with Tommy guns and tear-gas bombs. Radio code orders to the prowl cars in that district to stand off until we close in. We'll have that place entirely surrounded before we show ourselves. We're leaving within ten minutes!"

Hazzard stood back, appalled, as Trencher strode from the office. The inspector paused at the outer door, grim face turned back. His words drawled with ominous slowness:

"Drop around, Hazzard, after we've bagged those crooks. Judge Middlebrook will be here. You'll be very interested in meeting him, I'm sure."

Coldness stabbed Hazzard's heart as Trencher's heels beat away along the corridor. He glanced anxiously out the window, into his own office, but he did not find Ann Nash. Hurrying down the stone steps, toward his coupe, he saw her coming from the entrance of the courthouse. She came to his side at the car as he quickly slipped in.

"Mark—what is it?" She slid in beside him as the starter snarled. "Where are you going?"

THE CAR spurted away as Hazzard answered: "Trencher's located Leroy and the others. He's getting ready to close in on them now. It's only a matter of minutes. Bobby's gone to the hideaway in a car. She's putting herself in a trap!"

His hand closed tightly on Ann's as he sped. "Her whole life's wrecked if she gets caught. Not only hers, but Trencher's. He's sworn to get me—he may do it to-night. His lips curved wryly. "Perhaps it will be the end of both of us, Ann."

The girl's anguished eyes scanned his deep-lined face as he peered into the beams of the headlamps. The shafts cut far into sooty Terminal Street. It was flanked on one side with squalid tenements and stores, gloomy and deserted. Beyond the opposite curve, the railroad yards spread through the darkness, its web of tracks a gleaming pattern—reminding Mark Hazzard of the night that had branded him with murder.

He swung past the dirty, deserted store-building on the corner numbered eighty-six, and saw nothing through its cobwebbed windows. Half a block away, he braked at the curb and slipped out. He warned: "Better stay here, Ann, out of sight." He stepped into the shadows of the buildings. The very hush in the air was like the warning of an imminent storm. Hazzard paused, eyes sharpened, at the corner.

Eighty-six sat bleak and silent, with no sign of life around it. Two blocks along the cross-street a car had stopped, lightless. Hazzard had taken part in previous raids—he knew it was a headquarters machine. He had learned how cautiously, how skillfully, they could circle their mark without betraying their presence. Even now, he knew, Trencher's plan was in operation—grim men were approaching eighty-six from all angles, through back yards, through deep shadows.

A movement startled Hazzard—a car swinging around the far corner. It headed, lights dimmed, toward eighty-six. When it stopped, its driver remained at the wheel. Dimly Hazzard saw the white face of Roberta Trencher. Grim relief flooded his heart because she was not using her own car. The waiting sedan was evidently one the crooks had kept hidden, ready for an emergency. About to move toward it, Hazzard saw the door of eighty-six open stealthily.

The dark figure of a man appeared, but instantly vanished. The door shut as another car swung into Terminal Street. It purred past while the girl in the sedan shielded her face and the door of the store remained shut. Watching it swing to the curb near his coupe, Hazzard knew Dan Carey was at the wheel. He had found the girl's trail—and it had brought him within the jaws of a police trap about to spring!

HAZZARD'S LIPS pinched back a moan of despair. His move toward Carey was checked, his intention of warning the fugitive baffled, when the door of eighty-six again swung wide. He spun toward it. He eased his Webley into his hand as he recognized the lean figure of Jacques Leroy slinking out. He saw Roberta Trencher's widened, shining eyes while he strode direct to the car. Leroy jerked to a stop, and two other figures paused in the open door, when Hazzard turned toward them.

He ordered laconically, gun leveled: "Bobby! Get away from here— quick as you can."

Without warning the gun in the hand of Jacques Leroy slashed out flame. The bullet ripped past Hazzard's head as he sprang aside. Instantly Hallan and Sorley fired from the doorway—a fusillade that clanged flying lead against the girl's car. She uttered a stifled scream as she crouched down. Hazzard leaped beyond the corner of the building, firing twice swiftly, as slugs sang a song of death.

The window splintered at his side while dark figures dashed across the sidewalk. Through the jagged glass Hazzard saw Leroy leaping into the car, Hallan swiftly following. He aimed through the glass as Sorley sprang out. At his shot Sorley spun. Blazing fire turned upon Hazzard as the engine of the sedan thundered with a burst of power.

He fired twice at the spinning tires when the car spurted past. A new jangle of glass beside his head jerked him so that his bullets flew wild. As the sedan whined down the street Sorley crouched along the curb. Hazzard glimpsed Dan Carey sprinting from his car, service revolver gripped, in the flashes from Sorley's automatic. Unprotected, Hazzard smashed bullets at the crouching shadow. Carey's gun echoed the blasts—and Sorley slumped.

"After that car, Danny!"

One instant Hazzard paused on the corner. The storming reports were bringing a quick response out of the shadows along the cross-street. Men came running from dark doorways—headquarters detectives. Gruff commands echoed from the dark yards behind the buildings. Hazzard identified Trencher's booming tones as he leaped toward his coupe:

"Close 'em in!"

Ann Nash stared in dismay as Hazzard flung himself behind the wheel. Plainclothes men were rushing into Terminal Street when he kicked the motor into action; Peering at the red beacon of the fleeing sedan, he twisted from the curb. His thrust at the gas pedal sent the car rushing to top speed. Hazzard glanced back to see Carey's roadster spurting after him, dark figures swarming around eighty-six. Again, the crimson shine reflecting in his eyes, he raced grimly after the escaping sedan.

Hazzard's car jounced off the cobbles of Terminal Street, onto the smooth cement of a main highway, as the sedan streaked ahead. A gleam of flame flashed from it. A bullet hissed past Hazzard. He commanded: "Get down, Ann—down!" Leaning out, Webley glittering, he squeezed two quick shots at the black car. He heard the clang of the striking bullets—but the speed of the race did not diminish.

Again Hazzard turned a desperate glance backward. Carey's roadster was speeding close behind. Farther back, red headlamps were gleaming—the lights of a prowl car. The whine of another bullet turned Hazzard's eyes forward. With a jarring shock, a milky star appeared on his non-shatterable windshield. While Ann Nash peered up, white-faced, Hazzard aimed carefully into the roaring wind.

A new flash of flame showed him Jacques Leroy leaning out with leveled automatic. The bolt of bullet lightning became Hazzard's target the instant it vanished. He fired twice—and saw the crimson tail-light sway. He drove at fastest speed while the sedan wavered, slowing. A gasp of dismay broke from his lips when he saw it skid off the edge of the pavement. The crash of a collision carried on the cyclone howling around Hazzard.

He braked, desperately signaling Carey, as his headlamps showed him the wrecked sedan. It had slammed into a telephone pole that now was leaning askew, hanging on singing wires. The driver's door had burst open. Jacques Leroy, red streaking his forehead, was sprawled motionless in rank grass. Hazzard, slipping from the wheel, glimpsed a feeble motion inside the shattered car—the girl.

CAREY'S BRAKES squealed as Hazzard jerked the sedan's door open. On the front seat, Miller Hallan was leaning forward, head lolling—his skull crushed by its violent impact with the dash. His gun arm dangled limp. On the rear seat Roberta Trencher was groping for a support, trying to get up. Hazzard gripped her wrist and raised her—glancing back to see the red headlamps of the prowl car speeding close.

"Hurry it, Danny!"

With desperate haste the ex-cop helped Hazzard carry the stunned girl. Ann Nash switched off the lights of the coupe, to cover their movements of bundling Roberta Trencher into the roadster. She was staring, inarticulate with terror, as Carey sprang to the wheel. Hazzard ordered:

"Get her back, Danny—and keep out of sight! Cover her in every way possible! Step on it!"

Hazzard whirled back as the roadster leaped off. Ann Nash had hurried from the coupe. While the prowl car sped close, Hazzard peered at her, his mind working with lightning speed. Suddenly he snatched her hat from her head, disarranged her hair, ripped the collar of her waist. She was gazing at him in bewilderment when the red-lighted car reached the coupe and slammed to a stop.

Inspector Trencher wheezed out of it. His smoldering black eyes jerked from the demolished sedan, to Hazzard, to the girl, then down the road. Carey's roadster was a fleet, lightless shadow rapidly diminishing on the stretch of pavement. Trencher's blunt forefinger jabbed toward it as he growled:

"After that car! Stop it! Arrest anybody in it!"

The prowl car flashed off as Trencher turned. He strode to the sedan, looked down at Leroy, grunted at sight of Hallan's smashed head. When he turned back, Hazzard was listening to the faint, vanishing whirr of Carey's roadster, the whine of the prowl car chasing it. Hazzard smiled tightly into the inspector's ominous gaze.

"I think our case is cracked, Trencher," he said quietly. "But not strictly according to the book."

TRENCHER STRODE first into his office in police headquarters. Mark Hazzard and Ann Nash paused behind him as he stared at the girl waiting beside his desk. Roberta Trencher was pale and shaken—but her presence told Mark Hazzard that Carey had succeeded in eluding the prowl car. Her hostile eyes turned on Hazzard as her father asked bluntly:

"Bobby—where have you been?"

"I'm all right, dad," she answered in a low tone. "I can explain everything—quite clearly."

Trencher turned on Hazzard. "I'll finish with you first. I don't quite understand a couple of things about this case, Hazzard. Why did you beat me to the hideaway and blow up my plans? There's a girl mixed up in this. Who is she?" He placed a blue powder compact on his desk, still eyeing Hazzard. His daughter paled. "I found this in the sedan. The girl got away in the other car. Who is she, Hazzard?"

Ann Nash said quietly, her eyes shining at Roberta Trencher: "That's mine, inspector. I'm the girl in the case."

Hazzard spoke rapidly while Trencher's dark eyes scrutinized him. "Just after I left here, inspector, I found Ann was gone from the office. I got a telephone call warning me to lay off because Hallan was holding her as hostage. They'd snatched her after getting her out of the office with a fake call. They were going to use her as a cover for getting out of town. That, of course, is why I jumped the gun. Does that explanation satisfy you, inspector?"

Trencher growled his displeasure. "You're not afraid of going too far, are you, Hazzard?" His gaze turned to his daughter. "You owe me an explanation too, Bobby. Where have you been? What happened?"

The hostility in the girl's eyes had not faded. Gazing intently at Hazzard, she answered coldly: "Kidnaping is a serious crime, isn't it, dad—even for a district attorney?"

The inspector stared. Hazzard's crushed lips suppressed a groan. Inexorably the girl went on:

"That explains why I've been missing. Mark Hazzard forced me out of the house—actually hit me, knocked me unconscious. For the past twenty-four hours he kept me a prisoner in his home. That's not all, dad. My jailer was—"

The name of Dan Carey was on her lips. Her words were to condemn an innocent man to the electric chair, to bring the whole world of Mark Hazzard crashing to destruction—but Trencher's fist, smashing to the desk, interrupted.

"Hazzard—you have gone too far! That's your finish! You can't get away with that! I'll take Bobby before the Grand Jury and get you charged with—"

"Wait a minute, inspector." Hazzard's tone was incisive, brittle. "Is Bobby willing to go before them and tell the truth—the *whole* truth?"

Roberta Trencher's eyes flickered. Silence held in the office while Trencher glowered, while Hazzard waited with caught breath. Ann Nash, hand raised in dismay to her parted lips, stood rigid. When Roberta Trencher spoke, it was with a threatening, gloating ring in her voice:

"I—I can't do that, dad. Perhaps it will be better if I don't. Perhaps there's a way of getting Mark Hazzard without involving ourselves."

The glitter in Roberta Trencher's eyes chilled Mark Hazzard. Consternation filled him at the thought that this vindictive girl held the power to crush him utterly. Her challenge was one which some day must be met. His heart frozen, Hazzard turned from her. While the hand of Ann Nash curled reassuringly through his, he forced a smile and said bitterly:

"Good-night."

He stopped short in the outer office, gazing stunned at two men who had come into the room. One was the portly, grizzle-headed Commissioner Brook. The other was an older man, white-haired, grave-faced. Hazzard remembered his features vividly—remembered seeing them across a court bench. As clearly as he recalled the face of Judge Middlebrook he heard again the solemn voice that had doomed him:

"This court sentences the defendant, Dennis Grant, to imprisonment for life in the state prison."

Hazzard saw nothing but Judge Middlebrook's sharp eyes as Commissioner Brook mumbled an introduction. He was aware that the connecting door had opened, that Inspector Trencher was watching. He heard Middlebrook say:

"I have heard a great deal about you, Mr. Hazzard. Your methods are not quite conventional, but the results you get are very pleasing to one who has been on the bench as long as I. I know all the weaknesess, all the injustices of the statutes only too well. It was Chief Justice Taft who once said: 'The administration of the criminal law in the United States is a disgrace to civilization'—too true. I'm very proud, Mr. Hazzard, to shake your hand and wish you success."

Hazzard answered without realizing he spoke. Dazed, aware that Trencher's eyes were smoldering at him, he made excuses for himself and Ann. The girl's hand tightened on his proudly as he stepped out, closing the door. He stood near, heart icy, and heard through the panels:

"Now, Inspector Trencher, since the hour is late, where is the man you believe to be Dennis Grant?"

Trencher's answer was a defeated growl. Hazzard, with an anxious glance at Ann, hurried her away. He paused at the top of the stairs as she asked: "What was the name Judge Middlebrook said? I didn't quite catch it." His pleading eyes denied her question as he turned back. Again at the door of Trencher's office he heard Middlebrook exclaim:

"Mark Hazzard—Dennis Grant? There is no resemblance whatever, inspector. If the impossible is true, and he is Grant, I for one will be happy to let him remain Hazzard!"

Mark Hazzard, alias Dennis Grant, went back to the girl he loved with a smile.

BOOK VI

THE DEATH-CHAIR CHALLENGE

King Krager's brother was scheduled for hot seat payoff. But King Krager sent out a vengeance-laden warning that the governor's wife would balance the death scales. And he ordered Mark Hazzard, D.A., to lead her to her doom. For if Hazzard wouldn't give murder help, Krager schemed to explode a bloody secret that would send the D.A. to the chair.

CHAPTER I

HELL ON WHEELS!

THE RED-HEADED, keen-eyed young man at the wheel of the roadster listened intently to the voice whispering from the car radio—a pronouncement of doom upon a prisoner of the state.

" 'Babe' Krager must die in the electric chair. Governor Bryant has just announced he will not intervene. In exactly twenty-four hours the death sentence will be executed upon Krager."

The driver of the roadster was the man who had sent Krager to the death house. He was the two-fisted, hot-tempered District Attorney of King's County, the youngest prosecutor ever to fight the People's cause—the man known as Mark Hazzard.

"With Babe Krager waiting behind bars for the green door of the execution chamber to open and beckon him to his doom, his brother 'King' Krager, ruling power of the underworld of the city, desperately exerted every effort to save the prisoner. The governor's statement tonight destroys the convicted man's last futile hope.

" 'The damning evidence presented at the trial by Prosecutor Hazzard convinced me beyond all doubt that Krager deserves the death penalty,' Governor Bryant announced tonight. 'My duty demands that I take no action.' "

The tense curve of Mark Hazzard's lips persisted as he turned the roadster into the drive of his modest home. He was champion of a justice higher than the written law. Though his office was to convict those accused of crimes against the state, no man fought more earnestly than he to free them if he believed them innocent. If musty courtroom procedure failed to convict a prisoner whom Hazzard believed guilty, he took a lone wolf's trail to mete out the punishment the guilty deserved. He was a terror to the lawless, a hard-hitting guardian angel of the wronged, a fearless wielder of his own brand of justice.

But in all his tempestuous career, Mark Hazzard had never been more firmly convinced of a prisoner's guilt, more grimly satisfied with the rightness of the death sentence pronounced upon the cold-blooded killer, Babe Krager.

A cold, warning prickle played across Hazzard's scalp as he unlocked the entrance of the little house. It was silent save for an intermittent, metallic purr—the telephone. Unconsciously touching the Webley automatic holstered under his left arm, he lifted the receiver and listened alertly in the hush. Answering his guarded "Hello?" a whisper came:

"Skipper. This is Danny. I've got news—and I don't like it."

Dan Carey was an ex-patrolman, a convicted murderer, a fugitive from justice—and the district attorney's secret comrade at arms. Hazzard urged him softly:

"Spring it, copper."

"I've been trying to spot King Krager and some of Krager's mob, skipper, but they're keeping under cover. Not a sign of 'em, but there are some ugly new faces showing up in the dives where Krager usually hangs out. They look like imported rod men."

"Know any of them, Danny?"

"No. But they're bad customers. They hang around a while, get a tip-off, then disappear. They're ducking into a hideout somewhere, and taking no chances on having it spotted. Something big's in the wind, skipper. It means trouble."

Hazzard answered as he gazed warily through the dark doorways connecting with his study: "Stay on the job, copper."

"Listen, skipper." Carey's voice rang anxiously. "King Krager hates you for sending his brother up the river. You've got to watch yourself. He won't stop at killing you."

Hazzard chuckled. "Thanks, Danny. The King's sure to make another play—the most desperate yet, though I don't know what it will be. That's why I want you to keep your eyes peeled and report the minute you have something."

"Okay, skipper," Carey answered, "but—don't give him a chance! Watch behind you. I don't want you to get some of Krager's bullets in the back when—"

THE RECEIVER, suddenly jerked down, snatched Carey's voice away. A hand had darted over Hazzard's shoulder to grip his wrist. Another hand clutched his arm. "Watch behind you!" Carey had warned—and there were evil-eyed men behind Hazzard now. "Bullets in the back"—and now automatic muzzles were pressing against Hazzard's spine.

Two men whose eyes glittered through slitted black cloth, had materialized with ghost-like silence from the shadowed corners of the room. As anger pounded at Hazzard's temples, two more phantom figures glided through the doorways. Four gleaming weapons formed a deadly square around him.

"Take it easy, Hazzard," a whisper warned. "We're not going to kill you—here. That would be a bit crude. We're eliminating you from the picture in a special way. And you're going to have company on your way to hell."

A gloved hand reached inside Hazzard's coat, toward his Webley. As it slipped from its arm-pit holster, a wrathful impulse overwhelmed him. He grabbed at it. The masked four savagely drove out black knuckles. Hazzard strove to wrench away, hitting blindly. A snarl sounded. Steel clicked behind Hazzard's ear.

He thumped to his knees, sprawled on his face. While he was pinioned down, a black world whirling around him, he heard a liquid gurgle. His nostrils caught a sweet pungency. Chloroform! Cold, sodden cotton was slapped over his mouth and nose. He squirmed to escape it, but could not. He fought back in the only possible way—by holding his breath.

His lungs burned with the effort. He did not permit himself to breathe even when the wet pad was lifted. He lay inert, feeling masked eyes studying him, and heard a guttural voice whisper: "He's out."

Another directed huskily: "Get his clothes off. You, get busy with the telephone. We'll be ready by the time the other one arrives."

No names mentioned. The subdued voices were unrecognizable. Hazzard felt certain one of these masked men was King Krager, brother of the convicted murderer who was doomed to the chair, but he dared not risk a glance. He drew a long, slow breath into his stinging lungs while he was carried into the adjoining bedroom.

The gloved hands began to strip Hazzard of his clothing. In his study he heard a man moving about, rearranging the disturbed furniture. The windows were being opened to clear the air of the fumes of the anesthetic. Even his underwear was removed while he lay limp, simulating unconsciousness. Now other clothing was being pulled onto his body. It carried a rancid odor. The garments were worn and old.

A voice spoke in the next room: "Police headquarters." Hazzard controlled a startled jerk of his nerves—because it was amazingly like his own. It said into the telephone transmitter, imitating Hazzard's characteristic impatience: "Connect me with Inspector Trencher."

IN HIS office in police headquarters, Inspector Charles Trencher answered the ring of the bell. He was a seasoned veteran of the force whose lazy manner belied the alert penetration of his mind. He followed tried and true methods of procedure, with full regard to all the rules and regulations, and doggedly disapproved of the unorthodox means Mark Hazzard took to get results. His eyes lighted shrewdly when he heard the voice on the wire.

"Hullo, Hazzard, Burning up again, are you? Well, what are you going off half-cocked about this time?"

The voice answered: "I've found some new evidence in the Krager case, inspector. It proves we've both been wrong from the beginning. The Babe is innocent."

Trencher snorted. "Nothing in the world can prove Babe Krager is innocent of murder, Hazzard."

"You don't know what it is inspector," the voice insisted. "I want you to check on it right away. I'm at home. Come right over, will you—as fast as you can make it."

Trencher retorted: "You know Commissioner Brook left for a vacation in Bermuda three days ago, and I'm running the department. It's a day and night job and I ought to stay at this desk. Bring your evidence in and—"

"It's impossible, inspector. You'll realize why when you get here. I'll wait for you—and hurry it."

Trencher growled his disapproval, but he tramped down the broad stone steps of the headquarters building, heaved into a waiting police car, started off. By the most direct route he drove to the young district attorney's home.

He trudged to the entrance of the little house. The rattle of his knuckles brought no response. Puzzled by the silence, because a light was shining inside, he twisted the knob. "Hazzard!" Because there was still no answer, he sauntered in. Suddenly, facing the study door, the smoldering blackness of his eyes dangerously deepening, he paused.

At Mark Hazzard's desk a masked man was standing, leveling an automatic at Trencher's heart.

The inspector spun aside, grabbing at the police positive in his hip-pocket holster. A hand shot out of the darkness of the hall to grip his wrist. He twisted desperately again as steel streaked out of the gloom. The slashing gun-butt cracked sharply above Trencher's temple. He lurched, groaned, dived.

A voice in the gloom said: "Out cold."

Mark Hazzard lay lax on the bed in the room adjoining the study. Because a masked gunman was watching him with automatic leveled, while he had no weapon, he had not dared to cry out a warning to Trencher. Now, chancing a look through the blur of his eyelashes, he caught further details of the strange, daring plan of the masked men.

Trencher was carried sagging into the bedroom. He stirred fitfully as he was lowered to the floor. A wad of cotton soaked with chloroform was quickly pressed over his nose and mouth. He tried weakly to thrust it away, but could not. He lay still, drugged by the sticky vapor.

The masked men jerked Trencher's loose clothing off his limp body—this Mark Hazzard dimly saw. The inspector was stripped to the skin, then forced into tattered, oil-spotted trousers and a frayed coat that did not match. Broken shoes were pushed onto his feet. He lay entirely unconscious of what was happening to him while Hazzard continued to simulate a stupor.

"Take the clothes," a whispering voice said. "You, see that nothing's disturbed in the house. Be sure it's locked up when we leave. We've just about got time. Let's go."

One of the masked men bundled Hazzard's clothing with Trencher's. Another made sure no evidence of a struggle would remain. A third went to the front entrance. As though some sort of signal had been flashed, a heavy car immediately pulled into the drive. Two men lifted Trencher. Two more gripped Hazzard's shoulders and legs. He still pretended unconsciousness, torturously controlling his breathing, while he was carried out.

He was thrust into the rear of a big sedan, beside Trencher. The starter growled. As the car swayed into the street, Hazzard risked a brief glance. The tonneau curtains were pulled down. The two men on the rear seat were covered by thick darkness. Hazzard could see no face. The speed of the car quickened. The man at the wheel said:

"They'll look like a couple of tramps—if anything's left of 'em."

The sedan swayed around a bewildering succession of corners. It stopped at traffic lights, rolled at a moderate speed, at last quivered over a cobbled street. The tires ground through grit. It was stopped slowly, carefully. Hazzard sensed its lights were out.

"The telegrams are being delivered now," a whisper said. "One to Hazzard's office saying he's gone to Chicago. Another signed with Trencher's name saying he'll be in Elmira a while working on the Wilson case. Their friends'll be a long time waiting for 'em to come back."

A METALLIC sound came out of the gloom, then a slow, stealthy rattle. Trencher was lifted out of the car. Hazzard's arms and legs were gripped again. He felt himself heaved to a higher level, dragged across splintered wood. A few yards away in the darkness a match scratched. A sputtering hiss filled the hush. The rattle sounded again. Hazzard sensed he was now alone with Trencher in a closed space.

Somewhere near a locomotive was panting. A muffled voice said: "The seal's okay." The murmuring of the sedan's motor rose in pitch and faded. Hazzard cautiously drew himself up. He could see nothing in the thick darkness except a spot of light—a small spout of sparks shooting like a spray from a hose.

He knew what it was. It was the burning end of a fuse. Somewhere the blackness concealed a charge of dynamite set to explode at the first hot contact of a spark.

A jarring crash stumbled Hazzard against a wall he could not see. It shook as he leaned against it, while metallic clashes rolled like broken thunder into the distance. A quickening, rhythmic clicking came from below. With the floor rocking under him, knowing he was inside a moving freight car, Hazzard steadied—staring chilled at the sibilant tongue of flame.

He groped to it. His fingers closed on a curved, rope-like strand. By sense of touch alone he followed it away from the spitting nozzle of fire. The long fuse led to a tied bundle of gritty cylinders—half a dozen sticks of dynamite. It was explosive enough to destroy the car completely, to kill Hazzard and Trencher instantly, to hurl them out through broken walls unrecognizably mangled.

Hazzard's temper speeded his pulse as he pulled the end of the fuse out, carefully detached the detonator cap, slipped it into the pocket of the filthy coat he wore. Holding the burning end like a taper, he wavered past tracks of wooden boxes to the still, shabbily clad figure on the floor. He shook Trencher, sharply called the inspector's name. Trencher did not stir.

The wheels of the boxcar were clicking rapidly over the rails now. The train was shuttling out of the city. Hazzard tried to pry the broad door back. It was firmly fastened—not only bolted, Hazzard remembered, but sealed. He knew it would be impossible to force open. The train even now must be winding into open country.

Hazzard tried the opposite door—in vain. He climbed stacked boxes and tried to break through the smaller panels high at the ends of the car. It was hopeless. He was a prisoner with the unconscious Trencher while the passing minutes carried them miles from the city. The officer in command of the police, and the feared district attorney, removed from the scene—while shrewd, desperate crooks planned a daring coup!

A long haul with few stops—Krager must have arranged it that way. Hazzard could not guess how many hours must pass before he could try to attract the attention of the train crew. Perhaps he could not succeed in getting out of this sealed car until it reached its destination. It might be hundreds of miles distant. By that time Krager's diabolical plan would have achieved its sinister purpose.

Hazzard gripped the inspector's shoulders. "Trencher!" The man was inert. Hazzard waited, tortured with impatience—while the rails clicked, the car swayed, and miles were added to the distance. "Trencher!" No response came. The fuse burned slowly, thickening the air with pungent fumes.

Hazzard kicked a wooden crate open, levered at the big doors with the pieces of wood, saw them splinter in his hands. "Trencher!" The inspector's pulse was growing stronger, but he remained in a stupor. *Click, click click*—the sound meant added mileage and heated Hazzard's taut nerves. "Trencher!" When the fuse sputtered out and utter darkness filled the car, impatience overwhelmed Hazzard. The train was slowing—it meant a station was being approached.

Hazzard groped to the bundled sticks of dynamite. Carefully he untied them. He broke one in half, put part in the pocket of his evil-smelling coat. He felt his way with the others to the end of the car where Trencher lay.

He made a bed of sacks of grain, put the explosive on them, covered the sticks with more bags. Certain they were protected as much as possible, he stood beside Trencher with the half stick in his hand, poised to hurl it.

It whistled unseen from his fingers to the farther end of the car—and blasted!

Thundering power rocked the car. Blinding flame splashed. At the first roar and flash, Hazzard whirled to fling himself down on the unconscious man. His body protected Trencher as the destructive force wrenched through the car. Breaking wood screeched. Spilling boxes rumbled. Suffocating fumes clouded over Hazzard, flaming splinters rained. A heavy jolt twisted the car to a stop as cold air gusted in through shattered walls.

CHAPTER II

FIRST LADY
OF DEATH

HAZZARD PULLED up dizzily as couplings clashed. The explosion had ripped the trucks off the rails. Flickering tongues of fire lighted the burst doors. Hazzard gripped Trencher's shoulders, pulled him toward the open. Hopping down he saw startled men running from the engine and caboose, lanterns swinging. Farther ahead the lights of a small way-station shone. Hazzard dragged Trencher onto his back and started trudging.

He ignored the conductor who loped after him, gun in hand. When he was near the station he felt Trencher squirming. The fresh, cold air was reviving the inspector. Hazzard lugged him through the lighted door, paying no attention to the staring station master. He eased Trencher into a chair, defied the revolvers leveled at him, snatched up the station telephone.

"Connect me with the office of the district attorney. This is Mark Hazzard speaking. Get that call through fast!"

Trencher was muttering. Hazzard put the receiver down to take his arms. The inspector's smoldering black eyes blinked.

"Listen! The call that got you to my house was faked. King Krager tried to kill us both. We've got to let him think we're both blown to bits, but we're going back without his knowing it and play his own dirty game against him. He's gambling for desperate stakes and that's our best chance to get him."

Trencher gasped: "Krager?"

"He's hit at us because we sent Babe Krager to the death house, but it's not only that. You and I are the chief law officers in the city—his deadliest enemies. He tried to get us out of the way because we're the biggest danger he faces. Let him think he's done it. We've got to find out exactly what he's planning, take him by surprise, and hit back hard."

Trencher mumbled: "How do you know Krager—?"

Hazzard spun to the two men standing at the door. The angry quickness of his move so startled the conductor and the station master that they forgot their guns and recoiled.

"You're sending in a report that two tramps were killed in the explosion," he snapped at them. "It was caused by spontaneous combustion, grain dust, anything—but we're dead. Understand that?"

The telephone receiver was rasping. Hazzard grabbed it up to hear the anxious voice of his secretary. He began: "Ann, listen—" but her rushing words cut him off. He stooped at the desk, struck motionless with dismay, as he heard her breathless message:

"Mark! I've been trying everywhere to locate you. Governor Bryant has been turning the city inside out, trying to find Trencher. He's just received a horrible threat, Mark—and it's no bluff. He's been ordered to commute Babe Krager's sentence, and—"

"If he doesn't?" Hazzard demanded.

"If he doesn't Mark, if Krager dies in the chair tomorrow night, the lovely young wife of the governor is going to be killed at the same time!"

IN HIS luxuriously appointed office in the State House, Governor Bryant paced slowly past his desk and back—back and forth, trying to control the snapping tension of his nerves. He was a remarkably young man for his office, stalwart, honest, widely loved. His generous, far-sighted gubernatorial program had won him the enthusiastic acclaim of the people. He faced the problems of his position courageously, but tonight fear chilled his heart—fear of the vengeance of the underworld upon the wife he adored.

"Please don't worry, darling," a quiet voice urged him. "You know they won't dare touch me."

Striving to conceal his mounting anxiety, he gazed intently at the beautiful young woman he had married. Barbara Bryant had become endeared to millions through her generous contributions to charity. She was a charming first lady of the state. She shared her husband's dread, but she smiled reassurance at him—smiled while a threat of criminal savagery hung over her.

"I don't want to frighten you, Barbara," the governor answered softly, "but you don't realize these crooks are more dangerous than jungle beasts. King Krager is the most ruthless of them all. He's absolutely merciless, yet he's madly devoted to his younger brother—a cold-blooded killer. We can't ignore this—we've got to face it and take every precaution for your safety."

"I'm not afraid," the girl said, still smiling. "And of course you won't grant a commutation. You're not that kind of man."

A light knock sounded on the door. The governor's anxious "Come in!" brought his secretary, Hugh Durham, into the room. Durham announced quietly:

"Inspector Trencher and Prosecutor Hazzard are here, sir. They came in by a back entrance, I think without being seen. They suggest we draw the curtains, sir, in case someone is watching."

The governor hastily helped Durham close the window-drapes—and his concern for Barbara Bryant grew. It was natural that she should know little of the vicious characters of King Krager, dictator of the underworld. Krager controlled scores of rackets. Protected by the shrewdest criminal lawyers and backed with the power of wealth illegally gained, he feared no one while he ruled by fear. Shrewd, daring, hungry for the fawning admiration of his packs of underworld rats, he had openly boasted he could break any man who opposed him—yet District Attorney Mark Hazzard had actually sent King Krager's brother to the death house and Governor Bryant had refused to order the murderer taken out.

The death sentence imposed upon Babe Krager was a challenge which the king of crime had met with every legal resource. Step by step, while he brought all his evil influence to bear and spent bloody fortunes in one grim attempt after another, he had failed to win mercy for the contemptible killer of a woman and a child. Now his ruthlessness clashed directly with the governor's honor—the last possible appeal made by a merciless threat. The chill in Governor Bryant's heart grew sharper, as he blinded the windows, with the thought that even now some of Krager's malevolent gang were watching.

"Show Hazzard and Trencher in," he said huskily.

He stared in amazement at the two men who entered. He had already had a telephone call from Mark Hazzard, and he knew of the attempt on their lives, but he was not prepared to see them garbed as disreputable tramps. They had driven back to the city as swiftly as possible, not sparing a moment even to change the soiled clothing put on them by the masked murderers. They smiled reassurance to Mrs. Bryant and strode directly to the governor's desk.

"There is no possible doubt, gentlemen," he said levelly, "that King Krager is responsible for the attempt on your lives and the threat against my wife's, yet—"

"There is no evidence to prove it—we're only too aware of that, sir," Mark Hazzard answered grimly. "I can't identify any of the masked men who tried to kill us tonight, and neither can Inspector Trencher. In spite of that, I've been trying to induce the inspector to arrest Krager and in that way protect Mrs. Bryant, but—"

"On what evidence?" Trencher countered. "There isn't any. If I arrest Krager and his lieutenants on suspicion alone, their lawyers will have them out as fast as we bring them in. They've covered themselves too damned well. Without strong, concrete evidence, we're helpless to hold them. We've got to try some other way."

While Barbara Bryant listened anxiously, the governor spoke: "As soon as I heard from you, gentlemen, headquarters went into action. They're looking for evidence, but that's almost hopeless. Orders are out to pick up King Krager and his henchmen, but Krager hasn't been found. They're playing this desperate game very carefully, gentlemen—and time is short. It is less than twenty-four hours, now—"

THE ELECTRIC clock on the governor's desk indicated four-thirty A.M. In nineteen and one half hours the sentence of death would be executed upon Babe Krager. Hours of torturous anxiety to be faced by them all while the greatest power of the underworld marshaled against the forces of justice. The eyes of the three men grimly met.

"The threats reached me by telephone," Governor Bryant said. "They mean every word. They have not only promised to kill Mrs. Bryant if Babe Krager dies in the chair, but they have defied us to pin it on them after it's done. They've planned it with the utmost shrewdness, gentlemen, and they'll keep their promise—we can depend on that."

Mark Hazzard said tightly: "With your permission, governor, I'm going after Krager. Whether or not we have admissible evidence, I'm going to do my best to stop him. This job is up to Inspector Trencher and me, and I'm going to handle my end of it in my own way."

Trencher glowered. "I've warned you, Hazzard. You'll increase the danger to Mrs. Bryant if you try your usual hot-headed tactics. My aim is exactly the same as yours—to keep Mrs. Bryant safe at all costs—but we've got to take this slowly and carefully. If we don't—"

"Gentlemen." Governor Bryant gravely interrupted. "I am right, am I not, in believing that there is absolutely no honorable ground for reprieving Babe Krager, or commuting his death sentence to life imprisonment?"

The three men knew completely and finally the answer to that question. Babe Krager, in a drunken explosion of anger, had brutally assaulted Patrolman Tom Kennedy. While Kennedy lay in the hospital with a crushed skull, the police had combed the city for the braggartly prince of the underworld. For days he had remained in hiding—in a rented room not far from the scene of the attack.

The owner of the rooming house, Mrs. Blakeman and her daughter Dorothy, were quaint anachronisms who knew little of the crime-ridden world outside their door. They had not suspected that their new roomer, who paid them so handsomely, was a fugitive from the law until, belatedly, they had seen his photograph in a newspaper. They had been too frightened to report their discovery at once to the police—but Babe Krager had read the meaning of the fear in their eyes.

Slyly watching them, he had heard their whispered determination to inform headquarters. He had stopped them at the door with a leveled automatic. He had torn out the telephone, kept them prisoners for days in their own home, had swaggeringly forced them to serve him like slaves. When at last he had decided he could slip out of the city unseen, he had cold-bloodedly silenced them—with bullets.

He had not escaped the dragnet. Trencher's men had traced him to the rooming house—there to find a gray-haired woman and a pretty young girl with a killer's lead in their brains. Mark Hazzard had linked Babe Krager's gun directly with those slugs. A mass of conclusive evidence had made the death sentence for King Krager's brother inevitable. Governor Bryant's question had only one tenable answer.

"The courts never sentenced a man more justly," Inspector Trencher declared.

"Commuting Babe Krager's sentence to life imprisonment will mean his going free eventually, sir," Mark Hazzard pointed out. "He'd force himself to be a model prisoner. He'd earn time off for good behavior, then he'd be granted a parole. He'd come out to prey. I should never want that on my conscience, sir."

"Nor I," Governor Bryant answered tensely. "Well, then, gentlemen. The zero hour is tomorrow night. Until then we must take every precaution to safeguard Mrs. Bryant. I have already arranged for a police escort to accompany us home tonight. I'm quite sure nothing will happen to her as long as there is still time for a commutation to go through. But when tomorrow night comes—"

The telephone buzzed like a startled rattlesnake. Governor Bryant's hand jerked back, then drifted toward it. Hazzard and Trencher kept an anxious silence while he raised the instrument. Barbara Bryant gave him another calm, reassuring smile, but the dread in her clear eyes was too strong to conceal. The governor held the receiver so Hazzard and Trencher might hear—and rasping words sounded in the hush:

"Get every word, governor. This is the last time you'll hear from us. We're not going to try to snatch your wife. No matter what you do, or where she is, we'll reach her. You can't stop us. If Babe Krager fries tomorrow night, she'll be dead damn' soon afterward. That's final."

The connection broke. Mark Hazzard had listened with the galling certainty that it would be futile to try to trace that call. Trencher's black eyes burned with grim purpose as he met Governor Bryant's gaze. Barbara Bryant came quietly to her husband's side and placed her hand softly on his.

"I'm not afraid, darling. You've made your decision and you're going to stick to it because nothing else is possible for a man of your stature. Now, let's forget it—shall we?"

Forget it! Forget that the most daring, most ruthless criminal in the city had promised her death? Forget that a merciless killer was even now setting a trap for her in defiance of every precaution the police might take? Forget she was marked as the prey of a human jackal? Hazzard and Trencher and the governor gazed at each other with the certainty in their eyes that they could not avoid the dread thought an instant.

Suddenly Governor Bryant took up the telephone. His voice crackled into the transmitter: "Connect me with the state prison!" Hazzard and Trencher waited in a tense hush until: "Give me Warden

Wharton. No matter if he left orders not to be disturbed. This is the governor calling. Ring him!" Then, each word clear and incisive:

"Governor Bryant, warden. About the case of Babe Krager. I want to assure you right now that my decision is made and will stand. I will not order either a reprieve or a commutation of sentence. Do you understand that clearly?"

Hazzard heard Wharton's voice rattle in the receiver: "Yes, sir. I will execute the sentence accordingly, Mr. Governor. Krager is going to die in the chair at exactly one minute past twelve midnight tomorrow night. I beg your pardon, Governor Bryant. *Tonight*."

The hands of Mark Hazzard and Inspector Trencher gripped the governor's firmly—and Bryant smiled. They left the executive offices together—but not by way of the front entrance, where a police escort was waiting. They stole out the back of the building like the two disreputable characters they seemed, and silently separated in the rosy gloom of the street.

Dawn was breaking—the dawn of a day of reckoning.

CHAPTER III

KILLER'S BARGAIN

HAZZARD SLIPPED into the courthouse as cautiously as he had left the State Capitol. The somnolent hush filling the building was disturbed only by his quiet steps as he climbed to his office. A light was shining through the pebbled pane. He found his secretary, Ann Nash, dozing at his desk, her head resting on her arms.

As tireless as she was efficient, as devoted to the man Mark Hazzard as to the district attorney, she had remained at her post throughout the night. A proud, fond smile curved Hazzard's lips as he tip-toed to a closet. Because he spent many more hours at his office than at his home he kept a change of clothing here. Without awakening the girl he pulled off the filthy rags he had worn most of the night, and slipped into fresh linen and a smart suit.

The zing of the telephone spun him from the mirror as he was knotting his tie. Ann Nash, instantly awake, had the instrument at her ear before Hazzard could touch it. She gazed in amazement as he gently took it from her with: "Home and bed for you, sweet. You need rest."

"Mark!" she exclaimed in a relieved burst. "I'm so glad you're back—and all right!"

He pressed his lips to her hand as an urgent voice sang over the wire. He was laden with fatigue and nervous strain, but it tightened his alertness. The report of the ex-cop Dan Carey came in a rush:

"I've got a lead, skipper! I told you about these ugly looking birds showing up at Krager's old hangouts. A new one has just shown up. He's here now—at the Red Rooster."

"Keep your eye on him, Danny," Hazzard urged. "I'm coming."

"You'd better make it fast, skipper! One of Krager's men will connect with him in a few minutes, then he'll disappear like the others. He's waiting in one of the back rooms upstairs. I'll wait for you near the alley entrance."

"I'm on my way!"

Hazzard quickly took a gun-harness from a drawer of his desk. The holster contained a Webley automatic like the weapon he had lost to the masked murderers. Ann Nash's eyes widened with anxiety as he strapped it on.

"Mark—are you absolutely sure of what you're doing? Trencher's after your scalp, you know. If you should slip up—if the crooks should manage to reach Mrs. Bryant because of it—Trencher will break you. You're in between two fires, and you can't let yourself forget it for a second."

"I know, darling, but I don't trust Trencher's methods any more than he trusts mine." Hazzard pulled into his top-coat as he spoke. "Trencher will use all the usual means of protecting Mrs. Bryant, and that's exactly what Krager is counting on. Trencher's system may be thorough and good, but Krager can anticipate every move and find an opening. The way to stop him is to get him first, if it's possible." Jerking on his hat, he strode to the door. "That's my job."

"Please be careful, Mark!" the girl pled.

"Listen, Ann. Get some sleep, but come back as soon as you're rested up. I'm going to need your help."

Hazzard hurried down to the furnace room entrance of the court-house. He scanned the street carefully before he eased out. He was sure he was not being watched when, at the corner, he ducked into a taxi. It carried him rapidly across the city to the underworld hangout known as the Red Rooster.

It was a two-story building glaring with neon signs, housing a huge bar on the street level, the second floor devoted to suites of rooms used for dubious purposes. Hazzard sent the cab past it, got out at the far corner, walked back. His coat-collar shielding his face, he turned from the deserted street into the gloomy alley.

In a doorway a muscular man in patrolman's uniform was stand-ing—Dan Carey. Carey was being sought by the very force of which he had once been a member—hunted as an escaped murderer. Hazzard had convicted him of the crime and sent him up the river—a duty faithfully executed while in his heart the district attorney had believed Carey innocent.

Carey had made a desperate escape from the train that was carrying him to the death house. Hazzard, on one of his midnight prowls into the city's nether-world of crime, had found the fugitive lying sick—with exhaustion and hunger in an alley very like the one in which they stood together now.

Hazzard had not turned the ex-cop over to the law. Instead, he had sheltered Carey from the dogged search directed by Inspector Trencher. Carey was his under-cover assistant in the task of meting out a justice higher than the written law. Discovery constantly threatened him—and the same danger menaced the world of Mark Hazzard. If ever it became known that the district attorney was harboring a fugitive, it would mean the breaking of Mark Hazzard.

Side by side, prosecutor and wanted man, they gazed at the alley door of the Red Rooster. A single blinded window at the rear of the second floor was chinked with light. Carey said quietly:

"He's still up there, skipper. One of Krager's men just went in— Drost—must be with him now. They're due to fade in a minute, but they seem to be staying longer than the others did. That may mean something extra special is up."

HAZZARD DIRECTED: "Tail them when they leave, Danny. I want to get a closer view. If anything unexpected comes up, try to tip me off. Watch yourself, copper. I need you, you know."

"I'm not letting myself get spotted, skipper—not when I know what it'll do to you."

They crossed the alley together. Hazzard whispered instructions as they listened near the side door of the dive. He stepped back against the wall when Carey knocked. Slow steps approached. A safety chain rattled. A ratty eye looked out, narrowed with suspicion. Carey glanced up and down the alley warily.

"How about a glass of beer and a smoke?" he asked. "My feet hurt like hell."

"Sure."

The door rattled open and Carey sauntered in. Waiting outside, Hazzard heard the chain click back into its catch. Hushed moments passed. Hazzard knew Carey was staying in the rear of the place, near the door, with the beer and the cigarette. At last the rattle came again, so faint it was scarcely audible, and the knob turned.

Hazzard sidled in, closed the door silently. Another door shafted smoky light across the gloomy hall. Carey was blocking it, glass in hand, back turned. A few unsteady voices rumbled from the bar beyond. Hazzard glided past to the base of the stairs.

Silent steps took him up. The lighted room, closed, was at the end of the upper hall. Hazzard drifted to the door.

A low, husky tone came through the panel: "—takin' no chances at this stage of the game. Before we head for the Fahenstock place, the King's goin' to look you over himself."

Hazzard noted that. *Fahenstock place.*

"He knows he can trust Lou Garrow."

"He knows there's goin' to be a hell of a stink raised when the governor's fine lady gets pumped full of bullets, and he's takin' no chance."

Garrow. Somewhere Hazzard had heard that name. An imported gunman, certainly, but it tantalized the depths of his memory. Listening, he heard a knock below and another rattle of the safety chain. Quick steps sounded through a whisper. Startled, Hazzard saw Dan Carey coming up the stairs. Carey's face was white.

Hazzard hurried quietly to the ex-cop to hear: "Krager! He's here! He's coming up!"

Hazzard jerked Carey across the hall as a figure appeared at the base of the stairs. Footfalls climbed. The flight was the only way down—cut off by the ascending ruler of the underworld. Hazzard's swift gesture took Carey with him back along the hall. They darted to the door opposite that in which the voices had sounded.

It was bolted on the inside.

Hazzard's lips pressed down a moan of despair as he glanced back. King Krager had stopped short at the head of the stairs. His voice snapped like the lash of a whip: "Hazzard!" It was echoed in a husky whisper inside the closed corner room: "Hazzard!" The district attorney straightened, hand gliding to his Webley, trapped in the dead end of the hall.

Krager's voice lashed again: "Get Hazzard!"

Hazzard poised to sprint toward Krager. Carey's service gat flickered up. At the same instant the door of the corner room flashed open. Two men sprang out, automatics gripped—Drost, one of Krager's chief henchmen, and Lou Garrow, the imported rod man. They blocked the hallway as Krager ran closer. Hazzard whirled to the open door.

Carey bounded in beside him as he spun to slap it shut. The swift moves of the mobsters defeated the attempt. A shoulder thrust through the crack. Hazzard and Carey retreated when the two men crashed in. Krager lurched after them. Hazzard's automatic cracked twice as a heavy table reared up. He crashed down in the corner, Carey heaving upon him. The light went out.

Only feeble daylight slitted in through the blinded windows as three savage attackers fell on Hazzard and Carey. Neither could fire now for fear of wounding the other. A gun slashed down and cracked hard. Carey moaned. Hazzard kicked, fighting up. Thick arms clutched him in a gorilla hug. He fell with two men crushing upon him. The Webley was snatched away. He was pinioned by hard heels pressing on his wrists.

He lay still, breath sizzling, temper raging. A voice snarled: "Turn on the light." A snap sounded, a ceiling fixture blazed. Hazzard raised his throbbing head to see two automatics and four evil eyes watching him—Krager's and Garrow's. Drost's weapon had Carey cornered. Carey was glaring with fists clenched, a gash dripping red across his cheek. Aching muscles pulled Hazzard up.

"Maybe we can do a better job of it this time, Hazzard," King Krager rasped. "I owe it to you."

Garrow's eyes widened. "Hazzard? *He's* the D.A.? There's something screwy. I remember him—from about ten years back. His name wasn't Hazzard then. It was Grant—Dennis Grant!"

The steel-cold certainty stabbed into Hazzard's brain. Garrow! He had it now. Ten years ago—that was about right. Eleven, to be exact. The name connected directly with the narrow-jawed, close-eyed face he was staring at now. It was the face of a nightmare demon, leering in triumph.

Krager commanded: "What're you talking about, Garrow? Spill it!"

GARROW LAUGHED—AN ugly cackle, "We're not going to worry about the D.A. any more. He can't touch us, Krager. We've got him right where we want him. Because Dennis Grant is his name, see? He's wanted for murder back in Philly, and there's a life sentence still waiting for him."

Krager rapped: "Sure of that?"

"Sure? Say, I was in the cell right opposite his for a couple weeks. I couldn't forget him. He was up for murder, and he was convicted, but he escaped from the courtroom. They never did find him. Well, we have. Think of that! The D.A.—Mark Hazzard!"

"Hazzard stood rigid, fists clenched, overwhelmed with dismay, his stunned mind flooded with bitter memories.

It was a secret that had haunted his every living hour—the truth these killers now knew. He remembered with acrid clarity the chill Christmas Eve so many years ago when, broke and hungry, he had ridden the rods to Philadelphia so that he might spend the holidays with his mother. He had never reached his home. Instead, he had found himself trapped by cement walls and steel bars—charged with murder.

That fateful night, just as the freight pulled into the terminal, another tramp, apparently trailed by a criminal record, had shot a yard detective in order to escape arrest for vagrancy. The young man then known as Dennis Grant had never seen the dead man nor touched the murder weapon, but the searchers had closed in upon him.

"Life—that's what he got," Garrow was gloating. "Murder's never outlawed. All we have to do is tip off the cops and Hazzard will spend the rest of his days in prison."

The hungry shivering nights while he had not dared sleep because he must keep out of the hands of the law—Hazzard recalled them. At last he had found safety and a job. Endless nights he had studied law in order to learn its defects so that he might somehow make it mean true justice. His whole life as Mark Hazzard was summed up in the opportunity his office as district attorney gave him to justly wield punishment on the guilty and help the innocent.

Deep in the past the truth had lain hidden—the fact that Mark Hazzard, state prosecutor, was Dennis Grant, escaped convict—but now it was known to the merciless dictator of the city's underworld.

Krager asked tightly: "Can you prove that, Garrow?"

"Sure," Garrow answered confidently. "I'll swear to it. Every official of the criminal court of Delphia County, Pennsylvania, at the time Grant was tried, can back it up. There are records somewhere that will identify him—they'll show him up. If we tip off the cops, Hazzard hasn't got a chance."

Krager's thin lips were curling. "How about Inspector Trencher, Hazzard? Your old buddy, Trencher. He'll welcome this dope, won't he?"

FROM THE corner Drost blurted: "That's not all, chief! Take a look at this bird here!" He poked the gun at Dan Carey. "I've been trying to remember him—now I've got it. He's wanted for murder, same as Hazzard. And he came in here with the D.A.!"

Carey snapped: "If you open your trap about that, I'll kill you, you filthy rat!"

"Maybe," Drost drawled. "You'll fry just the same. Don't forget that. And this high and mighty D.A.—he'll never live to come out of the jug."

Krager's eyes were narrowed, calculating. Hazzard, fighting the turmoil of his temper, saw them light shrewdly. He straddled, fists still lumped, and asked huskily:

"All right, Krager. Let's have it." Krager nodded. "That's the idea, Hazzard. Cooperation. You're wise. Just lay low and let us alone, and you'll be all right. If you make a move against us, Trencher finds out about you, but while you keep mum you're safe. That's a bargain, isn't it, Hazzard?"

Hazzard snapped: "I'm admitting nothing."

"Listen. I'm not bluffing, Hazzard—you know that. I mean every word I say. That goes for what I've already told the governor. If Babe fries tonight, Bryant's wife is going to get it. If she gets it, you'll be helping us. You're going to follow orders—or else."

Hazzard challenged: "Go on, Krager."

"Mrs. Bryant is going to stay in town tonight. She's going to be at home. It's your job to see to that, Hazzard—or else. We've got our plan. You're just what I need to make it perfect. Remember this, Hazzard. Keep her with you, and turn left. Got it? Keep her with you and turn left."

"And if I don't?"

"If you don't do exactly that, Mark Hazzard becomes Dennis Grant—serving a life sentence. And your sidekick here goes to the chair. And we get the governor's wife anyway. Would you like your gun back, Hazzard?"

King Krager proffered the Webley with insolent confidence. Hazzard's hand closed on it coldly. A savage impulse seized him to jerk its trigger—to kill these crooks as mercilessly as they killed. He knew the attempt would cost Dan Carey's life and his own, that it could not halt Krager's diabolical scheme. He forced himself to return the automatic to its arm-pit holster—but the challenge remained glinting in his eyes.

"You can go now, Hazzard," Krager said levelly. "You and your friend the convicted murderer. Remember your instructions, that's all. Keep Mrs. Bryant in her house. Stay with her and turn left. I think we understand each other."

Hazzard's heart beat frigidly as he turned to the door. Carey stared in amazement as his service gat was put in his hand. They went into the hall together, down the stairs, out into the alley. They paused among the quickening sounds of the ascending day—the day of reckoning—haggard eyes on each other.

"Skipper—you're not going to let 'em get away with that!" Carey gasped. "If you're thinking of me, skipper, forget it. I'd rather go to the chair than see 'em do that to you."

Hazzard's hand closed hard on the ex-cop's arm. "I know you would, Danny—but there's no other way. I'm not thinking of myself—of going to prison for life. Some day it will happen—I'll go back—but I can't let it happen now. For your sake, and Ann's, and the governor's—in the name of everything decent I've fought for, Danny—I can't. I've got to play Krager's dirty game, but—" his lips tightened across clenched teeth— "we're not licked yet!"

"Count on me to the limit, skipper!"

"I've got to, Danny. Listen. Begin watching the Fahenstock place. It's a big estate on the same boulevard as the governor's home, to the left. Don't let yourself be spotted, but watch it every minute, and keep in touch with me by phone. That's the most you can do, Danny. The rest is up to me."

He watched Carey hurry from the alley. When the ex-cop was gone from sight he walked slowly along the squalid street seeking a taxi. Krager's command haunted his mind: "Keep her with you and turn left." The Fahenstock place—the hideout—to the left of the governor's mansion. "Turn left—or else."

Directions to death.

CHAPTER IV

DOOM BY THE CLOCK

MARK HAZZARD strode directly to the door of Inspector Trencher's office in police headquarters. He thrust in without knocking. Trencher ceased speaking, flashed hot eyes upon him. Governor Bryant, standing at the inspector's desk, turned red-shot eyes on Hazzard. The district attorney announced in clipped, bitter words:

"Our little strategy is wrecked, inspector. Krager knows now we weren't killed in the freight car. One of his men spotted me."

Trencher's heavy brows beetled. "Damn it, Hazzard! Our best advantage lost! That's what comes of your heading out alone. I warned you to stay under cover, but you wouldn't. Now we can't take Krager by surprise—he'll be watching our moves. What if your bungling costs Mrs. Bryant her life—how will you like that, Hazzard?"

Hazzard paled. "I have suggestions for safeguarding her against—"

"Keep them to yourself!" Trencher's fist crashed down. "Hazzard, you're out of bounds. This is strictly police work, and you have no hand in it. It's my responsibility, not yours, and I'm handling it as I see fit. If you don't keep hands off, your hot-headedness may upset my whole plan."

Hazzard's hot-headedness flushed his face. Rage kept him silent as Trencher turned to Governor Bryant.

"The safest place for Mrs. Bryant tonight is this headquarters building. No crooks can possibly reach her here. I'll have every door guarded and I'll surround you both with my best men. Krager may be smart, but he'll never be able to—"

"True, inspector, but you forget," Mark Hazzard broke in quietly, "that Mrs. Bryant will have to leave this building later. Your plan may delay Krager's move, but can't stop it. He'll wait his chance and strike

264

when you least expect. You'll never trap him unless you pretend to ignore his threat. You've actually got to invite him to make it good."

Trencher's eyes shone with the cold hardness of black diamonds. "I've warned you to keep hands off, Hazzard. I'll take no such risk as that. With Mrs. Bryant here—"

"I'm inclined, inspector," the governor interposed quietly, "to agree with Mr. Hazzard. It would be a mistake to betray our real fears. Bringing Mrs. Bryant here would show Krager we're afraid. We must take every possible precaution, of course, but less obviously. Krager is devilishly clever—and we've got to be as shrewd as he or it will cost Barbara's life."

"Exactly," Hazzard said with a tight smile. "The best place for Mrs. Bryant tonight, governor, is at home."

"Precisely. That is my own decision. Barbara and I must follow our usual routine, as though we believe Krager won't dare carry out his threat. In that way, by seeming to leave ourselves open to attack, we can best lay a trap. Actually invite Krager to make the attempt, as Mr. Hazzard says, though—pray heaven, if he succeeds—!"

Trencher's knuckles rattled as he glowered at Hazzard. "All right. You'll be at home, governor. But you're doing it at Hazzard's advice, not mine. I'll do my utmost to safeguard Mrs. Bryant. I'll build up an entirely new plan immediately. I'll take every possible precaution. When the time comes, governor, I'm going to ask you to check my preparations and agree that I have foreseen every contingency, so far as is possible in that location. Then, if Krager does succeed in reaching Mrs. Bryant—understand this distinctly—if he does make his threat good, her blood will be on Hazzard's hands, not mine."

"I accept that responsibility, inspector."

Hazzard spoke tensely, and glanced at the desk clock. Noon. The picture of those closed hands of the dial persisted as he turned away—twelve o'clock, the next minute creeping past.

He left the office with mocking voices echoing in his mind.

Krager's: "Mrs. Bryant is going to be at home—it's your job to see to that, Hazzard—or else." Trencher's: "Her blood will be on Hazzard's hands not mine." Krager's: "Stay with her and turn left." Trencher's: "Hazzard, your hot-headed bungling may cost Mrs. Bryant her life." Krager's: "If you don't follow orders, Mark Hazzard becomes Dennis Grant, serving a life sentence, and your sidekick goes to the chair." Trencher's: "Her blood will be on Hazzard's hands."

Babe Krager was scheduled to fry in the death house in exactly twelve hours....

ELEVEN-THIRTY-ONE—HALF AN hour until the stroke of doom.

The dash clock of Mark Hazzard's roadster was on the minute as he turned into the broad driveway of the home of Governor Bryant on Seymour Drive. He had scanned the dark grounds of the Fahenstock estate on the way without noting anything suspicious. Sensing hidden eyes watching him, he had realized that Inspector Trencher had guards secretly posted along the approach to the Bryant mansion. Leaving his roadster near the garage, Hazzard found only one indication of Trencher's grim preparations—a red star floating in the sky.

Alert headquarters men were stationed in the gardens and near the entrances, but darkness covered them. Cheery light glowed from the windows, through partly drawn drapes, but near them, inside, other men were standing ready. The darkness beyond the open door of the big garage looked empty, but it sheltered an entire squad prepared to repulse an attack with machine-guns, tear-gas and searchlights. The scene was cunningly serene—yet the hovering red star marked a further precaution planned by Trencher.

It was a blimp, especially chartered for the purpose, circling above the governor's home with all lights out but one. In its gondola, another squad of men was keeping an eagle's watch on the grounds while the bag silently patrolled.

A pause followed Hazzard's knock at the entrance of the huge house—a pause while unseen sentries made sure of his identity. A nervous man-servant opened the way. Inspector Trencher, standing arms akimbo in the library, smiled wryly as Hazzard entered. He drawled a protest:

"You insist on mixing in, do you, Hazzard? Think I can't handle this? I'm a pretty old dog at this game, you know. I think we're pretty well set,"

Hazzard said quietly: "Perhaps there's one thing you haven't thought of, inspector."

"We've considered everything. Every door and window of this house is under watch. There are men concealed in every room, in the attic, in the cellar. That's just routine. We've checked every inch of the place for hidden explosive, and we know there isn't any. I've got men guarding the light lines so they won't be cut. You may think my methods are slow and antiquated, Hazzard, but you've got to admit they're thorough."

"I hope so, inspector," Hazzard answered earnestly. "You're even prepared for the possibility that a bomb might be dropped from the sky, but have you thought—"

"That's what the blimp's up there for. It's watching the Drive and park. It'll spot any airplane that might come near, without being seen itself. It's carrying machine-guns and wireless. It can stop a plane and give us warning in time to get Mrs. Bryant into the wine cellar. Besides, it can come down fast in case of a ground attack. Three quick blinks of a flashlight will bring it swooping down in a hurry."

"But there is still one thing that can get past all your precautions, inspector—"

Trencher went on. "We're not going to be drawn away by a trick and leave the place unprotected. In case the crooks make a running attack, half my men are instructed to give chase, but the other half have explicit orders to stay at their posts. On top of that, any car beating it away from here can be kept in sight by the men in the blimp. Add to that prowl cars standing ready, the whole neighborhood policed—"

"One thing you've forgotten, inspector," Hazzard insisted. "One thing that can reach past all your defenses. Long-range bullets."

Trencher scowled. "They can't touch Mrs. Bryant that way."

Hazzard countered: "Look out the windows. There are four or five hills in sight, outside the district you've policed. Powerful rifles can cover the distance easily. Every one of these windows is a shining target. Krager knows he can't reach Mrs. Bryant as long as she's inside this house. But if those bullets—"

The quick opening of a door turned Hazzard. Governor Bryant, his face ashy, strode stiffly into the room. He jerked aside the portières of an arch and called huskily: "Durham!" Turning back, peering at a legal envelope in his trembling fingers, he came slowly to Trencher and Hazzard. He waited until Hugh Durham, his secretary, entered, then said slowly:

"Gentlemen, I know you've done everything possible—I know I'm betraying my honor and insulting your integrity by doing this—but it's a risk I can no longer face."

He gazed haggardly at the electric mantel clock. Its red hand was slowly spinning away tense seconds. The time lacked twenty-four minutes of the zero hour when a murderer was scheduled to pay the supreme penalty in the death house twenty miles away. Sight of that revolving red hand—red as blood—sent a shudder through Governor Bryant.

"Are you afraid, sir," Mark Hazzard asked quietly, "that Mrs. Bryant is not safe?"

"I am afraid. I admit that I am horribly afraid. Barbara is in her room, guarded by the most courageous detectives in the city. I can think of no way Krager might reach her—but there may be a way. He's planned it. He's waiting. Barbara means more to me than my office—more to me than anything else in the world. I can't—I can't take the chance!"

The governor turned to the telephone. His finger trembled as it spun the dial. Hazzard and Trencher watched his agonized eyes as he asked for: "Warden Wharton, quickly!" Then, his voice strained, his face deep-lined with self-condemnation:

"Wharton. The governor calling. Disregard all my previous statements in the Krager case. Delay the execution. I am sending my secretary to your office immediately with an executive order commuting Krager's sentence to life imprisonment. Durham should arrive by midnight. That's all."

Hazzard and Trencher gazed pityingly at a man crushed by fear, overwhelmed by his whole-hearted love for the girl he had married. Bryant proffered the sealed envelope to Hugh Durham. He said tightly:

"Drive fast."

Durham blinked his dismay, but hurried into the hall. Hazzard and Trencher, exchanging bitter glances, realized that argument with Bryant would be futile. Both men had labored grimly to convict Babe Krager. Their defiance of King Krager's power had jeopardized their lives. Now their earnest endeavor was being turned into a mockery by a man who was destroying himself in the eyes of an admiring public, who was granting the human wolves of the underworld a soul-searing triumph over true justice. And the agony in Governor Bryant's eyes revealed that he knew it.

He drew another envelope slowly from his pocket as Durham slammed out the entrance.

"This, gentlemen," he said in a hushed tone, "is my resignation—effective at two minutes past twelve tonight."

THE TELEPHONE shrilled into the tight silence. Bryant jerked the instrument up. "For you, Hazzard," he said. Hazzard answered hastily: "I'll take it in your study, sir, if you don't mind." He stepped in quickly, closed the door, took up the desk phone. Dan Carey's voice whispered over the wire:

"Skipper, I've got—"

"Hold it, Danny!"

Hazzard slammed the phone down, jerked desk drawers open. He snatched up several sheets of stationery, a long envelope bearing the engraved imprint of the executive offices. He shouldered out a side door of the study and hurried to the rear of the house, folding the sheets, stuffing them into the envelope, sealing it. He burst from the rear entrance, past startled guards he could not see, and sprinted to a car that was just backing from the garage.

"Durham!" The governor's secretary stopped the car. Hazzard gripped his arm. "Durham, the governor made a mistake. He had two envelopes you know, one containing his resignation. This is the right one." He slipped the sealed commutation of sentence from Durham's fingers, gave Durham the envelope he had prepared. "Step on it, old man!"

He smiled tightly as Durham backed to the Drive. Carefully tucking the commutation inside his coat, he re-entered the house. In the study the telephone instrument was still off its contact. Grimly he said over the line:

"Go ahead, Danny."

"Watching the Fahenstock place, skipper," Carey whispered. "Krager's there—a dozen others. The Fahenstocks are in Europe, I found out, and Krager must have rented the place through a false name. I don't get it, skipper. It's not even in sight of the governor's home. What the devil—"

"Keep watching it, Danny. If anything breaks, we'll need your help, but remember you've got to keep clear of Trencher's men. If it means bullets, copper, spend plenty."

He broke the connection. Immediately he spun the dial. He asked for: "Warden Wharton." When Wharton's heavy voice answered he talked quickly:

"Mark Hazzard calling for Governor Bryant from another phone. You're to disregard the governor's last message. He sent it because we suspect his telephone is tapped. We're letting Krager think the governor's cracked—but he hasn't. Durham's driving to the prison now, supposedly with the commutation, but there's only blank paper in the envelope. We've planned it as a trick to make Krager lower his guard, then we're going to close in on him. Understand that clearly?"

Wharton boomed: "That's more like it, all around! Babe Krager deserves the chair. If the governor's not sending the commutation, Krager gets fried on schedule."

"No commutation is coming, warden. Go ahead strictly as first planned. Don't call the governor back to check, because as I said, his wire may be tapped. You may hold me fully responsible."

Mark Hazzard's eyes glinted as he stepped from the study. Trencher, jaw clamped, was standing near the fireplace, staring at nothing. Governor Bryant was slumped in a huge leather chair. Barbara Bryant had come into the library. Her face was wan, but she was smiling. While her husband gazed at her speechlessly she said softly:

"Will it help a little if I say again I'm not afraid?"

It told Hazzard that Bryant had not spoken—had not revealed he had yielded to the dread threat. The governor's lips worked with an impulse to blurt out the truth, but he kept silent. Hazzard smiled with grim tightness as he gazed at the clock.

Twelve minutes until midnight—thirteen under the closing of the death house switch.

Hazzard strode to the radio, clicked it on. An announcer's voice faded up: "We wish to announce, ladies and gentlemen, that immediately word is received from the state prison, over our special wire, that the sentence of death has been executed on Babe Krager, we will broadcast the news to the radio audience." As the music of a string quartet resumed, Hazzard saw Governor Bryant wince—but the tight smile remained on Hazzard's lips.

A knock sounded at the front entrance. The district attorney and Trencher alertly watched the hallway. Ann Nash hurried into the library, carrying a brown-wrapped bundle under one arm. Barbara received her with gracious warmth. Ann placed the bundle in Hazzard's hand and his eyes thanked her. Putting it aside, he went quickly to the windows and drew the blinds.

Trencher demanded: "Why the devil are you doing that, when—" He broke off, with a quick glance at Barbara Bryant, confusion flushing his face. "There's nothing to worry about, Hazzard."

Hazzard made no answer. He stood by the radio, every sense alert.

His gaze turned again and again to the mantel clock. The music played on smoothly—the only sound. Bryant, Hazzard knew, was waiting in torment for the news announcement that Babe Krager had been granted a commutation of sentence. The minutes crawled past. The red hand spun toward the hour of doom.

Five minutes of twelve.... Four minutes.... Three.... Slowly the red hand whirled off another sixty seconds. Like scissors snipping upon a thread of life the clock hands closed upon the hour of twelve. Inexorable time shuttled on. Thirty seconds more.... Now one minute past.

It came with startling swiftness, with chilling abruptness, from the radio:

"Ladies and gentlemen! A special news dispatch direct from the state prison! At exactly one minute past twelve o'clock Babe Krager, condemned murderer, died in the electric chair!"

CHAPTER V

KILLER'S SIEGE

THE TELEPHONE shrilled.

Governor Bryant jerked up from his chair. He made no move to answer the call. He stood staring transfixed at the radio. He blurted aghast: "How is it possible? How is it—possible?"

The telephone jangled again.

Barbara Bryant's arm stole across her husband's shoulders. "They didn't break you, darling. I'm so proud they didn't. Because I'm not afraid, really I'm not, as long as I'm at your side. Well—it's their play now, isn't it? The governor stood by his guns, as I knew he would, and now it's up to them."

The telephone jangled a third time, and a stunned police inspector groped toward it.

Mark Hazzard was proffering a sealed envelope to Governor Bryant. Bryant stared at it blankly, then fiercely. His arm angled with a powerful impulse to drive his clamped fist into Hazzard's face—but he did not strike. He looked into the eyes of his wife, and a sob broke through his lips. He straightened, shoulders squaring. His hand, taking the envelope from the district attorney, did not tremble.

"Thank you, Hazzard," he said.

Trencher was snarling at the telephone. "Ambulance? Nobody here called an ambulance! I don't care what they said—it's a fake!"

He whirled away, loped to the front entrance, jerked it open. "Collins!" he barked into the darkness. "Draper! There's an ambulance heading this way. The driver got it past by saying it was called here because Mrs. Bryant's seriously hurt. It's a trick! Stop that car! Move, damn you!"

The ambulance was streaking nearer along the broad drive. Its red headlamps gleamed like a dragon's eyes, but it sped with siren silent.

As it whirred toward the Bryant estate, a dark-clad man pulled up from the front seat and dragged himself onto the flat top. While it slowed he straightened, a rifle snagged against his shoulder. With startling swiftness reports cracked from its bore.

The crashing of broken window panes filled the big Bryant house. Upstairs and down, glass shattered in the frames. As the ambulance rolled, a second man appeared inside the wide-thrown rear doors. Leveling a rifle, he pumped bullets at the house. Powder crashed through the windows on one side wall, then the front, then the other side. With tinkling fragments raining, the ambulance began to speed.

Police guns blasted along the street as plainclothes men sprang from the shadows. A radio car lurched from the darkness under a tree, careened across the lawn, darted out the gate. The red beacon of the patrol blimp made a streak in the sky as it dived toward the escaping ambulance. From its gondola a machine-gun stuttered out leaden defiance. Death hailed at the fleeing car.

Inside the governor's mansion—flames! Bullets ripping through the window drapes left fire on the fabric. Slugs smashing into the walls sprayed blinding, hissing light. Projectiles grooving into the floors left flaring trails clouding smoke. Each impact created a tuft of flames that swiftly spread. In every room, inside the walls, under the rugs and above the ceiling, sizzling destruction struck— incendiary bullets filled with blazing thermite.

As the choking fumes clouded, as the flare brightened in the mist, Hazzard sprang to Barbara Bryant's side with Webley drawn. His hand, closed hard on Ann Nash's arm, drew her close. He heard men scampering in the rooms above, someone shouting a fire alarm over the telephone. A headquarters man ran from the rear of the house carrying a streaming fire-extinguisher. Hazzard tore it from his hands, thrust into the study, turned the spray upon one flaming spot after another.

"Bring the bundle, Ann!" He sprang close to Barbara Bryant and the governor. "This is their plan working! Their object is to force you out. Once you're out you're open to attack. You've got just one chance— you've got to follow instructions. Here are two police uniforms—get into them, both of you!"

Bryant gasped: "Barbara? I?"

"Yes! Fast as you can make it!"

Hazzard dropped the extinguisher and hurried from the study, into a shouting bedlam. The small charges of thermite carried by the bullets quickly burned themselves out, and the spots of flame could be easily quenched, but their multiplicity was a nightmare. The house was not doomed, Hazzard realized, but the suffocating fumes must inevitably drive every breathing being into the open—while killers' guns waited.

He saw Trencher groping dismayed through the blinding vapor. The inspector blurted: "I was right in the first place. They should have stayed at headquarters. I'm going to take them down there now, Hazzard—and you're going to keep hands off!"

Hazzard answered quickly: "You've got to wait until they're in the uniforms. Let the other cars go first. It's their only chance. I'll drive the governor's car."

HE HURRIED into the clouded vestibule, snatched up a man's Chesterfield and derby. Going back, he pulled the coat on. Ann Nash came close, her eyes widened with consternation.

"What are you doing, Mark?"

"I've got to make them believe we're falling into their trap. If I'm at the wheel of the governor's car, they'll think Barbara Bryant is inside too. It's a chance, but if I don't play it they may sneak out and try to get her later."

"But if they don't actually see her, Mark—"

The telephone jangled. In the confusion of smoke and noise the sound chilled Hazzard's nerves. He groped to the instrument, jerked it up. A rasping voice carried over the wire, edged with evil determination:

"Remember orders, Hazzard. Turn left. She's going to get it now—or you're through."

Hazzard slammed the instrument down. His pulse pounded with anger as he turned back to Trencher and Ann. Ann had gone into the vestibule and had come back with a woman's fur coat and a smart felt hat. She said breathlessly:

"These are Mrs. Bryant's, Mark. I'll wear them and go with you. They won't suspect then that Mrs. Bryant isn't really with you. If they do suspect, and call off the rest of their plan, it will mean she's still in danger. In this way—"

"I can't let you do that, Ann!" Hazzard protested. "Don't you realize it will make you a target? I'll put the coat and hat beside me on the seat—that will be enough. Trencher, listen—"

The inspector, face crimson with anger, growled: "I told you to keep out of this, Hazzard. It's my job, not yours. If you gum up the works any more than you already have—"

"Listen to me!" Hazzard smiled wryly, "Krager's gang are waiting for you to make exactly the move you're going to make. So far we've no admissible evidence against them—we've got to make them spring their trap and catch them red-handed—but it's going to cost the lives of some of your men if you're not prepared—"

"I'm handling this!" Trencher challenged. "Whatever happens to my men, they're under my orders, not yours. I'll lead the cars to headquarters as I see fit."

"They're waiting, I tell you!" Hazzard insisted. "They'll open up on you from—" He was about to say— "the Fahenstock place." He knew the name would bring heated questions from Trencher. How did Hazzard know about the Fahenstock place? Why hadn't he spoken of it sooner? How was Trencher to know the use of that house wasn't another trick to draw some of his men off on a false lead while the governor and Mrs. Bryant were left inadequately protected? Yet, in spite of the danger, Hazzard began to press on. "They're camped in the—"

The door of the study opened quickly. Governor Bryant stepped out white-faced, buttoning the tunic of his patrolman's uniform. His wife, slender and trim, clad also in blue coat and trousers, was tucking her hair inside her helmet. Trencher stepped back, clipping orders.

"Get the cars ready! Start when I say the word. Be ready for an attack and if it comes, give them everything you've got."

Hazzard began again: "Trencher, you've got to listen—"

"Keep out of this, Hazzard! I'm not listening to a word you say!"

Hazzard gazed in dismay at Ann. She was still holding the fur coat and felt hat. "You stay here! It's the safest spot," he told the girl, turning to the entrance. He hurried toward the garage with Ann following.

Guns glittered in the light of the broken windows while fumes gushed out. Police cars had appeared and were lined up in the drive. Patrolmen were scurrying through the darkness. Hazzard heard one of them growl: "The ambulance is wrecked! Both sharpshooters dead!"

In the garage, Hazzard jerked open the left front door of the governor's sedan. Probing under the cushion, he found a screwdriver. He quickly loosened the hinge bolts of the door, pulled it free. Climbing to the wheel, he settled the door firmly in its socket. It remained

in place as he started the motor, hands curling white on the wheel—
the Chesterfield and derby lending him the appearance of Governor
Bryant.

Trencher was climbing into a police car at the head of the drive.
Men with bared weapons were crowding into the others. Starters were
snarling. Governor and Mrs. Bryant, surrounded by armed men and
safeguarded by their uniforms, were hurrying to a car near the garage.
A black parade began to move out of the driveway. Trencher was at
the wheel of the first. Hazzard saw in dismay that the inspector was
turning left!

The expanse of a public park spread on the opposite side of the
broad thoroughfare. It must be circled by the police cars in order to
reach headquarters. And the wheeled cavalcade must pass the Fahenstock place because Inspector Trencher had chosen the shorter way
and was turning left!

Hazzard meshed the gears. He was about to send the governor's
car past the others in the drive when its right front door opened. Ann
Nash slipped into the seat beside him. He stared in dismay—because
the girl was wearing the fur coat and modish felt hat belonging to
Mrs. Bryant. He blurted:

"Good Lord, Ann, you can't do that! They'll turn their guns directly on you. Leave me the coat and hat and stay here. Hurry it! I've
got to stick behind Trencher if—"

"Step on it, Mark," the girl said quietly. "I'm willing to take the
same chance you're taking. If the governor's wife isn't with him, Krager
will get wise. Trencher's on his way. Please hurry, Mark!"

Hazzard realized with a moan of consternation that there was no
time for argument. He spurted the big sedan to the broad drive. He
weaved past moving police cars, nosed into position directly ahead of
Trencher. The others lined up behind him. He said tensely, his fingers
tightening on Ann's while she smiled:

"Darling, listen. If anything happens—to either of us—I love you.
Remember that."

On the Drive the ambulance lay twisted on its side, two still,
white-coated figures spilled out of it, guarded by grim police. Overhead
a red star was hovering—the blimp, skirting along the route the cars
were taking. Ahead, near the corner of the park, the Fahenstock house
loomed lightless. The parade of cars was approaching it.

IN THE dark front rooms of the Fahenstock house, silent men were crouching at the windows overlooking the Drive. Tripoded machine-guns sat between each pair. Searchlights, connected with the house wiring, were looking downward while other men waited at the switches. Behind his killer army, King Krager, evil eyes narrowed, peered through the panes. The string of cars was moving now directly in front of the Fahenstock mansion.

Krager commanded: "Give it to 'em!"

Instantly a machine-gun tattooed. Glass splintered in front of the tripoded weapons. Slugs streaked down, their flight marked by the green glow of tracer bullets. Lead hailed from other windows of the big house, at the same moment, as other machine-guns chattered their song of death. A storm of doom broke upon the police cars in the street.

Windshields and side windows went white. Enamel flew from dented metal. Powerful projectiles ripped through car tops. Instantly brakes slammed, motors roared, bumpers clashed.

At the first sputter of a machine-gun, Mark Hazzard had slapped his foot to the brake pedal. He ducked down as slugs slammed against the car. "Out of sight, Ann! You'll be safe on the running board on the other side." He thrust the opposite door open, almost spilled the girl into the street in his anxiety. While lead whistled around him, he gripped the handle of the door near him and twisted. It sagged out of its frame. Holding it like a shield, bringing his Webley into his hand, Hazzard crouched low.

Trencher had hopped out of his police car. "Surround that place!" Uniformed men were ducking along the line of cars, skirmishing to the hedge, guns in hand. Hazzard hurried ahead of them. The heavy metal door quaked with the impact of raining bullets as he held it in front of him with one hand. He slipped into the drive while blue uniforms scurried around him and Trencher barked orders: "Cover every door!" Siege!

As Hazzard stumbled toward the side of the house, there came the added menace of blinding light! White beams shot down from the windows of the big house. The shafts swept along the hedges, into the gardens where Trencher's men were seeking shelter. Shouts of dismay gave quick answer to the glare and the renewed rattling of the guns in the windows. From one of the upper rooms a hoarse, exultant cry came: "We got her! She went down!"

The words flooded horror into Hazzard's heart while fury-sent he charged toward a side door. He drove the weighty square of steel at the panels. As the wood splintered, a uniformed figure brushed against him. "Skipper!" Hazzard peered alarmedly into the drawn face of Dan Carey. A fugitive of the law was at his side while the police who had long been hunting him swarmed the yard.

"Danny! Get under cover or they'll recognize you!"

"I'll risk it, skipper! Maybe they don't think I'm a cop any more, but I do. Those guys out there were my buddies once. I can't stand by and do nothing while Krager's gang mows 'em down! He's here, skipper—I saw him sneak in!"

Grimly, Hazzard again drove the heavy car door against the panels. A section of wood cracked out. He reached through, released a bolt. Webley ready, he sprang into a dark hall. Carey shouldered in beside him. Hazzard peered up a flight of stairs as he ordered:

"Watch down here, copper. Don't let any of 'em get out—but don't let Trencher see you!"

In Hazzard's mind that cry of evil triumph was still echoing: "We got her! She went down!" He dropped his steel shield, bounded up the stairs. Deafening gunfire was echoing inside and outside the house. He paused, peering into a front room of the second floor. Dark figures were huddling at the windows beside the spitting machine-guns. King Krager, commanding the onslaught, was standing back, gun in hand, just inside.

Hazzard snapped: "Krager!"

Krager spun. His eyes widened. The automatic in his hand swept level at Hazzard. Hazzard knew the gunners at the window had jerked startled eyes back, but he was seeing only Krager. The reflection of the searchlights bleared his vision as he leaped aside. His Webley spoke at the instant Krager's automatic spat. Swift shots clashed. Hazzard lurched against the wall, his left arm running hot red.

Swift footfalls—Krager stumbling out the door. Hazzard pulled up, eyes stinging with the glaring light, to see two men at one of the guns swinging its barrel toward him. They were Drost and Garrow. The gun jumped in jerky recoil. Black dots stitched into the wall toward Hazzard.

HE DROPPED, automatic cracking. One of the men at the machine-gun leaped to tip-toes. The other fell back, neck gushing, as the first went down like a length of chain. He spilled the tripod over.

The gun belched a shot into the ceiling, stopped—a metallic chant over the two men who lay dead.

Hazzard straightened, firing as he backed out the door. Men were loping down the stairs—some of the squad who had dropped from the blimp to the roof. Lead rocketed along the hall as they challenged the crooks at the guns. Hazzard stumbled down the lower flight. Through the windows, in the searchlight beams, he could see headquarters men crowding in. A door burst open in the rear of the house. Hazzard went along a hallway that was dark—then stopped short as an open door revealed a man in blue staggering before a killer's automatic.

Carey! Carey dropped to one knee as Hazzard glimpsed him, his service gat weighing his hand down. King Krager was facing him, automatic angling for a deadly shot. Carey withered, panting, as Hazzard snapped: "Krager!" Hazzard's automatic bolted when Krager jerked around. The bullet brought red to Krager's wrist.

The killer's gun spat in spite of his injury. Hazzard's burst out answering shots. They straddled, heads lowered, each blasting at the other, heedless of the coming bullets. Krager's left hand was reaching to a hip pocket. Hazzard knew he was going for another gun—freshly loaded. Hazzard's finger squeezed a trigger that did not respond. His Webley was empty. Then another gun clattered to Hazzard's feet. He leaped for it as Krager braced to fire once more.

A deafening shot cracked—but Krager's gun did not spit flames. Hazzard had sent a slug rocketing upward from the gun he was lifting from the floor. Krager snarled, took a deep, slow breath—and dropped.

"Danny!" Hazzard gripped the ex-cop's arm. "You saved my life— tossing your gun at me. Now, you've got to get out fast. Trencher'll recognize you the instant he sees you. Can you make it, copper? Out the back—go to the room."

"I can make it, skipper! As for that gun—I'd have killed Krager myself, but his slug knocked me dizzy!"

"You stopped him for me, Danny. Thanks for that! I'll hunt you up as soon as I can get away."

Hazzard steered the wounded ex-cop out the rear entrance of the big house. He circled toward the front while Carey tottered into the shadows. The searchlights were still beaming onto the lawn, but no machine-guns were pouring death out of the windows now. Headquarters men had crashed in a dozen ways. Whining cries of surrender answered their commands. The siege was over.

Hazzard saw Trencher howling orders. In the street, blue-coated men were surrounding another uniformed pair—Governor and Mrs. Bryant. They were unhurt. Hazzard knew that the three men who had learned his secret were dead—that their lips could never condemn him now—but he was thinking of Ann. Suddenly he saw her running toward him. "Mark! Mark!

His one arm went around her crushingly. He gasped: "I heard them say they'd got you! I thought—"

"They came close, Mark!" she said with a hysterical laugh. "I stood up to see what had happened to you and they fired at me. I just ducked down, that's all—they must have thought— Oh, darling, it doesn't matter! Just stay here with your arm around me."

Hazzard drew clean, cold air into his lungs. He heard men reporting: "Most of 'em sort of weighted down with lead, sir. Got a few small fry alive, imported rod men. We're saved the trouble of burning King Krager like his rat of a brother."

"Everything okay, Trencher?" Hazzard broke in.

Trencher was glaring at Hazzard. "Okay? You sound like you're sorry the whole gang's not dead. What did you want—a massacre? What's the matter with using the courts instead of guns and—oh, hell. Hazzard, I've said plenty of things about you, but I think maybe you're all right."

Hazzard grinned. He left Ann Nash only because Governor Bryant tugged him away.

"Hazzard, I want to thank you again. Your quick thinking not only saved Barbara, but—man, you helped me preserve my office and my self-respect."

Hazzard turned aside, to find the hideout of his wounded helper. There was his next job—with Danny.

ABOUT
THE AUTHOR

WRITERS ARE supposed to be interesting fellows who lead exciting lives. Some are and do. Unfortunately I'm not and don't. I've been told that I'm disgustingly normal.

I hail from St. Joseph, Missouri, land of the Pony Express and Jesse James. Off and on I took odd flings at odd jobs, all more or less usual. There's some newspaper reporting in the list, as well as magazine editing. But at an early age I contracted the writing fever; in fact, I earned my spending money while going through high school by writing short articles, and writing and selling short fiction was the only way I could pay my way through Dartmouth. Since getting married, almost seven years ago, I've done a bit of globe-trotting with my very globe-trottable wife, and we've had a swell time. Now I'm thirty-one years and one week old.

As for my fiction work—there is more of it than I can remember. My card index file of stories sold is about six inches long, most of the cards recording the sales of long stories. My stuff has been reprinted extensively in England, translated into French, Spanish and Czecho-slovakian. I have worked under three pen names besides my own, and recently a book of fiction was published under one of them, but I must keep that detail secret.

I think hard, plot carefully, and write fast, 6,000 words or more a day when I'm at the machine—which is, by the way, an electric one. (No one has ever invented an attachment to think up the story ideas.) I work systematically and produce on schedule. To me writing magazine stories is a business and a study, but also it's fun.

Where do story ideas come from? I happened to read an account of the devastation of Wandering Ants, and wrote "Once These Bones Were Men." One evening a friend of mine said, during a moment of quiet in the conversation, "How's this—men killed in alphabetical order?" Out of that came "The A B C Deaths." One day, sitting at my desk, I began to wonder, "Where would be a swell place to hide a body?" "Three Miles From Murder" was the result. A young woman told me, laughing, of how her old-time beau had once taken her for a ride in a buggy, and of how the horse stopped at every house along the road because it had once worked a milk-route. That made "Horse Sense."

I've written almost every type of story—but it's most fun to write detective and mystery stories. And I try to write 'em so the reader will have as much fun reading 'em.

And now to work!